I SHOULDN'T LOVE THIS WAY

I SHOULDN'T – VOLUME 2

MINA ALEXIA

Black Rose Writing | Texas

This is a work of fiction. Names, characters, businesses, places, events, and incidents are either the products of the author's imagination or used in a fictitious manner. Any resemblance to actual persons, living or dead, or actual events is purely coincidental.

ISBN: 978-1-68513-328-3
PUBLISHED BY BLACK ROSE WRITING
www.blackrosewriting.com

Printed in the United States of America
Suggested Retail Price (SRP) $27.95

I Shouldn't Love This Way is printed in Garamond

*As a planet-friendly publisher, Black Rose Writing does its best to eliminate unnecessary waste to reduce paper usage and energy costs, while never compromising the reading experience. As a result, the final word count vs. page count may not meet common expectations.

Dedicated to everyone who believed in Noah and Aria's love story. Thank you for encouraging me to publish and supporting me throughout my writing journey. I'm especially grateful to the divine beings who helped me revive this story after a long hiatus… you know who you are. Thank you for channeling me. I'm eternally grateful.

With love,

-M

I SHOULDN'T
LOVE
THIS WAY

PROLOGUE

November 29, 2002
2:16AM

To the love of my life,

Should this letter find its way to you one day, then I want you to know some things about me. Even though you don't know who I am at this moment and time, I need to reach out to you tonight because I'm afraid I'm losing faith in ever finding you. I'm twenty-three years old, in college, and I fear I'm becoming everything I've always hated in a man. Yesterday was Thanksgiving, and it was the worst holiday I've ever had because I spent it alone... getting high. I was supposed to go back home, but I can't stand being around my folks these days. We don't get along. We're the most dysfunctional family. I will tell you right now that I promise to protect you from all that toxicity when I find you one day. I won't let my mother poison our love—not like she did with my first love.

I know I'm not making much sense—my thoughts are all over the place. I'm sober at the moment, but most nights... I'm not. I'm sorry. Someday, I'll quit; I'm just not ready yet. I hope to God that when we finally meet, I'll be under better circumstances and will have put this addiction behind me. I never thought I'd be an addict. I'm too ashamed to tell you what my addiction is. But here's a truth: I'm a womanizing asshole. I've slept with more women than I can count. I'm irresponsible, and I've abandoned the one person who would love me forever, no matter what. Maybe I'll tell you about her one day. Her name's on my chest. I used to be a decent guy, but that's not who I am anymore. Despite popular opinion, I don't even love myself. I guess that explains my self-destructive tendencies. The only reason I'm still in school is because of my father. I don't want to let him down.

I'm terrified of falling in love with you. I'm scared because when you love someone, you should always be honest with them. My past is full of secrets and shame. I've done many things I'm not proud of—and normally I don't give a shit about what people say or think about me, but if you rejected me, it would crush me to the core. I haven't even met you, yet I feel unworthy of you. Perhaps it's best that we never meet. Who could ever love me after all I've done? I'll probably end up marrying someone just to settle, and you'll probably chase your dreams and fall in love with another man. I hope he treats you well, I really do, but I can promise you he could never love you as much as me.

Women say I'm heartless. Most times, I think they're right. Although, it's on nights like this that I'm rudely reminded that I'm not as stone cold as I wish to be. Whatever's ticking away in my chest is damaged, and the frost in my soul has touched it. I can't give away a frozen heart. No one really seems to understand that. I feel so empty. Every day, I've got all these people around me… but, I always feel alone. I think that's one of the worst forms of suffering: to be with someone who makes you feel lonely inside. I'm in so much pain and I mask it well, to my own detriment. It's self-inflicted, but you shouldn't have to fix me. I need to fix myself. I'm too weak, I guess.

I wanted to write you this letter as a cry for help, to convince myself that there is someone out there especially for me. But now that I recognize that possibility, all I want to do is prevent us from ever meeting. I wouldn't be able to live with myself if I broke your heart. Tragic, isn't it? I think it's sadder than "Romeo and Juliette." At least those two got to love each other before they faced their demise together. Romeo had the chance to express his love for Juliette. He held her, kissed her, made love to her… while you and I… we will never be fortunate enough to taste a kiss from each other's lips. I'll never be able to hold you through the night, and you'll never wake to find my eyes gazing at your beauty while you slept. I think this will be the most unselfish thing I've ever done in my life. You have your freedom now, and I'll never cage you. I'm undeserving of you.

This will be my last love letter. At least I can be content knowing that it's written for my soulmate. We've never met face to face, but I swear I've seen you in a dream. I'm giving you my heart. Take it with you wherever you are, wherever you go, because I don't need it anymore.

I hope you find happiness, beautiful. I'm sure you will without me.

Yours always,

Noah Hunter

CHAPTER ONE
NOAH

The grandfather clock in Dr. Grey's spacious office kept ticking while I reclined on his leather lounger and stared at the ceiling. A tight cord had finally snapped in my mind, choking me in torment. My psychological suffering was visible on my face. These dark red walls seemed like my prison and sanctuary; it was the only place where I could remove my mask and feel safe in doing so. I was living in Hell—and if not Hell, then purgatory. So much had happened. Why had life become so complicated?

Tick… tock… tick… tock…

"Think out loud, Noah," Grey said. Sitting across from me in a navy-blue suit, he had his usual notepad on his lap. The man always looked so composed—it was unnerving.

"I'm sorry." I turned my head in his direction. "My mind sort of wandered."

"Well, it's good that we got those wheels turning." His thin lips formed a subtle smile. "All you have to do now is share."

"Right—share." I rubbed my forehead. "A lot has happened. I might as well be straight with you. You're not gonna like it, and you'll probably be disappointed in me. I think that's why I've been delaying our visits and rescheduling."

"As I've said before, I am not here to judge you. I cannot stress that enough. I got the feeling that something had happened these past few weeks, but I wanted you to discuss it with me when you were ready."

Sitting up, I reached for the glass of water resting on the table. The cool liquid flowed down my throat, quenching my thirst before I placed it back and said, "I failed."

"Failed at what?" Grey asked.

"Taking your advice… failed at staying away from Aria."

"Explain."

My summarization was straight to the point as I took him through a timeline of events. I described all the conflicts that led to the rising action and inevitable climax of my first kiss with Aria on that carnival ride. He stayed quiet whenever I let him speak. I told him about how Aria and I had almost had sex when we returned home from the festival. Then I mentioned Ryan and everything that happened during Aria's birthday dinner.

The minutes passed, and I grew tired of hearing my voice. I stopped talking and looked at Dr. Grey, hoping for some feedback, but he stayed silent, gesturing with his hand for me to continue. I told him about my adoptive brother, Evan—how he'd randomly showed up at my doorstep.

"You never mentioned this brother to me," he said. "Not once during any of our sessions." He furrowed his brows.

"It was irrelevant."

"Hmm…" Doctor Grey pondered a response. I was irritated because I knew what he was thinking. "We shall return to this subject of your estranged brother at a later time."

"Evan was the least of my problems until he magically appeared out of nowhere."

"There's bad blood between you two?"

"To say the least." I scoffed and stared at a painting on the wall.

Grey scribbled something down. "Would you like to discuss it? You don't have to go into detail."

I briefly touched on my childhood with Evan, including the aftermath of that accident, before I candidly discussed my brother's psychopathy.

"I don't trust him," I admitted. "He's a sociopath, if not a psycho, and I don't want my daughter spending time with him. My parents put him in therapy as early as seven. Evan always had… behavioral problems—that's putting it nicely."

"When did he join your family?"

"He was five years old when my parents brought him home."

"You hold such negative beliefs about him, Noah. Why?"

"What do you mean, Doc?"

"I just mean this grudge you hold against him—I feel that deep down you know your father's death was an accident, and that Evan did not mean to shoot him."

I guess I'll never know.

"Are you envious of his relationship with Aria?"

I frowned and shook my head. "I'm not jealous of my brother. My hostility toward him is because of the horrible things he's done to my family. I've made a career for myself, despite the generous inheritance dad had left me with. I have a wife, a daughter, a family—I have no reason to be jealous of Evan."

You should tell him about the conversations you have with me… I tried to tune out that voice and poured myself another glass of water.

"What does Evan do for work?"

"He told me he's in contracting, and apparently he's in the business of building and renovating houses for the underprivileged in developing countries."

"So, he's making a good living for himself."

"Allegedly so." I sounded irritated.

"Does that bother you?"

Of course, Dr. Grey would pick up on it.

"I don't buy it, Doc. My sister told me he got into photography back when he was in college. And when I last visited, she showed me an extensive amount of his work. He's good, I'll give him that much. Although, I'm positive he chose that occupation to sleep with models. But that's beside the point. Aria told me about all the humanitarian work he's done after he abandoned his dream career as a fashion photographer. I just find it odd because that's not the brother I know and have grown up with. I don't know why she praises him so much. He's a compulsive liar."

"People change," Grey said. "Maybe you're worried he'll jeopardize your relationship with Aria. He's not your biological brother. He had flirted with your daughter, and that may have caused you to—"

"He thought she was my wife at first!" I cut him off.

"Ah. Well, I don't think you find it comforting to know that your brother would make advances on your wife behind your back."

"I'm incapable of trusting him."

"That's understandable. It seems you have quite a pattern going on in your life right now."

"What do you mean?"

"Repairing relationships."

"I want to repair my relationship with Aria, not that bastard."

"Let's focus on one person at a time. If she's going to rebel against you and see him regardless, then I suggest you meet him halfway and bridge the gap between you both." He then shared a famous quote. "… It's one of my favorite lines from Sun Tzu's book *The Art of War*. He was a Chinese general and an influential author…" Grey cleared his throat and smiled. "Not that you need the history lesson."

"So, you mean to say I should keep my friends close and my enemies closer?"

"Yes, exactly. Essentially, if you establish a closer relationship with Evan, you can keep a better eye on him *and* Aria."

"Thanks for sharing the wisdom."

"It's what you pay me for." He grinned.

I lay back and fixed my eyes on the ceiling again. That nagging craving to light up and smoke wouldn't go away.

"Are you all right, Noah?"

"Yeah, I just really need a cigarette at the moment."

"You've started smoking again?"

"Yes."

The sound of his fountain pen rolled over the notepad. "Share your thoughts," Grey said. "I won't interrupt you."

Sighing, I forced myself to get through the therapy session. "I suppose I should get you caught up on the latest drama between me and Aria… So, I'll rewind three weeks to Monday afternoon when she and I got into an argument over Vanessa." I paused and retrieved the memory. "Long story short… she gave me an ultimatum to choose between her or my wife. When I didn't tell her what she wanted to hear, she left the house and drove off. I wanted to go after her, but Vanessa had told me not to. She didn't know what we were arguing about. I couldn't tell her the truth.

"Anyway, I backed off and gave Aria some space, trusting that she wouldn't do anything reckless. But as the hours passed, I kept worrying, so I called her friend since my daughter refused to answer my calls and texts. Jessica didn't know where she was—which seemed like a big, fat lie. I know the rules of friendship: you don't snitch on each other. But anyway, by 10p.m., my every instinct told me to get in my car and drive to Ryan Taylor's house.

"I was dreading the possibility of her drinking, doing drugs, or having sex just to get back at me for hurting her. I don't trust Ryan or his intentions, even though *I'm* the one who's the actual demon here." I exhaled. "He could have easily taken advantage of her. I just wanted to put my concerns to rest. When I decided to find her, she finally texted me and told me she was okay and would be home by eleven. But she ended up coming home about half an hour late. I wouldn't have made such a big deal about it… I guess I was just jealous she had been with Ryan all evening and was answering me with pretentious, rhetorical questions when I wanted to talk.

"Her poor attitude pissed me off and caused us to argue again that night. My wife had overheard us and got involved, which inevitably led her to go ballistic on Aria. It was almost a cat fight. Vanessa had called her an 'ungrateful, little brat,' and Aria called her 'a materialistic, fake bitch.' My wife lost it even more and insulted her by saying she was an 'attention whore.' At that point, I had to step in and prevent my daughter from scratching Vanessa's eyes out.

"I know Nessa was only trying to help me discipline Aria, but everything just got worse. Aria lost her temper and kept running her mouth off at Nessa. It was out of character for her. I had no choice but to side with my wife and ground my daughter. She told me I could do no such thing because she's 'no longer a child.' I clarified that while she's living under *my* roof, she must abide by *my* rules. Therefore, I had every right to enforce consequences.

"The altercation further escalated when Vanessa confiscated Aria's laptop, iPod, and cellphone. I think taking her iPod was a little extreme, but I said nothing and tried to get into 'daddy mode.' I knew I'd give her gadgets back eventually, but I had to be supportive of my wife's decision. Aria expected me to jump to her defense, but I was so pissed off at her for ignoring my calls and staying at Ryan's house. My fatherly instincts were more dominant in the heat of the moment.

"I tried to explain that to her the next day when I drove her to school, but she gave me the silent treatment throughout the car ride. It was extremely unpleasant, and I hated having to go to work feeling hurt and disappointed in myself. She refused to understand and wouldn't talk to me. I hate silent treatments, you know? It triggers me and reminds me of the not-so-pleasant times in my childhood. My mother was *infamous* for giving me and my siblings the silent treatment."

I stopped talking and looked at Grey, hoping he would interrupt me. I didn't want to speak about my mother. But all I got was: "Hmm" and "Go on."

"Her coldness toward me made me feel unloved as a child. Who ignores their eight-year-old kid for days, just because they were misbehaving? *My* mother did, and all my emotional issues started from there. I remember apologizing and constantly begging her forgiveness, but she remained an eternal bitch until she felt I had learned my lesson. The old woman was proud and sadistic—still is. She takes pleasure in other people's pain. Of course, we later found out she had postpartum depression… Still didn't take my suffering away.

"If I ever have another child, I'd never treat them the way she treated me, Isaac, and Breanne. If my children were to misbehave, then they'd get time-outs—and I'd make sure to explain why I made them take a time-out. I'd always hug them and tell them I love them. I would never scream profanities at them or spank them. I would never become like my mother."

The agonizing sound of a little boy crying echoed in my mind as I fought to push back the memory. I didn't want to remember. I didn't want to reflect on all the ways my mother had failed me.

"Anyway, Doc"—I sat up and stretched—"I don't want to think about *sweet Mama Hunter.*" I fixed my eyes on the grandfather clock and tried to sort through my thoughts. I had to figure out a way to get through to Aria. I screwed myself over the second I let my guard down and abandoned my self-control. I never should have crossed any lines with her. I never should have kissed her on that Ferris wheel. But I couldn't stop myself. How could I possibly balance being a father and a lover to her at the same time? After all these events, she felt betrayed by me, which explained why weren't talking now.

Dr. Grey jotted some things down in his trusty notepad and readjusted his black-framed glasses before he asked, "Have you been intimate with your wife as of late?"

Hearing him say those words provoked a sense of shame in me. I was never prepared for his random questions, but I was thankful he had dropped the subject of my mother.

"I stopped sleeping with Vanessa after Aria and I kissed at the festival. We haven't had sex until a few days ago. As you know, my wife and I have been experiencing marriage problems, but I've screwed us up even more." Leaning forward, I hung my head down, resting my elbows over my knees.

"Your dishonesty complicates things," Grey commented.

"Believe me, I hate myself much more than you hate me right now."

"I don't hate you, Noah. I empathize with what you're going through. You're in a complicated situation. I was worried boundaries were crossed when you told me Aria was trying to seduce you. Honestly, I'm not surprised."

"But what do I do now? She refuses to get counseling and won't talk to me."

"I understand your frustration. You can't force her into therapy. She has to want it."

I didn't need a shrink to tell me that.

"Tell me more about your relationship with Vanessa," he said. "I remember your concerns about her addiction to plastic surgery."

"She's in counseling, as promised."

"And how do you feel about that? Is it helping?"

I shrugged. "I guess. I mean, she still feels insecure now and then. But I can tell she's attempting to change old habits."

"That's good news then," Dr. Grey remarked. He took a sip from his steaming cup of tea and placed it back on the saucer. "And what about your sex life?"

"It's a dishonest one."

"How so?"

"I think about Aria every time I'm having sex with my wife."

Straight to the point.

"How does that make you feel afterwards?" Grey continued his interrogation.

"Shitty. I feel guilty and emotionally detached. But I still show Vanessa affection. She doesn't know what's going on with me. I mask it well—I'm good at that."

"Is Aria aware of your rekindled intimacy with your wife?"

"I'm not sure."

I tried to explain the arrangement I had made with her—how I'd promised I wouldn't sleep with Vanessa if she stopped seeing Ryan. All of that changed when Evan showed up, and things went further downhill when Aria's hatred for Vanessa intensified after that fight three weeks ago. It caused a rift between me and her. We had stopped communicating, and she still continued to see Evan behind my back.

"… Eventually," I said, "I considered our agreement void and slept with my wife again. I know it's probably messed up. I feel like I'm betraying my daughter, but I'm married, and I know it's wrong to feel this way. Believe me, Doc. I know I screwed up. I never should have gone as far as I did with Aria, but it happened. And now that I'm trying to undo that damage, I keep making it worse. The closer I get to my wife, the more my daughter withdraws from me. She's been meeting up with Evan in secret. I know she's lying to me, and she feels justified because she believes I've betrayed her."

"Betrayed her as a father or a lover?" he questioned.

"A lover," I shamefully admitted.

"When you and Aria had confessed your feelings, you stopped having sex with your wife, correct?"

"Yes." Grey scribbled something on that damned yellow paper. It made me nervous.

"And you've recently been intimate again?" he reiterated.

"Yes."

"How did you avoid sex without making Vanessa feel rejected or suspicious in the past?"

"I occupied myself with work and fell asleep in my study most nights. Vanessa often complained, but I usually told her I had a big case I was working on and that it would all be over soon."

"Then these past three weeks have been mentally and emotionally taxing on you."

I nodded.

"How come you waited so long to be intimate with your wife again?"

"Because... I think a part of me was hoping to patch things up with Aria."

"When you say 'patch things up,' what do you mean, exactly? Explain."

I hesitated. "I'm still battling with myself. I feel so torn between two versions of who I am."

"I see. Continue," Dr. Grey said.

"I've known all along about Aria's visits with Evan. I don't know why, but it hurts. It hurts knowing she's dismissed my warnings and is pushing me away. The silent treatments had got to me. To be honest, the first night Vanessa and I rekindled our sex life, I was drunk. Aria had gone out, as usual—I rarely saw her home since we'd been feuding. Vanessa was with me that evening, and I was sexually frustrated. One thing led to another, and... Since then, the sex has been regular."

"How do you feel about that, Noah?"

My mind wanted to respond with: *Good! Everything is as it should be.* But my heart detected the lie and felt the exact opposite.

"I feel empty."

"Do you love your wife?"

"Yes."

"Are you still *in love* with your wife?"

I could hear his words, but they didn't seem to register. "If I wasn't in love with her, I wouldn't have married her."

"That doesn't answer my question. Are you still in love with Vanessa?"

"Yes!" I grew frustrated.

"That sounds more forced than honest."

"Are you trying to tell me *you* know how I feel about my wife?"

"No, I'm simply trying to help you be honest with yourself."

I groaned in annoyance and rubbed my temples. "I have romantic feelings for Aria, okay? I know I shouldn't, and I know I can't just turn them off. But they're real, and strong."

I hated it. Being this vulnerable made me feel so powerless.

"I know I probably broke several laws these past three weeks, but…"

"But what?"

"I don't know, Doc." I gravely looked at him.

"Do you regret going that far with your daughter?"

"I wish you'd stop saying that."

"Saying what?"

My voice was razor sharp. "The part where you refer to her as my daughter." Aware of the change in my disposition, I stood up and paced the floor.

"But that's who Aria is, your daughter."

"She doesn't feel like my daughter!" I erupted.

"Of course, she doesn't."

"Are you gonna have me arrested now? Because I don't care anymore—and I won't put up a fight."

"Noah, it's clear you genuinely love her. Your situation is convoluted. I understand you better than you think. Putting you behind bars is not only a waste of taxpayers' dollars, but it's not the right thing to do in this situation. Aria is an adult, so it's not like you started anything with a minor. Although, you bent the law. To commit incest, one must follow through with the act through a consummated union."

I felt sick to my stomach when he said that.

"But your relationship with Aria needs rehabilitating. Unfortunately, we live in a judgmental society. Everyone is trapped inside a 'system' and most of the population follows the rules. Disobeying those rules only shows antisocial behavior. However, that is not the case inside these walls of my practice. I specialize in exploring the gray areas of psychology with a blend of my own controversial ethics."

Great. I'm a lab rat, I thought, dipping my hands in my pockets as I leaned against the wall.

"What are you most afraid of?" he asked.

"I'm scared she'll leave me if I don't give her what she wants."

"Which is?"

"Sex. She wants me to sleep with her."

"Is that what *you* want?"

I stole a moment to think. "I find her insanely attractive—so, yes, I think about having sex with her—more than I should. But I would never take it that far. She's tested me many times, yet I've always shown restraint. I know she's eighteen now and can make her own choices, but in my mind, she's still a teenager and naïve about a lot of things in life. She needs guidance, and I'm a terrible role model right now." I sighed. "I'm scared she'll hate and resent me later on if we do it."

"Do what?" asked Grey.

"You know... *it.*"

"Define 'it.'" He stared at me impassively.

"Is this amusing to you?" I frowned. "You know exactly what I mean!"

"I want you to say it out loud."

"I'm scared she'll hate me if I give in to her advances and have sex with her! There! Happy now?" I didn't like losing my temper, but it was out of my control sometimes.

Dr. Grey blinked, sipping his tea.

"I should be stronger and resist our attraction," I expressed. "She's young and I'm her father. I should know better. It's so damn hard to think rationally around her. It's like she controls and manipulates my emotions, my every thought and action." The guilt was exhausting.

"You're damned if you do and damned if you don't."

"Yep."

"If Aria were older, would you sleep with her?"

"No. I don't know." I loosened my tie and took a deep breath. "Maybe… I mean, no!"

"Let's try to imagine a little hypothetical scenario for a moment. Suppose you were single and were to engage in a sexual relationship with Aria. Where does that take you down the road?"

I would never leave her side. I would never hurt her. I would love her and be devoted to her until the day I die, I answered in my head.

"We would have to keep our relationship low profile," I began. "No one could ever know about us. She won't ever be able to introduce me to her friends as her boyfriend. We won't be able to hold hands or kiss in public. An engagement proposal would be pointless because there's no way we could get a marriage license."

"You've entertained the prospects of marriage with your daughter?" Grey raised his eyebrows. "How interesting."

"What? No, I just"—I scrambled to find the words—"I was considering all the hypothetical situations."

"Go on," he encouraged.

"We could never have a child together. I'm sure I could impregnate her, but I don't want to, because the idea of bringing a genetically deformed child into this world scares the shit out of me. Excuse my language, Doc."

"Speak freely, Noah."

"I'm sixteen years older than her, and the more she blossoms into womanhood, the more I age into an ugly old man. It's bad enough that I have Dorian Gray Syndrome." I poked fun at myself. "Aria deserves to be with someone who is age appropriate and makes her happy."

There was a long silence between us as Dr. Grey wrote some things down.

"I can see that you truly want the best for her," he said.

"I really do."

"Would you mind if I emailed Aria? I'd like to reach out and encourage her to see me. She might refuse therapy because she feels intimidated or nervous."

"Go ahead."

He grabbed a piece of paper and pen from his desk and handed it to me. I wrote Aria's email address before sliding it back to him.

"What are you gonna say to her?"

"I just want her to know that if she's ever in trouble or needs to talk, my door is always open. If I can create an opportunity to gain her trust through one-on-one sessions, then I'm positive she'll be more willing to receive counseling with you as well." He smiled.

"I hope you can convince her. She's adamant about taking an oath of silence forever with me. What do you suggest I do?"

"Keep trying to open a conversation with her. Tell her that silent treatments fix nothing, and that you want her to communicate with you. She's exhibiting passive aggressive behavior. Have you thought about telling your wife about all this?"

"And destroy my marriage? No way! I know I messed up. I admit all my wrongs, which is why I put a stop to what was going on with me and Aria as quickly as it had started. These past three weeks… there's been no contact between me and her. I haven't even hugged her, and she hasn't been affectionate with me, either."

"Has Vanessa picked up on this?"

"Yeah, but she assumes it's because of my daughter's constant rebelling and the *Evan situation*."

"That's part of the reason, right?"

It took me a while to give an honest answer, but I finally said, "Yes."

"You feel angry and betrayed by her," Grey added. "At the same time, you feel you have no right to be."

"Yes," I sighed.

"Well, I don't want to force you to do anything you're not ready for. I can only offer you my professional opinion. I think it's good you've controlled your desires and have taken preventative measures to abstain from sex with Aria. Don't beat yourself up in feeling this attraction. Yes, you acted on it to an extent, but I believe there's still hope to heal.

"Genetic sexual attraction has detrimental side effects on the family unit. And you are right when you expressed that there would be a very limited future if you assume the role of her unlawful lover. Time and patience will mend your relationship with your daughter. I guarantee the moment she falls in love with another man, she won't desire you and will stop seducing you."

Is that what you really want? Do you truly want her to stop feeling this way about you? That taunting voice echoed in my head once more.

"I recommend increasing our visits to three times a week. I know this is going to be a struggle for you, which is why I feel it's best to discuss this more frequently, to make sure you keep a clear head and make rational decisions instead of impulsive ones."

"Sure, whatever you say, Doc."

"I'd also like to delve into your history with your brother next session. It would be helpful if you were to open up with no reservations."

"I'll try my best."

"That's all I can hope for." He smiled, glancing at his watch. "It appears our time is up."

"Thank you for seeing me on such short notice. I'm sorry I had to cancel yesterday."

"It's all right." He smiled warmly. "It's a beautiful Friday afternoon. You should take your wife out on a date."

"It's always beautiful in California," I said. "But yeah, that sounds like a good idea."

"I've scheduled you for Monday at 2p.m."

"That's fine. Thanks, Doc."

"You take care, Noah."

"I will. Have a good weekend." Grabbing my blazer, I walked out the door.

When I got in my car, I headed straight to the nearest gas station to buy myself a twenty deck of smokes.

CHAPTER TWO
ARIA

Almost four weeks had passed since my birthday. I was over at Steph's place on a Friday night. Jessica and Tammy were there, too. We had gone shopping after school and had stopped by the nail salon for a manicure and pedicure. Tonight was going to be amazing. Our exams were almost over (well, not really)—we just needed an excuse to go to this new club that opened in LA. Steph had said the place would not disappoint. I had been looking forward to it since last week.

"Are you sure these fake IDs will get us into the VIP section?" I asked, sitting on Steph's bed.

"Relax. We probably won't even get ID'd at the bar."

All eyes were on Jessica as she walked out of the bathroom. "Does this dress make me look fat?" she asked.

Her short halter dress was a dark plum color. "You look gorgeous!" I smiled in approval.

Steph stood in front of her and sipped on a rum and coke while she scrutinized her outfit. "I told her to stop overindulging on the fast-food," she rudely stated. "Now you're growing a muffin top! Honestly, Jessica, do you really want to end up looking like a fatso whose only hope is to attract a chubby chaser? Because we all know how *those* relationships go… It's not love when it's a fat fetish."

I was appalled and shocked by what she said as I yelled, "Jess is not fat!" The sheer outrage was visible on my face. "And even if she was, is that honestly the worst thing to be in the world? I don't think so! 'Fat' is just an adjective, not an insult. Stop making her feel so self-conscious about her body! You're not living in it, so what gives you the right to comment and judge?"

"Don't hate me because I love her enough to tell her the truth!" Steph seethed. "She's gaining weight, and I would be a terrible friend to not speak up about it and turn a blind eye. Fat people are disgusting, Aria. They're lazy, they smell, and the delusional idiots who are pushing for 'fat acceptance' are morons. They literally need to be shipped to an island and blown up! Is a human infant born the size of a whale? *No!* It's not natural to look like a blob of flabby flesh!"

"Would you please listen to yourself?" I shouted.

"Asking the world to sympathize and be tolerant of this disease is sickening. It's a sorry ass excuse they use to keep stuffing their face instead of cutting calories and working out. I will never, ever feel an ounce of compassion for a disgusting, lazy, tubby! Why should I, or anyone else, respect a fatty when they can't even respect themselves enough to take care of their body? If you want to bring good ol' Jesus into it, he'd say that it's sinful to eat so much like a gluttonous pig!"

No, he would *not* say that. Jesus preached love.

"If I were God," Steph continued, "I'd send them all to Hell where they belong! At least all that grease would melt down there!"

Tammy cut in and said, "Well, there you have it, ladies"—she gestured to Steph—"Adolf Hitler reincarnated as an angry white girl who hates big people."

"I feel sorry for you," I said to Steph. "It must be difficult living your life with so much hate in your heart. You give the word 'shallow' a whole new definition."

Tammy finished her shot of tequila and said, "She's just bitter because her ex dumped her last year and started dating Lilly Mullins."

"He did *not* date her!" Steph shouted. "He screwed that cow while he was drunk! It was a onetime deal, and *I* was the one who dumped him, so get your facts straight, Tammy!"

"Some guys like BBWs, Steph," Tammy retorted. "Get over it."

"BBW?" I asked in confusion.

"Big beautiful woman," she replied.

"More like *big bulging whale*! Lilly is an ugly cow who can only get a guy in bed with her if they're drunk."

Someone had struck a nerve. I knew who Lilly was; I sat next to her in biology. She was smart, beautiful, and clearly had an enemy because she was dating Stephanie's ex. According to my extremely shallow "friend," bigger people were subhuman and not worthy of love. I was so upset. I didn't know anyone who was battling obesity, but I'd been raised properly to know that you treat others with dignity and respect. Trying to fit in with the "in crowd" didn't seem all that important to me anymore—not after hearing Steph's bigoted rant.

"You know what?" I said to her. "Never mind the rest of the world—how can you stand there and criticize your best friend's weight when you know about her battle with bulimia? Do you really want her purging after every meal now? You're sick, Steph!"

"It's okay, Aria," Jess said. "I get her point. I really need to skip the drive-through."

"I'm only looking out for my bestie!" Steph flashed the smuggest smile.

I grabbed my handbag and headed for the door.

"Hey!" Steph shouted, blocking my exit. "Where do you think you're going?"

"Home."

"Why? Are you seriously that upset over what I said? It's a free country, Aria. I'm entitled to my opinion."

"Of course you are. And I have every right to say that you are full of shit."

"Don't leave!" Jess protested. "I never should have asked that stupid question. Please, Aria, you promised you would come out with us tonight."

Homesickness struck me like a hard slap in the face. I missed my mom. I missed Ally and Jade. I couldn't believe how Jess and Tammy could tolerate being around someone like Steph.

"Apologize to her," I said to the bitchy brunette.

"*What?*" Steph scowled at me.

"Apologize to Jessica now, or I'm gone."

Rolling her eyes, she faced Jess before sighing a pathetic apology.

"Now, apologize to me for making me listen to your revolting bigotry."

"Were you a fat girl once upon a time, Aria? Is that why you're all butt-hurt?"

I reached for the doorknob but Steph closed it shut and said, "Okay, I'm sorry! Jeez! Don't go! Look, I don't mean to be a bitch, and I don't mean to be so severe about this subject. I know you think I have no right to hate on fat people, but I have my reasons. I'm sorry—it just brings the ugly out of me."

Tammy nodded and said, "She's telling the truth, trust me—and it has nothing to do with Lilly Mullins."

"Keep your hateful comments to yourself next time." I scowled at Steph and pulled Jess into the bathroom, robbing her of a chance to respond.

A few seconds later, I heard a blast of rap music. Steph worshipped Nicki Minaj. I always wanted to go to her concerts. She's such a queen.

"Don't let her get to you, okay?" I shut the door, facing my friend. "You look amazing. Stephanie's whole *thin-spiration* is based on self-starvation. I don't want to see you skipping lunch on Monday because of her stupid opinions."

She eventually smiled. "Thanks for sticking up for me."

"Always." I hugged her. "I can't believe how ignorant she is."

Steph was a mean girl, and I hated myself for associating with someone like that. I was wise enough to know that "mean people" were just wounded souls in need of healing.

"Don't be so hard on her, Aria. There's a reason she's bothered by people who are noticeably overweight. Her dad had divorced her mother because she had let herself go. When Steph was twelve, her mother died because of her morbid obesity. It's like she needs to hold on to the hate and anger because she never properly mourned her death. Steph still blames her mom because her death could have been prevented. Her stepmom's kind of like yours… obsessed with body image."

"I guess we finally have something in common then." I sighed, listening to Steph rapping along to "Beez In The Trap." I'm sure Nicki would have told her to shut up if she knew she was a mean girl.

"She loves me," Jess said. "In her own demented way."

Demented indeed, I thought.

"Does your dad think you're sleeping over at Megan's place, too?" Jess asked.

"Yep."

We shared the bathroom mirror and fixed our makeup while chatting.

"Are you still not talking to him?"

"Nope," I answered while reapplying my lip gloss. "It's all because of Vanessa. I can't believe she tried to ground me for a month and take away my social life. I can't function without my phone, or my laptop, or my iPod. I can't survive without technology, period!"

Kind of sad, I know.

"Yeah, that was a little O.T.T. if you ask me. But at least your dad 'ungrounded' you and gave all your things back."

Uh, yeah! He freakin' had to! I was so mad at him.

"I can't stand my stepmom sometimes. I wish she would just disappear."

Okay, that was extreme—like—*Stephanie Cohen extreme.* I wouldn't wish death on anyone… except for Rob.

"Wow…" Jess glanced at me. "I didn't know you hated her that much."

"You don't want to know what it's like to live with her."

"She can't be worse than my mom. My mother is so damn strict about what I wear, who I talk to, who I go out with… The list goes on. I swear she's worse than my dad. Sometimes I feel like she's the one wearing the pants in the relationship."

I couldn't help but laugh. I had met her mother before, and she appeared as the control-freak type. "My stepmom doesn't give a crap about what I wear. I don't think she owns anything that hides her cleavage."

"Now you sound like a judgmental feminist." Jess laughed.

I had a hard time coming up with a legitimate reason to hate Vanessa without exposing Noah and me.

"I don't know. She just annoys me! Vanessa always sticks her nose in my business!"

"Okay, yeah," Jess replied. "That can be annoying. But I still think my mom is worse."

"Oh, hush! Let me bitch about her for a while, please!"

"Sure, babes, vent away." She laughed.

I playfully nudged her shoulder and grabbed my mascara out of my makeup bag.

"I still need to meet this infamous uncle of yours."

"You'll meet him soon." I smiled.

Evan and I had got so much closer throughout the weeks. Spending time with him took my mind off Noah; things between him and I weren't going so well at home. Technically, I still wasn't allowed to see my uncle, and I would have listened if Noah hadn't pushed me away again. He wanted things to be normal between us. While he focused on rebuilding his sham of a marriage, I focused on school, friends, and amazing Evan.

"We should go shopping for prom dresses this weekend," Jess said.

"Sounds good, I'm free."

My high school was hosting the big event on the 18th of May, which was three weeks away. Our prom had a modern masquerade theme and was going to be held at the Rouge Hotel in Beverly Hills. Jess was looking forward to it. I knew I couldn't ditch the event, so I said yes when Ryan asked me to go as his date.

"Are you girls ready?" Tammy asked from behind the door. "Our cab's here."

"Yeah, we'll be right out!" I put my cosmetics away and examined my outfit.

This skintight dress looks like a million bucks!

And I couldn't wait to go out and flaunt it.

∞

Originally, the girls and I had made plans to go to a club called Avalon. Apparently, this place had been in business since the 20s. The club was known as Hollywood's reining nightlife establishment, and we all wanted to go, except we had a big problem: we didn't have any hookups to get in. Steph and Jessica's birthdays were in the summer, so they weren't eighteen yet, like me and Tammy. Fortunately for us, Steph's friend, Marco, worked as a bouncer at Orca, and he had promised to get us into The Velvet Lounge with no problems. How Steph knew this thirty-something year old guy was beyond me.

"Whoa… look at that lineup," Steph said, stepping out of our cab.

Tammy stood on the sidewalk next to me. She was a platinum blonde, just like Vanessa. The only physical difference between her and my stepmom was that my friend was naturally blonde and had real blue eyes—oh, and minus the plastic surgery. She seemed anxious as she asked Steph, "Are you sure we'll be on the VIP list?"

"I didn't threaten to blackmail Marco for nothing!" Steph exclaimed. "Trust me. We'll get in."

It seemed the nature of Steph's relationship with this "Marco" character was strictly friends-with-benefits. She never went into detail about how they met. Walking ahead, Steph led the way as we followed behind her like groupies.

We skipped the long lineup and walked toward some bouncers who stood tall and intimidating next to a big, black door. Loud music was pounding away from inside the building. I got nervous when it was my turn to flash my fake ID. If you wanted to get into VIP, then you needed to be at least twenty-one. Just like Steph had promised, we got in with no hassle.

"See, ladies?" She beamed. "Didn't I tell you we'd get in? Tonight's gonna be a blast!"

We passed through security and walked down a long, dark corridor that had red neon floor lights. It was like walking through a red tunnel. If my gran were here, she would have compared it to a first-class trip to Hell. The irony was that she was looping in her own hell and completely ignorant of it—but that's a conversation I was saving for a therapy session. I was a sinner in her eyes, but I was more than fine with that. A night of drinking and partying was nothing compared to my long list of sins that had surely angered God with Noah.

"Now *this* is my kind of music!" Tammy cheered.

Booming bass and loud dance music blasted around us, synchronized in rhythm with a wicked laser light show. Approaching the main room, the bar looked incredible. The countertops were glowing in purple, with an amazing backdrop of running water pouring behind rows of gleaming liquor bottles. The glass shelving created an optical illusion, as if the bottles were floating. It was modern and impressive.

"Oh, my God!" Jess exclaimed. "I can't believe we're actually here! This is so F-ing awesome!" She could hardly contain her excitement, while I tried not to trip on my heels.

The dance floor was packed. A DJ was spinning some hot house tracks from the DJ booth. I don't think I had ever seen so many multicolored laser lights before in my life. The giant LCD screens mounted on the ceiling looked amazing. The visual effects were state-of-the art, and I stood in awe as a huge crowd of people were canon blasted with CO2 to cool off. A low haze of fog crept in below our feet while we took in the surrounding nightlife. Marco escorted us to the VIP section at the back of the club.

The main room had a red, green, and purple theme, divided into sections; it was upscale and screamed luxury. We sat on a moon sofa and ordered drinks when a server came by. I ordered a Cosmopolitan, Tammy got a Pear Martini, Jessica ordered a Strawberry Daiquiri, and Steph got a Sex On the Beach cocktail.

"Get ready to party it up, girls!" Tammy raised her glass. "Cheers!"

We clinked our drinks together before gulping back the liquor. The first sip felt icy and burned down my throat. But it had a sweet and tangy aftertaste, which I liked. The music was so loud that it made it hard to carry a conversation, so we kept on drinking, ordering Cherry Bomb vodka shots one after another. I had a low alcohol tolerance, which meant I had to take it easy on the booze that night. By the time I had my second shot, I was already buzzing. Scanning my surroundings, I listened to the drone chatter of people socializing with one another. Most of these "night crawlers" were just looking to hook up and have fun instead of walking out with a life partner.

We hadn't been sitting long when two guys randomly approached us and asked Tammy and Jess if they wanted to dance. My friends were more than willing to accept their invitation since the guys were their type. Steph and I sat back and had a few more drinks while Jess and Tammy disappeared in the dancing crowd. Before I could strike up a conversation, my phone vibrated.

Everything okay with you over there?

It was from Noah. Punching a response, I tried to hide my anxiety.

Everything's fine.

I was about to put my phone away when I got another incoming message:

Call me if you want to come home.

There was no way I was going home tonight. I messaged him back and told him I was staying. But then he texted me:

Okay… I was just saying.

Rolling my eyes, I sent him another text, hoping it would be my last.

We're watching a movie right now "DAD"-Bye.

Five seconds later:

Stop being a smartass.

My response:

Stop texting me.

His response:

Fine.

Me wanting the last word:

FINE.

Noah putting me in my place:

Now you're being childish.

No, I'm just acting my age :D

I was expecting another incoming message, but he didn't respond until minutes later.

Well, at least you're talking to me.

Technically, I'm not :/ We're texting, not talking.

I hoped I was getting a rise out of him. And then came his last text:

Right. Later.

No I love you, no kisses or hugs. Our text messages had undergone a drastic change during the past few weeks, and it stung inside.

"Was that your dad?" Steph craned her neck toward my phone and talked into my ear.

"Yeah."

"I need to tell you a secret!" She giggled, gulping another shot of vodka. "I probably shouldn't tell you this, but I'm buzzing as hell right now, so I don't care!"

I gave her a queer look.

"I *really* wanna smash your dad!"

That was no surprise.

"Steph, you're drunk."

"No, I'm dead serious, Aria. He's so sexy! I'm pretty sure you have the hottest daddy in California. I've wanted to sleep with him from the moment I saw him pick you up from school six months ago. I didn't know he was your father until you got in the car with him." She laughed.

"Quit grossing me out! I don't want to think about the two of you doing the nasty!" I knew I was the last person to say that, but it wasn't like I could say *hands off, he's mine!*

"I'm sorry! I have a weakness for older, married men." She laughed. "Especially sexy ones like your pops!"

"Okay, I think you need to slow down on the liquor." I shrugged her arm off my shoulder and moved her shot glass away.

"If you can just get me one night alone with him, I swear… I'll use my trust fund to buy you brand new wheels—any car you like!"

I knew Steph's family was loaded, but I highly doubted her intention to spend big bucks on buying me a Lambo or a Maserati. Even if she offered me a million dollars, there was no way I was going to "sell out" Noah like a pimp.

"You're crazy, Steph."

"And proud of it, bitch!" She knocked back another shot and stood up. "Oh, my God! I love this song!"

I was pulled on my feet by force, which almost caused me to spill my shot.

"Let's see how many hot guys you can pick up tonight!" Steph yanked my arm toward the crowded dance floor. I had no choice but to follow.

CHAPTER THREE
ENIGMATIC ENCOUNTER

Aria had been dancing the night away with her friends, unaware that she was being watched by someone who had been eyeing her all evening like a night stalker. A sharply dressed gentleman sat by the bar, sipping on Irish whiskey. He couldn't take his eyes off the entrancing beauty, dancing under the strobe lights. A crooked smile touched his lips as a flood of sexual images flashed in his mind while he checked out the gorgeous brunette in the strapless dress. Her outfit complimented her slim figure, he thought, and her black stilettos only heightened her sex appeal, accentuating her long, slender legs. Adjusting himself down below, he watched her snakelike movements as he strategized from a distance.

Can't wait to tap that, he thought to himself. *Fuck.*

His thoughts had no filter, and his fantasies often consumed him within his twisted universe that revolved around attractive women. He wanted to pull Aria away from the dance floor and find a private place where he could do the most scandalous things to her.

I'll make you scream…

A fantasy formed in his mind as he visualized sitting in the VIP section with Aria in his lap.

Kiss me and sit on it, he thought, imagining the sensation of filling her to the hilt when she would take him inside her.

Reverse cowgirl… nice and slow. He gulped back his drink. *Dancing on me so no one would notice… Then I'll slip into that tight, wet… Grabbing your hips and pushing until you'd shudder from pleasure. I won't let you off until I fill you up.*

His fantasy was lewdly inappropriate. If he were to express his sexual desires to Aria, she would have slapped him in the face and walked in the opposite direction.

The Velvet Lounge had a dress code. The handsome stranger was wearing a black blazer over a gray V neck shirt, and dark blue jeans. He matched his ensemble with a black leather belt and black combat boots—all brand names. He had gotten a haircut earlier that day and looked stylish in his tailored clothing.

Evan had always been confident in his ability to attract women, and as much as he desired to dance with the sexy brunette, the timing wasn't right yet. Hanging back in the shadows, he watched her like a hungry predator, waiting for the opportunity to pounce and capture its prey. Many women had flirted with him in turns at the bar, but they either ended up walking away with bruised egos, or reacted rudely to him since he was too distracted with someone else.

The DJ cross faded a new track into the mix, as the music changed to a nostalgic song that the young man was familiar with: "Make Me Feel" by Oliver Smith. Smiling, he watched Aria run her fingers through her wavy hair, dancing more carefree than before. Her body was hypnotizing; it captivated him. There were plenty of attractive women in the club, but he only had eyes for one.

A loud siren blared, triggering the CO_2 smoke machines. The dancing bodies disappeared under a cloud of colorful fog. Setting his glass on the bar counter, the stranger was about to head toward his target when a blonde in a red dress approached him.

"I'm gonna break many hearts tonight and give you an opportunity to buy me a drink." She sounded confident, flashing a smile as she moved in closer. To the average man, she appeared to be charismatic. Anyone with high intellect could see through her ego façade.

Pausing, he looked at her. He didn't like to have his personal space encroached on. She was a certified bombshell with a banging body, but not his type on an energetic level.

"I'm gonna have to pass. I don't do blondes."

The woman scoffed, looking offended. She half expected him to impress her with a seductive one liner, but he had flat out rejected her, wounding her ego. He didn't care; he never did. Leaving the broad at the bar, he walked off with a cheeky grin.

I don't have time for easy bimbos at the moment.

It was hard to find anyone beneath the thickening fog. But he used that advantage to slip through the crowd, smiling when Aria's perfume grew stronger.

Getting closer, he thought.

She was dancing near her friends; they each had a partner, except for her. A young man approached from the distance, but the stranger made him change direction when he moved in behind Aria and wrapped his arms around her waist. She was now his possession, *claimed.*

Aria smiled when she felt a pair of hands squeeze her hips. His energy felt amazing, she thought, surrendering to his touch. He easily matched her rhythm as they danced.

Curiosity tempted her to turn around, but she resisted. Part of her enjoyed the mystery of anonymity. All she knew was that the stranger was more than capable of keeping up with her. Arching her back against his toned chest, she slowly swayed her hips, keeping in time with the music as her face went flush. The thrill of not knowing who she was dancing with intensified her arousal. Her stomach tightened when he brushed his hand against her skin while it prickled with goosebumps. A breathy sigh escaped her lips. His cologne smelled familiar, but she was too drunk to focus and remember *who* she had smelled it on. Closing her eyes, she let the music carry her away as she danced on the "mysterious stranger."

The man's adrenaline kicked into overdrive. His spontaneous venture was risky, but he couldn't help himself. The last thing he wanted was to see her dancing with another guy. He secretly hoped the fog machines wouldn't let up soon, because as soon as that hazy barrier would evaporate, he would disappear with it.

It seemed as if they had been dancing with each other forever. No practice was required; they aligned and matched each other's vibration so perfectly, like two puzzle pieces fitting together.

Your body is mine, he thought, breathing in her intoxicating scent.

Raising her arms in the air, Aria felt a trail of goose bumps down her spine when his hands slid up her rib cage, brushing underneath her breasts. She tangled her fingers in her hair and shivered when she felt his breath on the nape of her neck. Her nipples had hardened. She trembled as he tightened his grip on her waist. Taking the lead, Aria rolled her hips while he kept up with her movement. She was so completely present, which rarely happened since she often battled a racing mind being high on the intellect scale. She wasn't sure if she was getting high off the music, the stranger, or the alcohol.

"What's your name?" she hollered.

He pressed his lips against her ear. "Matthias."

"I'm gonna turn around, Matthias…"

"Don't." He held her in place. "Not yet."

His voice sounds familiar, Aria thought.

"Just dance with me," he murmured again in that low, husky tone.

A third blast of CO_2 poured down to cool off the crowd, but she felt so warm against that masculine physique. His energy was dark, but captivated her in a seductive way. The music pulled them into a deep state of trance as the dance floor transformed into a wonderland of laser lights, smoke, and fog. Everyone went wild when the DJ filtered the track with some equalizing effects and dropped the bass again.

A wave of vibrations flowed through Aria's chest as her heartbeat pounded in rhythm with the music. Normally, she would have been more guarded, but she was intoxicated, which meant her logic was impaired. Temptation was nearly taking over as Matthias resisted the urge to kiss her neck.

She smells divine, he thought, breathing in her floral scent.

He restricted himself to subtle caresses down her arms, ignoring the urge to trespass her boundaries. Their bodies had connected and familiarized with each other, igniting a mating ritual. Aria had never experienced this before; it was new and exhilarating. She felt him change the pace while grinding against her. Something hard stiffened against her curves, which only stimulated a flood of sexual fantasies to unfold in her mind. She couldn't understand how this was happening, as if he was a warlock accessing her mind and filling it with thoughts that were so "unclean"… "unholy"… but pleasurable.

What if he's Noah? She entertained the idea for a second and quickly discarded it because she knew the chances of that happening were one in a billion. If he had shown up and seen her dancing like this, he would have made a scene and dragged her out of the nightclub.

Matthias felt a painful throb in his trousers as Aria teased him with her sensual movements. They danced through the entire song until the fog slowly evaporated around them.

"I'm Aria, by the way—"

She turned around, and he was gone. The attractive stranger had disappeared. Aria felt as if she had been dancing with a ghost. Scanning the crowd, she couldn't find him; he remained faceless.

"Come to the ladies' room with me!" Jessica shouted, grabbing her friend by the arm.

CHAPTER FOUR
ARIA

I was afraid that Jess and I would have had to wait *a million years* to get inside the restroom, but luckily that wasn't the case.

"Did you see who I was dancing with, by any chance?" I asked.

"Um, I noticed a tall guy dancing with you," Jess replied, washing her hands. "But I couldn't see his face—too much fog." She reached for some paper towels and dried her hands before she opened her clutch to retrieve her gloss. Fuchsia was definitely her color.

"Well," I sighed. "At least I didn't hallucinate the guy."

"Of course not, silly! We've been drinking alcohol, not shrooms!"

"You can drink shrooms?"

"Technically, you brew them first," she replied, powdering her nose. "I'm surprised you're still able to stand in those shoes!"

"I love these heels. I've never owned a pair of Louboutin's before."

"Having a rich daddy has its perks." Jess winked at me.

"I wanna know who I was dancing with. It's bugging me. I should have turned around sooner."

"Why didn't you?"

"The mystery of it all was more exciting."

"You sound like the type of girl who likes to be blindfolded, flogged, and spanked during sex!" Jess giggled.

"Oh God, that is *so* not me!" I laughed. "Definitely not into the whole BDSM thing. I'd never be into it."

"Never say never…"

"Be serious, Jess… He only gave me his name."

"Which was?"

"Matthias."

"*Ooh*, I like it!" She closed her clutch and turned away from the mirror. "Let's get our asses back out there and hopefully the 'mysterious stranger' will show up again."

∝∾

Returning to the lounge area, Jess and I sat down to find Steph and Tammy gossiping about me.

"Let's be real for a moment, shall we? Aria would have wound up sitting at the loser table if I hadn't taken her under my wing. She acts like she runs this group! We all know *I'm* queen bee! I don't understand how you girls could like her. I mean, I'm only friends with her because I wanna hook up with her dad."

The bitch was howling, not realizing that I was right behind her.

"I bet she was nobody back in New York… Unpopular and unimportant. She's lucky we're friends with her. I'm pretty sure Ryan only wants to date her because he wants to sleep with her. We all know she's a virgin, and he wants to pop that cherry! I hate how she acts all 'holier than thou.' *Ugh*! I can't stand her!"

"Um, Steph…" Tammy looked up at me.

This was it. I wasn't going to be nice to that broad any longer. I'd already given her way too many chances she didn't deserve.

"What?" Steph let out a ditsy laugh and twisted her head around. "Oh, shit. Aria…" She stood up and looked at me, dumbfounded. "I talk so much crap when I'm drunk. Please don't take it personally."

I'm not gullible.

"Save your sorry ass lies for your bathroom mirror because I'm sure that's the only way you can tolerate your pathetic existence and get out of bed every morning. What to do you tell yourself, Steph? 'I'm beautiful, I'm rich, I have everything, and all the boys want me?' Someone needs to give you a reality check, and as your 'friend' I'll honestly tell you that all they want is that used up *thing* that hangs loose between your legs… Because that's all you are to them, and all you will ever be: a cum dumpster!"

I didn't know I could say those things to her. The booze had made me braver.

"You bitch!" She lunged toward me, but Tammy grabbed her in time. "You better take that back!"

I was ready to fight her. In fact, I secretly wished she had laid her hands on me. I would have made her eat the floor. My inner rage monster was desperate to come out.

"Kiss your social life goodbye, Aria!"

Jessica got in between us to make sure I wouldn't attack.

"You're the nastiest bitch I've ever met!" I shouted. "You're a shallow slut! No one likes you! They pretend to like you! You have no real friends and I feel sorry for you. You hate me because you feel threatened by me. Consider us officially un-friended! And for the record, Ryan told me you were a lousy lay!" I annihilated her overgrown ego with my last comment.

Tammy seemed to struggle to restrain her, and Jess kept urging me to leave. My shadow side took gratification in humiliating Steph like that. I had always been passive as a child and let everyone bully me, but I wasn't a little girl anymore, nor was I going to be Stephanie Cohen's doormat any longer.

"There's one last thing I need to say to you before I stop wasting my breath," I added.

"Shut the F up and leave if you know what's good for you!" Steph screamed, slapping Tammy's hands away. She was really losing it.

Marco showed up just in time and locked his arms around her. "Cool it, Steph, or I'm gonna kick you out!"

"It's *her!* She's making me lose it!" Steph glared at me with murderous eyes.

"You're a two-faced twat! Noah would never sleep with a chick whose password to her vagina is as easy as one-two-three!" I gave one last blow, adding insult to injury, before I grabbed two shots from our table and left the VIP lounge. Jessica tried to match my stride as I threw back the vodka.

"Aria, wait! Where are you going?"

"Home!" A server brushed past me, giving me the chance to place the empty shot glasses on a tray.

"Don't let Steph ruin our night!" Jess finally caught up. "I know she said some shitty things, but she wasn't speaking on my behalf. We can party without her and go back to my place afterwards."

"I don't feel like partying anymore after hearing her say all that stuff— and we can't go back to your place. We'll get busted. I'm sure your mom would go ballistic. I'm calling a cab." I took out my cell and walked toward the nearest exit. Distracted with my phone, I didn't even look up to see who or what was in front of me, which led to me slamming into someone.

"Oh, my gosh! I'm so—"

"*Aria?*"

Evan...

I couldn't believe it. What were the odds of running into him at this place? Unlike all the times I had seen him in casual wear, Evan cleaned up nicely. His outfit was hot. I noticed a pretty brunette on his arm— presumably his date.

"What are you doing here?" he asked, looking just as stunned as I was.

"I, um..."

The music was so loud we had to shout over each other.

"It's a Friday night," I said. "We wanted to party." That was the best explanation I could come up with.

"I see."

The room was suddenly spinning.

"Hey, don't fall!" Jess grabbed my arm just in time, helping me regain my balance. Those Cherry Bombs were working faster than I had expected.

"Have you been drinking?" He suspiciously narrowed his eyes.

"No... it's these shoes. I've been dancing in them all night."

"Wait…" Jess spoke up. "Is *this* Evan? As in… your Uncle Evan?"

I guess she couldn't recognize him with the new haircut. The only time she'd seen him was when I had briefly pointed him out at the mall a while back.

"Yes, that would be me." He smiled. "I didn't realize I was that popular."

"Is everyone in your family good looking?" Jess flirted.

"Pretty much." I let out a laugh and felt my motor skills weaken as the alcohol worked its way into my bloodstream.

His date looked annoyed as she said, "Are we gonna dance or what?"

Evan leaned into her ear and murmured something while I watched her ruby lips curl into a grin. She handed him her cellphone, and he punched in his digits before he returned her device. I noticed the way she bit her lip and eyed him seductively, brushing her hand down his chest before walking away.

Awkward!

"Well… it was nice running into you!" I tried to wrap up the conversation as quickly as possible.

"Wait." Evan grabbed my arm.

A jolt of electricity sparked through my nervous system. I wasn't sure if it was because of his touch, or that I was heavily intoxicated.

"First off," he began, "you're drunk."

"I'm not!"

"Second, you look upset. What happened?" There was genuine concern in those honey brown eyes.

"She's fine," Jess said. "Our friend was just being a mega bitch."

"You don't need to tell him!" I complained.

"You're both underage. How'd you get in?" Evan switched glances from me to her while we stayed quiet.

"Please don't call Noah," I begged.

"Are you kidding me? He'd probably accuse me of bringing you here myself."

And right you are.

"You should have passed on the alcohol. Anyone could have easily slipped something into your drink." He gave me a worried look, then glanced at Jess and said, "Same to *you*."

"We bought all our drinks tonight and sat in the VIP section!" Jess beamed at him. I think she was more intoxicated than I was, though she held her liquor more gracefully than me.

"Wow, VIP, huh?" He flashed a teasing smile. "I should have partied with you tonight."

"Your uncle is so cool! Why didn't you introduce me to him sooner?"

"I was kidding about the partying." He lightly chuckled.

Shifting my weight to my other foot, my ankle twisted by accident.

"Whoa!" Evan caught me in his arms. "I got you." He helped me stand up.

Talk about quick reflexes.

"I… need to sit down."

"She was about to call a cab to go home," Jessica stated. "We're supposed to be at a sleepover tonight."

"But you got all dressed up and thought you'd walk right into the Velvet Lounge, huh?" Evan folded his arms in his chest and shook his head.

He seemed to handle my rebellion much better than Noah would.

"The fake IDs made it convenient," she answered.

"You… have…" I looked up at him, wrapping my arms around his neck. "*The mmmost… amaaaazinnng laugh!*" My speech was slightly slurred as I giggled the embarrassment away.

"She's definitely drunk." Evan simpered, glancing at Jess.

"And you smell *sooooooo* good!" I yelled out like an idiot, leaning toward his neck. I had a cologne fetish to satisfy.

"She's not going home." Evan shook his head. "Not when she's this drunk. Her dad will probably ground her until she's twenty-one."

"Screw Noah!" I blurted out in a drunken stupor. "I'm so mad at him!" Losing my balance once again, Evan caught me, wrapping his arm around my waist. I was glued to his body now.

"I think I better take her back to my place," he said.

"Yes! Let's go!" Sounding too eager, I rested my head in the crook of his neck and leaned on him for support. Drinking those last two shots was a bad idea.

"You should get home as well, Jessica," he advised. "It's not exactly the safest environment for you here."

"Uh, yeah… unfortunately, if I go home looking like this, my parents will kill me—well, not literally—you get the idea." She awkwardly laughed. "I'm gonna hang back until the girls are ready to leave. I'm not looking forward to staying at Steph's place tonight. I'll try to talk to her, Aria. You deserve an apology."

"I can't believe you risked getting grounded for life because of me."

"And I still would have accepted a cruel fate if your uncle hadn't shown up."

"I love you, girl!" I flung myself at Jess.

"Can't… breathe… lungs… collapsing."

"Sorry!" I released her from my deadly embrace and leaned on Evan again. "Just so you know, I don't want a lame ass apology from that cruel bitch! She can shove it someplace dark!"

"Right, Aria…" Evan gave me a queer look. "Let's get you out of here."

"Text me!" Jess demanded.

"I will!" I walked beside my uncle as he led me toward the exit. Losing my motor skills, I nearly tripped, but it helped to hold his shoulder.

"What about your date?" I asked. "You shouldn't ditch your plans because of me."

"She wasn't my date."

"Then what did you whisper in her ear?"

"Something extremely inappropriate." He smiled nonchalantly.

"Which explains why you whispered," I muttered to myself as he helped me walk without spraining my ankles.

"You're a funny drunk."

"I'm not drunk! I'm just… Everything's kind of in… *sloooowwwww…* motion."

"I'm sure." He laughed. "Hold on to me. I'll carry you once we're out of the club."

⊗

A warm breeze danced through my hair when we stepped onto the city street. In a couple of months, it would soon be summer. I felt abnormally feverish. Drinking all that liquor had spiked my body temperature.

"I'm parked underground," Evan said. "I'm gonna carry you now, okay?"

I nodded and let him scoop me up in his arms.

Reaching the parking lot, I was expecting to see his Impala, but it surprised me to find a black motorcycle in his parking space—a Harley Davidson model.

"Can you hold on to me?" Evan placed me on my feet and handed me a helmet.

"Yes!" I was excited to ride on the back of his bike with him, but nervous at the same time. "Wait… you won't get pulled over for a D.U.I. since I'm not sober at the moment?" I tried not to sound so drunk, though my question was stupid.

"No, but you can get charged with public intoxication."

"Oh. Well, that's a shitty deal."

Evan took off his blazer and helped me put it on. "It's gonna get windy on the road."

"What about you?"

"I don't need it. You can keep me warm." He smiled.

Sitting on his bike, he gave me one last glance. "Hop on and hold on to me—nice and tight, okay? Don't let go." He put on his helmet before I heard a thunderous retort. The engine was alive and revving. I wore the spare helmet he gave me and sat astride behind him, hugging his waist. This was going to be one hell of a thrill ride.

CHAPTER FIVE
GHOST GIRL

The apartment was dark and quiet that night as Natalie lay beside her snoring husband. She was wide awake. Despite her constant nagging to get him to do something about it, his weight gain had not helped his condition. Folding a pillow over her ear, she tried to drown out the incessant noise, but the disruptive sound kept vibrating her eardrums. Feeling frustrated, she pulled back the covers and got out of bed. There was a five second pause before the wheezing sound started again.

My life is so miserable, Natalie depressingly thought, walking down the hall.

She checked on Terry and Tiffany and then headed toward Aria's old bedroom. Rob had wanted to throw out his stepdaughter's things so it could be turned into a guestroom, but Natalie had fought him on the subject and rejected the idea. They rarely ever had any guests over, anyway. She had made him promise not to touch anything, hoping her daughter would move back in.

Switching on the lamp next to Aria's bed, Natalie sat on the white comforter. Through her absence, she found it strange to come home and not have her daughter there watching over the twins anymore. She felt bad for placing a lot of the house chores and babysitting duties on Aria.

If Rob had made more of an effort to help, her daughter would not have had to take on so many responsibilities.

Staring at the chipping paint on the wall, Natalie remembered that horrific night when Robert had lost his mind with rage and received a brutal beating from Noah. Aria had had to move her dresser to barricade the door, which explained why the paint had scraped off. If Rob had got his hands on her, there was nothing Natalie could have done to stop him. He always overpowered her in arguments, especially when things got physical. Someone always ended up with bruises if they retaliated against him.

"I feel like such a failure," she said to herself, tearing up.

Natalie could have easily wiped her tears away, but she knew she couldn't wipe the painful memories that plagued her mind. At every corner, she saw her daughter's pain within those walls; walls that did not speak but hid many secrets.

Last November had not been the only night that Rob had terrorized her daughter. Aria had endured a lot of verbal abuse and countless beatings at the hands of the man who was supposed to love and protect them…including the mother she fiercely protected. Natalie used to spank, verbally abuse, and hit her often as a child—covering her mouth with her hand to obstruct her airways when she would cry as a toddler. But Aria had blocked out most of the trauma to survive her toxic home environment. It was too terrifying to vilify her mother. It was easier to shift all the blame on Robert since his episodes of rage were more frequent. He had a list of shortcomings and had failed to fulfill his fatherly duties with Aria.

Natalie was aware of her husband's family problems. He had been a child of divorce, and when his mother remarried again, she had neglected him and nurtured her stepchildren more. This seeded an ugly resentment within Robert, which explained the reason he was so cruel to Aria. In his eyes, she was a walking trigger.

"Raising your biological children differs from raising someone else's," Rob would often say. That's why he was against adoption.

His raspy voice echoed in Natalie's mind as she glanced at her daughter's mirrored vanity and started crying. Aria had written quotes all over the glass in black marker:

Embrace who you are.
Love yourself.
You are worth it.
Once you hit rock bottom, there's nowhere to go but up.
I would rather suffer trying than to never put an ounce of effort, and suffer regretting the rest of my life.

The quotes were all positive affirmations. Grabbing a tissue, Natalie wiped her face. She realized right then that she should have been the one to tell her daughter these things every day. Somehow, Aria always persevered to stay strong no matter how horrible things had got at home. Wherever her daughter went, sunshine seemed to follow.

A black sketchbook was resting on Aria's night table; Natalie opened it in curiosity, as a wistful smile appeared on her tired face. There were hand drawn portraits of people her daughter had sketched: her grandparents, the twins, and celebrities. She had never taken art classes outside of school, but Aria was naturally gifted. Leafing through the pages, a loose piece of paper fell out on her lap. It had originally been scrunched up (since the paper was all wrinkled). Carefully, she straightened the folded edges and started reading.

Sometimes I feel so alone.
Quiet, empty, nothing left inside of me.
Nothing to give. Nothing to take.
I would cry if I had enough tears inside of me,
But I don't.
This life is a dry desert.
Endless walks through scorching sands that lead you nowhere… no place…
Only to find the world freezing over.
And once again, you're abandoned, alone, and frozen.

Incapable of dying, always awake,
Just to see the world desecrate
All your hopes and dreams.

Don't ask me to blind my eyes.
Don't make me believe in these lies
That suffocates me and burns my heart.
I wish I could tear this world apart.
Limb by limb like the Devil at war.
Until there is nothing.
Until it's no more.
Nothing left to salvage, no hope, no dreams…
Take a walk in my forest
What will you find?
No sparkling streams, no shimmering greens.
Hollow and desperate to feed on a soul,
But no soul is enough
To smoothen this diamond in the rough.

Natalie held back tears and folded her daughter's poem. She tucked it back inside the sketchbook and took a breath.

I'm so sorry, Aria. I'm sorry for not being a better mother to you.

She curled up in bed and hugged her daughter's old teddy bear. Natalie was unhappy in her marriage for a long time, but she didn't want her children to suffer the side effects of divorce, which was why she always stayed with Rob. She was missing Aria and prayed she would return to New York for university.

After twenty minutes of quiet reflection, Natalie finally fell asleep and dreamed about a life that could have been… with Noah Hunter.

CHAPTER SIX
ARIA

That motorcycle ride was a rush. It felt incredible to actually *feel* the speed of the bike. I had held on to Evan so tightly; I worried I had squeezed his diaphragm too hard, but we reached his place in one piece. He parked next to his Impala in the underground garage before we took an elevator up to his loft.

"You're gonna fall over again." He chuckled as I released his shoulder.

"I can stand."

Leaning against the steel surface, I watched the numbers in the elevator slowly light up in timed intervals. My feet were sore. I couldn't wait to take my shoes off.

"I didn't picture myself coming over to your place so drunk for the first time."

"That makes the two of us."

I stared at him, unsure of how to respond. "I like your hair—looks good."

"Thanks." He smiled as the elevator came to a stop. "After you."

Stepping out on his floor, I suddenly lost my balance, but Evan caught me just in time… again.

"I… am… *so* sorry."

"It's all right, love." He chuckled, carrying me in his arms down the hall.

I'm so embarrassed. I had never been this drunk.

Reaching his suite, I expected him to put me down, but he didn't.

"Can you do me a favor, Aria?"

I nodded.

"Reach into my front right pocket and grab my key."

"You can put me down. I'll use the wall to help me walk."

"No, it's fine, sweetheart. Grab my keys and open the door."

"Okay." I did as he asked and nearly touched his crotch before I found his pocket.

"The house key is the small—"

"This one?" I flashed a silver key in my hand.

"That's it. You officially have the key to my heart."

I blushed.

"Kidding."

Wait... what?

"You stole my heart long ago—and I mean that in a loving, paternal way—if you catch my drift."

"Noah would challenge you and accuse you of being heartless."

"My judgmental brother's not here. And he doesn't know my heart."

Evan was so charming. His confession moved me. I did my best to hide my gushing emotions. He brought me closer to the door so I could reach down and unlock it.

"That's it, sweetheart."

Carrying me inside, he kicked the door shut with his foot. "If you reach over to your left, you'll feel a light switch next to you."

I felt around the wall until my fingers brushed against a set of switches. The ceiling lights in his hallway suddenly lit up, and we could finally see.

"Thanks." He flashed a subtle smile and led the way to his kitchen.

Holy crap... his loft is huge!

"Fancy a cup of tea?" Evan offered.

"I didn't peg you for the tea drinking type."

"It's not for me, it's for you—a special blend I bought while I was in Shanghai not too long ago. It'll help sober you up."

Hovering near the island, Evan carefully placed me down on the black marble counter and brushed my hair out of my face.

"Don't fall over."

"*Ha-ha*, hilarious."

His blazer smelled amazing, but it was making me sweat. I took it off and placed it next to me. Hiding a smile, he crouched down low and reached for my left ankle.

"You could use these as a weapon," he said, pulling off my stiletto as I let out a nervous laugh.

"They're very expensive and worth all the pain."

"I bet." Evan placed my killer heels down and flashed a dimpled smile that made me melt.

"That feels so much better. Thank you," I sighed in relief. "See? I'm not that drunk. It was just these shoes." I flashed a coy smile.

"Hmm… right." He didn't sound convinced. "You have the cutest toes I've ever seen."

Sitting on his knees, he grabbed my left foot and massaged the sole. "Love the pedicure," Evan added.

"Thank you."

I blushed when he met my eyes. There was something about those deep depths of mahogany that made me feel as if he and I had shared a past life together once upon a time… like a soul recognition.

"It's nice to know there are guys out there who appreciate the effort a woman puts into looking… presentable."

Personally, I always thought that all feet were gross, but I tried to take care of mine.

"You're still a walking thesaurus." Evan chuckled. "Even when you're drunk."

"It's the little things that count, right?" I laughed with him.

He playfully pinched my toes before rising to his full height again, towering over me like an angelic being—minus the wings.

"I'll be right back, love," he said. "Don't move."

Evan's voice was so deep and soothing. Every time he spoke, something pulsed within me, as if he were reaching the darkest part of me; the part that I hid from the world.

I sat there for half a minute before the lights turned on in his living room. Evan returned soon after—minus our shoes and his blazer.

"I really love your crib."

"It's no mansion, but it's spacious," he said, washing his hands in the sink.

"It's perfect." I whipped my head around and met his eyes. We both smiled at one another.

"*Mi casa es su casa.*"

"Are you fluent in Spanish?

"No. Why?"

"Your accent sounded bang on."

And hot.

He grinned and said, "Your tea will be ready soon." Evan turned on the water cooker and opened one of his cabinets to pull out a packet of pre-grounded coffee.

"Mind if I look around?" I asked.

"As long as you won't take a tumble. I don't think I can reach you in time from where I'm standing. I'm no superman."

Superman's sexy… like you, I wanted to say but went with: "Batman's my guy."

"Don't say that at a Comic-Con convention."

"Noted." I laughed dryly, lifting my weight off the counter.

Everything was still spinning, but not as bad as before. Entering his living room, I let my eyes wander, admiring the open concept design, especially his furnishings and modern artwork.

"I didn't know you collected paintings," I said.

"I have a passion for abstract and contemporary pieces. I bought those paintings from some street artists in New York. Sorry if you were expecting Picasso."

"Not to discredit his talent, but his pieces don't really resonate with me," I mumbled. "Perhaps that will change as I age—love Michelangelo, though. When were you in New York?"

"About a year ago."

"Too bad you couldn't look me up."

"It would've been cool if you gave me a tour."

Expecting to see him in the kitchen, I turned around and was startled to find him standing right in front of me. "Oh, God!" I gasped, touching my chest. "You scared me!"

"Are you afraid of me, Aria?" Evan's mouth curved into a wicked smile.

"Why should I be? Of course not." I laughed.

He made me nervous, not scared.

"Good," he answered. "You have no reason to be. I'm only 'scary' in the morning."

"The morning?" I squinted in confusion. "How so?" I didn't think it was possible for him to look bad no matter the time of day—if that's what he was referring to.

"My voice gets… unusually deep. I've had ex-girlfriends tell me it's scary."

"Hmm… I like deep, though."

That sounded so wrong.

"How deep?" Evan laughed as I struggled to offer a witty response.

"I just meant…"

My face was feverish. I hated it.

"I know." He chuckled lightly, walking back to the kitchen. "Your tea's ready."

"That's great, but, um… I really need to pee more than anything at the moment." It embarrassed me to admit it.

"The bathroom's down that hallway on the left."

"Thanks." I followed his directions and was more than happy to relieve myself. You can't ignore when nature calls.

CHAPTER SEVEN
DARK PRINCE RISING

Evan had turned on some deep house music when Aria returned to the living room. He already knew all the lists of artists and bands that his niece listened to. He had hacked several of her social media accounts and her laptop last year, unbeknownst to Aria. Being an expert in seduction, he worried he was off his game; his niece made him nervous. For the first time in his life, he felt an indescribable chemistry that he had never encountered with another woman. It set his soul on fire. He could hardly believe that Aria was in his loft with him… how he had manifested her. His calculated planning and patience had paid off. Strategy was important in the game of chess, he thought to himself, pouring coffee into a dark mug. His evening had gone better than planned. He already knew about Aria's plans to sneak off to a club with her friends. Normally, Evan would have picked up a woman that resembled his niece to hook up with, but having the real deal in his home was even better.

His original scheme was to seduce Aria, hoping to get a kiss before bedtime. He had a gift for "setting the stage" for opportune moments, yet sensible enough not to force it.

"You can drink your tea now." He stepped toward his niece. "It's not too hot."

"Great!" Hoisting her weight up, she sat on the edge of the counter, crossing her leg over the other.

"Tired?" Evan watched her pretty face as she arched her back and stretched.

"Nope," Aria replied. "It's like"—she glanced at the time on his oven—"two in the morning. Wow, time flies."

She watched him open the refrigerator before he handed her a bottle of water. "Here. You need to flush the alcohol out of your system."

"I thought the tea was supposed to detox me?"

"H2O is the crucial catalyst here, love. Drink up."

"Yes, sir!" Struggling with the cap, her hands felt like Jell-O. Evan stealthily moved in between her legs right when she was about to get off the counter.

"Let me get that for you, sweetheart."

Handing him the bottle, she wrapped her thighs around his waist and pulled him closer, laughing when he spilled some water on his shirt.

"Oh, you think that's funny, huh?" He grinned while she giggled. "Need I remind you of who's holding the large quantity of water here?"

"Is that a threat?"

"Take it as you wish."

"Are you for real right now?"

"Look in my eyes, love. Do I look like I'm having a go at you?"

Fire and ice collided as Aria searched his gaze.

You're so handsome, and I hate it, she thought as he grinned.

"Wipe that smirk off your face."

"Why don't you wipe it for me?"

"With what, some bad news? *Oh, look… your brother's arrived!*"

With a kiss, is what Evan wanted to say, but kept his mouth shut.

"You smile a lot around me, don't you?"

"Would you prefer I brood in silence like Noah?" he asked.

"No."

"Good. Then we have no problems here."

"I'm ready to be replenished now with your *boujie* water, Uncle Evan." Aria opened her mouth and waited.

"You want me to help you drink your water, now? How old are you, two?" He chuckled, staring at her sultry lips. They were parted enough for him to slip something inside… His imagination was running wild again, but at least he stopped it from going further into x-rated territory.

"Right, here it comes… don't swallow too fast."

Not like the way you'll be swallowing my load when I shoot it down your throat, he wickedly thought, tipping the bottle so she could drink. A couple of droplets trickled down the corner of her mouth and onto her cleavage, which triggered some explicit scenarios to manifest in Evan's dirty mind.

Can't wait to see my cum dripping down your chin like that.

Wiping her mouth with her arm, Aria looked up at him and smiled.

"What are you thinking?" she asked.

"Nothing."

"You're staring at me funny."

"What else should I be looking at right now? You're living artwork. I'd like to admire."

If not touch…

"You need to stop showering me with compliments—makes me think you're insincere."

"Do I sound insincere, sweetheart?"

"Are you asking me that question as a psychopath trying to elevate his game, or…?"

Evan rolled his eyes and sighed. "I see my brother's been filling your mind with rubbish."

"I was teasing. Noah doesn't like to talk about you."

"Typical."

Gazing into his russet eyes, she noticed how they shimmered. Aria wondered what secrets he hid within them, oblivious to his perverted imagination.

"You smell like him," she said, untangling her legs from around his waist.

"Like who?"

Leaning into his neck, she breathed in his cologne. Then she looked up at Evan and said, "No one. I just thought"—she laughed—"… never mind."

Evan was about to respond when Aria retrieved the bottled water from his hand and gulped down the cool liquid.

Fuck-me. I wish you'd deep throat my cock like that.

"Thanks for the water."

"No problem, love." He stood between her legs, arms folded in his chest.

"I like this music. It's so chill."

"I should take you to my favorite lounge. They play a lot of deep house and chill out."

"I've got a fake ID now. I might as well put it to good use." They smirked at one another.

"I'll be monitoring your drinking next time."

"Does that mean you'll let me drink while we're out together?" She could hardly believe her ears.

"You know, in the UK, the legal drinking age is eighteen. But technically, anyone under sixteen may consume alcohol if purchased by parents or guardians."

"Wow, I didn't know that. But we're in the United States, not England."

"Well, we can pretend to be English foreigners for one night. What do you say?"

Her eyes lit up as she laughed. "I like that idea."

"By the way, how are things at home? Are you still giving Noah the silent treatment?"

"Yeah. I don't care, though."

Evan noticed her frown. "Now, *that* is a lie." He reached out and gently cupped her face. "You do care."

She shrugged. "It is what it is."

Honey seeped into aqua as he fixed his gaze on her, refusing to break their eye contact.

"He's being so mean to me," Aria confessed. "He thinks he can forbid me from seeing you, even though that's completely ridiculous. I'm not a child!"

"Then I guess bringing you to my place was a bad idea." Evan's hands reluctantly fell from her cheeks, landing on the counter.

"What Noah doesn't know won't hurt him."

"Look at you." He grinned. "All sly…"

"You have no idea."

"I do. You're a good girl who loves being bad… with the right one."

"Hacking my mind again?"

"You can't tell when I do it?" He peered into her eyes. "You're a lot smarter than you look. I'm surprised."

"Um… I don't know if I should be offended right now…"

He chuckled, adoring her whimsical laugh.

Magic, Evan thought. No one ever had this effect on him.

He didn't want to move, but his coffee was getting cold, and so was her tea.

"I'm sorry I ruined your night," said Aria.

"You didn't." He reassured her with a convincing smile.

"So, am I gonna cringe when I taste this *shamanic concoction*?"

"No." Evan chuckled. "It looks and tastes like green tea, actually."

Aria was on her feet again before she left the kitchen. Strolling into Evan's spacious living room, she lay down on his large leather sofa and made herself comfortable.

"Love the color." She stroked the dark leather.

"It's espresso," he added, walking toward her with a hot mug in each hand. "Uh oh, someone's tired," he said, setting her tea on the coffee table.

"I'm just testing your couch."

Evan sat at the end of the sofa and sipped his coffee, never taking his eyes off the angel he wished to corrupt. "One of my mates is a carpenter. Most of the furniture you see here is all handcrafted by him."

"I love it! It's so different." Aria sat up, reaching for her steaming mug.

"Thanks. I guess I'm kind of eccentric. I like to express my individuality. I've always been like that. Though it's got me into trouble more times than I can count."

She couldn't imagine him being violent or loud. Evan was always so calm. She had yet to discover the darkest parts of him he hid so well.

"I know the feeling," said Aria, sipping her tea. "It tastes very, um… *herbally.*"

Evan laughed out loud, smiling when she curled up next to him.

"Are you cold, sweetheart?" he asked.

"No, I just wanna cuddle."

"*That* I can definitely do." He wrapped an arm around her.

Resting her head against his chest, she listened to him delve into different topics, enjoying his company while he chatted about the times he had got into trouble in his high school years. When it was Aria's turn to share, Evan gave her his undivided attention as they sipped on their warm beverages. She opened up about her troubled childhood, which was a blend of happy and painful memories. They spent an hour and a half talking while Aria sobered up. The tea had served its purpose, just as he had promised.

Evan's stereo switched tracks as the music faded to something slow and sad. The male vocalist had a soothing, soul riveting voice. Aria was nearly moved to tears. Evan noticed the shift in her mood, and it worried him.

"Are you all right, love?" He tucked a lock of hair behind her ear.

"Yeah, I'm fine." Forcing a smile, she set her empty mug on the table. "This song…" She looked at him.

"You know it?"

"'High Green Grass' by Sebastien Schuller… it brings back memories."

"Not so great, I'm assuming?"

There was a palpable pain in Aria's aqua eyes. "I started learning contemporary dance a few years ago. It's closely related to ballet, classical and modern dance styles—in case you didn't know."

"I'm familiar with it."

"Oh, that's great. Then I don't need to explain."

Evan smiled and waited for her to continue. His mother had forced him to take ballroom dancing when he was younger, which explained his dance experience. Out of all the different artistic styles, contemporary was his favorite.

"Anyway," she continued. "My dance teacher had got us all prepared to do a big show at the end of the year, and there was this solo performance she had choreographed for me—it was to this song. For weeks I tried to learn the choreography. Ms. Geneva's vision was for me to narrate a story through the movement of my body and facial expressions."

"What story was that?"

"A young woman abandoned by her lover, praying he'd return and set her free from endless sorrows."

"That's deep," he remarked.

"Yeah, I remember that part well." Aria chuckled. "You know what the sad part is?"

Evan shook his head.

"I had difficulty connecting with this song at first. My instructor said I wasn't feeling the music. According to her, my movement was too rehearsed and mechanical. There was no fluidity when I danced—and that was because I couldn't connect with the song and the theme of the story. She wanted more emotion from me. I didn't want to be reminded of my breakup with my ex, so I had to dig up painful memories and use that as inspiration to execute my performance." Aria paused, blinking back tears. "I had to narrate a different story in my head… My father abandoning me."

"Just like he did when you were a baby." Evan's voice was gentle and comforting.

"Ms. Geneva was so impressed and blown away when I finally performed in front of an audience. She told me it was as if I had transformed from an ugly duckling to a beautiful swan overnight."

"You could never be ugly." Evan scoffed. "What an envious hag. How dare she. Give me her full name."

"Quit joking around." She giggled.

"I'm serious."

"Get off it."

She laughed when he gave her a stony expression.

"She meant my dancing. I poured my heart out on that stage, and my family never showed up. I was bummed about that. Mom had tried to make it to my performance but had to work late." She sighed heavily. "Anyway, it feels like ages ago, to be honest."

"Dance for me."

"What? No way!"

"You said no one had showed up at your recital. Well, I'm technically your family, and I'm here right now." He stood up and dragged the large coffee table to the other end of the room.

"What are you doing?" Aria followed his movement with her gaze as he walked over to the light switch in the corner.

"Creating a stage for you," Evan replied.

"Are you serious? I can hardly remember the routine!"

He dimmed the lights, creating a more ambient atmosphere. "Contemporary dance is all about freestyle," he said. "Let your emotions lead your movement."

Aria smiled and stood up. "And how would you know that?"

He ignored her question and walked over to his theater system to replay the song from the beginning. "Take center stage, Miss Hunter. Your audience awaits."

"Yeah, my audience of *one*." She giggled.

Evan turned up the volume as the soothing melody flowed from the speakers in surround sound.

"I don't know why I'm nervous."

"Don't be," he said. "Imagine me in my underwear, if that helps." Evan teased, sitting on the sofa. He leaned back and stretched his muscular arms along the edge of the sofa.

That definitely doesn't help, she thought.

Imagining him naked made her stomach flip like pancakes. Aria closed her eyes and tried to find that secret place in her mind where she compartmentalized all her pain. It was only her, Evan, and the music now.

He stared at her as she swayed her body side to side, motioning into a full spin, rotating on one foot, like a ballerina. She reached out for something in front of her, as if she were longing to hold someone she could never have: an invisible man, a ghostly lover. The piano melody in the song was touching; it made her tear up. Losing herself in the music, Aria visualized every bandaged wound on her body before she opened them one by one, allowing the blood to flow. Contemporary dance was a healing medium, allowing the dancer to move their energy to release emotional traumas; Aria's fluid movement reflected this. Arching her back, she raised her arms in the air and leaned forward, stretching her leg back in the second arabesque position. With her arms extended in front of her, she slid one leg into the second ballet position, twisting her body in a *fouette.*

Captivated by her flexibility, Evan watched her pirouette around the floor. When Aria slowed her spin, he noticed dark tear tracks down her cheeks. While her eyes were still closed, he stood up and walked around her.

Aria was lost in the music. With a heavy chest, she sifted through painful memories without Noah. Abandoned and alone, she had grown up never knowing what a father's love truly was.

She danced her heart out like a lost soul doomed in limbo. No matter how she gracefully moved her body, no matter how much she prayed and yearned for him to hold her, he would never come back. She felt alone with her sorrows. Aria welcomed those feelings and allowed them to be the driving force that influenced her choreography, which made her performance so believable. Twirling like a spinning top, she slowed down and opened her eyes to see an empty sofa across from her.

Where'd he go?

Blinking in confusion, she felt a powerful pair of arms envelop her waist. Her heart fluttered when he lifted her, sliding his hand underneath her thigh. Evan coaxed her body forward in a fish dive as she bent her leg into a *parallel passé*. Using her strength, she pulled herself upright before she arched her back against his chest. He gently let her body slip out of his grasp while sliding his hands around her waist. Tightening his grip, Evan lifted her on his right shoulder in a shoulder-sit position. Like a flower blooming, she raised her arms and opened them.

Balancing her weight, Aria curved her back over his shoulder, as if she were taking her last breath. Evan held her firmly and spun her body while her hair whipped around. The story in Aria's mind had magically taken a new twist. The depressing tale of the abandoned young woman was now rewritten: a mysterious man had seen her dancing in a crowd, but no one noticed her. She was invisible to everyone but that man. He was her masculine mirror who embodied her shadow side, the rejected aspects of self.

Tears welled up in her eyes as she envisioned the story unfolding. The man who had seen her was a soldier who had returned home, burdened by haunting memories. All his pain was forgotten when he saw that beautiful girl dancing in the street. Their fingers interlocked when he approached her from behind and lifted her body as if she were light as a feather. He slid her down his shoulder with ease, hugging her to his chest. Evan had a healing touch, if only in that moment, that balanced music and fantasy. If the Italian choreographer Bruno Tonioli had seen their dance, he might have commented about how the pair had stunningly portrayed "oneness" through the art of dance.

Evan entwined his fingers through Aria's and lifted her up again. She stretched her legs into the splits, tightening her calf muscles and holding that position while he rotated her in a full turn. Still buzzing, she felt like she was flying every time Evan lifted her. A part of her never wanted the song to end. He had taken one of her most painful memories and transformed it into something beautiful. The pain had faded. Aria no longer felt abandoned and forgotten. When the song finished, Evan lowered her down, feeling her soft breasts brush against his chest. She gave him goosebumps, which never happened when other women touched him.

"You never told me you have a dance background!"

"My mum forced me to take a bit of ballroom when I was younger. I hated it at first, but changed my mind when girls fancied me more."

"Of course." Aria laughed.

The energy between them had shifted, and they were aware of it.

"You dance exquisitely, Aria. I'm glad I was lucky enough to watch you tonight."

"You pleasantly surprised me."

His tone sounded low and seductive as he said, "I'm full of surprises."

She felt a thrilling pull in the pit of her stomach when he gently caressed her hip. His touch had aroused her. Feeling conflicted, she withdrew from him.

"I guess I'm crashing here tonight?"

"You guessed right." Evan sauntered to the coffee table and carried their empty mugs to the kitchen.

When he returned, Aria flashed a timid smile and said, "Thanks for the tea—it helped."

"Don't mention it."

"I guess we better go to bed then."

"I guess so." He grinned, sensing her nervousness.

"Where exactly will I be sleeping?"

In my bed—naked, he wished.

"I have a guestroom. Everything you need is in there. Unfortunately, I don't have any PJs for you, love."

"Oh. That's fine."

"You can wear one of my shirts," he offered. "I doubt my shorts will fit around your tiny waist."

"That's okay. I just need to get out of this dress."

Evan frowned. "Why didn't you tell me sooner?"

"Because I wasn't sober enough to notice the discomfort? It's so tight, I have to peel it off me." She blushed when he arched his eyebrow and chuckled.

"Follow me."

☙❧

Walking into Evan's bedroom was like entering an art exhibit, Aria thought, standing in awe. The wall behind his bed was covered with erotic pictures. She studied them while he walked into his closet and found her a shirt. "… *Yeah…* the artwork in my room is a bit risqué."

"I wasn't expecting to see a bunch of naked women on your wall." She laughed nervously.

"I appreciate erotic photography."

"The models are beautiful."

"They're all right." Evan glanced at the photos.

Say what? You must find them gorgeous, otherwise you wouldn't have displayed their pictures, thought Aria.

"Photography used to be my thing before I got into contracting," he expressed.

"Really?"

"It's always been a hobby of mine. I took some courses back in my college days."

"I've always wanted to model," she said. "Noah promised he would hook me up with a well-known modeling agency here in LA. But so far that hasn't happened."

"Do you have a portfolio?"

"No." She frowned.

"Well, you're gonna need one before you walk into any agency. I could help you with that if you like. I can set up my studio stuff and camera equipment here, and we can do a full day photo shoot sometime."

"That would be amazing!" She beamed, hugging his waist. "You're the best!"

"Anything to help you, love." Evan breathed her in.

I'd love taking pictures of you in lingerie, he thought to himself. It was all part of his plan to seduce her.

"What do you think of the male model?" he asked, pointing at a photo on the wall.

Stepping closer, Aria admired the erotic display of women that had been dominated in bed sheets, blindfolds, and ropes.

"He's definitely fit."

"Do you like his body?" He glanced at her, noticing a rosy shade of pink spread across her cheeks.

"Obviously." She giggled.

"What do you like about his physique?"

"His muscles, shoulders… he's totally ripped."

"You like muscular guys?"

"Well, muscles aren't mandatory, but always a bonus!" She quietly reflected on the photo. "He seems like a dominant, alpha type, based on how he's holding these women—they're all in submissive positions." Aria paused. "How come his face isn't visible in any of the photos?"

"Maybe his face was ugly." Evan stifled a laugh.

"Were all these people actually… *doing it,* or making it *look* like they were doing it?"

He shifted his eyes on his niece and folded his arms in his chest. "Doing what, exactly?"

"You know…"—she lowered her voice—"*it.*"

"I don't know what you mean, love?" He feigned ignorance, wanting her to be direct.

"Um…"—she cleared her throat—"Sex."

An attractive grin appeared on his face as Evan glanced at the picture again. "It's all in the eye of the beholder—whatever you want to believe."

Aria observed every detail, from the diamonds around the woman's neck, to every undulating muscle on the man's body. She noticed a black crucifix tattooed on his back with a crescent moon above it. There was also a pentacle inked in the middle of the cross. She found the pictures mentally stimulating and darkly beautiful, the longer she stared at them.

"I like how they're in black and white."

"Are you into photography at all, Aria?"

"A bit, yes. Though I've never taken pictures of naked people." She turned away from the erotic artwork and met Evan's gaze.

"Why do you like them in black and white?" he asked, amused by her awkwardness.

"I don't know. I guess because it makes you recognize the potential of a certain object or person when it's not in color. It alters the interpretation, including your perception of the picture, so to speak... Makes you look beyond the spectrum of color. For example, if these photos were not in black and white, I'd immediately associate it with lewd pornography. But because they're in black and white, it accents the artwork with soft sensuality and saturates it with emotion—which is ironic because feelings are never black and white; they're colorful and complicated."

"You went all deep on me again. I'm speechless. There's so much depth to your personality."

"Thank you."

"You're welcome." His lips curved into a half smile as he held her gaze and undressed her in his mind.

So bloody gorgeous.

"I should get some sleep," Aria said. "I'm sure you're tired as well."

"You'll find everything you need in the guestroom. I've got brand new toothbrushes in the medicine cabinet."

"For your sleepovers, I suppose?" she teased.

"Always best to be prepared."

"In that case, consider purchasing some night gowns for your lady friends."

"My lady friends sleep naked, and they don't occupy the guestroom. Let's put it that way."

Her cheeks flared up in heat. "T.M.I., Evan!"

"I was just being honest, love." He examined her body language and wondered if she felt the slightest bit of jealousy.

"Well," said Aria. "I'm off to sleep." She glanced at his bed, questioning his "body count."

Why does my mind go there?

"Goodnight."

"I like pancakes in the morning!" she hollered, walking out.

Evan leaned against the doorframe and watched her disappear down the hall, staring at her shapely bottom.

I'll give you something better than pancakes… soon.

⚜

It had rained through the night as Aria kept tossing and turning in her sleep. A nightmare had plagued her peaceful slumber, terrorizing her as she mumbled in her sleep.

"No… no… please don't!" she whimpered, rolling on her side.

Thunder clapped in the sky as Evan's eyes snapped wide open when he heard a scream. Immediately, he threw his body out of bed and rushed toward the guestroom. Not bothering to knock, he stormed in, half panicked.

"Aria!"

Sitting up in the darkness, she tried to calm her breathing.

"Are you okay, love?" He approached her.

"I had a nightmare. I'm sorry I woke you."

"Don't apologize."

She ran her fingers through her tousled hair and met his worried gaze.

The lightning lit up the room at random intervals while Evan walked toward the window and closed it. "I just panicked when I heard you scream. You scared me. I thought someone was trying to murder you." He looked back at her in relief, retracing his steps to the bed. "Do you want to talk about it?"

"No. Thanks, though. I'm sorry I woke you up."

"Stop saying sorry. I was already awake."

Another loud crash of thunder roared in the sky. Aria hugged her knees to her chest.

"This storm sounds angry," he added.

"Are you a light sleeper?"

"The slightest sounds can wake me."

"That sucks."

"Sometimes." Evan paused. "I'm gonna get you a glass of water. That usually calms me down when I have nightmares."

"Do you have them frequently?"

"I used to get bad night terrors when I was a kid. Not so much anymore." He placed a hand on her knee. "Sit tight, love." Lightning flashed outside the window and lit up the room.

Aria's heart suddenly dropped when she recognized a tattoo on Evan's back. Blinking, she was sure it was no delusion. A black cross had been inked on his back with a pentacle drawn through it, and a crescent moon above—identical to the one she had seen on the male model in the photos.

The man in the pictures… is Evan. She concluded in silence.

Returning shortly, he noticed his niece wasn't in bed anymore. He found her standing by the window as lightning buzzed behind her.

"Why'd you get out of bed?" he asked, noticing her knotted shirt, exposing her midriff, which only triggered movement below when his eyes cascaded to her thong.

"I needed to stretch my legs," she replied.

"Here"—he handed her the glass—"drink this. You'll feel better."

"Thanks." Aria took a couple sips and drank it all down, not realizing how thirsty she was. A calm silence fell between them as her mind wandered.

Those photos… why did Evan hide his identity?

"You okay?" he asked. "You seem bothered by something."

"No, I'm fine—just shaken up from that nightmare." She walked back to bed, placing the glass on the nightstand. "I'm gonna try to sleep." Aria slipped under the covers. "Sorry again for waking you."

"Don't sweat it. Sweet dreams, love."

As Evan walked out, Aria gazed at his tattoo.

Were all those women his lovers? Why do I even care? I need to sleep.

∞∞

An hour had passed, and Aria still couldn't shut off her thoughts as she tossed and turned. That nightmare was still fresh in her mind. Painful memories had risen to the surface. Her face was wet with tears. She was about to get up and go to the bathroom when something furry hopped on the bed and purred.

"Hey, little guy!"

The cat rubbed himself against her before he scurried away.

"Baxter!" Aria whispered.

Having him around eased her anxiety. Animals were so therapeutic, she thought, getting out of bed to follow the playful feline; he stealthily turned a corner and slipped into another room.

Aria's late-night pursuit led her straight into Evan's bedroom. Her pupils had adjusted to the darkness, which made it easier to see him under the sheets, lying on his back with an arm hanging over his eyes. She paused and wondered if he was hovering between dreams and consciousness. She needed to be held and assured that everything was going to be all right. More than anything, she needed Noah. Having sobered up, all she felt was emptiness. Tears stung her eyes as Aria blinked them away.

I need to get out of here.

Turning to leave, Baxter let out a startled yowl. He had been standing right behind her, and she had almost trampled him.

"Baxter," she whispered. "Come here…"

Evan stirred and raised himself on an elbow.

"Aria?" He squinted in the darkness.

She whipped her head around, feeling like a trespasser. "I'm sorry, I couldn't fall asleep. Baxter came into the room—then he left—and I was trying to look for him—and he came in here—but it was dark—so I didn't realize I was in your—"

"It's okay." He chuckled at her disjointed speech.

She must be anxious, Evan thought, charmed by her awkwardness.

"Come here." He pulled back his sheets and patted the mattress. Having heard the tremor in her voice, Evan sensed she needed him.

"I didn't mean to disturb you," she said. "I should go."

"Come... *here*."

Making her way to his bed, she crawled in. Evan stretched out his arm and allowed her to mold herself against his body. His heart glowed to life when he felt her energy radiating through his vessel. There had been many nights when she yearned to be held and cuddled. The dominant topics in Aria's childhood memories were physical, psychological, and emotional abuse. Rob had been a monster to live with, and she could never forget his cruelty. The trauma always haunted her, even at eighteen, even in her dreams.

Resting her head on Evan's chest, she hugged his waist and sighed. There was nothing but a lulled quietness between them. Though, it didn't last long, as she whispered, "Would you ever hit me if I made you mad?"

"Don't be silly." He tilted her chin up. "Where did that come from?"

"I just wanted to know."

"This is about your nightmare, isn't it?"

"It's nothing."

"Come on, Aria."

She shook her head and slid her leg over his.

Evan let out an exasperated sigh, ignoring his arousal.

"Your heart's beating fast." She noticed.

"I'm frustrated." He glided his hand down her lower back. "I want to help you feel better."

"You are. I just don't want to talk about it."

The rainfall was heavy, hitting the rooftop as thunder rumbled in the distance.

"You're the man in the photos. Aren't you?" Aria changed the subject.

"Yes."

"Are those women your trophy ex-girlfriends or what?"

"Trophies?" He chuckled. "No. More like *one* ex-girlfriend."

"Is it the woman with the diamonds?"

"Yes."

She stayed quiet. "Why didn't you tell me it was you?"

"I wasn't planning on you finding out. I assume you saw my tattoo."

"Yes." Aria paused. "I didn't know you were so…"

"I'm a sex addict," he shamelessly confessed. "I love sex."

She felt a squeezing pull in her stomach when he said that three letter word.

"Oh. I, um… didn't know that. I'm sorry if I'm prying." She sat up and tried not to stare at his naked body. "I shouldn't be in here. Sorry again for waking you." Aria was about to leave when Evan grabbed her arm.

"Like I said before"—his gaze was intense—"you really need to stop apologizing for things that aren't your fault. Does it bother you I have pictures of naked women hanging on my wall?"

"No, it's your life. You can do what you want."

"You said you liked his physique."

"Yeah, that was before I knew it was you."

"Otherwise, you wouldn't have confessed?"

She stayed silent.

"We're not related, Aria."

"I know that."

"You're attracted to me."

"*What?*" She laughed.

"I know you're attracted to me. I can see it in the way you look at me."

"I think you need to go back to sleep." Turning to leave, she gasped when Evan yanked her on top of him with his chest pressed against hers. The heat coming off his body aroused her.

This is so the worst time to not be wearing a bra…

"Stop fighting it," he murmured, holding her waist. "Sit up, Aria."

"Evan, I—"

"Sit… *up.*" It wasn't a polite request.

Raising her upper body, she carefully mounted him, feeling his manhood harden beneath her. Evan untied the knot in her shirt while Aria raised her arms and let him pull the garment off her body. She couldn't understand why she was being so compliant—as if she were possessed by an entity.

"I don't know what I'm doing." She hugged herself, hiding her perky breasts.

"You don't need to know. Leave that to me."

"How… did you—"

The kiss was sudden.

Heat.

Lust.

Desire.

Evan's lips glided over Aria's as he kissed her with everything he had. He groaned in pleasure when he tasted her, decimating her resistance by the force of his passion. He ravished her in his arms as if she always belonged to him. Sucking on her nipples, he hardened them with his expert tongue.

"*Oh my God...* that feels…" Aria moaned, eyes rolling back.

She glided her fingers through his brown hair and pulled him in when he grabbed a fistful of her juicy peach. Their faces were inches apart as Evan positioned himself between her legs.

"You're so bloody gorgeous. I'm in two minds when it comes to punishing you…"

"Why punish?"

"For possessing my soul."

Desperate to kiss her, he let their lips collide in passion. Aria was breathless when he finally withdrew. Shutting her eyes, she surrendered as Evan licked the center of her chest, leaving a trail of kisses down her navel. He hooked his fingers on the edges of her thong and tugged them down.

Staring at her smooth sex, Evan was mesmerized; he needed to taste her.

"What a gorgeous little kitty… fuck."

Crouching, he stretched her folds until he found her pearl; a line of spit fell from his lips onto her swollen flesh. Teasingly, he stimulated the area of sensitive nerve endings until she moaned in ecstasy.

"Do you like that?" His voice was thick with desire as he looked up at her.

Clutching the sheets, Aria tried to find her voice; her arousal was uncontrollable. Evan slipped his middle finger into her tight entry, careful not to penetrate too deeply.

"You're soaking wet"—he sucked on his finger—"and you taste so sweet."

Teasing her, he gave her swift licks, making her pant for more. A feral moan escaped her as he got more aggressive with his technique: kissing and sucking on wet folds of flesh.

"Evan," Aria breathed. "Stop… we have to… stop."

Noah suddenly appeared in her mind, triggering a small voice in her head.

How is this happening?

Her pleasurable moans echoed around them as Evan buried his face in her dripping sex, licking her faster until her legs trembled. A powerful orgasm was on the horizon, as she curled her toes and dug her nails into the mattress.

"I bet you're so tight." Evan panted, pulling out his aching shaft. He stroked himself before he slapped his tip against her, reveling in the wet sound of primal desire. A rope of clear quartz dripped out of him onto her vulnerable entrance.

"Bloody hell… you have such a pretty pussy. Do you know that?"

Aria was speechless. She had fallen into a dark chasm, mind numbingly lost in pleasure. She didn't want to be like those nude models, photographed and mounted on his wall. She didn't want to be a short-lived conquest. Evan wasn't the man she wanted to sleep with, but her body begged to differ.

"Please," she said. "Let's stop." Opening her eyes, she cupped her breasts to cover her nudity.

But Evan refused to give up. He was aching for release. He needed to penetrate her.

"Let's play a little game, my love," he said, leaning over her body. "It's more of a challenge for *you*. But if you succeed, I'll stop."

"Evan, no, I—" She inhaled sharply when he pressed his thumb against her sweet spot, rolling it around. He massaged her until her breathing became harsh and jagged. Ignoring the red flags, Aria snaked her arms around his neck and stared into his eyes.

"Spell the letters out for me."

"What do you mean?" she asked.

"Spell out what I'm writing, and we'll stop. I promise."

Her breathing grew shallower as she closed her eyes and waited for further torture. Evan spread her outer lips and found that pink valley of nerves. He slowly traced the first letter with his index finger, right against her swollen flesh.

"E…" she started.

He traced the second letter just as slowly.

"V…"

Then the third:

"A…"

And fourth:

"N…"

"Good girl," he said. "Here comes the second word." Taking pleasure in watching her squirm, Evan moved his finger again.

"I… S."

"Third word…"

"G… O… I… N… G…" She took her time and spelled each letter correctly, as he continued to trace the remaining ones. "T… O… F… U… C… K…"

"Last one, now. Don't mess up."

"M… E."

The shocking realization was visible on her face as she repeated the words in her head.

"Did you solve the puzzle, Aria?"

"You're… gonna…"

"That's right." Evan smiled darkly. "*I am.*" Gripping his cock, he slammed into her without warning and made her scream in pain… and pleasure.

₧₨

Aria gasped for air as her eyes snapped open. The rain had let up. She was alone in bed, with no sign of Evan, and a dull ache in her stomach. The sensation of being painfully penetrated still pulsed inside of her. Her panties were soaked, and she had broken a sweat. Their entire sexual encounter had been nothing but a dream. But it felt disturbingly real. She almost wondered if he had put a dark spell on her while she slept.

God, this is so embarrassing, she thought, knowing she would have to wash the sheets and her clothes in the morning. The empty glass on her nightstand let her know that everything had been real until the part where she had dreamed about entering Evan's bedroom.

Perplexed by her unexplainable arousal, Aria could not understand why she had dreamed of having sex with him. But she was relieved it wasn't real, because as angry as she was at Noah, she still loved him.

Stepping into the bathroom, she filled her empty glass with water, taking eager gulps before she got back in bed.

It meant nothing. It was just a stupid dream. She repeated this mantra as she slowly drifted off to sleep.

CHAPTER EIGHT
ARIA

It would have been nice to have started my morning with a positive attitude, but as soon as I got out of the shower, my mood shifted like a swinging pendulum. Noah and Evan were arguing outside my door, and it sounded far from pleasant.

How did he know where I was?

I didn't think Evan would have contacted him. And then it hit me: maybe Jess had accidentally revealed my whereabouts this morning… or Steph might have called and told him where I was. That bitch probably wanted to get me in trouble since she knew about Noah not wanting Evan around me.

"Where is she?" Noah yelled. "Where is my daughter?"

"Calm down, bro."

"Don't tell me to calm down! You had no right bringing her back here! You should have called me!"

"She begged me not to contact you. That's how terrified she is of you, and I don't blame her. You've got a hell of a temper."

"Aria!"

I was panicking.

"She's in the shower," Evan said. "You need to cool it."

"You find my daughter drinking underage at some sleazy nightclub, and you didn't even think to call me first? I'm her father, not you!"

"I don't understand why you're so upset. I took care of her."

"You're not her guardian!"

"See, this is exactly why she didn't want me contacting you. She wanted to avoid *this*. You're completely losing it, mate. You would've flipped the lid had I called you last night. Getting mad at a teenager while they're drunk is counterproductive. I brought her back to my place so she could sober up in a safe environment."

"Safe environment?" Noah let out a patronizing chuckle. "Being around *you* is dangerous, not safe! You're reckless, Evan. I'm on to you. Don't you dare think for a second that I—"

"Stop it!" I screamed, opening the door. "Stop yelling at him, Noah!"

Standing across from the brawling brothers, I was dripping wet, wrapped in a white towel. Noah fixed his scornful gaze on me while I stared him down. That calm ocean in his eyes was polluted with gasoline, and I was the spark that had set the waters ablaze. I could almost feel his fury, which made me want to back off, but I quickly recovered my strength and straightened my posture. That magnetic attraction I felt was uncomfortably pulling at my insides. He was still so seductively desirable, even while he was unbelievably angry.

"You're in big trouble, young lady."

"I figured as much," I calmly replied. "I know you're angry and—"

"Angry doesn't even *describe* what I'm feeling right now."

"Just don't take it out on Evan."

"I can handle my brother," Evan stated.

"I know you can," I said, switching my gaze to Noah. "If you want to lose it, then go off on *me*, because going to that 'sleazy nightclub' was *my* idea. Coincidentally, Evan was there—and he certainly hadn't shoved a shot full of vodka down my throat. We ran into each other right when I was about to leave. He noticed I was a bit drunk and—"

"*A bit?*" Noah mocked me with his maddened glare.

"… he brought me back to his place after I pleaded with him not to call you."

"Stop making excuses for him!" He fumed. "Evan's the adult, you're just a—" He stopped mid-sentence and sighed.

"Just a…?" I was certain he was going to say *child*. "Well? Go on. Say it, Noah."

We stared each other down without blinking. I knew he was raging inside; everything in his body language showed this.

He wants me to comply like a "good girl" and shut up. Well, that ain't happening.

My heart pounded as Noah closed the gap between us. Every time he was close to me, all I could think about was ripping his shirt off and kissing him.

"*You*," he stressed, "are my *very* irresponsible teenage daughter, and I'm extremely disappointed in you."

Something had changed in his eyes; I couldn't see the ripples of blazing water anymore. The ocean was still again, and eerily lifeless. He looked… hurt.

"Get dressed," Noah demanded. "I'm taking you home."

I wanted to argue back and shout at him; to be a drama queen and get under his skin to push him over the edge. But I couldn't. It was bad enough that he had scolded me in front of Evan. Swallowing my pride, I turned around, and did as I was told.

"Stay away from my daughter, Evan. I mean it."

"What are you gonna do, get a restraining order?"

"That's a great idea."

"She's my niece!"

"The next time you try to pull a stunt like this as a favor to me, I'll thank you with my fist!"

Their nonstop arguing was beyond irritating. Marching out of the guestroom, I steeled myself and shouted, "Will you please just stop?"

Noah had this look of horror on his face when he saw what I was wearing: a skimpy club outfit and heels. His jaw dropped. Evan looked amused.

"You wore *that* last night?"

"Um, yeah. The club had a dress code, so—"

"I can't believe you wore that! It's nearly see through! Every asshole could have swarmed you!"

"I didn't get swarmed!"

"We're leaving." Noah glared at me. "*Now.*" Grabbing my hand, he faced Evan with a murderous gaze. "Stay out of our lives."

I mouthed a silent apology to my uncle, just before Noah dragged me down the hallway. Glancing at Evan, he gestured he would call me. I was sick of Noah demonizing him. He wasn't the bad guy.

⋘⋙

The ride back home was awkward. I was expecting Noah to let loose and blow up, but he didn't say a word. There was nothing but this uncomfortable silence between us, and he wasn't even road raging—not yet, anyway.

It's the calm before the storm, I despairingly thought.

The stillness was bothering me. Turning on the radio, I switched stations to get a rise out of him. While most people got migraines from "obnoxious" dubstep music, Noah didn't mind the genre—which I seemed to have forgotten, since he didn't shut off the stereo. The music had loud, thudding bass, synthesized melodies, and reverberating vocals. Some songs were really mellow and well-paced, and others were dark with distorted instrumentals. If *Transformers* were to have an orgasm, that's what dubstep sounded like.

Will you please just say something?

I blasted the song to piss him off. But all he did was lower the volume on his steering wheel. Feeling frustrated, I sat back, watching the passing palm trees from my window. The flicking sound of a lighter caught my attention as I turned my head. Cigarette smoke suddenly wafted into my nostrils.

"Since when do you smoke?" Now I had every right to be angry at him.

"That's none of your concern." Noah devotedly took a deep puff, tapping the ashes out the window.

"It *is* my concern! You're exposing me to second-hand smoke!" I coughed.

Cursing under his breath, he took another drag before he put out the butt in an empty coffee cup.

"I've never seen you smoke." I looked at him in disbelief.

"You've never seen me do a lot of things," he replied, sounding irritated. "And that's a good thing."

The darkness in his voice did something to me.

"That's not the answer I was looking for."

"But still an answer." Noah's mocking undertone was so annoying.

"You're gonna smell like an ashtray," I muttered, turning my gaze out the window, only to jump when he slammed on the brakes and pounded the car horn.

"Take it easy!"

He stopped at a red light and continued to ignore me.

Probably raging on the inside.

"Why don't you just yell at me since you're so obviously pissed off? I'm sure you'll feel a lot better."

No response. No reaction. Noah seemed determined to torture me with silence as he stared straight ahead.

"Are you ignoring me now to punish me for giving you the silent treatment?"

"I'm using logic. Stop fucking with my emotions."

"*Oooh*... he cussed."

The tables were turned. I felt horrible for treating him like this for weeks. I had no clue how I could ever endure his cold indifference for an extended period. But thankfully, Noah finally spoke.

"We both know what happens when we argue."

"Yeah, I know. I push your buttons, you push mine. I hurt you, you hurt me, and then we..." I froze.

"And then we what?" He glanced at me with a seductive gaze.

Kiss and makeup, I wanted to say, but I couldn't tell him that. Our relationship had so much negative tension lately, and I felt like he didn't love me the same anymore.

"Finish what you were gonna say, Aria." Stopping at another light, Noah locked his eyes on me.

"We come to a resolution."

"Yeah, we're awesome at that lately, aren't we?"

"I'd rather have you express your anger healthily than to bottle it up inside—that's how resentment builds. Why are you smoking?"

"Why do you think everyone else does? I'm trying to manage my stress."

"You're sabotaging your health, Noah."

"Tell me something I don't already know."

The light turned green, and we were moving again.

"I didn't know I stressed you out that much," I said, feeling sad.

"Is that what you think you do, stress me?"

"Are you trying to sound condescending?"

He sighed and flexed his fingers around the steering wheel while I tried to find some common ground with him.

"Can we just get past everything that's happened?"

"I don't know, Aria. You tell me. Can you get over your little feud with Vanessa?"

"The same way I'm expected to get over what happened between you and me?"

"You're digressing from the subject at hand."

"No, I am not," I denied.

"Why did you lie to me? Why were you drinking? And why did you go to Evan's place?"

He didn't even give me the opportunity to answer the first question.

"We're not in a courtroom, Noah—and this isn't a deposition, so stop cross-examining me."

"Are you considering a law career as well?" he spoke with that same lofty tone, triggering me.

"I don't need to go to law school to know what a deposition is. I'm not stupid."

"Your actions last night prove otherwise."

"You want me to apologize for drinking underage? Fine! I'm sorry! But I refuse to apologize to Vanessa!"

"It's not healthy holding a grudge."

"Wow." I scoffed. "Says the guy who unjustly hates his own brother. You're the last person to lecture me about 'holding a grudge.'"

"Don't drag Evan into this."

"Too late. He's been *dragged.*"

Noah gripped the steering wheel tightly, taking a deep breath. I prayed he would blow a gasket.

"Talking to you is pointless when you're being so immature," he said.

"That's rich coming from you. Anytime you hear something you don't like, you conveniently call me 'immature.' Would you like to add anything else?"

"Annoying as fuck."

"Look in the mirror."

"Extremely disobedient."

"Good. I'm glad. Someone has to stand up to you."

"A princess brat—edit: *my* princess brat."

"I'm not yours. I belong to me."

He laughed. "You're hilarious!"

"This isn't a laughing matter."

"Would you prefer I road rage?"

"Do it."

BEEEEEEEEEEEEEEEEEEEP!

"LEARN HOW TO DRIVE OR GET OFF THE ROAD, ASSHOLE!"

I hadn't been expecting that.

"Control your rage."

"Jeezuz, Aria!" Noah shouted furiously. "Did you give your stepdad this much attitude daily? I don't think so!" He honked his horn when someone else cut him off. "Son of a bitch!" he yelled out the window while I rolled my eyes. Robert's violent temper tantrums had made me numb to acts of aggression; it was part of my norm while living with the monster.

I was quiet now. I had never seen Noah this angry before. Surely all his rage was meant to be directed at me instead of that clueless driver. Rob had nothing to do with our argument. It hurt that Noah had brought him into it.

"Look," he sighed. "I'm sorry. I didn't mean to mention him."

"Whatever."

He seemed to have read my mind.

"It was a low blow. I'm sorry." He sounded sincere, but it didn't make me feel any better.

"Aria."

"Just drop it!"

Numb yourself. No tears. Change the subject: This had always been my pattern of coping with pain.

"You want me to *make nice* with Vanessa? You can forget it—not happening. Everything she had said to me was out of line and she knows it. She never even apologized!"

Noah stayed quiet, but it didn't last long.

"You say you want to be treated like an adult…"

"I *am* an adult!"

"Then act like one! Adults communicate. Adults listen to each other and work together when repairing relationships."

"The same way you're trying to *repair* things with Evan?" It was my turn to throw some spite and sarcasm in his face.

"Don't go there," he warned.

"Why not? You're hardly a role model, and you don't practice what you preach. Your hostility toward him is destructive and your threats are meaningless. It's funny how you call me immature when you're the one who stormed into your brother's place, made a huge scene as if we were in some stupid soap opera—oh, and let's not forget about how you abducted me like a crazy psychopath."

"*Psychopath?* Really? I'm your legal guardian, not him!"

"I'm not a child! I don't need a guardian anymore!"

"*My* house, *my* rules!"

"You're such a control freak!"

Noah hit the brakes again as my body jerked forward. He'd almost driven through a red light. I'm sure if I didn't have a seat belt on, I would have gone right through the windshield. I had provoked him to lose his temper, and it sucked being stuck in traffic with someone who was pissed off.

"She doesn't really care about me."

"I think you have it the other way around," Noah said.

I let his words sink in and felt a little guilty because it wasn't like my stepmom had it out for me. From the moment I moved in with them, she was nothing but overly nice. My feelings for Noah had clouded my judgment and turned me into a villainous uber-bitch. People do desperate things for love, especially when they can't control their thoughts, fears, and projections. Was I just a jealous, desperate lover? Maybe the only viable explanation was that I was so starved of love that I couldn't fathom sharing him with someone else. Maybe loving Noah brought out the worst in me, not the best.

The next ten minutes had given us enough time to calm down, and thankfully, he didn't ask me anymore questions. We had forfeited our argument. A powerful gust of wind blew through my hair as the roof of the car retracted. Noah put on his sunglasses and turned up the stereo once we got on the freeway. My heart felt heavy as I tried to drown in the music instead of my despairing thoughts.

CHAPTER NINE
NOAH

My wife wasn't home when I got through the door, which was for the best, since Aria was still angry. I'd had enough of arguing with her in the car. I didn't want to mediate between her and my wife if either of them snapped. On a positive note, Vanessa had taken yoga classes in the mornings, and I was happy about this because she'd said it cleared her mind and stopped her from obsessing over plastic surgery. She had kept her promise and was following through on improving our marriage. I owed her my support.

Walking through the door, Aria took off her heels. She was about to head to her bedroom when I stopped her.

"I'm assuming you haven't had breakfast yet?"

Our eyes locked.

Goddammit. She is so beautiful.

"Evan was in the middle of making some, but…"

"Get changed. I'll fix us some scrambled eggs."

"You haven't eaten?" She looked surprised.

"I woke up, showered, received an anonymous text about your whereabouts, and knew I had to hunt you down. Eating breakfast wasn't exactly first on my list of priorities."

"An anonymous text? What was the number?"

"Does it matter?"

"I'm really not that hungry," she said, disappearing down the hall.

I was certain my daughter was famished. She was probably too stubborn to sit down and have a meal with me. However, I was confident that the smell of French toast would lure her into the kitchen soon. My tactics never failed.

⋇

As a young boy growing up in my father's house gave me a privileged upbringing. Every morning, a gourmet chef would cook us breakfast, which included all our meals throughout the day. My mother never lifted a finger with house chores. She always hired catering services and party planners when hosting events. Acquiring extra help was the sensible thing to do, considering we lived in a mansion. I don't have any memories of my mother fixing breakfast for me and my siblings or packing my lunch. I remember the first time Vanessa tried to make me breakfast in bed… she nearly burned the house down. It's laughable now when I recall. Crazy how you can find the comedy in not so pleasant moments in hindsight.

Moving away from the stove, I felt a pair of arms slide around my waist. Her fragrant perfume was recognizable. After weeks of sensory deprivation, I was overwhelmed to feel her touch again. I couldn't understand why she had this effect on me. She made my heart shiver.

"I'm sorry, Noah. I didn't mean to worry you."

How could I stay mad at her? It was impossible. She had a way of controlling my emotions, even the ones I thought I could never feel. I stood there quietly, feeling like I could breathe again. Feeling her body against mine only reminded me of what I had been missing all this time: contact, closeness.

"Please don't stay mad at me."

I tensed up when she kissed my back, triggering a sensation below.

"I'm not mad, Aria. I'm disappointed. You lied to me. I trusted you enough to let you go to your friend's place when I could have kept you grounded. Your silent treatment hasn't exactly been fun to deal with, and I know you've been sneaking around to see Evan."

"I wouldn't have to sneak around if you would just let us hang out like family." She loosened her arms.

"I told you why I don't want you associating with him."

Turning around, I instantly regretted it. She was wearing ripped shorts and a black bikini top that showed way too much cleavage. Ignoring the distraction, I cupped her face and avoided looking down. "You've only known Evan for a few weeks. I've known him all my life. Why can't you trust what I tell you?"

"Because I believe people can change. It's not like he's murdered anyone."

"That's debatable."

"Come on, Noah. He hadn't deliberately killed your father."

Such a sweet, naïve girl, I thought. She did not know how twisted people could be.

"Aria, I'm trying to look out for you."

"I don't want or need your protection. All I'm asking is that you give him a chance. He saved me last night."

How did my brother always end up looking like a hero and making me the villain? I was so sick of it.

"Fine," I sighed, dropping my hands from her face.

"Seriously?"

"Yeah, but on one condition."

She looked at me, waiting for my response.

"You can see him as long as I'm there with you."

"I have no problem with that. Both of you need to bond—being brothers and all."

"I'm not interested in bonding with him. I'm interested in making sure he doesn't become a negative influence."

This conversation was exhausting—anything related to Evan was.

"You need to forgive people you care about," said Aria.

"I don't care about Evan."

She arched an eyebrow.

You could take her right here, Noah. Just lift her up on that counter and—

"I think your eggs are burning."

Shit. Those steamy images quickly evaporated as I switched off the stove.

"There goes breakfast," I muttered, dumping the eggs in the garbage.

"I'm more of a fruit salad person, anyway."

"You distracted me." I placed the pan in the sink.

"It's nice to know I still can." She flirted.

It was tempting to reciprocate, but I remembered Grey's advice during our last session.

"Aria, I—"

"I miss you." She snaked her arms around my neck and pulled me closer.

Feeling her breasts against my body aroused me. This was so wrong and frustrating as hell. I had never felt such a magnetic pull like this in my life. There was no explanation.

"I'm not letting you off the hook that easily," I said. "I'm still mad at you for what you did last night." I saw my reflection when I stared into her eyes.

Am I narcissistic to love her to this degree because she's a part of me? I questioned.

"Tell me how to make it up to you." She left a trail of soft kisses along my jaw, making my heart sigh.

I knew exactly what she was doing. I didn't want her to stop; that's what messed with me so much.

"Get along with Vanessa," I said.

"Done." Aria let out a long-winded sigh.

Her lips glided down my neck, as I battled with myself. My demon was still alive; he wanted her.

"No more silent treatments," I added, caressing her hips.

So much for remaining frigid…

"You got it." Aria pressed her palm against my chest and took her time kissing my neck.

The way she touched me was beyond inappropriate. Allowing her to kiss me like this was even more disturbing. It seemed impossible to resist our chemistry. My animal instincts were beckoning me to relinquish control and ravage her, but I ignored those impulses and gently eased her arms away.

Tame that monster, Noah… tame him.

"*And,*" I added. "We can't do *this* anymore." I felt horrible for hurting her, but I had no other choice.

"Because you're married?" She sulked.

"No, Aria, because I'm your dad, and you're my daughter."

"Is that the only barrier keeping you from being with me?"

"Everything we did with each other—all the inappropriate stuff…" I exhaled my frustration. "It was wrong. I'm a man of morals. My entire professional career is based on upholding the law. I can't contradict everything I believe in."

"Spare me the criminal law bullshit, Noah, please. You close cases, you're not a district attorney."

"I was an associate working under the D.A. of LA County before I transferred to my firm. And I'll have you know they had promoted me to head litigator, so I'm familiar with the criminal justice system. I used to help put bad guys away, and now look at me. I'm the biggest hypocrite ever."

"Fuck the law!" she cried out in anger. "You've already broken so many rules! You can't take it all back now—it's too late! I can't pretend like everything we shared didn't happen." Her eyes betrayed her inner turmoil. I felt horrible.

"Can we ever go a day without arguing?" I said, unsure of how to rectify the situation.

As a man, it was my duty to be a problem solver by honoring my word and following through with actions. But with my daughter, I was looping in a moral dilemma and felt stuck. How could I normalize things between us? I'd always excelled at resolving just about anything, especially in my area of expertise. I needed help. Aria was my weakness. I couldn't bend the truth and be manipulative like I was on the job. It was a necessary evil to be a successful lawyer, which was why I'd been promoted to senior partner two years ago.

"You're right about one thing, Noah." She gave me a stony stare. "You *are* a hypocrite. I'll give step-mommy 'dearest' a fake apology. And don't worry—I'll even keep my hands off you from now on."

My heart sank as she turned around and left the kitchen. I wanted to follow her. Every part of me was desperate to show her exactly what she meant to me, but I resisted and decided it was best to keep my distance for the moment. I didn't trust myself around her. She had no idea how many times I'd had sex with her in my dreams, undressed her in my mind, and passionately kissed her to the point of soul intoxication. She wasn't aware of the ugly monster I hid within: my personal shame. This inward corruption grew stronger every day, and it was getting harder to ignore.

Improving my intimate relationship with my wife hadn't fixed my problem. Every time I was in proximity to Aria, all I could feel was magnetic attraction—like I couldn't think. My logic would shut down. Being a man with high intellect, I wasn't used to tapping into my heart space like this; the depth of emotions she made me feel were on another level. This attraction wasn't built on foundations of lust; it was forbidden love. Everything reminded me of her, to where I found it hard to focus on work. I had to resist that natural pull and ignore the way my body gravitated toward her. This dance we did around each other was mentally draining.

Will it ever end?

I craved redemption, but I was losing all hope.

CHAPTER TEN
ARIA

April 27, 2013
12:03 AM

Dear Diary,

Saturday morning was mega shitty. I really don't feel like summarizing everything that had happened, but ever since Noah had brought me back from Evan's place, things between us remained awkward. I think he's been avoiding me on purpose. I had kept my promise and apologized to my stepmom, which hadn't been easy, but she wasn't mean about it, and accepted my apology. I was grateful.

Yesterday, I called Jess and invited her over. We hung out by the pool and sipped on virgin cocktails while sunbathing all afternoon. When I had mentioned Noah's "anonymous text," she told me that Steph had been the one who contacted him because she had boasted about it the following morning. I'm no longer friends with that backstabbing bitch anymore. Thankfully, I'll be graduating soon and won't have to see her face again.

I got accepted at two of the three universities I had applied to. I wanted to go to Berkley because it's in California, and that means I wouldn't have to leave Noah. But ever since the drastic revolution in our relationship, I decided to accept Columbia's offer of admission last week. I would have been happy to study abroad, if only it were possible. My chosen field was liberal arts. I'd love to learn languages, though—Italian, Greek, Spanish, Arabic, French—that's not an exhaustive list. I didn't think it would be possible to be fluent in world languages within this lifetime. Living in Paris or Italy to launch a modeling career would be amazing… But it's a farfetched dream. However, Evan could always help me reach it (should I decide to ditch academics).

I guess I'll figure out my major next year. I'm hoping to qualify for that entrance scholarship once my marks are submitted to Columbia. It would be such a relief because I won't have to depend on Noah to pay for my education. I'd rather bus tables part time than to accept a penny from him. I just need a clean break. I can't be in his life, and he can't be in mine. Not when I feel this way about him. It hurts too much, and he can't understand it no matter how many times I explain.

I was surprised to find a professional email from a "Dr. A. Grey" in my inbox this evening. I wasn't sure how to respond, so I didn't reply—but I archived his email for later reference. I hate how Noah is still pushing therapy on me. I don't want or need counseling. I know exactly what's going on with us, and I don't need some quack to lecture me about it. Yes, it's hard to feel this way about Noah, but it's not like I can magically make it disappear. I'm in love with him, and I thought he was in love with me, too. I never thought I'd be in a situation like this. I'm positive that if Noah had raised me, I never would have felt this attraction. I can't look at him as a father figure. One: he's dead handsome, and two: the sexual attraction I feel is too intense. It's so hard to ignore. Most days I want to cry, and usually I do… at night… like I am right now. How many more diary entries do I need to smudge with tears before I give up altogether? I'm done. I'm just <u>DONE.</u>

Yours truly,

-A tortured soul :(

I closed my diary and wiped my tears before I turned on my crystal lamp and reclined in bed.

Why do I always do this to myself? I glanced at my iPod. *People listen to music to feel better, not to trigger more pain and cry their eyes out.*

Maybe I really was an emotional masochist. I'd been raping the replay on this one song for the past week: "Killing Me Inside" by ATB & Sean Ryan. It was remixed by Amurai, and it made me cry every time. Sean's voice was too amazing to skip on my playlist, even though his lyrics opened the flood gates inside.

My room looked cozy, bathed in warmth from the flickering flames of cinnamon scented candles along my dresser and nightstand. Sleep would not sneak up on me soon. Staring at the ceiling, I lost myself in a maze of thoughts when someone knocked on my door.

That better not be Vanessa. I'm not in the mood for some lame-o girl talk, I thought, warding off a mood swing.

"Aria, it's me."

Oh no…

"May I enter?" Noah asked.

Why did he want to see me? I wasn't blasting my music, so that couldn't have been the reason. Sitting up, I ran my fingers through my hair before I answered him.

"Come in."

My bedroom door opened, and I stopped breathing. I was in the presence of a god. His attire was nothing special—ripped jeans and a black undershirt. But he still looked out of this world attractive.

"Hey." Noah smiled sheepishly.

"Hi." I tried to mime his expression but failed. "You don't look like you're dressed for bed."

"I know," he answered. "I was about to turn in—thought I'd check on you first."

"I'm all right… just can't sleep—listening to music."

"I used to do that whenever I had trouble sleeping—wasn't the case when I got locked up in solitary confinement once upon a time." He slid his hands in his pockets and scanned my room.

"Wait, what?" I looked at him in shock. "You were incarcerated?"

"Cocaine possession and bar fights. It's not on my record, fortunately."

"Are you okay?"

"Yeah, it was years ago—gave me the kick in the ass I needed to get my shit together. Anyway, let's drop that subject."

"You sure? I'm here if you need to talk about it."

"I'm good."

Noah had an intoxicating sex appeal. I didn't think I'd ever tire of staring at him. In my eyes, he was the epitome of perfection. I was confident he could change anyone's sexuality if he really wanted to.

Lesbians would go straight, and straight men would turn gay at the sight of Noah. The LGBTQ community might criticize my biased beliefs if I voiced them, but I didn't care. Polarizing opinions spark academic debates, which were good in my books. I was all for social critique.

"Is that apple cinnamon?" he asked.

"Yeah, I'm sort of obsessed with scented candles."

"Smells amazing."

Not as amazing as your scent.

Noah sat on the edge of my bed and met my eyes. It was hard to read his expression. He was always so stoic—like that was his baseline. The only thing I could focus on was the buffalo stampede occurring in my stomach.

"I wanted to talk to you earlier," he said. "But I didn't want to disrupt your time with Jess. Are you doing okay?"

"I'm fine."

No, I wasn't. I was dying inside and craving his touch. Three weeks of Noah deprivation felt like months of crawling the Sahara Desert with a dangerous shortage of water. I was down to my last few drops. How was I going to survive knowing that he didn't want me anymore? It was torture because I wanted to reach out and touch him so badly, but I knew I couldn't. He was nothing more than a mirage now—like he was there, but not really; not in the way I wanted him to be. Whatever hopes and dreams I had of him quickly turned into an illusion, and the realization was depressing as hell.

"You don't look fine." Noah frowned. "You look like you've been crying."

"I haven't."

I hated how he could read me so well.

"I feel like crap," he admitted. "I want you to know that."

"And that's supposed to help me feel better?" I glowered at him, smelling faint traces of cigarette smoke. "You need to quit before you get addicted."

"Well, it's either get addicted to smoking or get addicted to—" He halted.

"Addicted to…?"

"Nothing."

I sighed, lying down. He always made me feel so vulnerable; I hated it, but I knew I was wrong to push him away. Maybe it was time I pulled him closer and made him realize how right it was to feel this way about each other.

His eyes never left my face as he said, "I don't enjoy making you cry."

"That's cocky of you to assume I've been crying over you."

"I'm not trying to be cocky. I just know that I hurt you."

"Really, now?" I said sarcastically.

"Yes. I understand how you feel, Aria."

"Do you? I mean, do you *actually* understand me? Or are you just saying that to make yourself feel better?"

"You think this isn't hard for me?" He grimaced. "You honestly believe I'm not torn about what's happened to us? My conscience weighs heavier than yours, and you don't know how unbearable this burden is to carry."

I was so mad. The only way I could justify my rage was because I was hurting deep down. My automatic response was to withdraw and push him away, but deep down, I just wanted to be held and comforted. I missed him so much. Ignoring him for so long hadn't been easy, but my anger fueled me during moments of weakness. Letting all that go made me feel as if I didn't have any armor on anymore. My eyes welled with tears as I stared at the ceiling again.

I wish I was a robot, I desperately thought.

"Please don't cry."

"I'm not."

Noah lay next to me and softened his tone as he said, "Hey, look at me." He coaxed my chin in his direction, noticing a tear roll down my cheek.

No denying the obvious now.

I was slowly falling apart and tired of pushing him away.

"I know I said I don't need you to protect me, but can we forget about that tonight? I really need you right now."

At last, I placed my pride beneath my feet and exposed my weakness.

"Sweetheart," Noah spoke in a soothing voice. "I'll always protect you, whether or not you want me to, it's like second nature to me."

He pulled me in his arms as I buried my face in his chest and cried in silence. All the hurt and agony that I had bottled up inside was finally pouring out.

"*Shhh…*"—Noah rubbed my back—"it's okay. I'm here, baby."

He held me for the longest while, whispering comforting words in my ear. The warmth of his body and gentle caresses were healing and injuring me at the same time. It felt good to be close again. His affection had ripped open wounds that were nowhere near healed in my heart. He made me crave more from him. I desired things he could never give. It was a crushing reality, but one I had to accept. You can't force someone to want you or love you the same way.

I often remembered that night on the Ferris wheel… That look in Noah's eyes when I told him I was going back to New York. He didn't want to lose me. Maybe the only reason he had crossed so many boundaries with me was because he was afraid I'd leave him. Did he have abandonment wounds, as well? If yes, then I felt a thousand times worse. My desolate thoughts only made me cry more.

"Aria, talk to me."

His chest was my only shield as I hid my face in it.

"Aria…"

A painful lump swelled in the back of my throat.

"You should go. I'm sure Vanessa's waiting up for you."

"She's passed out on sleeping pills upstairs—and even if she wasn't, I wouldn't leave you while you're crying like this." Noah ran his fingers through my hair. "What's going on in that pretty little head of yours?"

"A train wreck," I whispered into his shirt. "I wish I could hold you."

"You can," he whispered back, guiding my arm around his waist.

How did I ever end up in a modern-day tragedy? What did I do wrong in life to deserve this?

"Open up to me, Aria. I promise I won't lecture you. I'll listen." Noah's bedroom voice was unbelievably sexy, even though he wasn't trying to be sexy.

His hand brushed down my spine, sending chills through my body as I hugged him closer.

"I'm a mess, Noah."

"Don't think. Talk. You'll feel better afterwards."

I doubt that. If only he were telepathic. It would have saved me the trouble of having to actually say the words.

"I'm afraid."

"What are you afraid of, angel?" He caressed my back with a lazy hand.

Oh God, not again. Why am I turned on right now? If there was ever a moment where I wished I were asexual, that was it right there. An absent interest in sex would have made me immune to carnal desires.

"Aria, look at me."

He lifted my chin. There was no way to avoid his penetrating gaze now.

"I know I can pull off a hell of a poker face," Noah said, "but I'm not heartless."

"I'm afraid of losing you."

"You will *never* lose me. I have a hard time balancing everything I feel for you. Half the time I feel like I need to check myself into a psychiatric ward. I battle with myself daily because every time I'm around you, I can't focus on anything apart from this raw, intense…" He paused. "It's wrong on levels I can't even describe. Aside from our blood relation and the fact that I'm married, you're only eighteen. You're still a baby. Had I met you under different circumstances, I still wouldn't have gotten involved with you."

"I don't believe you." I glared at him. "Our attraction is hot enough to set this roof on fire. You're telling me that 'under different circumstances' you could ignore that, simply because I'm not 'old enough?'"

He stayed quiet.

"There's no point in going through hypothetical situations," Noah stated, "because it doesn't matter. The law is the law, and I'm a man of the law. I'm married and I'm your father. I can't be your lover. I'm genuinely sorry for acting on some of my desires for you. That's entirely my fault."

Some *of his desires? Is there a list?* I wondered, feeling oddly better.

"Learning about GSA and coping with it has been hard," Noah added. "But therapy is helping me. I won't force you, but I wish you would give it a shot."

The saddest sigh fled from my lips as I surrendered to silence. There wasn't much I could say, but Noah wasn't done.

"I'm responsible for your wellbeing, Aria. What I did with you…"— he stopped—"it was wrong. Fathers aren't supposed to lust after their teenage daughters."

"I'm not a teenager anymore!"

"You're *eighteen*. Did you hear that word properly, or do you need me to keep emphasizing the last syllable until it sinks in?"

Gawd.

"Besides, you're not really an adult until you're at least twenty-one. Personally, I'd bump that up another decade."

There was no use in arguing with him, so I changed the subject and said, "You didn't force me to kiss you."

"No. But again, it doesn't matter."

"I want a lot more than what goes beyond this…" I brushed my hand down his stomach.

"Stop that." Noah sighed, grabbing my hand, guiding it to his chest. "Look, no matter how old you get, I'm your father and you're my daughter. You're a part of me. You're my flesh and blood. It's not the natural way of things to engage in a relationship with a blood relative."

"Cousins marry cousins in some countries."

"We're not cousins, and we live in the United States of America."

Obviously.

"I'm never getting married," I openly expressed. The idea of marriage gave me extreme anxiety because of what I'd witnessed between Mom and Rob.

"Why do you say that? Marriage is wonderful."

"Are you seriously gonna preach to me about how great married life is?"

"A piece of paper and a ring don't solidify the lifelong commitment two people make when they pledge their eternal love for each other," he explained. "That's just social and religious customs. I like to look at marriage as a union of souls. Everyone wants to find their soul mate. And when you find them, you never want to let them go. So, you make it official and get hitched. Of course, every relationship takes work and has difficulties, but true love will always survive all trials and tribulations."

"Are you a love guru now? Because last time I checked, your relationship direly needs an intervention."

He gave me a stern look. "My marriage is not up for debate."

"Marriage is overrated. Everybody gets married for the wrong reasons these days, and no one stays true to their vows. What's the point in spending thousands of dollars on a huge wedding ceremony, only to get screwed over by your 'one true love' and get divorced a few years later? Some couples don't even last a year. Divorce statistics aren't that high anymore because less couples are getting married. Personally, I think that's wise. It seems like anyone who 'ties the knot' ends up miserable down the road. People get married and separated as easy as breathing air."

"Relationships are complicated," Noah responded. "People constantly change, and nothing stays constant… but that's what marriage is all about, for better or for worse, in—"

"*Sickness and in health*… yeah, I know how it goes," I impatiently answered. "That's exactly my point, though. If people are always changing, what's the point in taking anyone's feelings at face value when you know they'll inevitably stop loving you the same way? Are they without fault because they've reconsidered?"

"I didn't know you were so cynical about love and marriage." He looked surprised.

"Can you blame me? It's not like my mom and stepdad are the perfect example of a blissfully married couple. I rarely saw them express affection for each other while I was growing up. If they ever shared their relationship problems on the *Dr. Phil* show, no one would ever want to get married."

Noah was silent.

"The way I see it," I added, "marriage is a lie. I'm already disillusioned. Couples never stay faithful. I'd rather die an old maid."

He quirked an eyebrow. "Have you reached that conclusion based on what's been going on with us?"

I shrugged.

"Aria, I want to be a good father to you because that's what you deserve: someone to love you unconditionally, with no self-serving motives. I want to see you succeed and be happy in life."

"I'm never gonna commit."

"Well, as your father, I have no problem with that. It actually eases my mind to know that you won't be parading a boyfriend around the house soon."

I rolled my eyes. "I said I wouldn't commit. I didn't say I wouldn't date."

"I don't mind you dating." He seemed to hide his sadness with a smile. "It'll help you get over your feelings for me."

No way. Impossible.

"But seeing as you're a reflection of myself, I can tell you exactly why you don't want to commit."

"Enlighten me."

"You're not scared of commitment, you're just afraid of committing to someone who won't commit to you."

Damn it. I hated how he was always right. Disturbing as it was, I was prepared to give him all of me forever. It hurt being rejected. Somewhere deep inside, my heart found its voice and whispered, *if I can't have you, then I want no one else.*

"I probably shouldn't discuss this with you," he went on. "But it's a harsh reality, and I want you to learn how to protect yourself when you make a lifelong commitment."

"What do you mean?"

"Before Vanessa and I got married, we signed a prenuptial agreement. There was an infidelity clause in our documents, to be specific. Vanessa was the one who wanted it. If I ever cheated in the marriage, she would receive a financial reward, followed by a divorce."

I wondered exactly how much that financial reward was. Big bucks, no doubt.

"And if she ever cheated on me, then I'd get to keep all my assets. We would sell the house, split the money in half, and she would have no choice but to give me a quick and easy divorce. The purpose of a prenup is to protect you. Everything is sorted out ahead of time in the event of a divorce: division of property, spousal support, infidelity, and so on."

It surprised me she hadn't demanded him to give up all his assets if he committed adultery—probably because she knew he would never sign it. That financial reward must have been a ballpark figure of… millions? Maybe that's why he had been so paranoid about crossing boundaries with me because my stepmom had dug her claws in deep. It made sense that he'd want to protect himself. Noah had inherited a huge chunk of money, and his salary was higher than hers. If it were up to me, I'd give her nothing and go my separate way. I wondered what other assets he had… dream houses across Europe?

"Doesn't that make things awkward and destroy the whole meaning of marriage?" I asked. "Kind of like: 'I love you, honey, and I want to spend the rest of my life with you… Will you marry me?… Great! I need you to sign *here, here*, and *here* because I don't want you screwing me over down the road—just in case we—you know—wind up with a divorce.'"

Noah laughed. "Well, I've never heard a marriage proposal done like that before. I'm sure if I had proposed to Vanessa your way, I would have got a slap in the face then left high and dry."

"I doubt she would have left you on your knee, regardless."

"I never got down on my knee and proposed," he admitted.

"Why not?"

"I don't know That's not how it happened."

"How did you propose to her, then?"

He seemed uncertain of how to respond as he said, "Are you sure you want to have this conversation with me right now?"

"I'm just curious."

Noah released a lengthy sigh. "It wasn't anything huge, Aria. It was more like a conversation. We'd often had discussions about settling down because we felt we were compatible… And then one night, I took her out for dinner, flashed her the ring, and popped the question."

I guess that was better than hearing him say he took her on an eighty-day trip around the world before he proposed on top of the Eiffel Tower, or the sand dunes of Morocco, or a beach sunset in Bali. The romantic in me was still alive.

Romance is smoke and mirrors. I lamented my reality.

"You've gone quiet again." Noah stroked my face. "What are you mulling over in your mind?"

"You mentioned earlier that I'm a part of you."

"You are."

"I feel like I've found the missing piece of my soul when I look at you. Don't you see that when you look at me?"

Silence surrounded us as we stared into each other's eyes. Was he contemplating a confession? Or was he searching for the most effective way to bury the truth somewhere within his tormented soul?

"I look at you," Noah said, "and I stand in awe because I don't know how I created such a beautiful person who outmatches not only her mother in terms of attractiveness, but her father as well. Sometimes I feel like Natalie and I never made you." He bent an elbow and rested his head in his hand.

"Why do you say that?"

"How could two people who are so imperfect create such perfection?"

"You're the one who's perfect, not me," I candidly confessed.

Noah let out a mirthless laugh. "We both know that's not true."

"I don't feel like an average human being."

"That's because you're not. You're far from average. You're too mature for your age in every aspect. How could I have made you? I often wish I hadn't."

At least that was something we could both agree on.

"I'm an alien," I sighed. "From a faraway planet called Dysturbia."

"Nope."

"I'm a sex-crazed forest nymph, reincarnated..."

He furrowed his brows and gave me *the look,* as if to say I had lost my mind.

"Is this the part where I'm supposed to L-O-L and not actually mean it?" Noah said.

"That won't work; we're not texting."

"Ah."

The song changed to "Sirens of the Sea" by Above & Beyond and Ocean Lab; it was one of my favorites.

I took a deep breath and said, "I'm not sure if it's my fatally flawed humanity that makes me feel like such an outcast, or the possibility that I really might be part of some other world."

Noah pressed his lips to my forehead and murmured, "You're a Siren."

"A Siren?"

"Are you familiar with Greek mythology?"

"A little."

"Sirens were known to be beautiful and dangerous creatures. You could compare them to modern day *femme fatales* who lured men that were voyaging by sea. They used their enchanting music and voices to shipwreck the sailors on their island. The Siren's song had an appeal that was hard to resist. Once a man was drawn in... the outcome was not exactly a happy one."

"Are you saying I'd shipwreck you?"

"You've already shipwrecked me."

Staring deeply into his eyes, neither of us breathed a word. I glanced at Noah's perfect lips and felt a burning desire to kiss him.

"When I'm around you," he began, "I feel like I'm floating in the middle of an ocean, stranded with no life jacket… just clutching a piece of driftwood. I'm helpless. I hear you calling out to me, I can see you…"—he caressed my cheek—"but I can't swim to shore."

"They call it Greek Mythology for a reason," I said. "It's only a myth. Besides, a rational minded Noah would swim to shore."

"A 'rational minded Noah' would rather drown alone at sea and become shark food than to allow that Siren's voice to lure him toward her island."

Oh, how I loved speaking in metaphors.

"Why? It's not like she'd be the death of him. What sort of 'doom and gloom' entails this silly myth?"

"Think of it this way: if he were to reach that island, he'd never want to leave."

"So, she would hold him hostage?"

"Not exactly. He'd know he would fall head over heels in love with her if he swam to shore. She's a Siren and incredibly beautiful; to where she would enslave him with her allure. And how could any man leave behind the woman he loves once a ship would come to his rescue?"

"That's easy. He could take her with him."

"She's trapped and bound to that island."

"Then he should stay there with her. Voluntary exile doesn't seem like such a bad idea. I'm sure society was boring enough to abandon back then."

"You're missing the point." Noah chuckled light heartedly.

"I'm not. I get your point. I guess I'd just rather be a Siren than your daughter."

He gave me a sympathetic smile and brushed my hair off my face.

"He would want to stay with her. He wouldn't even have to think twice about it. In fact, he would give up his life, his wealth—everything if it meant he could live with her forever on that island. Now, would you like to know why he refuses to make those sacrifices?"

I nodded.

"Because he knows that enchantingly beautiful Siren is his daughter. He had set sail looking for her for many years, but no matter where he looked, he never found her. When he heard the Siren's song in the middle of the sea, the melody entranced him. And when he approached her island and saw her beautiful face through his telescope, he was mesmerized and heartbroken because he knew who she was."

"How did he know?"

"She was a broken part of his soul. When one half finds the other… they just know."

I tried to hide my smile. "Why was he heartbroken?"

"Because he was in—" He paused.

I could've sworn he was going to say, "in love."

"He was in despair," Noah said. "He wanted to save her, and knew he should have resisted the Siren's call, but he couldn't."

The song continued to play in the background, adding to the magical atmosphere of Noah's story. I kept imagining myself as this seductive Siren, sitting on top of a rock while giant waves crashed on the shore like *The Little Mermaid*.

"So, what did he do?" I caressed his chest, gazing up at him.

"He jumped ship and chose a torturous fate. Her face was the last face he wanted to see, and her voice was the last voice he wanted to hear before he died."

"But why did he choose to die?"

"Because he knew that a Siren's life span was short-lived. If a mortal ignored her song and passed the island, she would die. Therefore, he wanted to die with her."

"That's so sad."

His story would have been perfect for Lana Del Rey's "Born to Die" video.

"Well," Noah said. "I told you the conclusion wouldn't be a happy ending."

"I would swim to shore and save you."

"I know you would." He smiled.

I felt so exposed admitting this to him as I stared into his eyes and lost all sense of time.

"Just off the record… that Siren didn't shipwreck him. He shipwrecked himself."

"If he never heard her song and saw her face, he never would have shipwrecked himself to begin with. She's entirely accountable for that." Noah smirked.

"I'm not a danger to you."

"You are. You have no idea how dangerous."

He made me shiver when he touched my hip. Was now a good time to reveal how I saw him in my eyes? He was a perfect reincarnation of an immortal being in human form.

"Do you feel any better?" Noah asked.

I wasn't crying anymore, so that was a plus.

"Do you regret going as far as you did with me?" I asked.

"I'm gonna plead the fifth and decline to answer that question."

"I thought we were speaking off the record?"

"Yes, but if I told you the truth, I'd be incriminating myself."

I sighed, hiding my face in his chest again. "I wish I could kiss you."

"I know." He stroked my face with a gentle hand.

"I don't know how to stop these feelings, Noah." My voice cracked as I teared up. "How can I forget about everything that happened between us?"

"It's my fault, baby. I don't blame you for any of this." There was sadness in his eyes. He wanted to comfort me, despite his obvious pain.

"Maybe you should stop blaming yourself and just accept it," I said.

"I tried to. I can't. I don't want to destroy you. I've already corrupted your innocence to a traumatic degree."

"I was already corrupted way before I met you."

"Then I've scarred you for life." Noah released a heavy sigh.

"You haven't." Moving my leg, I tangled it between his and hugged his body. The contact made me feel so complete. All my life, I never felt like I fit in anywhere, but when I was in Noah's arms, I felt like I belonged. "I wish you could stay with me."

"I'll stay right here next to you until you fall asleep."

I was calmer now, but the pain was still there. Loving him was breaking me. I couldn't stop myself from shattering. I couldn't stop loving him.

"Do you want me to switch off your iPod?"

"No." I shook my head. "Leave it."

Betsie Larkin's voice made every trance track epic, and I loved that Andy Moor tune she was singing on: "Love Again."

"What?" I let out a short laugh. "Why are you smiling at me like that?"

"No reason." He rubbed my hip. "You're just so… beautiful. I could stare at you all day."

Flashbacks of erotic memories flickered in my mind as I closed my eyes and enjoyed his touch. Being up on that cliff with him that night had been too amazing to describe. That was the furthest we had ever gone with each other on a physical level, and sadly, it was our last intimate encounter together. Part of me wished it had never happened, because it only made me want him more.

"Your therapist emailed me," I blurted out at random.

"Did you respond?"

"No, but I didn't delete his email, either."

"You should talk to him."

"No lectures tonight, remember?"

I guess I had set myself up for that.

"All right, all right."

Snuggling closer, I let out a contented sigh.

"Close your eyes, angel," Noah warmly murmured.

Being in his arms felt like Heaven. I didn't want to wake up and find him gone in the morning. Having lost the battle to stay awake, I eventually faded. I dreamed of the ocean, and Sirens, and shipwrecked sailors that night.

CHAPTER ELEVEN
ARIA

Mondays always sucked. But on this day, I wanted to bang my head against my locker when I realized I had left my social studies project on my desk… in my bedroom. I had spent a week and a half researching socioeconomic disparities in education, and I was supposed to give a presentation that day. If I didn't get my ass home, Ms. Conrad was going to give me a zero—no excuses. There was no point in calling Noah or Vanessa because they were both at work, so Ryan gave me a lift during lunch.

We drove over to the house together. He waited for me in the driveway while I stepped inside to get what I needed.

Halfway down the hall, I suddenly stopped dead in my tracks.

Oh God, oh God, oh God…

Vanessa and Noah were home. Judging by the shameless moaning and groaning, they were really going at it upstairs. Cursing myself in my head, I wanted to run out the door, but I couldn't; my project was worth fifty percent of my final grade.

Don't self-sabotage, Aria.

F it.

Wiping my burning tears, I ran out of the house. *Screw the grade*, I thought.

Ryan noticed I was upset as soon as I got in the car.

"Hey," he said. "Are you all right?"

"I'm fine." I avoided his eyes, strapping on my seat belt.

"Wow, your dad's car is sick! The license plate is kind of, um…" He laughed.

I did not know what he was talking about until I looked at the vehicle parked in front of us. It was a yellow Mustang with the following license plate: COM N 4U.

I realized three facts right there:

1. That wasn't Noah's car.

2. That wasn't Vanessa's car.

3. That wasn't Noah upstairs in the bedroom with my stepmom.

"I'll be right back," I said to Ryan. "I forgot something."

Unfastening my seat belt, I bolted toward the front door.

What if I'm wrong? I don't want to walk in on them having kinky sex! I couldn't shut off the paranoia.

Vanessa's moans were like rough, manly grunts that only got louder when I reached the top of the stairs. Edging closer to the bedroom, I noticed the door was slightly open as I glimpsed at a man's hairy buttocks and a buzzed haircut.

She's in bed with Amir! I couldn't believe she was cheating on Noah. But more than anything, I needed to tell him the truth.

What if he doesn't believe you? My conscience warned.

I needed proof. Reaching into my pocket, I was about to pull out my phone when I remembered it was in Ryan's car.

Fleeing the house, I grabbed what I needed, and quickly took a snap of Amir's vehicle and license plate.

That should be enough evidence, I concluded.

Um, no! Get your ass back inside and go all Joey Greco on that bitch!

That television host was always so calm while confronting cheaters. I was shaky with adrenaline—which meant all pending actions *and* reactions were unpredictable.

"You got what you needed?" Ryan asked, turning the ignition.

Stop stalling and go back! My mind screamed at me.

"Aria?"

"Yeah"—I snapped out of it—"let's head back to school."

How could you wimp out like that? Take down that bitch! The little voice in my head wouldn't stop harassing me.

Reaching the end of the driveway, Ryan was about to make a right turn when I unfastened my seat belt and cried out in panic, "Wait! Go back!"

"Forgot something?"

"Yes! Turn around, please!"

"All right, take it easy." He put the car in reverse, as the whirring sound of the spur gears got louder with speed.

Adrenaline was coursing through my veins; I desperately needed it for my next move. As soon as he put the vehicle in park, I opened the passenger door and stepped out.

"Do you need me to come in with you?"

"No, I'll be right back."

"You sure? You're acting strange."

I didn't have time to answer him as I slammed the door shut. Seconds later, I strode inside the house like a soldier invading enemy territory— minus the firearms.

The sex noises got louder as I retraced my steps. Pulling out my cellphone, I crept closer to the bedroom door and braced myself. This was it: the confrontation.

"Oh, Amir! Harder…"

I could have sworn I was walking in on a shoddy porn set, starring amateur wannabes. Traumatizing as it was to hear *and* see my stepmother having sex, it was worth all the gratification I would feel once I'd show Noah the pictures.

How long has she been screwing this guy?

Vanessa was riding him, going buck wild, as her hair bounced around her shoulders. They didn't even notice when I slipped inside the room. Edging closer, I stood at the foot of the bed and collected the evidence.

One snapshot… three, four…

"Shit, Vanessa! Stop!" Amir pointed at me.

"Oh, my God!" She froze, whispering, "It's him… isn't it?"

"Nope," I casually replied. "It's your lovely stepdaughter, Aria."

Vanessa got up and covered her nakedness. There was a long pause before she sat next to her partner in crime as I took more photos just to piss her off.

"What are you doing?" she furiously shouted. "Delete those pictures, *now!*"

This wasn't the same stepmom I had met when I'd first moved in. She had flipped the script on me. Her fake façade had slipped at last.

"You're a cheating whore!" I shouted. "How can you do this to Noah?"

Venom dripped from my voice as I glared at her.

"Aria, please let me just—"

I made a run for it when they got out of bed.

"Come back here, you sneaky bitch!" screamed Vanessa.

She chased me downstairs while I rushed for the front door; it suddenly slammed shut once I opened it. My stepmom's clawed hand was firmly against the barrier. Her pointy, purple acrylics could have easily blinded someone if she used them as a weapon.

"Give me that phone!" She tried to yank it out of my hand as I pulled my arm away.

"You're completely psycho!"

Grabbing the door handle again, she suddenly pulled my hair and threw me down on the ground.

"Get off of me!" I yelled, refusing to let go of my phone. I called out for help repeatedly, hoping Ryan would storm in, but it was useless; he couldn't hear me over the loud rap music blasting from his car.

"Give me the phone *now*, Aria, and we can talk about this rationally!"

"You're hurting me!" I yelped in pain.

Vanessa sat on top of me while we struggled. Some lessons in martial arts would have helped me out here.

"Give it to me, you little bitch!" She demanded, pulling my iPhone out of my hands.

"LET GO!" I was about to win the tug of war when Amir yanked my phone away. Dragging me on my feet, he restrained my arms like a dirty cop enforcing police brutality on an innocent citizen.

"Don't bother deleting the pictures," he said to Vanessa. "Destroy the phone."

"Good idea." She vanished down the hall.

"Let go of me, you assholes!"

"Hold still!"

My stepmom shortly returned, gloating at my desperation.

"*Oops!* Aria lost her cellphone!" she said, getting in my face. "We better get her a new one, Noah." Vanessa mocked me with a stupid smile. She would have been the best candidate on *The Bachelor*—psycho bitches series.

"What did you do to my phone? Give it back!"

"Can't." She grinned. "It's burning in the fireplace."

Fuming with rage, I screamed profanities at her when my temper snapped. All I needed was a pair of horns and I would have head-butted her right in the chest like the hot-headed Aries I was. Botching her expensive boob-job would have made my day.

"I hate you! He'll never believe you!" I yelled, struggling for freedom.

When the bastard released me, I was so enraged I could have caused an earthquake (if only I was telekinetic). It was too late to recover my broken cellphone. I thought about running to my room to grab my iPod since it had a camera. But then I remembered I had left it in my locker at school. And then it hit me: Ryan's phone.

Dashing out of the house, I flung open my passenger door and faced my friend in a panic. "I need your cell! Please, hurry!"

He turned down the volume on his stereo and looked at me. "What's going on?"

"I'll explain later. Just give me your phone!"

"My battery's dead."

Why is this happening now? Right when I caught her red-handed!

Before I could answer Ryan's questions, Vanessa's voice blasted behind me.

"Come back inside and we can talk about this, Aria!"

I had no intention of sitting anywhere near her after what had happened. She probably wanted to negotiate a deal to cover up her lies.

Without wasting another minute, I got inside Ryan's car and put on my seat belt.

"Will you please just tell me what happened already?"

"I'll tell you about it once we leave. Drive!"

Stepping on the gas, we disappeared in seconds. I had to stop by Noah's firm as soon as possible. He would believe me—evidence or no evidence. Vanessa was done.

CHAPTER TWELVE
ARIA

Noah's law firm was a big corporate building—not as big as the skyscrapers in New York, but still a concrete tower. Taking the elevator up to his floor, I stepped out and got lost, standing out like a sore thumb. A blur of gray suits and dark pencil skirts brushed past me. The scent of perfume, cologne, and coffee had thickened the air. Noah's work environment was a place to which I could never adapt. I mean, imagine spending hours reading law books and constructing convincing arguments to win a case in court. I could never manage the stress that came with that profession, and I certainly didn't have the dedication and passion for it.

Explaining the whole cheating scandal to Ryan had been frustrating. After he had dropped me off, I insisted he head back to school, since I planned to stay with Noah for the rest of the day. Thankfully, my friend had been nice enough to hand in my project for me. I really didn't want to attend the rest of my classes. This was a family emergency.

Navigating the busy space, I was about to walk into Noah's office when I heard a woman's voice.

"Miss—um, hello? Excuse me…"

I whipped my head around and noticed a lady with jet black hair and shiny dark eyes, sitting in a small cubicle. She was of Asian descent and had attractive features. I liked her smoky gray eye shadow; and the way she had tied her hair up in a high bun accentuated her elegant cheekbones.

"You can't go in there without an appointment," she politely said.

"I'm Noah's daughter."

"Oh! Hi, Aria!" She smiled and got up from her seat to greet me. "Honey, your father's not in at the moment. He's at a meeting with a client. I'm Dianne. I've been curious to meet you! He always talks about you."

He does? I wondered what those discussions were like.

Noah's secretary had amazing fashion sense, I noticed, taking notes in my mind. She wore a long navy-blue pencil skirt, fastened high at the waist with a gold belt. Her silk, ivory shirt was stylish, and I loved her heels and accessories. Dianne was pure sophistication.

"Do you know when he'll be back?"

"Maybe an hour," she replied, "depending on how the meeting goes."

My disappointment was visible, but I tried not to show any signs of distress.

"Isn't it a school day for you, young lady?"

"I have a last period spare. I need to see my dad."

"Is it an emergency?"

"Sort of."

"I'll let you in," she said, escorting me. "If all goes well, he should be back within the hour."

Noah's office was more than spacious. The first thing that caught my eye was his name inscribed on the glass wall that had separated his workspace from the rest of the firm:

NOAH HUNTER
SENIOR PARTNER

How was I ever going to measure up to his success? His work desk was enormous, with a laptop resting on it—some pens, and a phone. The black leather office chair was nerve-racking to stare at. How was he able to manage the pressure of his job? I wondered. Then again… it was Noah. He could handle just about anything, except for me.

Observing my surroundings, his office had a modern theme with a shelf full of law books in one corner. I could see palm trees and the ocean in the distance as I looked out the window. The view was gorgeous.

Noah's office was quiet. The glass barrier was soundproof. I couldn't hear the buzzing noise of workplace traffic any longer. An office job was not for me. I had yet to find my true calling.

As I sat on a loveseat, Dianne suddenly walked in bearing gifts: fashion magazines. Her perfume smelled amazing, and I loved her energy.

"I've got a little something for you to read while you wait."

"That's kind of you." I smiled.

"Would you like anything to eat or drink?"

"No, thank you. I don't wish to distract you from work."

"I want to make sure you're taken care of. You're my boss's daughter—and between you and me, he's the most loved and respected senior partner at this firm."

That didn't surprise me. Who wouldn't love Noah?

"Well," she sighed. "Back to work! Give me a shout if you need me."

Seating myself, I flipped through pages of *Vogue* and tried to stop overthinking.

CHAPTER THIRTEEN
INNOCENT UNTIL PROVEN GUILTY

A pair of guilty adulterers sat in a yellow Mustang parked in a private lot of an establishment. Amir and Vanessa had been arguing nonstop for the past ten minutes. Prior to leaving the house, she had thrown out the remains of Aria's burned cellphone and called for maid service to tidy up the mess they had made in the bedroom.

"Shit!" cursed Vanessa. "What are we gonna do?" She ran her fingers through her hair in distress.

"Relax, babe. We destroyed the cellphone and trashed it out of the house. I've already got an alibi if Noah confronts me. I told you it was risky coming over."

"That annoying bitch is gonna ruin everything! Not only will she destroy my life if Noah finds out, but yours as well!"

"Calm down." Amir touched her thigh. "As long as we stick to our story, we'll be fine. It's been over a year, and he still hasn't clued in. We've done it this long. He's never suspected a thing… neither has my wife."

But Vanessa refused to drop the subject. "We never should have started this affair. What were we thinking? What are you gonna tell him?"

"That his kid's acting out and trying to hurt you. She made up a fictitious story and got rid of her phone to make it sound more believable. It's the typical case of 'I hate the stepmom, so I'm gonna disrupt marital harmony and make her disappear.' And that's the same excuse you need to use. Tell him the brat's deliberately trying to destroy your marriage."

Vanessa took a deep breath. "Okay, I can do this." She pulled down the visor to fix her makeup in the mirror and said, "Did you interact with Noah at all today?"

"I told him I was heading out to lunch before I came over. I know this guy who owns a restaurant downtown. When I tell him to *jump*, he says, 'how high?' He'll vouch for me. I'm not worried."

Vanessa shut the visor.

"Don't stress," he reassured her. "Everything's gonna be fine."

"What if she gets that boy involved?"

"Please." Amir scoffed. "Is Noah actually gonna believe him? The kid is best friends with his rebel daughter. Besides, he already told me he doesn't like him." He calmly took a sip of his coffee and set it back in the cup holder. "Noah decides based on facts. He's a lawyer; he needs proof. Innocent until proven guilty, remember? The brat has no proof. It's her word against yours."

Vanessa marinated in misery.

"You're gonna get wrinkles if you keep frowning like that," Amir teased.

"Shoot!" she gasped, turning down the mirrored visor. "I got injections last week, too!"

"All the more reason to stay cool as a cucumber."

"I don't want to go in for another visit until next month." She stretched the skin across her forehead and felt satisfied when no age lines appeared. Fixing her cleavage, Vanessa opened the passenger door and looked back at her lover. "Don't contact me until I reach out, okay?"

He turned the key in the ignition. "Done."

CHAPTER FOURTEEN
ARIA

An hour had passed since I had entered Noah's office when he finally appeared. He was reading a document as he approached the glass door and didn't notice me. I stayed quiet and waited for his eyes to find mine. Dressed in a navy-blue pinstriped suit and silver tie, he looked so sexy. I'm sure I wasn't the only one in this office who was guilty of fantasizing about him. Noah placed his briefcase on the desk and paused when he looked up and saw me sitting on the sofa.

"Aria?"

There it was: my anxiety kicking in.

"What are you doing here?" He smiled, surprised to see me. Too bad I had to be the bearer of bad news.

Hopefully, he won't shoot the messenger.

"Is everything okay?" He looked concerned, opening his briefcase. "Shouldn't you be at school?"

"Yes." I wished I could hug him. "Do you have time to talk?"

He pulled out some files and sat at his desk. "Yes, I do. What's up?"

This was such a bad idea, I regretfully thought. *I should not be bringing family drama to his workplace. Abort mission!*

"I, um…" I fidgeted with my fingers. "I wanted to interview you for my careers class."

White lies…

"So,"—he shot me a quizzical stare—"you ditched school to come all the way here to do it? Come on, Aria, out with it. And this time, the truth."

I lowered my head and muttered, "I don't think you want to know right now. I made a mistake coming here."

Way to go Miss Smarty-pants! It took you nearly an hour to figure that out?

"I should have waited for you to get home," I said. "I'm sorry."

Noah frowned and made his way around the desk before he leaned back on it. "Now I'm concerned. What happened?"

"I'd rather discuss it when we get home." Grabbing my school bag, I started toward the door.

"Hey—hold up, young lady," Noah demanded.

I stopped and faced him.

"Did something happen at school? Someone hurt you?"

Someone didn't hurt me… someone hurt you, I wanted to say.

"I'll tell you about it when you come home later."

"How did you get here?"

"Ryan drove me."

"Why was Ryan driving you?" He narrowed his eyes.

"It's a long story."

"I have time to listen."

This was pointless; he wouldn't drop it. I was about to respond when that backstabbing bastard walked into his office.

"Hey, Noah, just dropping in to relay a message: Zuckerman wants you collaborating with me on that Global Tech case." Amir placed a folder on Noah's desk and smiled at me as if nothing had happened. "Oh, your daughter's here! How are you, Aria?" His enthusiasm was as fake as Vanessa's tits.

"Don't talk to me," I shrewdly replied. "If you think you've shut me up from telling the truth about you two, think again."

Mister Douchey-Asshole laughed and looked at us.

"I don't know what she's talking about. Do you, Noah?"

"Aria, what's going on?" His blue eyes penetrated mine. "Why are you being rude?"

There was no way to keep quiet now. Amir had forced my hand. The truth had to come out.

"I caught him in bed with Vanessa about an hour ago at our house… in *your* bed," I added.

Amir snorted in disbelief. "She's kidding, right?" He laughed. "Kids these days… doing all kinds of drugs."

"Sweetheart," Noah said. "That's a serious accusation."

"I took photos of them in bed together on my phone. When I tried to leave the house, they got physical with me—I'm talking tag-team effort. Vanessa stole my cell and burned it in the fireplace!"

"Wait—*physical?*" Noah looked confused.

"She was hurting me, and *he* helped her."

"Are you insane?" Amir faked his outrage.

That bastard pretended to play the victim when he damn well knew he was lying. He was so twisted in real life, which only proved he was just as sly and manipulative on the job. If I were a killer, I'd hire him as my attorney. He would have helped me lie my way out of death row.

"Ryan drove me home during lunch so I could pick up my project, when I got through the door, I heard noises upstairs. I went up and found them in your bed… having sex."

Noah stared at me with an impassive expression, as if I were crazy.

"Did you not hear me?" I raised my voice. "They were fucking!"

"Don't use that kind of language around here," he cautioned.

Amir snickered under his breath. "Noah, buddy, I was at Casey's restaurant for lunch this afternoon. Let's swing by his joint right now if you don't believe me. I've brought back leftovers if you're hungry."

"What?" I cried out. "He's lying!"

Noah looked at Amir and then stared at me. I could see the disappointment spreading over his face, and it made me shrink inside myself.

"That won't be necessary, Amir," Noah said. "I'm sorry you're getting dragged into this."

"So… are we cool, then?"

"Yes," he replied, glaring at me. "We're cool."

I worried he would unleash his wrath once that lying prick was gone.

"All-righty then." Amir cleared his throat. "I'll leave you two to chitchat."

I couldn't contain my anger any longer. All afternoon, I felt like an active volcano that was ready to erupt.

"How can you stand there and lie to his face like that? What kind of friend are you?"

"Aria!" Noah's raging uproar startled me. "Must I remind you where you are?"

Amir looked at me with a smug smile. I bet he was laughing on the inside.

Tame your shadow, Aria. Tame it.

"Apologize to my colleague!" Noah demanded.

"What? No way! He's sleeping with your wife!"

"Don't worry about it, man," Amir said. "I'm gonna get out of—"

"I said, *now*, Aria!" Noah's voice sounded threatening, but his scornful stare was far worse.

My intention was never to humiliate him; I just wanted him to believe me. Pulling off a sticky note from Noah's desk, I snatched a pen and started writing.

"A yellow Mustang with *this* license plate was parked in the driveway of our home," I stated, showing off the note. "This is Amir's car."

"I don't own a yellow Mustang."

"I know you don't." Noah glanced at him, folding his arms in his chest. "I'll look over the case file you left me. I'm gonna have that chat now with my daughter, Amir. And since she's not willing to say she's sorry, I'll apologize on her behalf."

"Don't bother."

"I have a teenage daughter, too," Amir replied. "They can be a handful. Good luck, bro." He faked an empathetic smile and finally left.

Noah's heated eyes bore into mine, as if he were holding back his fury.

"You're gonna regret this once you find out I'm telling the truth."

"I don't know what kind of stunt you're trying to pull here, Aria—but compromising an innocent man's reputation is wrong."

"I'm not trying to pull anything!"

Well, except for that attractive silver tie around his neck. *That* I didn't mind pulling.

"I thought you and Vanessa had settled things. Why are you making such outrageous accusations? Is this your way of taking revenge to get back at her?"

It hurt that he thought I would stoop to such levels.

"I can't believe you would think that about me."

"We'll discuss this later. My driver will take you home since the school day's over." He picked up his office phone and dialed.

"Hang up. I'm out." I walked toward the door and noticed Dianne looking at us; she seemed worried.

She didn't hear our argument, did she?

My heart didn't want to leave, but my pride was screaming to run.

"Aria, wait." Noah appeared behind me.

"Why? You don't believe me." I refused to face him.

"Look at me."

"No. I'm leaving."

He gently grabbed my arm and pulled me away from the door. My heart sped up from the contact. As angry as I was, Noah just had this ability to touch something deep within me; something that made me shiver.

"Don't be so difficult, please," he begged.

I met his pleading eyes and wanted to cry. It was devastating to know he didn't trust me.

"Aria, is this about us?"

"There is no *us* anymore." My eyes brimmed with tears.

"Look, I know you were hurting last night. I know you want us to—" Noah stopped, lowering his voice. "You know…" He caressed my face, but I withdrew.

"I can't. I can't stand here another second knowing you don't believe me." Stepping back, I convinced myself that his touch was toxic. "I can get my own cab home."

"Don't leave yet."

"Goodbye, Noah."

"Hey! I'm talking to you!"

His fuming voice caught everyone's attention as they stopped what they were doing and looked at us. My embarrassment didn't stop me from heading straight toward the elevators. I didn't care about how loud and angry he got. He had no authority over me. Not anymore.

CHAPTER FIFTEEN
NO STRINGS ATTACHED

Evan Hunter entered his loft around eight in the evening; but he wasn't alone. A blue-eyed brunette was accompanying him. He had met her at a bar last weekend. Being the charismatic man he was, he successfully lured her back to his place after their dinner date. She seemed interested in a night of steamy, spontaneous sex.

"Wow, nice crib!" Lindsay said, scanning her surroundings, unaware that she had walked right into the wolf's den.

Evan made his way to the mini-bar and asked her if she would like a drink.

"What do you have?"

"I make an impressive Amaretto Sour."

"Sounds good to me."

While Evan was fixing their drinks, Lindsay strolled around his living room and admired all the artwork on the walls. "I didn't think you were the artistic type."

"I get that a lot," he answered, grabbing two glasses before he entered the kitchen. Filling the cocktail shaker with ice cubes, he poured some Amaretto and added the sweet and sour mix.

"Are you sure you're single?" she asked, facing him.

"If I wasn't, I wouldn't have hit on you."

"I'm just surprised. A good-looking guy who is well-established doesn't stay on the market for long."

"I don't believe in monogamy," Evan replied, mixing the cocktail shaker.

"Maybe I can change your mind." She smirked.

I doubt that.

What he really wanted was to sleep with her and send her on her way.

The drinks were finally ready to be served as Evan approached his date. He handed Lindsay a glass and smiled. "Cheers!"

They clinked their glasses together and sipped on the liquor.

"It's great! You weren't kidding." Her open cleavage caught his eye.

"I'm a man of many talents. You'll get to experience a good majority of them tonight, if you're lucky." He winked.

"*If* I'm lucky? *You're* lucky I'm even here with you."

Her sassy attitude amused him.

"Let me be the judge of that." He took a step closer and grazed her cheek with his hand. His touch was gentle, as he slowly glided his thumb over her bottom lip and lowered his face to hers.

Lindsay felt her knees weaken as they kissed. Taking control, she bit his bottom lip, igniting their sexual attraction. When she pulled back from his powerful kiss, she beamed with hearts in her eyes.

"Yep, I'm definitely lucky," said Evan, humoring her.

"Can we have some music?"

"Turn on my stereo." He pointed at the remote on the coffee table. "I'm gonna change out of my clothes. Be right back."

Strolling into his bedroom, he pulled off his V neck shirt and was about to open his closet when he froze. Something snapped inside of him as he heard the haunting trance music and minor melodies: "The Rapture Pt. III" by &ME, Black Coffee. It was "Aria's song"—and no one listened to Aria's songs except for him, he thought. Evan had a personal playlist dedicated to her. Her music always shifted him closer to her frequency, or so he believed.

Evan often fantasized about making love to her while that dark melody played in the background. It had become sacred to him in a twisted way, as if it were an ominous anthem that would transform Aria into his earthbound sex goddess: the rise of the dark feminine, proudly mounting him, riding him to euphoria in all her glory.

Leaving the bedroom, he appeared behind Lindsay and startled her when he demanded she change the track.

"It was on your playlist," she nervously uttered.

He grabbed the remote and changed the song.

"Sorry." She backed away from him. "I think I better go."

Things had gotten awkward fast, and Lindsay felt uncomfortable. Evan's reaction had been over the top, and he knew it. Rolling his eyes in annoyance, he put on the "nice guy mask" and went after her.

"Lindsay, I'm sorry. I didn't realize I still had that song on my playlist—reminds me of my ex," he lied.

His explanation seemed convincing enough as she sympathized with him.

"Please don't go." He tried to sound sincere, reaching for her hands. "I'd like for you to say." His eyes were deceptively genuine. "I'd *really* like for you to stay."

Lindsay bought the entire act. Wrapping her arms around Evan's naked shoulders, she surrendered to lust before she kissed him softly. Evan knew where this kiss would take them: straight to the bedroom. And that was exactly where they headed. He took her to the gates of ecstasy before he was filled with shame and regret. It always happened post orgasm. He had no choice but to file it away, enslaved to his darkest desires.

CHAPTER SIXTEEN
ARIA

The confrontation in Noah's office was bad, but what took place at home was much worse. Vanessa and I had been arguing. It was her word against mine, and honestly, I wasn't doing too well.

"I'm telling you I caught her in bed with your 'so called best friend!'" I furiously yelled at Noah.

He sat in an armchair, scowling at me.

"Why won't you believe me?"

"He doesn't believe you because it's obvious you're trying to sabotage our marriage! Your accusations are absurd! Where is your proof, Aria? You have none!"

"Because you destroyed my phone!"

"I did no such thing! You're hiding it!"

I met Noah's eyes and desperately begged him to believe me. "Why would I lie about this? Ryan was with me; he'll verify—"

"I was at work the entire day, Noah," Vanessa cut in. "Check our home security footage. Please, you *know* what she's trying to do here."

The three of us argued for the next ten minutes, hurling insults at each other while Noah tried to mediate between us.

"Check her phone!" I frantically cried out. "I'm sure there are plenty of incriminating texts. Better yet: check her phone records!"

Vanessa flashed a condescending smile as she handed her cellphone to Noah and said, "I have nothing to hide, honey."

"That won't be necessary," he declined. "It's clear what's going on here."

He was taking her side over mine; it made me want to expose all our "trysts," but I'd swore I would never stoop that low. I didn't want him to hate me. I had to bite the bullet.

"She put her hands on me!" I exclaimed. "She literally yanked my hair, pulled me down on the floor, and beat me!"

"Aria," he said, rubbing his temples. Noah seemed frustrated, but I had to summarize what had happened.

"Amir restrained me while she took my phone and burned the evidence!"

"Stop!" he shouted.

"Who knows if that's what she actually did?"

"You have the most outrageous imagination, Aria. Just because you're angry at me doesn't give you the right to spin a web of lies!" Vanessa looked at Noah and said, "I know you and I are still working on things—and I'm doing my best, but to be accused of sleeping with your best friend is just..."—she released a heavy sob—"extremely hurtful!"

Vanessa deserved an Emmy; I'll give her that much.

"I've been nothing but kind to you, Aria."

Noah hugged my stepmom and comforted her while she cried before he glared at me and said, "I want a word with you, *alone.*"

"You're actually buying all those crocodile tears?" I couldn't believe it. "Well done, step-mommy!" I applauded her with mock enthusiasm. "You deserve a standing ovation!"

"I want her out of my house! She's no longer your responsibility. She's disrespected me long enough!"

"Nessa," he said. "Calm down."

"You should be grateful to be living here with us!" she yelled at me. "You don't deserve this privileged lifestyle, and that's the truth."

"*Vanessa!*" He shouted. "Step outside and cool down."

"No! She needs to hear this!" The bitch locked her murderous gaze on me and said, "My husband may have been absent for most of your life, but he's saved you from poverty, abuse, and your pathetic excuse for a mother!"

"Shut up!" I screamed in tears.

"This is how you repay him? By deliberately destroying his happiness?"

Noah demanded that she stop.

"You must have been plotting revenge from the moment you stepped into this house."

"I have not!"

"And like fools, we welcomed you with open arms. All you've done is take advantage of our kindness and generosity!"

"Enough!" Noah thundered, more enraged than ever.

"I won't allow you to destroy my marriage. *I* am his wife, and *you* need to accept that!"

That steaming kettle in my mind was screaming as I lunged toward her. But Noah stepped in, and bear hugged me. I guess he feared I'd put my hands on his *precious wifey.*

"Let go!"

"Violence won't fix this," he urged. If he was concealing his anger, he was doing an amazing job.

"I'm not some delinquent!"

Vanessa continued to cry, causing my temper to shatter.

"I can't believe how you are victimizing yourself, you lying bitch!" I yelled. "You don't deserve him! You're gonna regret lying to his face. The truth will come out. It always does!"

That was my last exchange with her before I stormed out and fled from the house in my Firebird. I didn't want to stay under the same roof as that tramp for a minute longer.

Hopefully, he won't follow me.

ଓଞ୦

Racing down the street, I kept checking my rear-view mirror like a paranoid carjacker. I didn't enjoy running away from conflict, but there was no point arguing with a liar. I also realized my pattern, how I ran when things got bad. Reaching a red light, I weighed my options:

sleepover at Jess or Tammy's. Even though Jessica would have happily let me stay over, I didn't want to impose. Evan's place was also an option, and he was technically family. Once the light went green, I stepped on the gas and headed toward his loft.

⛥

Progressive house music echoed down the narrow hallway that led to Evan's unit. At least I wasn't drunk like last time, I thought, approaching his front door. Composing myself, I gave three knocks and waited.

Why am I so nervous? Maybe he didn't hear me. Making a second attempt, the door suddenly swung open.

"Aria, hey!" Evan's brown eyes lit up. He looked happy to see me. I didn't know whether to stare at his face or his abs; his jeans hung low at his hips, revealing his trim waist.

Is he flaunting his physique? I wondered. *Oh God, why did I come here?* It was too late to regret it now.

"I'm sorry for not calling first," I said. "But—"

"Come back to bed, you sexy beast!" a woman yelled from inside. "I'm ready for another round!"

Crap! He's got a chick over.

Evan seemed embarrassed as he laughed uncomfortably.

"I'm really sorry." My face went flush. "This was such a stupid idea." I turned to leave.

"Wait!" He grabbed my wrist.

"But you have company, and I—"

"She was just about to go, actually."

I'm not convinced.

"Stay, Aria."

Meeting his eyes, I chewed the inside of my cheek.

"Please," he insisted. "Please, stay."

Reluctantly, I stepped inside.

CHAPTER SEVENTEEN
DATE OVER

Evan was in a hurry to get his date out of his place. The last thing he wanted was for Aria to leave. Entering his bedroom, he found Lindsay lying naked in bed, waiting for him.

"You need to leave," he said, picking her clothes from off the floor. "My niece is here, and I can't kick her out."

Lindsay sat up, irritated by the news. "You're kicking *me* out?"

"Pretty much."

"Unbelievable," she scoffed, getting out of bed. "Will you call me at least?"

"I've got your number saved, don't I?"

"Yeah, but will you use it?"

"Of course." His smile was convincing enough, but Evan knew he wouldn't call her again. She lacked EQ and IQ from what he gathered throughout their date.

Sighing, Lindsay promptly dressed herself before she walked out of his bedroom. She stole a quick glance at Aria, intimidated by her beauty. "*You* are his niece?"

Aria nodded.

"Aren't you too old to be babysat?"

"I, um…"

"I'm kidding," Lindsay said, putting on her shoes. "Family comes first."

"Sorry to spoil the fun."

The sassy brunette turned around and looked at Evan. "Don't forget to call me!"

"Good night, Lindsay!" he hollered over the music.

Now he had Aria all to himself. At last.

☙

Dark house music echoed around Evan's loft while he rolled a joint. The pungent scent of cannabis was in the air. Aria couldn't help but notice.

"Is that marijuana I smell?"

"Uh… no…" Evan flashed a guilty smile, cracking open a window.

"You're high, aren't you? Were you guys smoking weed?"

That wasn't all we were doing, he thought with a smirk. "Don't tell your dad."

"I won't be telling him anything anymore."

She finished her soda and sunk back into the sofa.

Evan studied her face and asked, "What happened?"

"It's a long story."

"I've got time."

Hesitant at first, she eventually summarized what happened when she discovered Vanessa's infidelity.

"That's unfortunate," Evan replied.

"He thinks I'm lying. He refuses to believe me."

"Welcome to my world, sweetheart. You and I are in the same boat," he sighed. "Noah never takes me seriously. He always thinks I'm lying; even when the truth is staring him in the face." Reaching for the Mason jar, Evan grabbed it off the coffee table and stood up.

"Where are you going?"

"I'll be right back."

"I know what's in the jar."

Evan paused.

"Can you roll another blunt?" asked Aria.

"Is that what you think is in here?" He flashed a crooked smile.

"Well, let's see: you're holding a silver painted jar, and running off to hide it somewhere… What could be in there aside from the obvious?"

Evan chuckled, sitting back down. "Clever girl." He twisted the lid.

"Wow! That is strong!"—she fanned the air—"I can smell it from here."

"They grew this strain in the West Coast." Evan measured the marijuana bud on a digital scale before he dropped it inside his titanium herb grinder. "You'll feel a nice, relaxing body high," he added, "easing into euphoria."

"Let's puff the magic dragon!"

"You're not supposed to be smoking this stuff."

"I've done worse." Aria shrugged.

"Really, love? Like what?"

Like trying to sleep with Noah.

"Well?" He waited.

"Like cigarettes and booze," she answered. "They're more harmful in comparison, if you ask me. At least cannabis has health benefits."

Evan chortled to himself while preparing his joint. "Does your dad know you're here?"

"Nope. And I don't care." She stretched, scanning the living room. "Where's Baxter?"

"Sleeping in a closet somewhere, most likely." Evan was nervous, but he hid it well. Aria's visit had been unexpected, though he had no qualms about kicking out his date. "You realize my place is probably first on Noah's list once he comes looking for you, right?"

"You could always lie and say I'm not here. Or… just don't let him in."

I love how conniving you can be, Evan thought.

"Is this something you do frequently?"

"Smoking pot?"

"Yeah."

"No." He licked the rolling paper. "Why?"

"Because you look like you know what you're doing."

You have no idea *what else I can do with these fingers.* Evan tried to hide his wicked smile and said, "I started smoking weed when I was young. I guess you could say I went through a stoner phase. But now I smoke it occasionally." He lighted the joint and took a deep puff before he handed it to her. "This stuff is powerful. You might cough up a lung or two."

"I can manage." She took the joint from his fingers and smoked it. Suppressing the irritation in her lungs, Aria coughed twice.

"Can't say I didn't warn you." He laughed.

Recovering from another hit, she slowly exhaled and passed the joint back to Evan.

His private thoughts were too scandalous to share, though he was sober enough to keep those fantasies to himself. Blowing out hoops of smoke, he passed the joint back to his niece. They continued this ritual until there was nothing left to inhale.

"Were you doing a photo-shoot?" Aria noticed the camera equipment and backdrop in the corner.

"No," Evan replied. "I had set up that equipment for you. I meant what I said last time about helping you make a modeling portfolio."

"Can we do a shoot right now?"

"I don't exactly have a rack full of chick gear in size zero."

"I'm not a size zero." Aria stood up and boldly took off her top.

Evan's eyes widened.

"I'm gonna need some lingerie shots, right?" She wiggled out of her shorts.

He was speechless, checking her out from head to toe as she confidently stood in a black push-up bra and panties that had rhinestones around the front fringe.

"Well?" Aria tugged on her hair elastic, shaking her locks. "Are you game?"

"Let's do it." He grinned.

Instead of using the backdrop, Evan suggested she pose on the sofa. He grabbed his professional camera and took pictures of her from different angles while she reclined on her side.

"Bend your elbow and rest your head in your hand," he instructed.

Aria listened and allowed him to coach her to pose more provocatively.

"Beautiful… now hold that pose and cross your left thigh over your knee so that your ankle hangs over the couch a bit."

"Like this?"

"No." He walked toward her and guided her leg into position. It wasn't easy for him to conceal his arousal; her skin felt so soft, and he desperately wanted to caress it.

"How about now?" Aria looked at him for approval.

"Perfect."

The camera flashed at high shutter speed as he took racy shots.

I would love to bang your brains out on that couch, Evan fantasized.

"Don't move," he said, walking into his bedroom. He stepped out holding a pillow in his hands… and a knife.

"Whoa… Are you gonna stab me or suffocate me?" She giggled, sitting up.

"Do I look like a psychopath to you?"

"If you were, you'd be a sexy one."

Would you fuck me, too? He wanted to say but held his tongue.

Evan grinned, stabbing the pillow and dragging the blade down, ripping the cotton casing.

"What are you doing?"

"Watch." He placed the knife on the table and reached into the pillow. "I'm gonna make it snow."

Aria's laughter echoed in his ears like a pleasant melody as he tossed a fistful of feathers over her head. He loved her voice. Maneuvering around her, Evan took snapshots from different angles.

"I love this song!" She stood up, dancing seductively. "It sounds like… toxic, angry sex."

I'll give you angry sex, thought Evan. *Just wait.*

"Papa Roach is an amazing band," he said. "I love 'Getting Away With Murder' and 'Between Angels and Insects.'"

"Epic tracks! Have you heard of Korn?"

"Jonathan Davis is a G," said Evan, scrolling down his playlist to "Freak On A Leash."

Sitting up on her knees, Aria danced and got lost in her own world while Evan crouched and took more pictures.

"How are you doing that?" he asked, mesmerized.

"What do you mean?"

"The way you roll your hips like a cobra queen… it's insane!"

"I just let the music guide my movements."

Jonathan Davis's voice blasted from the speakers, screaming through the chorus of his dark rock anthem, as if he were a deity, awakening souls to the darkest aspects of self. Music was a powerful catalyst for shifting consciousness. Evan was aware of this; he used it to his advantage like a dark warlock. It seemed like synchronicity when Crazy Town's "Butterfly" was next to play.

Leaving the sofa, Aria grabbed the tattered pillow and shook it, watching the feathers float around her. "God, I feel amazing!"—she spun around—"Are you sure that was weed we smoked?"

"I'm sure." Evan laughed, watching her transform into a wild rose. His insidious plan was working: she seemed to surrender to the sinister influence of the music.

"You look like an angel that's escaped her snow globe," he said.

"Freedom!" Aria spun around with her arms in the air. She had lost herself in the heavy metal, tapping into dark feminine energy.

"You know, Evan… I think you're the only one who really gets me."

Hypnotized by her snakelike movements, he stalked her every move, taking pictures like the paparazzi.

"Bend your elbows over your shoulders, love. Hold your hair up."

"Like this?" Aria playfully bit her lip and winked at him, holding the pose.

"Perfect! I love it!"

She laughed, snatching the camera away. "We took enough photos of me. It's your turn now."

"Definitely not." Evan chuckled, reaching for his camera, but she blinded him with a flash.

"*Oops!* You blinked!"

Covering his face, he avoided another flash.

"Someone's photogenic."

"Hand it over."

"Make me!"

"Oh, I'll make you all right…"

Evan laughed, matching her steps while she walked in reverse, taking pictures. Before she knew it, she was slammed against a brick wall. Evan trapped her, closing the space.

"Nowhere to go now, love." He took the camera out of her hands and snapped a photo of her.

"I don't want to go, anyway." She raised her arms above her head and crossed her wrists, as if she were bound by invisible chains.

So sexy, Evan thought.

Possessed by the music, Aria coiled her arms around his neck and pulled him closer. She wanted to seduce him; she wanted to be reckless and stupid; but most of all, she wanted to hurt Noah. Despite the warnings in her mind, she brushed her hands down Evan's naked chest and slid them up his shoulders.

"What are you doing, Aria?" He searched her eyes, never blinking.

"Touching you."

"Why?"

"Why not?"

He stayed still and said nothing, welcoming her healing caresses.

Pulling him closer, she closed her eyes as she braced herself for his kiss. Their lips were inches away from touching when someone pounded on the door.

"Right on time," Evan sighed disappointingly. "Hide out in my room. I'll handle your dad."

But she didn't want to hide. She wanted Noah to see how reckless she had been. She wanted to be vindictive and cut into his heart the same way he had cut into hers.

"Let me in, Evan!" Noah shouted from the other side of the door. "I know she's there!"

Someone was getting beat up that night, badly.

CHAPTER EIGHTEEN
ARIA

I was high, half naked, and I didn't care. This was *my* rebellion.

"Open the Goddamn door!" Noah yelled like a madman.

"You better leave, love," Evan whispered. "Before shit hits the fan."

"No," I protested. "I can face confrontation. What's the worst he can do? Spank me?" (I wished he would).

Strengthening my weakened ego was harder than I'd thought. Marching to the entrance door, I unlocked it and opened it.

"Well, hello there, Noah." I met his seething eyes with a sardonic smile. "How nice of you to drop in and spoil the fun."

His stunned expression shifted into a grimace as he eyed me up and down.

"Why aren't you dressed?" he said, looking furious.

"I got hot."

"Are you high?"

I could have sworn he did a double take at my cleavage before he met my gaze with a perpetual frown.

"Don't make me ask you again, Aria."

"I'm not."

"Don't lie to me." Noah stepped inside and sniffed that musky scent of marijuana. Turning around, he glowered at Evan and shouted, "You let her smoke weed with you?"

"He didn't make me do anything." I shut the door, facing him. "It was *my* decision."

Noah ignored me and kept his murderous gaze on his brother, shouting expletives. There was nothing stopping him from pounding Evan's face in. I had never intended for violence to break out.

Turning into a human shield, I parked myself between both brothers.

"Don't you dare touch him!" I warned Noah.

"Move!"

"No!"

"Move aside, Aria!" he shouted again. "*Now!*"

You sound so hot when you curse out loud, I thought, knowing it was wrong for my mind to go there.

"You don't need to fight my battles for me, sweetheart," Evan said, gently moving me to the side. But I wouldn't budge.

"He'll put you in the hospital like he did to my stepdad! I'm not moving!"

I stood up to Noah, unaffected by his rage. Everything in his body language suggested that he wanted retribution.

"What the hell were you doing with her? Why isn't she dressed?" His interrogation had only begun.

I couldn't tell if he was angry because I was partially indecent and high, or because I had scandalously disrobed myself around his "arch nemesis."

"I was photographing her," Evan replied. "I promised Aria I'd help her make a portfolio since she wants to pursue a modelling career."

"So, you gave her drugs and let her prance around your place in her bra and underwear? Who do you think you are? Hugh Hefner?"

"*I* wanted to smoke a joint," I cut in. "You think you can control my life, but I don't need your consent anymore!"

"Really?" Noah raised a doubtful eyebrow. "I could've sworn I was the one with the law degree"—he folded his arms in his chest—"And last time I checked, possession of marijuana is *illegal* unless it's prescribed by a licensed physician."

He sounded so patronizing.

"Perhaps I should remind you of all the laws *you* have broken lately," I countered.

He ignored my pathetic threat and continued to scold Evan like a child. "How could you be so irresponsible? And *you*"—his eyes darted in my direction—"you're not some teenage runaway. You have a father in your life." He raised his voice for dramatic effect and said: "A very *pissed off* father who's staring right at you!"

"I'm not deaf. I can hear you just fine."

"You want to be a Cover Girl? Then trust in *me* to make that happen." *Noah lecture in three... two...*

"The industry is so corrupt," he added. "And you can easily become victimized by media hungry hyenas that only care about dollar signs when they look at you."

Sigh. I had so called it.

"They don't give a fuck about your best interest, but I do!"

His nonstop cursing had got out of control.

"... That's why I've been taking my time to research a good agency," Noah said. "I want to make sure you're in good hands and will not be taken advantage of."

"How can you expect me to trust you when you don't even trust me?" I cried out. "You refuse to believe me about Vanessa!"

"Don't drag her into this, please."

Evan finally came to my defense. "Your daughter finds your whore of a wife in bed with your best mate, and you stick your head in the sand. What kind of man are you?"

"You told him?" Noah looked at me with betrayal in his eyes.

"Yes."

No point in denying.

"And he believes me."

"You're making a big mistake, my brother," warned Evan.

"My personal life is none of your business. I warned you last time to stay away from my daughter."

"Your 'daughter' wouldn't have been here in the first place if you had listened to her. Instead, you chose to be a bloody idiot and hurt her. You must be proud of yourself."

Noah looked ready to kill him.

"Aria, get out of the way!" He balled his fists.

"Stop this!" I said. "I'll never forgive either of you if you get violent!" I stood in between them, holding their chests. This wasn't a simple task since I was pushing back approximately two-hundred-something pounds of muscle on both ends.

Noah's tone was hostile as he asked Evan if he had "touched me."

"Answer me!" he demanded.

"He only took pictures," I spoke up. "He wasn't trying to get in my pants!"

"That's funny," Noah scoffed, "considering you don't have any pants on!"

Okay, to be fair, he had a point. But I was telling the truth. If anything, *I* was the one who had tried to seduce Evan, not the other way around. Feeling guilty, he didn't exactly stop me, either. We would have kissed if Noah hadn't interrupted us. Even if we had gone as far as hooking up, it wouldn't have been wrong from a moral standpoint; we weren't biologically related. However, Noah and I were… but I still wanted him, regardless.

"Notice how she keeps coming to *me* every time you have a parenting fail?" Evan said.

Please don't provoke him, I quietly begged, holding Evan's gaze, hoping he'd understand my desperate plea. The last person Noah had roughed up was Rob. My stepdad had almost been left in critical condition. I loved Noah's gentle nature, but he also had a violent side that was aggressive, animalistic, and difficult to tame.

"Get your clothes on, Aria," Noah demanded. "We're leaving."

Hesitant to move, I worried if I resigned my position as referee, they'd end up killing each other. All I had to do was step away and it would have led to a potential fatality. They were both experienced in boxing and mixed martial arts. If they wound up in a fist fight, I feared they would ruin their attractive faces and knock a few teeth out. I couldn't imagine Noah with a black eye. He appeared so invincible in my eyes, like nothing and no one could break him. But I knew everyone has a story of pain and suffering. We all break down in life before we experience a breakthrough.

"You need to stop treating her like a dog on a leash," Evan ranted, which only angered Noah as he cursed at him.

"Shut the hell up! You don't know what you're talking about."

"I don't? The more you try to control her life, the further you'll push her away. I'm trying to help you out here."

"I don't need your help! I need you out of our lives!"

"Hey!" I pushed Noah back; he was getting short fused. "If I get dressed, will you promise not to hurt him?"

"He can't hurt me," Evan cut in. "He's the one who's gonna have broken bones and stitches. You should hold *me* back."

"I beg to differ," Noah argued. "Get out of the way, Aria."

My God, there was way too much testosterone in the room… more than I could handle.

"I'm gonna play the 'teen card' here and remind you both that you'd be setting a terrible example if you brawled out in front of me. Not to mention how I'd be traumatized by witnessing it."

The tension in the air had not evaporated, as they both stayed silent, seemingly plotting ways of getting away with murder.

Cautiously, I lowered my hands from Noah's chest and said, "I'm gonna get changed now. Please don't kill each other."

Rushing toward the sofa, I threw on my T-shirt and shorts before I slipped on my flip-flops.

"You ready, Aria?" Noah asked, never taking his eyes off Evan.

They exchanged silent threats: a toxic display of masculine pride through "Alpha male-glaring." I imagined Noah as a big white wolf, baring his fangs and snarling at the black wolf across from him, who was ready to attack.

"I'm ready," I finally answered.

"Good," Noah replied.

The next thing I knew, I was thrown over his shoulder with my body dangling like a ragdoll.

"Oh, my God! Put me down!"

From wolf-man to cave dweller, I thought. *Territorial or what?*

"Stay the fuck away from my daughter," he said to Evan. "We're leaving now."

"Noah!" I yelled in frustration.

There was no use in kicking and screaming. He would not let me down. Maybe he wanted to humiliate me. Marching out the door, he headed for the elevator at the end of the hall.

"What is this?" I shouted. "A military operation? Let go of me!"

"Stop talking."

"Don't tell me what to do!"

"You're so annoying. You're lucky I love you so much."

"Put me down! *Now!*"

Noah stopped and pressed a button on the elevator while I continued to rant.

"Noah!"

"She came to *me*," Evan explained, catching up. "I wasn't gonna kick her out when she needed me."

The elevator reached our floor with a *ding* before Noah stepped inside, ignoring his brother.

"I'm so sorry!"

"It's all right, love. You're always welcome here."

Evan's handsome face disappeared when Noah turned around, forcing me to face my reflection in the mirror.

"This is the last time she'll ever come to you." He sounded resentful. "I promise you that."

The doors closed shut, cutting off all communication with my uncle. There was nothing but silence between Noah and me as he clenched my thighs.

"What are you, a Neanderthal?" I ridiculed. "You can put me down now. You made your point."

I waited while he gripped my thighs like I was his private property.

"You said no silent treatments."

"You need to learn when to shut up."

"Don't talk to me like that! How dare you?"

"I'm your father. I'll speak to you as I please."

"You're abusing your authority."

Noah let out a mirthless laugh. "She's funny... 'abusing my authority'... *right*."

"Your reaction was so over the top."

"*O.T.T.*, really? This is me being tame. I could do so much worse."

"Is that a threat?"

"Projecting that chessboard into your reality again, Aria? If you wanna play chess, learn it properly... from the Master."

"You're an annoying, arrogant prick!"

"What else?"

"You're so overbearing and overprotective! I hate it!"

"What else?"

"You can't just decide for me all the time!"

"I know what's best for my baby. What else?"

"No, you don't!"

Sighing in defeat, I waited for the elevator to take us down. Arguing like this was a waste of energy, but I hated the silence between us; it triggered me. Even if we were arguing, it was better than him not speaking to me.

"Will you please let me down? We've reached our floor. I don't need you to embarrass me further."

"You embarrassed yourself."

"Finally! He speaks!"

Noah kept walking, unphased by my temper tantrum.

"What's next?" I asked. "A spanking?"

"You mention that a lot, Aria. You must really want it, huh?"

Ignoring me, he strode toward the lobby doors and stepped outside while I dangled over his shoulder. It was raining, I noticed, feeling a light drizzle.

"I drove here. You should at least let me drive the Firebird back home."

"I don't give a shit about the car right now." Noah placed me on my feet, staring at me with fury in his icy gaze. "I'm so unbelievably mad at you. I could pull my hair out!"

I was horrified at the thought.

"Look at you"—he cupped my face—"your eyes are all bloodshot."

"It's just weed!"

"Since when did I say it was okay for you to smoke pot? I had a cocaine addiction for years! Do you really want to follow the same path? Are you hell-bent on messing up your life like I had?"

"I wasn't shooting up or snorting anything!"

"What the hell do you think I was smoking before I turned to coke? It's a gateway drug!"

"A gateway to *healing* if you don't abuse it!"

Standing next to his Audi, we argued back and forth while a light mist of rain drizzled over us.

"Get in the car," Noah demanded. "We're going home." He looked and sounded less than friendly as he walked to my passenger door and opened it.

"Did you not hear me?"

Loud and clear, master.

"In the car, Aria. *Now!*"

His angry outburst had knocked some fear in me as I instinctively obeyed him. The stereo came to life as soon as he started the ignition, but he quickly switched it off. The rain was pouring harder, which was weird because normally the forecast in LA was sunny with blue skies. However, that night, I was worried a freak storm was advancing toward us. Noah turned on the windshield wipers before he pulled out on the road.

——

The silence between us was painfully awkward as rain pelted the roof of the car. Ten minutes had passed, and my temperamental father was silent, so I spoke up.

"I don't want to live with you anymore."

I waited, hoping he'd say something—*anything.*

"I want to go back to New York."

Noah gripped the steering wheel and exhaled harshly.

"I'm grateful for all you've done for me, but I think it's time for me to—"

"Am I that much of a monster? Why do you constantly hold that threat over my head?"

"It's not a threat. I'm serious."

Being so close to him seemed to be toxic for both of us.

"You want to leave me, Aria?"

"Yes!" I cried out in tears, not caring if it hurt him.

"You want to go back and live in that shitty apartment with that abusive asshole?"

"Yes! I'd rather get beaten and bruised everyday than to endure the emotional pain you put me through."

"Don't talk nonsense."

"It's torture and I can't take it anymore!"

"You think I'm not suffering?" he shouted. "Every time I'm around you, all I can think about is…"

I waited for him to finish, but he stayed quiet. My patience was wearing thin.

"Well? Say it!"

"Forget it."

"Why not?" I yelled.

"Because it's wrong!"

"You're such a coward, Noah."

"Yeah, that's right." He scoffed. "I'm the coward for loving you so much; I'm the coward for ignoring my own selfish desires because I would rather grieve over my heartbreak than to make you suffer long-term trauma by giving you what you *think* you want!"

"You're already making me suffer long-term trauma! Do you honestly believe I can forget everything we did?"

"Of course not!"

"Just because we haven't had sex doesn't mean I can get over everything else!"

"You think I don't know that?" He glanced at me. "Why else am I pushing for therapy so much?"

"To hell with your stupid therapy!"

The rain poured down harder than ever while we took an oath of silence. After a brief minute, Noah felt the need to have the last word.

"You're so stubborn, Aria. I don't know how to discipline you. And I don't think it's possible to make you see the light."

Ouch.

"Trust me, I see the light. *You're* the one who's blind."

"You're right, I am blind." He kept his eyes on the road. "Blinded by my love for you."

Noah's tone had changed, as if he had magically purged all his anger and frustration. He sounded warm and gentle. It was like a switch.

How does he do that?

I had no words or insults to throw at him. How could I keep stabbing him with daggers when he was clearly bleeding inside? His confession had miraculously doused my flaming temper.

Have I truly blinded him? I tried to rationalize.

Weaving in and out of traffic, visibility worsened as the storm poured down like buckets of water splashing over the windshield. I was used to this kind of weather in New York, but not here.

Once we reached a traffic light, I let loose and finally let him have it.

"Why won't you believe me about Vanessa? I wasn't lying about what I said!"

"You've lied to me before," Noah sighed in frustration.

"Because I wanted to go to a club with my friends—but that has nothing to do with Vanessa and Amir!"

"Stop."

"I admit I dislike my stepmom, especially after discovering she's been cheating on you. However, I—"

"And what about me?" he shouted. "You're so quick to judge my wife, you're forgetting about all my past transgressions."

"Our situation is totally different."

"If anyone's guilty, it's me."

"Are you serious? You haven't had sex with me!"

"I kissed you!"

"She's probably been screwing Amir for God knows how long!"

We came to a slow halt as we approached another traffic light. Noah seemed calm but refused to look in my direction.

"Do you really believe I would lie to you just to get Vanessa out of the picture? How could you think so low of me? Why would I sabotage what we have through lies and deceit?" I angrily wiped my tears, resenting how fragile I felt around him.

"That's already our reality, Aria—what we've become: liars."

"Because of what happened?"

"You're too possessive of me."

"Oh, and you're not? You didn't answer my first question."

Maybe his mind was racing, and he had tuned me out. I hated the idea of clinginess. "Clingy" was not in my personality. But Noah kept going.

"You want to claim ownership over somebody who is wrong for you in every way! Well, I've got news for you, sweetheart: you can't have me! Sorry! Not in the ways you want! Never! Do you hear me? You can never have me that way, and I refuse to give in to your head games and screw us over by fucking the fuck out of you! Because that's what you want, right?"

"No!" I sobbed.

"You want me to stop being your dad and start looking at you as some piece of ass?"

"No! Stop it!" I cried even harder. "How can you say that to me?"

He looked so enraged but focused on driving.

"You're so cruel!"

"Maybe so." He switched gears. "My only regret is having missed out on raising you. I could have spared us both from turning into psychotic people."

My tears kept flowing as I tried to calm down. "It's never been about sex for me, Noah. I'm in love with you… and it hurts. It makes me crazy."

"You don't know what you're saying."

"I do!"

"You're a damaged young girl who needs help just as much as I do."

"I know what I feel, and it won't change! It never will!" I desperately needed him to believe that.

"I'm not in love with you, Aria!"

I'm not in love with you... His words echoed through my soul and snuffed out the light.

This was the part where everything became still, as if time had suddenly frozen and the only sound I heard was my heartbeat thudding in my ears, slowing down and weakening before it flat lined and died. He had spiritually killed me. But I still dared to hope for a full resurrection. I believed I was his flaming phoenix.

"Look me in the eye, Noah, and say that to me. Say you're not in love with me."

He took his time to respond before he said, "I can't."

"Why not?"

"Because I have to keep my eyes on the road!" he yelled out in rage.

"You said you were blinded by your love for me. You lied."

"And you clearly misunderstood what I meant."

"You're worse than Rob." I sniveled.

"Yep, I'm the biggest asshole in the world—and a liar. What else would you like to add to that list?" His condescending tone only wounded me deeper.

My feelings were beyond hurt. I had two choices now: stay silent or hurt him back.

Tick... tick... *BOOM!*

"I wish I never met you! I wish I wasn't your daughter! And I wish you never came into my life!" I cried hysterically. "I hate you, Noah! I hate you so much!"

The light turned green, and he stepped on the gas so hard I feared we would hydroplane. You know that terrifying feeling you get when someone scares the crap out of you unexpectedly? You jump; your heart rate instantly spikes; and you tremble all over because your nervous system has been shocked. That's exactly what happened to me as soon as

I heard metal scraping against metal and crunching upon impact… deafening car horns and shattering glass.

Consumed with panic, I whipped my head behind me and witnessed the most graphic on-road collision I had ever seen. A fatal car crash occurred as soon as we had passed the intersection at the traffic light. Noah and I had cheated death. It could have been us. Our lives had been spared in that three second period.

To my horror, a huge white four-by-four had slammed into a black sports car. It was a T-Bone collision that had caused the car to flip off the road. The driver in the pickup truck could have been drunk texting or speeding. But they were entirely responsible for the accident because they had run a red light. Overwhelmed by emotion, I started crying. We could have been roadkill that night, and the last words I had said to Noah were "I hate you so much."

"Oh, my God!" I covered my mouth in shock. "Oh, my God…"

"Don't look at it," Noah calmly advised. He slowed down and occasionally glanced at the accident through his rear-view mirror.

My skin felt icy, and I was shaking.

"Hey," he said, catching my attention. "Sit back in your seat, please. I'm still driving."

Avoiding the traumatizing scene, I buried my face in my hands and broke down. I just couldn't hold it in anymore. The ticking sound of a turn signal caught my attention as we pulled into a parking space on the street. Noah said my name in a gentle tone, which was a relief since he had sounded so mean earlier.

"Come here," he said. "Let me hold you."

I didn't want to move, though. A part of me wanted to shut him out and stay angry. But more than anything, I needed his comfort. Nothing felt better than being in his arms. His energy was so masculine, protective, and healing.

"*Shhh…* you're okay. I've got you."

Unfastening my seat belt, he wrapped his arms around me.

"I'm s-sorry," I stammered in tears. "I'm sorry for what I said. I d-don't hate you. I could… n-never hate [*sniffle*]… you."

"Hey," he murmured in my ear. "I know, baby. Try to calm down. You're having a panic attack. You're safe. We're safe."

Vulnerability was not something I liked to feel, but how could I have stayed so prideful after almost dying?

"I love you, Noah. I love you so much it hurts." I clung on to him and had the biggest cry of my life.

"It's all right," he said in a soothing tone. "I know you don't hate me. We're bound forever, Aria. There's a blood contract between us."

A contract I wish never existed, I thought, weeping even more. I loved breathing him in this way: so close. He felt like he was mine, if only for a brief minute.

"That could have been us."

"But it wasn't. We're here, we're alive, and we're okay." Noah stroked my hair, kissing my forehead before he slipped away from my arms.

"It wasn't our time to go yet," he said. "I'm gonna be here when you graduate from college; I'm gonna give you away when you walk down the aisle; and you're gonna make me a proud grandfather one day when you take on motherhood."

I didn't want to think about either of those possibilities; I was still shaken up.

Noah handed me a tissue as I wiped my tears and tried to relax.

"It's the first time I've ever seen a car accident up close," I expressed.

"Me too. That was scary." Noah paused. "On a side note… you're high, so you're gonna feel everything at a more amplified level."

Tears misted my vision as I apologized again. "I never wanted to upset you. I just wanted you to believe me. It hurts that you don't."

"Look, I can't throw Vanessa under the bus with no evidence to prove your accusations."

"I know what I saw!"

"That's why I've hired a private investigator."

Best decision ever. She was bound to get caught.

"Noah, I would never lie to you and deliberately wreck your relationship just to get you all to myself. That wouldn't be a genuine victory for me."

"Sweetheart, you don't have to compete for my love"—he caressed my cheek—"you already have it."

"Not how I want."

"We keep running in circles about this. You know I can't go there with you, and I explained why." Noah exhaled his frustration. "Please, let's not fight. Not after what happened. I'm not even mad at you anymore. I'm just grateful we weren't involved in that car crash."

Police cruisers, a fire truck, and two ambulances sped past our car as the blaring sound of the sirens filled the streets.

"Do you think those people are okay?" I asked.

"Hopefully, no one died tonight." He looked out at the road. The rain had finally let up. "Let's go home—and please don't pick a fight with Vanessa."

I wasn't going to. I was done fighting for someone who didn't want me. After graduation, I was going to take the first flight out of sunny California and trade my luxurious accommodation for that crappy apartment on Conduit Avenue. Yep, I was planning to return to the polluted streets of NYC. I missed Times Square; it was gorgeous at night with all those flashing neon lights, and cars rushing by. The skyline at sunset was incredible, and I missed riding the ferry. All those skyscrapers just made me feel so enclosed inside this vast dome—and the city itself was so diverse. China town always smelled delicious, and little Italy was heaven to me... I was so homesick and missed my best friends. Running from Noah was the only way I could move on from these feelings I had for him. I had no other choice.

CHAPTER NINETEEN
ARIA

May 25, 2013

Dear Diary,

I really don't know how to start because I'm feeling so many mixed emotions right now. My prom is tonight, and like any girl my age, I should glow with excitement and be happy to have reached this milestone… except all I can feel is an unbearable sadness that only dulls when I think about dying. No, I'm not going to kill myself. I just feel an odd sense of comfort knowing that I won't be alive forever. Who wants to feel the way I do… <u>forever</u>? I wouldn't wish this on my enemy.

To share the latest news, I've finally graduated. The ceremony isn't until the second week of June. I should look forward to walking across that stage with pride and receiving my diploma in front of my friends and family… but I'm not… because I won't be there. I won't be attending, and my parents don't know. I'll get to the reason after I finish sharing my racing thoughts. I'll try my best to piece this puzzle together, despite my splitting migraine. It's hard to focus when my feelings get in the way. My head is all over the place. (Deep breath.)

Starting my first year at Columbia University is exciting and scary at the same time. New environment, new people, and harder expectations. The messed-up part is that I lied to Noah and Mom about where I'll be going to school. Yeah, I've been lying about a lot of things lately. But it's not because I want to hurt anyone; it's because I've been hurt enough, and I just need to be on my own. They think I've accepted my offer at Berkley. The reason I lied is because I didn't want to have to explain my choice and argue about it with Noah; and I didn't want my mother doing extra shifts to help me with finances—nor did I want her arguing with my stepdad about me moving in again. That's not my plan, anyway. I'm returning to New York, but I will not live with them. Jade had offered to let me stay at her place for the summer. I'm planning to get a job and save up for living expenses before school starts.

So, what has my life been like these past four weeks? Well, there's been a lot of tension between Noah and I, but that's nothing new. We can't seem to get along. One minute he's close, the next minute he's miles away, and this pattern never ends. I'm so done with all our fighting. We keep pretending not to feel attracted to one another—the usual song and dance. It's been difficult to stay on good terms with my stepmom. I just don't respect her. She probably ended her affair with Amir, since Noah's P.I. failed to catch her in scandalous acts. Once I leave LA, no one will know but me. And that's exactly how I'm going to keep it: top secret.

Speaking of which… Noah's flying out of the city tonight—it's work related. He mentioned having to meet with a client in Seattle and won't be back until Monday afternoon. This makes it convenient for me, because I plan to fly back to New York tomorrow evening. I've bought my ticket in advance, and no one knows about it. That's why I won't be attending grad. I don't want to stay here unless I have to. Now that I've finished my exams, I've technically graduated. My diploma will be sent in the mail.

Mom and Rob won't be expecting me, of course. I suppose I'll visit eventually as an "unwelcome surprise"—just to say hi. It can't be that bad. Not as bad as what I go through when I'm around Noah. I'll have to survive the humid months of summer until school starts. Then I can move into a dorm with a roommate. Noah will inevitably find out that I've left, but it'll be too late. He'll get on the next flight out to New York and try to convince me to come back, but I'll refuse. I can't live like this anymore. We're constantly around each other, the sexual tension never goes away, and I'm madly in love with him. It's morally wrong, but it's what my heart feels, and I can't change it. I can't hug him and feel normal, daughterly feelings. They just don't exist, and no amount of therapy will ever fix that.

Every time I look at him, I think about undressing him. Every time I kiss his cheek, the memories of our passionate kisses flicker in my mind. Anytime he touches me, my skin flares up in heat. I'm in love with him, and I wish I wasn't. I've been trying to keep things amicable between us, but that has been an epic fail. I'm his biological daughter, but I blind myself to it. Noah feels like my twin flame, and I wish he could see me the same way I see him. We constantly see through each other; we finish each other's sentences; and we think the same thoughts (most of the time). We're so compatible, it's unreal, despite our age difference and the tragic genetic factors.

I don't want kids. He and I could always adopt. I just want him. All of him. Maybe it's selfish of me to leave like this but loving him this way is agonizing. It's wrong in the eyes of God and society, but it doesn't feel wrong in my heart and soul.

Last week, Jess and I went shopping and finally picked out our prom dresses. I bought this beautiful red gown with sequins along the train of the dress. It's strapless with a slim fitting bodice and open back. The gown seemed as if it were made just for me when I had tried it on at the dress shop. Jess had told me I looked like a beauty pageant winner. She's such a sweetheart and has been a good friend to me. I'll miss her when I leave California, but I'll make sure to keep in touch with her.

Anyway, I digress… I've calculated a way to hook up with Ryan Taylor. As cliché and disastrous as it sounds to have sex on prom night, I really don't care, even if I am self-sabotaging. Ryan thinks I'll be attending Berkley as well in the fall, but we're not officially an item, so I don't feel obligated to tell him about my plans to run away. We'll have a little after-party of our own when the prom is over. It was nice of him to reserve us a suite at the hotel. Noah will be away all weekend, so I won't have to worry about him finding out—and Vanessa just doesn't give a shit about what I do and where I go. She'll probably end up going out tonight or will most likely meet up with that asshole she's been spreading her legs for. It's so unfair how she's getting away with this. I wish Noah would believe me. I'm done trying to convince him.

He replaced my phone weeks ago and told me that if I ever contacted Evan or saw him again, he would confiscate my cell, effective immediately. I had sent my uncle an email explaining the circumstances I was in—that's why I haven't seen him in weeks. It doesn't matter, anyway; once I'm in New York, I'm free to do whatever and won't be using this stupid iPhone.

These past two weeks have been strange. I'm not sure if it's just paranoia, but I keep thinking I'm being followed every time I'm out in public. I constantly look over my shoulder and no one will be there, of course. It doesn't help that I keep having these reoccurring nightmares about Rob. I guess that's because I'm returning to New York.

Steph and I haven't been on speaking terms since that incident at The Velvet Lounge. She tried to isolate me from everybody at school, just as I suspected, but Ryan's friends love me, so the tramp failed in that aspect.

It's almost time to go, and I still have to finish getting ready. Jessica's dress is so beautiful. The design is almost like mine, except it's royal blue and has a shoulder strap. The open back isn't as revealing, and the train of the dress is shorter. All those hours shopping for the perfect prom dress were worth it.

I don't know why I want to sleep with Ryan. Maybe I just want to destroy what remains of my innocence. Maybe I want to get back at Noah… or maybe I genuinely don't give a shit anymore. I wish I could wake up to an alternate reality where Noah would be mine, and we could live on this beautiful island, far away from the rest of the world, in our own little paradise. We'd make love on the sand as the ocean tide turned in, soaking our bodies while we coupled together. My love for him would flow into his body as fast as the water flowing upon the shore. I would gaze up at a vanilla sky and surrender to every pleasurable sensation.

Insert sigh here:_____________ (IN BIG CAPITAL LETTERS.)

I need to get him out of my head. Why can't I be a normal person and obsess over sexy artists and actors?

Until next time… which will probably be in The Big Apple,

-Eternally depressed :((((

Closing my diary, I forced myself to cheer up. I still had half an hour to kill before my friends would arrive. Spending time at the spa and beauty salon with Jess had been fun (aside from the painful Brazilian wax). That was the price to pay for beauty. I just wanted to look and feel perfect because it was my big night. I don't think any guy would want to go down on a girl, only to cringe and realize he needs a weed whacker before engaging in sexual activities. I'm all for girl power, but refusing to groom your lady parts and armpits is just wrong! I mean, sure, we're born with all this hair on our body—some more than others, but doesn't it feel more hygienic when you wax or shave? I can't imagine feeling sexy wearing lingerie and strutting around with prickly legs. Maybe it truly is all social construct and gender norms. Imagine a world where people are made fun of for having no hair on their body, and the super hairy individuals are only labeled as beautiful and sexy. Okay, that made me laugh a little inside.

Forcing myself to come back down from whatever warped universe I had ventured to, all my weird and un-sexy thoughts instantly disappeared when Noah stepped into my room.

"Wow!" he said, admiring my figure. "You look…"

I turned away from my tall length mirror and met his gaze, holding my breath.

"Stunning," he confessed with a smile. "Absolutely breathtaking."

"Thank you," I muttered.

"You are beyond the vision of beauty."

Why do you have to be so charming right now?

Because it's your prom, and he's trying to be a wonderful dad! My conscience answered.

I was still low-key mad at him, but my expression gave nothing away. In the passing months, I had studied the eternal poker face of Noah Hunter, taking notes to master his body language. After much needed practice as his silent apprentice, I was now a master at disguising my emotions. I could hide my feelings just as well as he could.

The lady from the salon had done an amazing job of styling my hair. I'd gone against the traditional look and had it down in big bouncy waves and curls. The makeup artist had glued a temporary tattoo of a masquerade mask around my forehead and cheekbones. It was all black and elegantly designed to augment my eyes and winged eyeliner, which added a pleasant contrast to the ruby gloss that shimmered on my lips. The smoky eye shadow bumped up my age a couple years. My entire ensemble made me feel beautiful.

Noah was staring at me, which made me nervous. Rubbing my arm out of habit, I noticed him pull out a long velvet box from his back jean pocket.

"I got you something." He smiled.

"Why?"

"Because you aced your SAT, passed your most crucial academic year, and earned yourself a scholarship. Let's not forget that tonight's a big deal for you." Stepping closer, he was now inches away from my face. "I guess you could say the main reason I'm gifting you with this extravagant piece of jewelry is because you're my daughter, and I love to spoil you." He opened the box. "You deserve this."

My jaw dropped. It was a diamond necklace with a pear-shaped ruby pendant hanging in the middle.

"Oh, my God! Noah, I…"

"Turn around."

Facing the mirror, I stared at my reflection.

He stood behind me and removed the choker I'd had on. Tonight was the first night I wasn't wearing that leather wristband he had given me a month ago.

"This must have cost you a fortune!" I gently brushed my fingers across the sparkling stones.

"Don't worry about that. Your value has no measure." He smiled. "You are beyond limitation."

I felt like crying, not because I had thousands of dollars' worth of jewelry around my neck, but because he loved me enough to spend so much money on me. My stepdad always had a hard time giving me loose change to spend on things I liked when I was little. I remember when we used to go grocery shopping, we would always pass these toy vending machines filled with plastic capsules full of cheap costume jewelry. I often begged him to give me money so I could get the princess necklace I'd wanted for a while. The frugal bastard couldn't donate a measly fifty cents. He would always rage and get grumpy when I'd ask for things he couldn't afford. A good parent would gently explain their financial situation to a child, or calmly tell them "no" and give their kid a short time out if they throw a tantrum.

Early in life, I learned to stop asking for my needs and wants, because I already knew how the monster would respond, anyway. Yes, the "princess necklace" was nothing great, and I probably would have thrown it out later, but it would have made me happy at that age. Rob would have made me feel loved if he'd only cared enough to nurture my self-worth and not stomp on it. I'm not saying that a person's value is defined by how much money they possess, but from a child's perspective, if a parent cannot afford to buy them something they want, then there are better ways to make them understand that money is tight. My stepdad had always yelled at me, humiliated me in public, and told me I was a dumb, spoiled little bitch who was going to burn holes in his wallet by the time I'd turn eighteen. At eight years old, his cruelty had done nothing for my self-esteem.

And now here I was, ten years later, wearing diamonds around my neck—and I didn't even have to beg or ask for it. Sadly, Noah's generous gesture would only be accepted for tonight. I didn't want to keep that exquisite necklace. I planned to return his gift, put it back inside that black velvet box, and place it on his desk in his study before I'd leave tomorrow. I wouldn't take the things he had bought me. All my expensive designer clothes, accessories, brand name bags, shoes… everything would stay here in this house, like a showroom put on display at a furniture store. All this stuff represented memories of him, and it would hold a constant haunting presence if I took a single item with me. I was sure it would hurt Noah, but I planned to leave him a note to make him understand; hopefully, he would.

Making several attempts, I tried to write my farewell letter. But whenever I got to the part where I wrote, "Don't come for me. Don't look for me. Don't think of me." I ended up scrunching up the note in a paper ball and scrapping it because I'd panic, get frustrated, and cry. I didn't want him to forget me. I didn't want him to live his life as if I didn't exist. I wanted Noah to come after me like the way Jerry Maguire did when he realized Dorothy completed him. I'd stare into Noah's misty blue eyes the same way Renee Zellweger did in that movie when she pulled off the most epic line in that scene.

Okay, maybe I wouldn't phrase it exactly like she had, but I truly desired a monumental declaration of love that would take our relationship to the next level with no fears, reservations, or guilt. I wanted Noah to realize that I had completed him. *Love Potion No.9* perhaps? Hmm… only in Hollywood. Unfortunately, making him fall for me would not happen, and that was a harsh reality I had to accept.

"You look deep in thought," he said, massaging my shoulders. "What are you thinking?" His voice sounded soothing. I loved listening to him talk.

"I'm admiring this necklace. It's so beautiful."

"*You* make it look beautiful."

We locked eyes in the mirror, and I wanted to shy away when he closed the space between us and wrapped his arms around my waist.

"I'm so proud of you, Aria."

The pink blush that had spread across my face darkened to a plum color when he kissed my cheek. I didn't want to get so emotional, but I couldn't help it whenever I was around him. Tonight was going to be the last time I'd ever see him again. I didn't want him to find me. Our separation would be difficult at first, but I prayed it would get easier. Time heals all wounds, and I had to believe it would heal the ones that Noah Hunter had left in my heart.

Studying him through the mirror, I said, "You look as if *you're* the one who is lost in a mist of memories."

"I just wish I was there during your early years. Then I could look at you now and say that my little girl is all grown up. You grew up without me, and regretfully, I was never there."

"It's okay. It doesn't matter now."

It felt like an instinct to console him. This was the first time in weeks that we'd actually touched and now that he was holding me, I didn't want him to let go. I wanted to enjoy it for as long as I could before my heart would ache from the loss of contact.

Staring at our reflections, I listened to the music playing in the background. I felt so connected to Noah through music. Every lyric always seemed relatable to us. Some people wear their heart on their sleeve, but I've always had a way of expressing how I feel through music.

Sometimes all you need is one perfect song to express exactly how you feel when words escape you.

"How did you get to be so beautiful?" He touched my shoulders.

"I guess I can thank your genes for that." I replied, staring into his arctic eyes.

"No." He shook his head. "Thank your mom. All your beauty is from your mother's side. She was the hottest girl at my high school."

"What was your prom like?"

"You don't want to know. It was full of um"—he paused—"wild excursions."

"Did that involve Mom?"

"Yes."

"I guess that shouldn't surprise me."

Noah chuckled, changing the subject. "So, are you all set?"

"Almost."

"In that case…" He took my hand and kissed it. "I'm gonna leave and let you get to it."

My heart was breaking from despair. This was going to be the last time I would ever see him again.

"I'm gonna miss you," I confessed, hugging him tightly.

"I'll only be gone for the weekend."

"I know—but still."

Noah kissed my forehead and said, "You'll be home by curfew, right? Because if you're late, Vanessa's gonna kill you."

I was prepared to go all Bruce Lee or Jackie Chan on her ass if she so much as lifted a finger on me again.

"I'll be home on time. Don't worry."

My stepmom and I had made a pact: I would stay out of her way, and she would stay out of mine. That's how we kept the peace… well, *tried to*. I made a deal with her and asked her to cover for me tonight. If Noah were to call and ask about my whereabouts, she had promised me she'd tell him I came home by curfew and was sleeping. In return, I had promised to stay out of her marriage problems. Vanessa had been hesitant at first, but we eventually shook on it. It would have been easier if I'd told her I was planning to move back to New York, but I didn't trust her with that knowledge; I didn't trust her at all.

Searching Noah's gaze, I was uncertain of what I was looking for. Maybe I was in search of hope; a sign that would let me know he loved me the same way I loved him. But he was hard to read at the moment. He was so good at masking his emotions, and the extraordinary thing was that he didn't need an actual mask to do it.

My stepmom's voice suddenly echoed in the background, letting us know the limo was here.

I looked at Noah and tried to hide my sadness as he dropped his hands from my shoulders. "I'll let Ryan know you're getting ready," he said.

"Thanks."

Once he was gone, I did another quick take in front of the mirror and grabbed my sparkly red clutch before I left my bedroom.

೦೨೦

Ryan was waiting for me in the foyer, holding a fancy plastic box that had my red corsage inside of it. He looked so handsome in his black suit and red satin tie. The biggest smile appeared on his face when he saw me. Vanessa had her phone out and kept taking photos of us until the flash blinded us.

"Take good care of my daughter," Noah said. "Or else." He threatened Ryan in a *joking-but-I'm-actually-serious* sort of way.

"Don't worry, Mr. Hunter. I'm a perfect gentleman," Ryan reassured him, reaching for my hand.

I didn't want to go to this stupid prom. All I wanted was Noah. I wished he could abduct me from this lame event and fly me out to a secluded place where we could be together, no Vanessa, no Ryan, and no other judgmental eyes.

"Have fun, sweetie." Noah smiled.

I gave him one last glance before I walked out the door with my date.

Our friends were waiting for us in the limo. I heard their laughter as we approached the vehicle. Unable to resist, I turned around and met Noah's eyes. This was it… our last lingering gaze.

I imagined a strong ocean current crashing upon the shore, erasing the enormous heart I had drawn in the sand that read:

NOAH + ARIA
FOREVER

I was going to leave his life forever. This was goodbye.

CHAPTER TWENTY
ARIA

Dance music echoed from the banquet hall, as I held Ryan's arm and walked through a set of white French doors. Glittering confetti dusted over our heads when we stepped inside, entering a fantasy world of colorful fog and strobe lights.

"All right, party people!" The DJ took the mic. "I wanna see everyone on the dance floor!"

"Oh, my God!" Jess gushed. "Isn't this amazing?" She brushed past us with her date, while Ryan and I scanned our surroundings in awe. So many people had arrived.

Standing at the top of a marble stone staircase, I fixated on the ivory-colored balustrade. They decorated the hall in baroque furnishings, which had transformed the space; it was a revival of the renaissance era. Floor candelabras were lit near the terrace doors and columns. Crystal chandeliers majestically hung from the ceiling, with the lights dimmed to create a more romantic atmosphere.

Sheer gold curtains were draped across the walls and arched windows, adding a warmer tone. I was impressed by the beautiful floral arrangements. The tables were covered in silk, overlapping in black, violet, and gold, which didn't take away from the exquisite center pieces: white orchids dusted with gold glitter, meticulously arranged inside a crystal vase that was placed in a large basin of water. Dancing flames flickered from the bowls of floating tea light candles.

A colorful spectrum of satin gowns spun around the dance floor, as if they were exotic flowers coming to full bloom. Everyone was wearing intricate masks, and from what I could see, no other girl had painted or tattooed her mask on her face like I had. The DJ faded another track into the mix and got everybody hyped up. I actually felt… happy.

"You ready?" Ryan smiled.

"This is our last night as seniors. Let's enjoy it to the fullest." I hooked my arm around his while we descended the stairs.

"Look at Coach Carter's tux." He laughed, pointing at the fashion crime. "It's orange!"

I spotted him and giggled. "Wait—how do you know that's him? He's wearing a mask."

"Because Carter's got the biggest beer gut in the entire school faculty."

Laughing, I tried not to trip over my open toe Gucci's. We were almost halfway down the steps when I suddenly froze. A tall man dressed in a black tux and dark mask was standing next to my English teacher, Ms. Perez. His short brown hair was slicked back, and he looked oddly familiar. He was staring right at me.

"You okay, Aria?" Ryan asked. "You look like you've seen a ghost."

My friend's voice faded into the background as I watched the stranger carefully remove his mask.

Oh… my… God. It was Evan.

"Aria?" Ryan's voice was audible again.

"I'm fine," I answered, snapping out of it before we started down the steps. Those dark eyes never left my face, and I couldn't look away from his gaze.

When we finally reached the main floor, I walked toward my uncle and greeted him in good spirits.

"Evan, what are you doing here?"

He smiled, glancing at Ms. Perez. "I'm Claudia's date."

When did this happen? I wondered. Evan had never told me he was seeing her.

"Aria, you look so gorgeous tonight!" Ms. Perez said, hugging me. "I'm gonna miss having you in my classroom."

Originally a native of Venezuela, Ms. Perez was known as the hottest teacher at my high school. She was one of my favorites among the faculty.

"Are you dating my uncle?" I boldly asked.

"We met at the gym two weeks ago," she said, looking smitten by him. "Nothing's serious yet, but he's an ideal candidate. Let's put it that way." She winked at Evan, followed by a subtle exchange of flirtatious smiles.

"Why didn't you tell me you were coming to my prom?" I asked my uncle.

"I wanted it to be a surprise."

Ms. Perez explained how she had asked him if he wanted to chaperone when she had found out I was his niece.

"That's an excuse," Evan stated. "She just wanted me here as her date."

"Guilty as charged." Ms. Perez blushed.

I was about to ask Evan a question when he turned his attention on Ryan and said, "So, Aria, care to introduce this young man to me?"

"Of course! Ryan, this is Evan. Evan—Ryan."

"*Ah*, the star athlete… now I remember." He reached out and shook his hand. "Nice to meet you."

"Aria's told me a lot about you, Mr. Hunter." Ryan offered a smile.

"Good things, I hope." Evan smirked at me. "And please call me Evan. I'm still too young for that 'Mister' crap."

We all laughed.

"Treat my niece well."

"I will."

"Good. I've got my eye on you."

God, he was just as protective and territorial as Noah. Maybe it ran in the family or something. I often wondered what my other uncle was like.

Ms. Perez took a sip of her fruity beverage and told us how proud she was of our achievements. She had high hopes for our academic futures and wished us an amazing night.

"Go," Evan said. "Frolic amongst your peers."

"You just wanna get rid of me so you can hang out with your hot date," I teased in a low voice.

"Come here," he said. "Give me a hug." He pulled me into his arms and whispered, "I missed you."

"I missed you, too." I hugged him back and recognized the scent of his cologne. It was the same cologne that Noah often used: *Eternity*, by Calvin Klein. If I closed my eyes, I could have convinced myself that it was Noah I was hugging.

Reluctantly, I withdrew and slipped my hand into Ryan's before I politely said my goodbyes to Ms. Perez. She smiled and gave me a little wave as I walked off with the most popular guy at school. Turning my head, I caught the way Evan gestured two fingers at his eyes and then pointed them at Ryan with this serious look on his face.

Is that supposed to be a friendly threat?

Ryan looked uneasy as he looked at me and chuckled. "We might have a hard time sneaking off while your uncle's here."

"Don't worry about him."

"If you say so."

Hopefully, he wouldn't sabotage our plans. I hadn't expected him to be here, but I wasn't disappointed.

Ryan led me to our table, where the rest of our friends were seated. We sat down, socialized, and indulged in the delicious dinner our hundred dollar tickets had covered.

☙◗◖❧

Time had flown much quicker than I expected, which meant I was enjoying myself. It made me sad knowing this would be the last time I would ever see anyone here again. All my friends thought I was going to Berkeley in the fall. I didn't want to explain why I was moving back to New York, especially since I had expressed how much I hated living there.

Whoever hired our DJ had made an excellent choice. He had played many of my favorite songs: "We Are Young" by Fun, "World Hold On" by Bob Sinclar, "Get Lucky" by Daft Punk, "Koko" by Sander van Doorn, and so much more.

I couldn't keep my eyes off Evan all evening. I was crushing on him. He was laid back, funny, charismatic, not to mention good looking. He and I... we had this understanding: a bond. Throughout the weeks of getting to know him, I realized he had quickly gained my trust. Evan's place had become my haven. I still remember that evening when he took photos of me. In hindsight, I'm certain he was going to let me kiss him. We weren't biologically related, so it wouldn't have been the worst thing if that kiss had actually happened. I couldn't help but wonder if Evan was actually attracted to me. Maybe we had been so high that night that we didn't care about the rules anymore. He'd had a chick over, and I'd disrupted things...

Ugh, I didn't want to analyze it. All I knew was that my stomach twisted in knots every time he looked at me with those alluring brown eyes. Perhaps the reason we'd connected right off the bat was because we both felt like outcasts in the family.

Slow dancing in Ryan's arms, I kept wishing it was Evan I was dancing with as we swayed to a beautiful love ballad.

The music suddenly faded, as Jenna Connelly (our student council president) took the podium and tapped on the mic.

"Hello, everyone! Can I have your attention, please?"

We stopped dancing and turned toward the stage. Jen's blonde hair and champagne gown looked amazing that evening.

"Thank you all for voting tonight! I have tallied the ballots, which means it's time to announce this year's prom king and queen!"

A crowd of students cheered and clapped, waiting for the results. As for the voting... I had voted for Jessica and her new boy toy, Matt Kensington.

"All right, class of 2013," Jen announced. "Your prom king and queen are..."

There was a lengthy pause before she revealed the names.

"Ryan Taylor and Stephanie Cohen!"

Everyone applauded as a blinding spotlight flooded my face. And then I realized why I was centered out: Ryan was next to me.

"What the hell?" He looked confused. "I swear the votes were rigged. There's no way she could have won!"

I was a little pissed that Steph was voted as prom queen—not because I wanted to win the crown, but because I felt she didn't deserve it. "Don't worry about it," I said to Ryan. "Get up there and fulfill your duties. You only get to be prom king once in your life!" I smiled and tried to be the supportive "girlfriend."

Before he headed to the stage, I gave him the sexiest kiss while the spotlight was still on us. I just wanted Steph to go green with envy since she had *the hots* for Ryan.

Jessica soon appeared at my side, chatting my ear off.

"I can't believe Steph won! I bet she rigged the votes."

I suppose it was possible.

"It's okay," I said. "This is probably the only event that will be her most memorable achievement in life. Let her have her five minutes of 'fame and glory.'"

"If you can't beat'em, join'em!"

We stitched on a smile and blended in with the crowd, applauding.

After Ryan and Steph got crowned, they posed for pictures and walked off the stage. The lights were dimmed as Jen announced it was time for their first dance together as "prom royalty." Everyone cleared the way for the pair and watched them dance while others joined in. I was expecting the DJ to play something by Savage Garden, Ed Sheeran, or Christina Perri, but he played a Chris Isaac song that was covered by Gemma Hayes: "Wicked Game."

"I'm gonna grab some more punch," Jess said. "Do you want me to bring you a glass?"

"No, I'm good. Thanks." I smiled, watching my friend disappear before fixing my eyes on the "happy couple."

Steph's prom dress looked more like fancy lingerie than a formal gown. There were slits on both sides of the black silk fabric, reaching up to her thighs; and the front of her dress had a plunging neckline that showed off her "twins" and pierced navel. I was reminded of J-Lo's millennium fashion moment, when she had worn that green Versace gown at the Grammy Awards. There was a bit of a resemblance between the dresses in terms of design, but the Latina goddess certainly wore it better. I liked Steph's mask: black and red feathers, with rhinestones around the eyeholes. Steph had a beautiful face and body, though I couldn't say the same about her personality. Hot girls who are mean are like bananas: yellow, ripe, visually pleasing, and good enough to eat… until you peel back the layers, and it's all rotten inside.

I couldn't help but feel sad as the music played on. Gemma's voice was so soft and lovely. My head was filled with thoughts of Noah, despite my distractive evening.

I need some fresh air.

No one noticed me slip away as my heels clicked behind me. Headed toward a pair of double doors, I opened them and stepped outside.

ଓଃ୫ଠ

Standing on the terrace, I could finally breathe again. The architectural design reminded me of the Venetian balconies of Italy. A warm spring breeze played with my hair as I absorbed the surrounding beauty around me. The garden was glowing with fairy lights, and the fragrant smell of roses had permeated the air. My eyes roamed toward the lampposts, illuminating the darkness along a park path. The breathtaking view overlooked a lush landscape that made me feel as if I had walked through a portal to a different dimension. An orchestra of crickets performed a prelude to nature's musical score.

Surrounded by palm trees, I gazed at a marble fountain in the center of the garden. The water kept changing colors from red to pink, purple, and blue. I appreciated all the labor that went into creating such a luxurious outdoor atmosphere. A blanket of stars sparkled like diamonds above me. The garden was tranquil, decorated with solar lamps, flowers, and chaise lounges. Fireflies floated around me, reminding me of the first time I'd seen those glowing insects… It had been a hot summer in July, and I'd spent the evening playing in my grandparent's garden. I was five years old. I remembered being fascinated by these pretty glowing bugs, thinking they were fairies. Funny how gullible and naïve we are as children; ignorant of the corruption in the world; so easily… trusting.

"What are you doing out here all alone?"

Evan's charismatic voice echoed behind me, snapping me out of my thoughts.

"I needed some air," I replied, turning around to meet his dark eyes. "This is a masquerade prom. Where's your mask?"

"I don't need to wear a mask around you," he said, smiling.

Xylophone melodies echoed outside, amplifying the romantic ambiance.

"It's so beautiful out here," Evan expressed.

"This hotel is pretty amazing."

He stepped beside me and said, "You should have been crowned prom queen."

"I'm not disappointed."

"Drink this." He offered me a glass of punch.

"No, thanks."

"I think you'll want to drink *this* glass." He grinned, placing his drink on the railing before he flashed a silver flask concealed in his tux.

"You smuggled alcohol inside?"

"What can I say?" Evan chuckled. "Old habits die hard."

"You spiked the punch bowl?"

"No. Only our drinks."

"Now I feel special." I beamed. "We should make a toast."

"Allow me the honor." He raised his glass and cleared his throat. "To my beautiful niece, and her promising career in the modeling industry. You're gonna give all those veterans a run for their money."

"Oh, I don't know about that." I blushed and shied away.

"I have full confidence in you."

His dark eyes hypnotized me as he tapped his glass against mine.

"Cheers, love!"

I felt the typical burn in my throat when I drank it down. It was strong—whatever it was.

"So," Evan said, "you're not disappointed in the slightest that you didn't get to be prom queen?"

"Nope," I answered. "I was actually hoping that Jess would win the votes." I paused and changed the subject. "Why didn't you tell me you were dating my teacher?"

"Well, you and I haven't exactly been communicating regularly."

That was true. "I'm sorry about that night, Evan. I was a mess."

"You were hurt. I get it."

We locked eyes, and I suddenly felt naked, worried he could read my thoughts. "Shouldn't you be chaperoning inside with your date?" I said.

"Claudia's taking care of a little fiasco in the lady's room with some students."

"What happened?"

"Catfight over a boy."

"Wow… girls these days. I would never fight over a guy if he were indecisive about wanting to be with me—*especially* if another girl was in the picture."

It quickly occurred to me that I had contradicted myself. I was exactly in that sort of situation: me, Noah, and Vanessa. A love triangle from Hell.

"I can't imagine how you could ever find yourself in that predicament," Evan expressed.

"Why do you say that?"

"Because you're stunningly attractive, smart, funny… You're the entire package, Aria. Any guy that would hesitate to be with you would have to be gay."

"You're flattering me. And that's not true—everyone has their 'type.' Chemistry is hard to explain. I don't know if it's because of physical appearance or energetic alignment. Maybe both."

"First, I never give meaningless compliments. And second, I think you're onto something here…"

"Thank you." I smiled.

"This garden is huge." He reached out his hand. "Let's explore it."

☙❧

A stone cobbled pathway lit up with lanterns as I walked in the darkness. I strangely felt like Cinderella… all this magic would disappear at the stroke of midnight (including the fantasy of my perfect life). I would return to a reality of rags and endless hardships, minus Prince Charming.

Walking hand in hand with Evan, we headed toward a gazebo in the distance, decorated with string lights. It was more like a fancy garden tent with a polished wooden platform. Music echoed in the distance as we walked up the steps. The running sound of the water fountain was so soothing.

"I'm surprised no one else is out here," I said, looking around.

"Well, technically, we're supposed to be watching 'the royals' have their first dance."

I laughed, glancing at the twinkling lights above me. "The sucky part is that Steph's dancing with my date to one of my favorite songs," I sighed. "Someone up there wants to torture me tonight."

Like Noah does every night, I thought in dismay, fixating on the fountain in the distance.

"Dance with me," Evan said.

"What?"

He took the drink out of my hand and placed it on the railing.

"Are you serious?"

"It's not like we haven't danced before." He flashed a charming smile. "I'd be honored if you had this dance with me."

What a gentleman.

Accepting his hand, I smiled when he wrapped his arm around my waist and pulled me closer. We slowly swayed with the music, falling under what seemed like a love spell. Closing my eyes, I rested my head in the crook of Evan's neck and surrendered to how safe he made me feel. I couldn't understand why Noah always said he was dangerous.

"What was your high school prom like?" I asked.

"Lame." Evan chuckled.

"You didn't go?"

"I did, but my friends and I ditched our prom and drove up to my family's lake house. All six of us had got baked out of our minds that weekend, and… well, the rest… you don't want to know."

"I do."

"… inappropriate activities."

"Ah. Okay." I nervously laughed. "If you think proms are lame, then what are you doing here? You must be trying to score some serious points with Ms. Perez, huh?"

"I don't need to help her chaperone to score points. I came because of you."

My cheeks reddened.

"Are you blushing?"

Hiding my embarrassment, I stared at the black buttons of his shirt.

"I really have missed you, Aria."

"I missed you too, Evan."

His fingertips brushed against my lower back, sending chills down my body.

"I have a bit of a confession to make."

"Tell me." I met his captivating eyes.

"For most of my life, I've always felt so left out. I hated not being biologically related to my family. I can't tell you how many times I got into heated arguments because of this. But right now, being here with you… it's made me realize how grateful I am to not share the same DNA."

My heart was racing.

"You and I…" he broke off, whispering, "We have something."

I wasn't sure why my palms were sweaty.

"Don't we, Aria?"

Evan stopped dancing and looked straight through me. He brought his face closer to mine, paralyzing me with an unseen power.

How is this happening?

Releasing my hand, he traced the pulsing vein in my neck with his thumb before he cupped my face. I closed my eyes, letting him coax my chin upwards.

"Evan…"

He pulled me in and pressed his lips against mine, pouring passion into the kiss, which triggered a transformation within. Memories of Noah flickered in my mind: his eyes, his smile, the way he furrowed his brows whenever he was ticked off at me, the way he'd rub the back of his neck when he was nervous; his lips, his laughter, his body, the sexy things he'd said and done to me… Everything hit me at once.

A tear drop fell from the corner of my eye as I wrapped my arms around Evan's neck. I was letting go… of Noah. This was my last goodbye to the man I was hopelessly in love with. There was no point in holding on to something that would never work; no point in loving someone who would never love me the same. I realized this way too late.

Eventually, I'd get married one day, have children, grow old, and look back on my youth. I'd remember a time when I was eighteen and in love. I would remember Noah and smile because at least I was lucky enough to experience that feeling. At least I'd been able to explore what it means to love someone unconditionally, even if that included breaking rules and defying the will of God.

"We shouldn't be doing this here," I said, pulling back.

"I can't express how badly I've been dying to kiss you," Evan admitted.

I was speechless.

"From the moment I set my eyes on you, I…"

"Evan, I think—" I stopped when I heard someone approaching.

"There you are!" said Jess. "Ryan's been looking all over for you. He's worried you're upset at him." She climbed the steps and waved at Evan with a smile.

"I'm not upset," I answered. "I was just talking to my uncle."

Talking… right.

"Oh." She seemed confused. "Okay, well… I'll just let him know you're all right."

"We're done with our conversation. I'll head back with you."

Evan and I exchanged a secret glance before I walked away and followed Jess. We were halfway down the path when our prom dates started toward us.

"Where did you go?" asked Ryan. "I got worried." He removed his mask and kissed my cheek.

"I was just chatting in the garden with Evan."

Turning around, I noticed he had disappeared.

"Steph's perfume gave me a headache," Ryan complained.

"You're lucky she didn't chat your ear off through the dance!" Jess laughed.

"I was so tempted to step on her feet."

"Well," I said to Ryan. "How noble of you to refrain from temptation."

He smiled and offered me his arm before we walked back to the banquet hall with our friends.

ৎৎ৪৩

Watching my classmates dance to Psy's "Gangnam Style" was hilarious. I remember when his music video had gone viral and skyrocketed him to fame on YouTube. Everybody knew the crazy choreography—including Coach Carter. Sometimes you need to let loose and have fun, no matter how ridiculous you look.

As midnight approached, Ryan and I had one last dance together. Boyce Avenue had covered a song that was originally sung by U2. I loved this acoustic version, even though Bono's vocals were incredible. Resting my head in the crook of Ryan's neck, he held me close and danced with me.

The riveting lyrics echoed around us as I closed my eyes and let my mind wander. Noah instantly appeared. I hated how he had this effect on me. Evan had kissed me two hours ago, and you would think I would try to process that through the rest of my evening. But no... all thoughts were strictly Noah related. I wondered if he was thinking about me at all—whether he missed me. As hard as it was to leave him, I did not regret coming to California. I didn't regret a single moment I had shared with him. Our relationship was beyond complicated, and even though he couldn't return my feelings, at least I knew he cared about me. That should have been enough, right? Except it wasn't. Not for me. I was selfish that way. I could have stayed. I could have gone to Berkley, dated Ryan, or a nice guy in college; I could have had a normal life, but I didn't want that. I had never been privileged with normalcy. Now that I had all these opportunities that gave me exactly that: security, stability, *normalcy*... I wanted to run. I wasn't sure if I was deliberately trying to sabotage my life off course and set myself up for failure, or if I genuinely thought this was the best alternative for me. Would I ever feel normal again? Had I ever even felt normal?

Nope, my subconscious answered. *You are anything but normal, Aria.*

I would have replied with a witty French quote, but my linguistic knowledge in that department was… how do you say… *le suck?*

Ugh, way to butcher a language. I love French culture—don't come for me.

I was supposed to be enjoying this last dance, but I was having conversations with myself like a neurotic person. Thankfully, the song ended, and I was no longer relating the lyrics to Noah.

"Thank you for the dance." Ryan smiled, kissing my hand. "Do you mind waiting while I use the restroom?"

"Yeah, no worries," I said.

"Don't disappear."

"I won't."

Not tonight, anyway. Not until tomorrow.

When Ryan left, I looked for Evan through the crowd, but couldn't track him. I spotted Ms. Perez sitting at a table, talking with her colleagues, but my uncle wasn't with her.

Where did he go? Is he upset? My paranoid thoughts consumed me. Opening my clutch, I pulled out my cellphone and noticed Evan's text message.

Sorry for bailing. Something came up. Emergency. Don't worry. Let's talk 2morrow or whenever ur free this weekend. I need 2 c u.

But I wouldn't be there tomorrow. I didn't want to imagine how mad he would be once he'd find out I had flown back to New York without saying goodbye. To complicate things more, we had kissed. I didn't know how to feel about it.

Let's go through my list of facts, shall we?

Can we please ditch your irritating habit of listing things already? It's getting annoying, my ego complained.

I guess I just needed to reiterate the fact that I was still in love with Noah, and despite everything I had planned tonight, sleeping with Ryan wouldn't change my feelings. That kiss with Evan had left me feeling…

hot and bothered, but it didn't break the love spell I was under. Regardless, I was still going to sleep with Ryan. My mind was made up, as if it was the only way to purge Noah's energy from my body.

Hopefully I can get over my all-consuming love for this man. I need to get over him. I sighed, spamming my mind with sad emojis when I realized I would never get over him. Maybe having my head probed, prodded, and psychoanalyzed by a doctor was not such a bad idea.

"Aria?" Ryan said, pulling me back to reality.

"Sorry." I blinked. "Zoned out."

"I noticed." He gave me a worried look. "Are you sure you're okay?"

"Yeah, I'm just… a little nervous."

"About tonight?"

I nodded bashfully.

"We don't have to. You know that, right?"

"Yes, but it's what I want. Trust me."

He was such a nice guy; the only good-looking guy at school who wasn't an arrogant douchebag—which was a rarity. Had I never met Noah, I would have dated Ryan and made our relationship official.

Determined to destroy my "purity," I gave my virtue the middle finger. There was nothing innocent about me. It seemed so foolish to hold on to my chastity. I could have pretended to be like Anastasia Steele from *Fifty Shades of Grey.* She stayed celibate for like twenty-one… twenty-three years of her life? And then she gave her virginity away like it was nothing to notorious billionaire Christian Grey: a guy she had known for what seemed like two days or a week. He'd served her up with some creepy BDSM contract prior to Ana dropping her panties.

Desperate?

I realized I was practically doing the same thing, except Ryan wasn't a billionaire; there was no contract; I had known him for much longer than a week; and he didn't have a "red room of pain." (Not that I knew of, anyway.)

Hypocrite much, Aria?

Maybe that's what happens when you fall in love. You lose your mind. Nothing and no one else matters. The entire world could be against you, but as long as you and your love are tuned into each other, committed, and loyal… everything else fades away.

Love is madness.

"Are you ready to leave?" Ryan asked.

"Yes. I'd much rather party with you, *alone*." I smirked seductively as he led me away from the dance floor.

We said our goodbyes to our friends and headed for the staircase. Jessica knew about my plans with Ryan. She was supportive of my decision because she thought we were compatible. If I had told her I was moving back to New York, she would have advised me not to have sex with him that night. I hated not having anyone to talk to about Noah. I mean, who could I confide in? My best friends? My mother? I guess fate had never been in my favor since the second I was born. I must have truly been an abomination. Mom should have aborted me; it would have spared everyone from so much hurt and broken dreams.

Reaching the top of the stairs, I took one last look at the beautiful banquet hall. This venue was better than whatever crappy prom I would have had at my old high school.

"Let's go pop that bottle of Dom Pérignon," Ryan said, escorting me out.

⳹⳾

Wasting no time, we went straight to the front desk to get our room keys. While Ryan was busy checking in, I told him I needed to call my uncle, since I was worried about him disappearing.

"We're all finished here."

"You head upstairs. I'll be right with you," I said.

"No, problem. Don't rush. Actually…" He paused. "Take your time."

"Why? What's up?"

"You'll find out soon." He grinned, heading for the elevators.

"No crazy surprises, please!"

"Just trust me."

Once Ryan disappeared, I sat on a cream sofa in the lobby and gave Evan a call. But he wasn't picking up, so I texted him.

Hey, r u ok?

I couldn't shake the feeling that something serious had happened. Unable to sit, I paced the lobby and waited for him to text me back. After about a minute, I received an incoming message:

I'm fine, love. Call me 2morrow. I'm free all day.

I felt so bad. He didn't know I was leaving.

Should I tell him? I wondered.

Have a good night. xx

Well, I guess that settled it.

I figured it would be best to call him once I was in New York. I'd have to explain how things weren't working out for me while living with Noah. I wouldn't go into detail about the reasons, but our "irreconcilable differences" were a perfect excuse to want to move out of state.

Scrolling down to Noah's name on my contact list, I considered calling him.

Forget it.

My nerves were getting the best of me as I made my way to the elevators and stepped inside. This was not how I wanted to be intimate with a man. I wanted to share my temple with Noah. But he didn't want me. He was almost a thousand miles away. Even if I wanted to seduce him, I couldn't. Vanessa had won. Everyone had their happy ending, except for me. I needed to stop feeling sorry for myself.

෪

Stepping onto the floor of our suite, I walked down a dimly lit hallway. Fancy light fixtures hung from the ceiling; and unlike most hotels that covered their floors with carpeting, this establishment had an intricate style of marble tiles, which only made the interior design more elegant. It was a five-star luxury hotel, so I shouldn't have been surprised. Leisurely, I passed several suites that had gold plated numbers on the doors until I stood across room 518. Calming my nerves, I took a deep breath and inserted my keycard in the security slot.

No turning back now…

All the lights were off when I stepped into the suite, except for a lamp on a nightstand.

"Ryan?"

He didn't answer.

"Hello?"

Something caught my eye as I entered the room: a piece of paper was folded on the bed. Edging closer, I noticed a silver dollar resting on it, with a single white rose tucked between the note. No wonder Ryan had told me to "take my time;" he'd been planning a surprise. Smiling, I held the rose and avoided pricking my fingers. I could have sat there smelling it for the next five minutes, but I didn't want to keep Ryan waiting.

How did he know I love white roses?

Jess must have told him.

I laid the rose down on the bed and read the mysterious love letter. The handwriting looked unrecognizable to me. I was familiar with Ryan's handwriting, and it didn't look like it belonged to him. Maybe he had got someone else to write it to throw me off.

Aria,

You deserve so much more than this little hotel room. Take this keycard and meet me at room #1206. It's the penthouse suite on the top floor. But before you get here, I want you to do me a favor. Please visit the fountain in the hotel garden and make a wish. Toss that silver dollar in the water and come find me. I'm waiting for you. I hope your wish comes true.

I loved his romantic side. It felt nice to be courted. Placing the coin and letter in my purse, I grabbed the rose before I left the suite to fulfill Ryan's romantic request. He had put so much effort into making this night special. The least I could do was show my appreciation.

CHAPTER TWENTY-ONE
ARIA

Strolling through the labyrinth of the hotel garden, I thought about my amazing evening. Even though prom night was almost over, it wasn't as bad as I thought. Overall, I was glad I went. At least I could leave my friends on good terms with fun memories. I must have meant a lot to Ryan for him to have gone to such great lengths to impress me with sentimental gestures.

You're crazy to abandon the prospect of being with a guy like him, I told myself. But my heart wanted Noah. I couldn't help it.

Retracing my steps, I made my way to the four-tier fountain and sat on the edge. I listened to the splashing patter of water spraying out into the marble basin as the lights changed colors. A pool of loose change was resting at the bottom. These shiny coins represented wishes that belonged to strangers who had once stood or sat at this same spot.

This seems like such a waste of time.

I sounded just as cynical as my stepdad. Grabbing the silver dollar from my purse, I held it in my palm, noticing an eagle engraved into the coin. Sitting there, I reflected on what I wanted most.

I wish…

All I could think about was Noah. It frustrated me how I couldn't delete him from my brain as all my anguish resurfaced. A hurricane of memories swept me by storm and left me incapable of finding any solace. No matter where I turned, I was confronted with images of me and him: the man who had once abandoned me, only to return through a wall of mist, disoriented, mirroring me. I was everything he hadn't expected: broken and destructive beyond repair. He could have turned his back on me. He could have walked into that fog again and left me stranded. I'm sure whatever life he had on the other side was much better than standing in a hollow chasm of emptiness with me: a young woman who could look after herself. But he didn't leave. Even after assessing these facts, he still wanted to be the father I always deserved.

Now look what you've done, my conscience whispered.

I was planning to abandon Noah, when all he wanted was to hold my hand and lead me through that heavy mist to the other side together. We could have peacefully stood in the sunshine, knowing our wounds had healed along the way. All he ever wanted was to obliterate the darkness in my life. And all I ever wanted was to be found by a man who would love me unconditionally.

Now that Noah had found me, I was heartlessly ignoring all the Hell he'd gone through to get here. I didn't want to accept the possibility of happiness waiting for us beyond the fog. I didn't want to walk the same path as him. I guess I was at war with God and my destiny. How could the Creator bring such an attractive, accomplished man into my life, and expect me not to feel attraction? How could God forbid me from falling in love with him? If the Lord was truly omniscient, omnipotent, and omnibenevolent, then how come he had not expected the pending avalanche that would come when Noah and I would cross paths? Had he not foreseen the way I would abominate the definition of love? How I would twist and contort the meaning just to manipulate my way into getting what I'd want? Was this a test? If so, I had epically failed. Despite this realization, I still dared to hope. I had two choices: take Noah's hand and follow him into the light or turn my back on him and pray he would follow me into the darkness.

Feeling burdened, I stared into the pristine water and faintly whispered, "I wish Noah was in love with me."

A vibrating ringing sound echoed in my ears when I flipped the dollar, watching it rotate before it found its place over a coin at the bottom of the fountain: one of many wishes that most likely had never come true. Feeling oddly lighter, I stood up, straightened my dress, and headed toward my new destination: the penthouse suite.

❀

Riding the elevator, I sent Ryan a text.

I'm on my way up. u didn't have to go through all this trouble for me... But I'm so touched. See u soon! xox

I didn't realize how nervous I was until the elevator stopped. The doors retracted before I stepped out. The hallway was almost identical to the previous one I had walked down, except the ceiling was taller, with skylights between the light fixtures.

My cellphone suddenly vibrated as I approached room #1206

I'm sorry. He told me not to text u... we got caught. I'm lucky he didn't beat the shit out of me. Text me when ur home.

Oh, God... the note, the rose, and the room key... Was it really from Ryan, or Evan? I wondered in shock. That explained why he'd left so suddenly. I didn't know how he had found out about my plans with Ryan, but maybe he just wanted to sabotage our night so that I wouldn't do something I would later regret.

Standing across a pair of dark mahogany doors, I noticed the intricate design, admiring the giant archway. Music played from inside the suite as I inserted the gold keycard. I recognized the song: "Your Love Is An Echo" by Aiiso. The doors unlocked, unleashing a quiet terror in my chest. I wasn't sure why I was so nervous suddenly.

Entering the threshold, I paused and took in the modern luxury of my posh environment. There was no way Ryan could have afforded this. I was convinced it was Evan's doing. All the lights were off, with only a trail of white pillar candles placed along the marble tiles, leading the way to the master bedroom; I just needed to follow the flickering flames. The music was so beautiful with romantic lyrics that touched me.

My heels echoed behind me as I passed a fully furnished living room through an archway leading to another gathering room; the windows were wide, reaching the ceiling. Stopping in my tracks, I noticed the terrace doors were open, inviting a cool breeze inside. A pink moon was high in the sky. The picturesque landscape was an artist's dream.

The vocalist seemed so sure of his feelings, but I couldn't relate. I felt so lost.

What should I say to Evan?

Heading closer, I wasn't sure where my heart would guide me by walking through that threshold. The door was wide open, giving me a glimpse of the bedroom bathed in warm candlelight. I noticed a king-size bed, covered in red and white rose petals; a white canopy hung right above it. Tall white pillar candles surrounded the bed, which looked more romantic and beautiful. I felt as if I had walked in on the set of a timeless romance movie.

Entering the bedroom, I suddenly froze.

Breathe...

I had two choices: black out and faint, or voluntarily call up the psychiatric ward and tell them to rush over and strap me in a straitjacket... Because the person who was standing across from me could have easily been a hallucination. I unquestionably doubted my sanity.

Clad in a black tuxedo, he stood on the threshold of the balcony door, gazing at the ocean with his hands in his pockets. I was afraid to move, fearing he would vanish. It wasn't until he turned around that I melted. Half of his face was covered by a black mask, but he was handsome beyond words—more perfect than ever.

"So," he said with a smile. "Did you get what you wished for?"

His deep voice and ocean eyes were a dead giveaway.

"Please tell me you wished for this."

Keep breathing...

Stepping closer, he removed his mask and looked at me while I stood statuesque, tears filling my eyes. He was desirable in every aspect; standing before me like the god I envisioned him as. It was a miracle.

Is he real?

Staring in disbelief, I was speechless, begging my brain to re-coordinate the wires that had gone haywire.

"Noah… how… how did you—"

"How could you ever consider leaving me, Aria?" Closing the distance, he held my face.

I noticed a palpable sadness in his eyes.

"Don't you understand I need you here with me?" The intensity of his gaze made my soul shiver. "How could you go behind my back and get a one-way ticket to New York?"

I was about to explain when I realized there was no way he could have discovered my escape plans, unless he…

No… Please tell me you didn't!

"Wait," I said. "How did you find out about me flying back to New York?"

He seemed hesitant to answer.

"I read your diary."

"You *what?*" I couldn't believe it. I was outraged.

"It happened by accident." Noah took a breath and dropped his hands. "After you left for prom, I came in your room to leave you one last present on your nightstand. That's when I saw your diary right there in front of me—it was wide open." He paused and took a breath. "I was tempted, okay? I didn't mean to read it, but as soon as I noticed my name on that page… I couldn't resist."

How could I have forgotten to put my diary away? I wanted to bury my head under a rock and never come out.

"I can't believe you violated my privacy like that!" I teared up. All those private, personal thoughts were no longer a secret. He knew them all.

"I just read one page, Aria," he tried to reason. "But it was enough for me to cancel my trip and come save you from making a big mistake."

"Save me?" I frowned in confusion.

How long had he been waiting for me? Does Vanessa know he's here? My mind was racing. I could hardly register anything that had happened in the last half hour.

"So," I said with contempt. "You came here to stop me from sleeping with Ryan, is that it? Well, mission accomplished. Thanks for making a complete fool out of me!"

There was my spitfire temper again.

"You're a smart girl." Noah darkened his gaze. "How could you even think about having sex with a guy you don't love?"

"You're the last person to be lecturing me on this topic." I shot him a scornful stare.

"I'm not here to lecture you." He frowned again.

"I've made my feelings for you crystal clear, Noah. You don't want me. You refuse to love me the same way. You've told me that repeatedly. And now you refuse to let me try to love someone else? How do you expect me to get over you if you won't even let me? Are you that selfish?"

Battling my pride, I blinked back hot tears and tried to keep my composure.

"Tell me you want this relationship," I said. "Or let go of me completely."

All I wanted was to hide myself in his chest and hug him forever. I missed him so much. There was always this magnetic attraction between us, and I was like a moth to the flame: inevitably getting burned.

"Just hear me out," he pleaded.

"No. You have a wife to get home to," I coldly replied.

My snippy attitude was deliberate. I just felt so embarrassed that he'd read my diary. All those things I had said about him… *God!*

"It's over between me and Vanessa. I'm so sorry for ever doubting you." He caressed my cheek. "You were right. She had been unfaithful to me all along. Three days ago, my private investigator caught those two hooking up on tape. I had mentioned nothing to Vanessa because I wanted to blindside her with legal papers this Monday."

While I was happy the truth was out, his decision still hadn't eliminated my insecurities.

"I'm not a rebound, Noah. I'm going home." Turning away, he grabbed my arm and pulled me closer.

"God damn it, Aria! Can you please leave your stubborn pride outside of this bedroom and just listen to me? I'm trying to show you how I feel about you."

You just wanted to stop me from sleeping with Ryan, I blasted in my mind.

"Look around you"—he motioned with his hands—"what do you think this means? Do you honestly believe that Ryan could have pulled this off? It was all me, sweetheart. I was waiting for the two of you to enter your suite to stop things from escalating. When I saw he had come alone… Let's just say I used that opportunity to make him abandon his plans. I assume he thought I'd take you home and ground you—and believe me, I certainly gave him that impression before he left."

That sounded like something Noah would do.

"I knew you'd be heading up to the room, and I wanted to avoid a confrontation with you, so I opted for romantic spontaneity. A bellhop had been delivering room service in the hallway, and when I saw a vase full of white roses on his cart, I paid him for a favor. I didn't want you to recognize my handwriting; I asked him to write that note on my behalf. That silver dollar I left behind for you was a special coin my father had given me.

"I've always carried it in my wallet in remembrance of him. When I saw the fountain from the balcony, I thought it was an appropriate time to part with it and leave it in your hands. I swear to God, Aria, as soon as I read your diary, I left the house, drove to my friend's tailor shop, and suited up in a tux. I have no regrets about coming here and sabotaging your plans with a boy that you *think* you love."

But I wasn't in love with Ryan; this I already knew.

"Do you understand what I'm trying to say here?" Noah sounded serious. "I had made my decision hours ago. There was no way I could leave knowing you were leaving me. I called the hotel and booked this penthouse suite as soon as I'd discovered your plans. I showed up ahead of time and waited for the right moment to intervene." He swallowed hard, searching my eyes. I had never seen him so vulnerable before. It was a whole new side to him.

"Allow me to reiterate some facts so that it's crystal clear to you on where I stand with my feelings: that note was from me. I left you that rose; I asked you to make that wish by the fountain; and I was hoping you'd wish for me to be here… for me to be the one who was waiting for you." He held my hands and caressed them with his thumbs, never taking his heated gaze off me. "All that matters now is that you're here and I'm here," he added. "Together, like we're meant to be."

This situation was difficult for me to digest.

"Aria, I'm gonna ask you again… Did your wish come true?" His voice was gentle, and his eyes looked so beautiful in the burning glow of the candlelight, reminding me of the sun setting across the ocean.

"I'm not sure," I replied, looking at our hands. "I wished…"

Noah tilted my chin up. "Tell me. I want you to look at me when you say it."

But I was still afraid to express myself.

"I wished that you… would fall in love with me… like I am with you."

The truth was out. His eyes had become warm, as if he were caressing my soul as he said, "If I wasn't in love with you, I wouldn't be here trying to pour my heart out to you." His confession was fearless, shaking me to my core.

No… this can't be happening. The Devil loves doubt, I thought; he was alive and on my shoulder.

"It's been an endless power struggle between us for a while now, Aria." Noah cupped my face. "But you win." He wiped my tears and murmured, "You win."

All my guards came crashing down when I noticed a flicker of emotion in his misty gaze.

"You own every part of me," he confessed. "And I want to possess every part of you. I can't ignore the way I feel about you any longer. I'm ready to give you what you need. I'm ready to give you what you've needed from me all this time." Removing his blazer, he threw it over an armchair in the corner of the room. "I'm sorry it took me this long. I can't stand the possibility of you loving another man the way you love me—that thought alone just makes me want to stop breathing. Every day I've had to ignore my heart, even though it's been constantly screaming for me to tell you how I feel whenever you're around me." Noah loosened his tie and unbuttoned his shirt.

"It killed me knowing I could never touch you the way I wanted. I love you with every fiber of my being," he continued. "When I look at you, I see my reflection, and it tears me up inside because I can't figure out how it's possible to be in love with a reflection of myself—it's narcissistic—it's wrong, but my heart begs to differ. You are a part of me. You complete me. I don't want to live without you. You were right when you said that we can't go back." He caressed my face.

"You breathed life into my broken soul the first day I cast my haunted eyes on you." Noah paused. "You truly haunted me all my life, Aria. I always felt your presence and had long dreamed of reuniting with you. I just never thought it would be like this"—he stared at my lips—"this love I feel for you… it's so… forbidden… It sets my soul on fire."

Noah's declaration was unbelievably moving as I tried to control the surge of dopamine rushing into my bloodstream.

"You saved me, Aria. All these months I've been scared, convinced I would damn us both to Hell if I so much as touched you. But how could two people who love each other so purely belong in Hell? How could God punish us when my love for you transcends the meaning of love? What I feel for you exceeds everything I've ever felt with loving a woman. I love you so purely and deeply. I would die for you, and I'd gladly welcome resurrection to die a thousand more painful deaths, if it meant you'd be safe from danger. That's how protective I am of you."

There was no way I'd let him die for me. The death of him meant the death of me.

Noah took my hand and placed it on his chest, right against the phoenix tattoo. Resting his hand over mine, he said, "Do you feel that?"

I felt his heartbeat pounding strongly against my palm.

"There's no room for any other woman inside—not romantically," he clarified. "The key to my heart is your fingerprint. I don't care what the world thinks anymore. If love is madness, then consider me a madman. I want to take you in my arms, and I want to kiss you, and touch you, and show you how desperately in love I am with you."

Tears spilled down my face as I looked at him in shock. This was the ultimate expression of love. My words could never surpass his confession. What could I say?

"Noah, I—"

"Let me finish, baby." He stroked my cheek. "I felt a powerful pull from the second I saw your beautiful face last year. I didn't know what it meant, but as our relationship progressed, I knew I had wrongful desires for you. Once I wrapped my mind around it, I ignored our attraction because I love you too much to hurt you and take advantage of you. That's why I never acted on those desires until you had. I just wanted to snuff out those flames. But I realize now that loving you the way I want isn't wrong."

Noah paused, intensifying his stare. "It's so right. My heart knows it, my soul knows it, and my body yearns to feel it." He held my hands. "You are embedded in me, and if you find me worthy enough to give yourself to me, I promise to show you how much I worship and adore you. I promise to give you all of me. No barriers, no resistance. Not anymore."

I couldn't stop crying as he patiently wiped my tears away, leaving me speechless. Many times, I had daydreamed about Noah confessing his love for me. Living in this moment was a thousand times better than anything I ever envisioned.

"Please say something," he whispered, looking worried. His eyes betrayed his vulnerability. "I'm sorry if I've overwhelmed you."

This was a lot to process.

"Why the sudden change of heart?" I asked, aware of my demon of doubt.

"I've felt this way about you for a while now. I just didn't want to admit it. You're my daughter, and this unchangeable fact has always messed with my mind. When I read what you wrote in your diary, it hurt me badly. I understood why you wanted to be with Ryan, but it absolutely crushed me inside. You were planning to fly back the next day without telling me… This isn't some desperate attempt to make you stay; this is me revealing my feelings with no mask, no rules, and no third party in the equation. Vanessa's out of the picture. It's just you and me, Aria. I'm risking it all for you."

The truth was in his eyes, and I believed him. Maybe all my suffering had been for a reason: how can you appreciate the best moments in life if you never experienced the worst?

"I'm in love with you," he openly confessed. "I want to protect you the way a father protects his daughter, but I can't love you the same way because my every instinct tells me to show you my affection in romantic ways." Reaching for my hips, Noah murmured, "It's been tremendously hard for me to ignore these impulses. You've been the biggest test of my life, Aria."

Staring into his eyes, I was afraid to trust his truth as he squeezed my waist and said, "I wish I could read your mind. Please tell me what you're thinking."

Lost in his handsome features, it took me a while to find my voice.

"Noah, you know how I feel about you—that's no secret. I've just been waiting… hoping you would return my feelings, too. I'm so happy… and in shock. I wasn't expecting this. Nothing I say can describe how I feel right now."

I was dying for his kiss.

"If anyone found out about us, they'd be quick to judge and accuse me of the worst things," he continued. "But my love for you is real; it's the purest thing I've ever felt in my life. We don't even have to cross any physical boundaries with each other. I could sacrifice those needs for you. I just want to love you and make you happy without hiding my feelings. I can hide them from the world, but I don't want to hide them from you."

There was no way I was going to walk out of this lavish hotel room without kissing him. I wanted him. I always wanted him.

"I don't want to fight fate any longer," Noah said. "I don't want to have to convince myself day in and day out that I shouldn't love you this way"—he pulled me closer—"because I should." The seduction in his voice made my heart palpitate as he caressed my back.

All this time I had been waiting, wishing, and praying for this moment. And now that it was here, I was terrified.

What if I won't be good enough for him?

"You're shaking," he said. "Are you cold?"

I withdrew my trembling hands from his chest, but he took them into his own and warmed me up. Noah's body was always like a furnace.

"Aria, I would never force you, you know that. We could just order room service, cuddle all night, and I would be happy."

God, no! I was so done with the PG stuff between us.

"I want you. I'm just nervous."

I was about to be intimate with the sexiest man in the universe. Who wouldn't be freaking out if they were in my shoes?

Noah smiled faintly, removing his shirt before he dropped it on the floor.

Staring at his muscled chest, I fixated on his tattoo and couldn't wait to cover his flawless skin with kisses, like I'd often imagined in my head.

"We'll move at your pace." He reached for my hips. "I want to take my time with you. You're in control."

How was I related to such a magnificent human being? Were we truly children of God, loving and pure? Or spawn of Satan, selfish and evil? Was I to blame for all this? Did I cause Noah to stray from a righteous path? Would he be denied entry through Heaven's gates because his love for me was wrong in the eyes of God? Would he be thrown out of Hell, too? Would Satan reject him once he'd discovered how pure Noah's heart is? Where was our place in the afterlife? Would Noah and I be stuck in limbo together when we died? Or were we already there? My questions were endless, and I had no right or wrong answer.

In the grand scheme of things, this flawless man had come to me as a fallen angel. That's who Noah Hunter was underneath his cloaked humanity. He had rescued me from the nightmare of my life back in New York. A depressing revelation occurred to me while he unzipped my dress:

Noah had shown me more love in the seven months he'd known me than my stepdad ever did.

My gown loosened as it slid off my body with a sigh. Standing in heels with a strapless red bra and matching thong, I felt nervous and naked. The necklace he gave me sparkled around my neck as I touched it.

"I need to kiss you." Noah's deep voice sounded husky as he whispered, "I've been so deprived."

I had never seen him this transparent. My anxiety had fled, replaced by a feeling that rippled through my body: *arousal.* Stepping out of my dress, I wrapped my arms around his neck and pulled myself flush against him.

"No more deprivation," I murmured.

Noah never took his eyes off me as he reached back and expertly unhooked my bra. The garment slipped off me, removing the barrier between us. My breasts were pressed against his firm pectorals. I wasn't sure if my skin was on fire or his.

The music switched tracks, changing to something slower: Sade's legendary song.

No ordinary love…

Was this divine intervention? There was no one here to stop us.

"You consume me, Aria." He lowered his voice. "I'm gonna consume you… all night." His hot lips grazed my neck, making my stomach twist into knots.

Why did he have this effect on me? This man was strikingly handsome. I felt intimidated. I often wondered if he felt the same. Brushing my hands down his chest, I stared into his hypnotic eyes.

"Please let me kiss you."

Holding his gaze, I gave his thumb a brief peck when he rolled it over my bottom lip.

"Stop holding back," I whispered.

"You're the only woman who makes me feel this nervous."

Sliding his hands up my neck, Noah caressed the curve of my jaw and grazed his lips against mine. My breathing grew shallow as I teased him back, licking his lips until our tongues made contact: an erotic dance of sensation. We continued our playful foreplay until we finally surrendered to a sweeping kiss of passion that made me weak in the knees.

This kiss differed from other intimate encounters; it was wild and uncontrollable… liminal. My heart exploded in ecstasy every time he swept his lips against mine, as if it were the ultimate high I was chasing all my life. Was it even healthy to pursue euphoria? I just wanted to *feel* alive. Why else would I incarnate here if not to experience the greatest love ever?

Noah took his time with my lips, kissing me slowly and sensually before I felt the sweet intrusion of his minty tongue. Our breathing got more labored the longer he deepened the kiss. Unfastening his belt, I reached for his fly, but Noah lifted me up in his arms and carried me to bed. We stripped down, and it was the first time I had seen his naked body. Every part of him was perfect, from head to toe. Our clothes and shoes laid in a pile on the floor by the bed. Staring into each other's eyes, we were dangerously in love. I raised myself on my elbows, watching as he kissed his way up my leg, over my knee, parting my thighs and kissing my vulnerable flesh.

"We don't have to do this," said Noah, hovering above me.

"I want you. I'm ready."

"I don't want you to regret this."

"I won't. Why would I regret it?"

"Because of the obvious."

"I love you. I want you."

He hooked his fingers on the edges of my thong, looking up at me. "May I?"

I consented with a nod.

"You're so beautiful, Aria." He caressed my thigh. "Look at me, baby. Don't close your eyes. I want you to see what you do to me."

This is actually happening…

Curiously, I lowered my gaze, admiring the generous size of Noah's cock.

"Lie back," he demanded.

I obeyed him, ignoring my burning desire to please him first.

"Do you trust me?" he asked.

"Always."

"Spread your sexy legs for me."

I focused on my breathing as he crouched between my thighs and lowered his face to my sweet spot. His tongue brushed against my pearl, scorching me from the waist down. Holding my breath, I shut my eyes and felt Noah's warm tongue teasing my velvet folds, making me moan.

"You taste so sweet."

The stimulation was beyond pleasurable. Reaching down, I tangled my fingers through his thick brown hair. It seemed as if he was already familiar with my body, like an experienced lover who knew how I desired to be touched. Nothing felt awkward. Everything felt natural, and that fire between us only burned brighter.

I cried out in ecstasy, clutching the bed sheets to ground myself. Not only was he gifted with a quick-witted tongue, but he knew how to use it in the bedroom as he took me to new heights of bliss, unexplored territories of the soul. Powerful waves of pleasure flowed through me as I curled my toes into the mattress, surrendering to his probing tongue.

"Noah… *oh, my God…*"

Gripping my thighs, he refused to release me until I'd go over the edge. My tummy tightened as I felt a mind-bending release. Our sexual chemistry had no explanation.

"Feel good?" He peered up at me with a smug smile.

I was too breathless to respond. How was it possible that he desired to worship my body? I should have been the one worshipping *him*. And I planned to do just that as I sat up, but he trapped me beneath him.

"I want to please you tonight. There will be plenty of opportunity for you to return the favor, but you should know that my pleasure is derived from pleasing you."

Oh god of all sex gods, have you reincarnated your favorite son in a human body just for me?

"Let me show you how I love you," Noah whispered in my ear.

Our eyes locked first, and then… came… *the inferno*. His kiss was deep and flaming with desire. That slow, sensual movement of our lips grew wilder, igniting passion as he reached below and rubbed my core, teasing me with his fingers until I was soaked. We both seemed possessed by animalistic lust.

"Are you ready for me?" He breathed between needy kisses.

"I want you." I bit his lower lip, snaking my arms around his neck.

"I'm gonna give it to you, nice and slow… even though I'm tempted to punish you."

"What for?"

"For scheming behind my back."

"Yeah, but you know why."

"Doesn't matter." He stared at my lips. "I love kissing you. I've never felt this way about anybody. I can't tell if fate is screwing with us or liberating us."

"I'd like to believe in the latter."

Supporting his weight above me, he teased my entry with his magnum shaft in slow strokes.

"What are you doing?" I breathed.

"Conquering what's rightfully mine."

"Is that all you see me as? A piece of property?"

"I'm guilty of fucking you in my head like that multiple times, I'll admit."

"He's so uncensored."

"You love me this way. Raw. Unfiltered. Cutthroat with the delivery of truth."

"I love you unconditionally."

"I know you do, and I love you for it. Your demon loves mine."

"My demon is desperately in love with yours."

"Can you handle my shadow, Aria?"

"I was born to tame your monster within."

"Kissing you doesn't feel like sin."

"Because I let you in."

"We really are love drunk fools, aren't we? Rhyming stanzas in bed…"

"Angels and demons dance in my head…"

Noah's beautiful eyes lit up as he chuckled and kissed me.

There was no turning back now. How could we, after this?

"Are you on the pill?"

"No. I read about the harmful effects of birth control."

"I'm not pulling out"—he kissed me passionately—"*Ever.*"

"What?"

Holy hell. I couldn't take it anymore. Kissing him back, I slid my hands down his shoulders and chest in a massaging motion. I loved touching his skin and feeling his toned muscles. I couldn't believe his body was mine.

"Does that feel good?" he asked, grinding into me.

"*So… good,*" I breathed, licking his lips.

"Do you want me inside you?"

"I do."

He was luring me into submission.

"I am so in love with you, Aria."

I prayed that love would last forever; it was my biggest fear: abandonment.

"I won't be able to stop once we do this," Noah warned, thinking I'd change my mind.

"I don't want you to stop."

"I'll say this again… we have blood ties."

"I don't care. I love that I'm bound forever to you by DNA."

"You really are my kind of 'fucked up,' aren't you?"

"Just be grateful you found me."

"I am. Every day. I promise."

The idea of letting someone invade your body so intimately seems awkward, scary, and gross when you take sexual arousal out of the equation. But when you're turned on beyond comprehension, all you can think about is surrendering to that powerful drive to procreate. It's like an instinct.

"I don't want to hurt you," Noah said, gripping his swollen cock.

"Make it hurt... *so good*."

"You always know which buttons to press."

Staring up at him, I felt his base push in as my body resisted the intrusion.

"Fuck. You are tight..."

Noah took his time penetrating me, stretching my tight, fleshy walls. Halfway in, I was grateful when he allowed me to get over the shock of his invasion.

"Are you okay?" he asked, pushing himself deeper. "Am I hurting you?"

"No." I wrapped my legs around his waist, pulling him forward until he was fully submerged. The deed was done. It felt like a burning sting, but my arousal served as a numbing agent to the pain.

"I can't believe I'm inside you right now..." Noah panted, staying still. His violent throbs sent waves of pleasure through my body.

"I'm okay," I breathed. "It's not as bad as I thought."

"I promise I'll make you feel better soon." Closing his hands over mine, he slid my arms above my head. I felt his cool, minty breath against my neck as he fondly worked his way into my body.

I had been a wilting rose, withering away in a gloomy garden, with no gardener to tend to me; no one to water me and give me the sunshine I desperately needed. It seemed a miracle that Noah had found me, placed me in the sunlight, and revitalized me. I had transformed into a beautiful white rose. Right there in that moment, I had finally opened and blossomed for him. Just for him, always for him.

His voice seemed caught in his throat as he said, "Never leave me." Tear drops fell from his eyes and landed on my cheeks. "You're the only one who has the power to break me, Aria."

"Please don't cry." I felt a tight tug at my heartstrings.

"I'm not made of stone," he admitted, keeping a slow grind.

"Your poker face is so convincing."

"But you see right through it; that's your gift. I wish you could be in my mind for a day to understand all the ways I love you. My words will never be enough."

His confession made me tremble inside as I held his face and kissed him with everything I had.

Noah filled me to the hilt and stayed in control of his gentle rhythm. "I need this with you," he breathed. "I need to feel you like this every day." He kissed me deeply.

Overwhelmed with happiness, I never wanted to leave this euphoric plane of passion with him.

His expressive eyes were gentle but heated as he said, "No one has to know what we mean to each other." Noah hid his face in the crook of my neck. "No one can take you away from me," he whispered. "No one."

A surge of pleasure rippled through my body while I surrendered to the sinful sensation. Rocking his hips into me, I moaned, dragging my nails down his back.

"You can go faster," I said, lost in a haze of lust and longing.

"Are you sure?"

"Yes." I kissed him hard and felt his speed. His inner beast had finally come out to play, and I loved every second.

Cursing under his breath, Noah slammed into me. He kissed my lips, bending his elbows on the mattress to avoid crushing me. "Do you promise... to be mine?"

"I promise."

"I'm so... addicted to you." He panted. "You know this... makes it worse... right?"

"Uh huh."

"I need to slow down—I'm close."

"Do I make you feel good?" I held his handsome face.

"I can't even describe... how this feels... it's alchemy."

I smiled, kissing him.

"Do you want more?"

I breathed an inaudible "yes" and whimpered when he impaled me with a single thrust.

"Harder?" Noah huffed, rocking into me. "Deeper?"

The lioness within stirred in her cage; I had locked her up for far too long. It was time to let her out.

"Do you love me?" I asked. "Forever?"

Slowing down, he brushed my hair to the side and murmured, "Love doesn't even describe what I feel for you. I think this is way too evolved for anyone to understand, let alone us." He kissed me with a promise, as if he were pledging his undying love. We burned together in our sinful passions, and from our ashes, our love became immortal. A divine prophecy had been fulfilled.

"I want you on top of me." Noah rolled on his back.

But I didn't feel confident enough to take control. Not wanting to disappoint, I carefully shifted my weight and mounted him. A gratifying groan rumbled from his chest when I stroked his length.

"Do you want me to ride you?"

"I want you to do whatever you want with me," he replied. "You're in control, remember?" His voice was thick with lust and sexy as hell. Impatiently, he reached down below and rubbed me, making me moan.

Gripping his shaft, he looked at me with a heated stare. "Sit on it."

His voice was enough to make me orgasm without penetration. I lowered myself on him and felt his intrusion piercing into me. It would take a while before I'd adjust to his size, but everything felt so good once the pain subsided. Quickening my pace, I held on to his chest, noticing a hunger in his eyes.

Noah kissed me hard and passionately. It seemed impossible to pull away. Caressing my hips, he slid his hands past my ribcage, cupping my perky breasts. I traced his chiseled abs and rocked back and forth, harder and faster. In a united effort, we worked toward our mutual goal.

Through jagged breaths, I asked him if he would love me forever this way.

"I swear on your life."

"Do you promise to never… push me away?"

"I couldn't... even if I—tried..." Noah groaned. "I don't want to talk anymore." Locking eyes, he grabbed my hips and pounded into me, making my breasts bounce.

I gripped his firm pectorals and let him ravish me. His powerful thrusts sent me over the edge. The stimulation felt incredible, as if we had discovered an extra dimension of pleasure.

"I have to take my time with you," Noah said, catching his breath. "Lie down beside me, beautiful."

I wanted to stay where I was, but I enjoyed having him in control.

"Turn on your side, baby."

Spoon sex?

I was familiar with this position. But the idea of anal sex terrified me... if that's where we were headed.

"Wait," I said. "You're not gonna... you know... stick it in the other..."

Noah quietly chuckled. I felt so embarrassed. His lips hovered toward my ear as he softly said, "I wouldn't put you through something as demeaning as that—ever." He kissed my shoulder, rubbing my hip.

I didn't think anal sex was demeaning. It just looked... uncomfortable and scary.

"Just relax, Aria. This won't hurt, it's gonna feel good. I promise."

Spooning with me from behind, he lifted my right leg as I closed my eyes and listened to the sound of his voice. He told me how much he loved and desired me, all while teasing my dripping gateway.

"Tell me you want me," Noah whispered, wrapping his fist around my throat.

"You know I want you."

"Then say it."

My body tensed up, surrendering to sensation. He bent his arm under my thigh, raising it so he could go deeper. I whimpered as he bit my shoulder, panting. Our uncontrollable moans got louder, the more he made me feel his powerful thrusts. I needed to feel his lips again—all that sexual energy had to go somewhere. Craving his tongue in my mouth, I twisted my neck and hoped he would give me what I wanted.

A colorful supernova exploded in my mind when our lips crashed together, like an intergalactic experience that opened a new timeline. Hiding in his body felt amazing. Our tongues caressed each other in a teasing dance, heightening my arousal. To be an amazing kisser, one had to master the art. It was not a science. Noah had met his match.

A spark had ignited between us as it burst into flames. We kissed each other with such a desperate need, as if we were deprived for an eternity. Our passion transformed into a fight for dominance as our tongues twisted and collided.

Noah pulled out of me and sat up, reclining on a pillow. Stretching his legs, he said, "Sit on top of me, baby."

He gripped his cock, enticing me.

"Your body is so perfect. It's not fair."

"And you think yours isn't?"

"Compared to you… um…"

"Shut up and mount me. You're lucky I get turned on when you speak nonsense."

Grabbing his shoulders, I carefully lowered my weight and felt that familiar intrusion that was no longer painful. He whispered sweet nothings in my ear as I wrapped myself around him in a lotus position. I could see him, kiss him, and dominate his body at the same time; I loved it. We were finally connected in every aspect.

Noah's lips smoothed over mine while he grabbed my hips. He'd breathe in, and I'd breathe out like a synchronized pattern as our sex became tantric. If it was possible to change a person's DNA and make them evolve into superior beings, then Noah had succeeded. He was changing my genetic code, transforming me into whatever divine being he was. That's all I'd ever wanted: to exist in his world and be a part of him. Making love to this man made me feel immortal. My fear of aging did not exist anymore. We were kindred spirits, mirror souls in union. Our youth was forever preserved by our love. We would always see each other this way, as young and attractive, regardless of how time would age us.

"Look at me, Noah." I pressed my forehead against his. "Please."

Opening his eyes, he let me peer into his soul; no mask, no poker face, just pure Noah—vulnerabilities and all.

"No one's judging us," I said. "It's just you and me against the world."

"I want you to come with me," he said, moving my hips faster.

"I'm close…" I held my breath as a mind-blowing orgasm approached.

Slamming into my G-spot, he made me scream. A waterfall suddenly appeared in my mind. I was free falling at 3000 feet, but I wasn't going over the edge alone. Noah was holding my hand, ready to plummet to the dark waters with me.

"Oh, G-God… Noah, I'm…" My body trembled with forbidden pleasure.

He kissed me hard as I moaned in his mouth, feeling an explosive blast. He had finally achieved his release. Sighing, I closed my eyes and envisioned us resurfacing from the emerald waters. The sun had set like a powerful symphony quieting down, becoming more magnificent, as the alluring beauty of the darkness approached, casting its shadow over coral-colored clouds, turning day into night. Looking up at the sky, it was just the two of us now in our hidden paradise. The tranquil wilderness felt so surreal, as if we had entered another dimension, like a painting on canvas that had come to life. All I could feel was bliss.

Recovering from his sweet rapture, I watched his chest rise and fall as he kept his eyes closed. Our passionate lovemaking had exhausted him.

How are you so perfect? I wondered.

"I can feel your eyes on me," he said with a smile.

"That's because I'm gazing." I caressed the flaming phoenix.

"My post-orgasm face isn't very gaze-worthy." Noah chuckled.

"Your every expression is gaze-worthy. You're devastatingly handsome and you know it, so don't even try to deny it."

He laughed.

"You could easily melt a heart with a smile," I added. "You're gifted that way."

"I think you're talking about yourself… I'm gifted? Or cursed?" He suppressed a smirk, allowing me to stare into his brilliant sea.

"You're not cursed."

"You place me on too high of a pedestal. I'm just an ordinary man who's extremely flawed." He kissed my open palm, caressing it against his cheek.

"You're not flawed. That's not how I see you."

Ghosting his fingers down my back, my body flared up in heat.

"Don't deprive me of your eyes," Noah said. "Why is it so hard for you to look at me?"

"Because you're so attractive, it makes me shy away. I just feel so exposed around you—like you can see right through me."

"You don't like being admired?"

"Feels more like I'm being scrutinized and picked apart."

"The damaged inner critic. I need to kick her ass and tell her to get the hell out of your head."

"She's been the bane of my existence."

"You don't have to be afraid anymore, Aria. I never want to hurt you. I'm sorry that I had all those times before. It was unintentional, you know that."

I did.

"Every time I made you cry, I was hurting myself a thousand times worse. It felt like chest rape."

I kissed him, hugging him tightly.

"You're an exquisite work of art," he whispered.

"I'm *your* work of art."

"And I'm a fucked-up artist." Noah pulled me closer to his lips. "You're my greatest masterpiece. That sounds messed, huh?"

"I don't care."

There was a long pause before he asked, "How do you feel?"

"Like I've been initiated as your forbidden lover."

His lighted hearted chuckle made me glow inside.

"How do you like your promotion?"

"Oh, shut up!" I smacked his chest. "I'm not a business transaction."

"I didn't say you are. I just highlighted the fact that you've been promoted."

"As?"

"My sex slave."

"Is that right?"

"Mhm."

"And you were waiting to drop this bomb on me after…"

"You spread your sexy thighs for me."

"What a daunting revelation." I laughed. "I'm not your sex slave, and I'm not 'your main chick' or your 'side piece.'"

"There's my fierce kitty. Here we go… I love this. Lay it on me, baby. What are your conditions in this partnership?"

"Why are we having this conversation *after* we've had sex?"

"Because there's nothing traditional about us. In fact, we defy orthodoxy in every way. We are officially the non-conformists of society."

"I'm good with that."

"Was it that good for you? You're stroking my ego, Aria."

"You don't need the ego strokes."

"True. I'd much rather you stroke my… snake."

I giggled as he left a trail of kisses down my neck, awakening my desire for him.

"Did I hurt you?" Noah asked, caressing my cheek.

"I should check the damage."

All the color suddenly drained from his face, and I couldn't help but laugh a bit.

"Relax, Noah. I'm kidding. I'm fine."

"I didn't want it to be painful for you."

"It wasn't. It was amazing."

"I hate that someone else had you."

"I can say the same about you and all your past lovers. Now I'm constantly worried about your exes reaching out and going through *Noah-withdrawal*. I don't want a third party in our relationship—or multiple parties."

"That's not your reality. You have no idea what you do to me."

But how long will that last? I feared.

"Aria, I love you." He kissed my forehead. "Which means I have no intention of dishonoring you and what we have."

"I love you more." I teared up, admiring his attractive features. "Be right back."

Wrapping the sheets around me, I disappeared into the bathroom, replaying the past hour in my head.

CHAPTER TWENTY-TWO
ARIA

Soft music played in the background, setting the mood as we basked in the afterglow of our erotic lovemaking. I lay on Noah's chest while he reclined on his back with a hand folded behind his head. Releasing a sigh, I enjoyed our nakedness, humming when he grazed his fingertips down my spine. His heartbeat sounded like a calm, drumming rhythm.

"Your skin is so soft," he murmured.

Hugging his body tighter, I left a chaste kiss on his chest near his phoenix tattoo. I couldn't imagine any other man touching me; all I wanted was him. We lay like this for the longest while, tangled in each other's arms.

"I'm so in love with you," Noah confessed. "I can't say it enough."

I caressed his ribs and looked at his handsome face. Had God created this beautiful man just for me? Was I ever meant to have him this way? Were we destined to be together? I thought about Sophocles' *Oedipus the King*: the tragic play of incestuous love. No, I was not like Oedipus; he didn't know that the woman he'd married was his mother. That poor man met an ill fate and became permanently blind because he'd stabbed himself in the eyes once he had discovered the horrifying truth. But what if that was just a metaphor? What if Oedipus didn't physically blind himself? What if it was just an allusion to how love is blind? Does true love blind you, too?

It should liberate, my higher self-answered. *True love heals.*

If my relationship with Noah was to be written as a true romance novel, would people perceive it as the most nightmarish love story? Would it be banned from the world of literature? Would the reading audience be disgusted by our relationship and crucify us for loving each other this way? I couldn't imagine loving him any other way—not like a daughter. It seemed impossible in my mind.

"I can't change the way I feel about you," he said. "I can't fight it anymore. I've tried. I don't care that it's wrong. I don't care that it's wrong to love you this way. It takes a real man to have the courage to honor his truth."

"Thank you for your bravery." I stole a kiss from his addictive lips and rested my head on his chest. "Tell me a secret, Noah."

"A secret?" He played with my hair. "Hmm. Okay." Noah paused. "All my life, I was searching for you, not knowing how blind I was… all the poor decisions I made while seeking this love… all the hearts I trampled on—the karma I collected. True love doesn't have a destination. You've been with me all along, inside of me… my mirror." He sighed. "That one sucked. I can come up with something better."

"That was beautiful." I blushed.

"Pull me into your sea. Find true love within you, within me."

"I love your poetic soul. You should write that one down." I kissed his chest, relaxing in his arms.

"I'll remember it. I used to write a lot of poetry. You inspire me."

"Is that a sign of true love?"

"The most passionate poets of the past were deeply in love."

We stayed silent for a while until I asked, "Are you afraid?"

Noah seemed to waver. "Yes. Honestly, I'm afraid you'll leave and won't love me anymore once I'm old and feeble."

It saddened me to see such hopelessness in his eyes.

"You are Noah Mason Hunter, and you'll always be young and desirable. Besides"—I simpered—"you only get hotter with age."

"You're puffing up my pride." He chuckled.

"I'm serious. You're like those types of men who become more attractive as they get older."

"Well, thank you. That's a major compliment."

He shifted his body from underneath me, and the next thing I knew, he was in between my legs again.

"Round two already?" I giggled.

"Can't handle my sex drive? I think it's safe to say you've woken something in me I can never put to sleep. Take accountability for my sudden affliction."

I couldn't stop smiling. I loved this side of him: so unguarded. Our lips collided before Noah thrust into me. Drowning in sensation, he gave me deep strokes, staring into my eyes.

"I want you," he whispered, panting in pleasure.

"You have me," I whispered back.

"I want you all the time."

"I'll make you work for it."

"Is that right?"

"Guaranteed."

"That's fine. I'm good with that—just turns me on more."

Our kiss was on fire as he controlled his passion and slowed down, breathing with me, as if we shared one set of lungs.

"I've never… loved anyone… this way," Noah confessed.

Holding his face, I drowned in him all over again. He kissed me fervently as we coupled together. His pleasurable groans filled my ears like a sensual symphony that made me tremble. Hearing him whisper my name was enough to have me fully aroused.

"I'm never letting you go," he said, supporting his weight above me.

"What if I run?"

"I'll chase your ass down faster than you can blink."

"Is that right?" I laughed, kissing him.

"You're mine."

He steered himself into my core with a powerful thrust, as if to assert his alpha being. Every muscle on his body tightened and flexed; a stunning display of his godhood. I felt the force of his speed slamming into my cervix, causing a numbing pain mixed with pleasure as he showed off his unstoppable stamina. Noah groaned and cursed under his breath, holding back his release.

"That's it, baby." He kissed my neck. "Come for me again."

My body surrendered to his will, releasing an earth-shattering orgasm as I writhed in euphoria.

Guiding my thighs off his shoulders, Noah kissed my forehead and made my skin tingle.

"I love the way you moan for me."

I wanted love marks all over my body; I would have proudly shown mine off.

Hickies: the visible war wounds of passionate lovemaking. (Cited from Aria Hunter's "Personal Definitions.")

"I'm sorry I got wild," Noah murmured in my ear.

"I think you should get wild more often." I pulled his face to my lips. "Do you really love me?"

I knew the answer. I just liked to hear him say it.

"Love isn't an adequate word to express what I feel for you." He kissed me, as if he were unburdening his soul.

We made love through the night until the early hours of the morning. It was sinful; it was passionate; it was everything I ever wanted. All I felt was love. Uncontaminated love.

CHAPTER TWENTY-THREE
ARIA

At dawn, the blackness of the sky had faded, welcoming a beautiful sunrise on the horizon, bathing our bedroom with warmth. The melting wax had snuffed out the flames of the candles, but the aromatic scent of incense and roses still permeated the air. A live podcast quietly played in the background while I lay in bed next to Noah.

"*… And our next track is by Amurai, 'Love & Light (Downtempo Mix)' taken from 'Armada Lounge, Volume six' album,*" said the radio host. "*You're listening to Anjunadeep, live on Digital Airway!*"

Satellite radio was so much better. You wouldn't have to listen to ten minutes of annoying advertisements.

The sound of the ocean blended beautifully with the soothing instrumentals as I listened to the tide crashing upon the shore. This moment was perfect. It was a little piece of Heaven with the man I loved.

"Your eyes are gorgeous in the sunlight," Noah said, brushing my hair out of my face. "I could stare at you for hours. Your beauty is unmatched." His voice sounded deeper than usual, but I found it sexy.

"Even without makeup?"

"*Especially* without makeup."

Lying on his side, he bent an elbow and rested his head in his hand.

"Holy biceps…" I gripped his arm.

Noah chuckled.

"You. Are. Perfection," he sighed.

"Stop." I hid my face.

"Stop what? Telling you how beautiful you are… how you've got me wrapped around your little finger?"

I loved the way he touched my body.

"You keep making me blush. It's embarrassing."

"I like making you blush." Noah grinned.

"Do you feel weird?"

"I feel…" He exhaled deeply. "Complete."

We were on the same wavelength.

"Was I okay?" I didn't want to feel incompetent in the bedroom. Noah was an amazing lover. His stamina and his ability to give so much of himself had proven this.

"Aria, making love to you was like… entering the temple of a goddess. I don't think I can ever function properly at work anymore. I'll just be thinking about us and the next time I can…" He lowered his lips to mine, kissing me softly.

A crazy heat spread between my thighs as Noah took my hand in his and kissed my knuckles. I loved how affectionate he was, though he didn't give this impression in public.

"Don't look at me like that." I hid my face in a pillow.

"I think I've told you this before, but I don't know how else to look at you." Noah chuckled, pulling me into his body.

"I'm not used to this. Experiencing this side of you…"

"Well, you better get used to it because there is *no way* we can go back to having a platonic relationship after all that mind blowing sex. I can't, nor do I want to."

I kissed his chest and left clavicle before my lips grazed his throat and jaw. A light brush of stubble had grown, but I liked it. He had major sex hair going on, which only made him a thousand times sexier. Wrapping my leg over his, I kissed his neck for as long as I could while something throbbed against me.

"Oh, my God, Noah! Seriously?"

"I can't help it I want you so much." He smirked.

"You know, when we first saw each other, I thought your lawyer was you."

"That old guy?" Noah laughed.

"Yeah, I was so confused when you had apologized to me."

"I understand." He affectionately kissed my hand.

It made me sad knowing there were many women who got to experience intimacy with him. I wished I was his one and only. But even then, I was plagued by a demon in my head who told me I could never measure up to all his past lovers. His high "body count" messed with me.

They're in his past for a reason. Not present, my higher self tried to console me.

"Baby," Noah said. "Please be honest." His eyes were serious as he caressed my cheek. "Do you regret last night? I can't help but feel this nagging guilt, like I took something from you."

My innocence? No.

Cuddling closer, I said, "I love you, Noah. You're everything I've ever wanted and more. I have no regrets."

"You're so young, though."

"I know that makes you feel apprehensive about us being together—but I'm eighteen, not sixteen."

"You're not even at the legal drinking age yet."

"I know."

"Not for another three years." He groaned.

"Look," I sighed. "I want to be with you, even if that means we'd have to hide our relationship from the world and live in secrecy."

"I can't ever tell anyone I'm your boyfriend. I can't kiss you in public—can't hold your hand without people thinking we're dating..."

"I don't care. Let's leave the country and live someplace in Europe. We could get new IDs... It could be an adventure! You're a lawyer. I'm sure you could pull it off. No one would have to know. We can make this work."

"You're such a hopeless romantic." He flashed a hint of a smile. "You remind me of myself when I was your age."

"You're still a romantic. I mean, look at what you did for me last night. I didn't expect that at all."

"You bring out that side in me."

I quirked an eyebrow. "How many sides do you hide from the world?"

"Too many." He chuckled. "I'm like a complicated Rubik's cube, Aria."

"So am I."

"I'm a hundred times more complicated."

"Maybe so, but a Rubik's cube can always be solved."

His attractive lips curved into a devilish smile before he kissed me and ran his palm along my stomach.

"What did you think when you read my note?" Noah asked.

"I couldn't recognize the writing. I suspected it was from Ryan."

Good thing I hadn't mentioned Evan's cameo appearance.

"Well"—he rolled on top of me—"I hope I was a better surprise than him."

"You know you are."

Noah kissed my neck, delighting my senses. I laughed when he playfully growled. We both felt so happy and carefree.

"You… [*kiss*]… are… [*kiss*]… mine… [*kiss*]…"

Wrapping my arms over his shoulders, I stared into his eyes and said, "Please never walk out on me."

"That's never going to happen."

"It hurt so much knowing I could never have you. When you said you weren't in love with me, it jus—"

"I didn't mean it. I lied to you because I didn't want to admit the truth. I can never love another woman the way I love you, Aria. I hope you realize that. You've ruined me."

Holding his gaze, I lightly traced his eyebrows. "I haven't ruined you. I want to love you forever."

"Promise me you'll pull the plug on my respirator if that day should ever come."

I rolled my eyes. "Don't be so morbid, please."

"At least promise me you won't get mad when I off myself once I'm old and dependent on Medicare."

"Quit the crazy talk!"

"I don't want to be a decrepit old man, sweetie. You're young. You shouldn't ever have to look after me and nurse me in my old age."

"You're only sixteen years older than me."

"*Only* sixteen?" Noah cringed. "Jeezuz, that's ancient in my books."

"It's not that bad. You still have another thirty years to go before you hit sixty. We'll both look after each other." I took my time kissing him, hoping he'd cheer up.

"You have all this power over me, and it freaks me out. I'm not used to it. It's terrifying."

"I won't abuse that power. You don't have to worry." I reassured him with a smile, massaging his shoulders.

Lowering his face to mine, he let our lips reunite in a tender kiss while thunder crashed in the distance.

"I wish I could stay in this moment with you." Noah broke our kiss. "If I could freeze this memory and relive it forever, I would."

"Why do you say that? I look forward to creating more amazing memories with you. You still have to take me to Italy this summer."

Sadness suddenly seeped into his eyes.

"Why are you looking at me like that?" I said. "What's wrong?"

"It's nothing."

"It doesn't look like 'nothing.' What's on your mind, Noah?"

Panic filled my heart as our bedroom darkened. A freak storm was moving in, as if we had angered the gods by our lovemaking.

"Promise me you won't forget about last night," Noah said, looking anxious.

"What do you mean?"

"*Promise me, Aria.*"

How could I ever forget?

A loud lightning bolt crashed above us, startling me as the wind forced its way through the windows, whipping the curtains in the air.

What the hell is going on?

"Was there a hurricane warning overnight?" I asked as the rain pelted down. "We should probably close the—"

"We don't have much longer, baby."

Wanting to get up, Noah stopped me by trapping me beneath his buff body. He stroked my hair and stared right through me.

"Noah, you're confusing me. What's wrong?"—I reached for his face—"Why are you crying?"

"I don't want to let you go."

A teardrop fell on my cheek.

"… But you have to wake up."

There was another loud crackle, as thunder shredded the sky. Had we angered God?

"You need to wake up, Aria. Please…"

"Noah, I…"

Spiraling in panic, the room was suddenly fading into darkness.

"Look in my eyes, baby." His fingers whispered across my forehead. "Don't be afraid. I'm with you."

The ceiling suddenly disappeared when I looked up. An army of onyx clouds had invaded our paradise, glowing with lightning, chanting in thunderous voices. It was terrifying, but Noah stayed calm throughout the chaos. Holding my face, he demanded I ignore the surrounding danger, as if he were hypnotizing me to dissociate from reality.

"I'm right next to you," he said. "Wake up, sweetheart."

Fear in its rawest form was all I could feel, as it mutated within me.

"We can't stay here forever, Aria. I'm so sorry. I just wanted to give you this night. I wanted it just as much as you did."

Noah's voice had become nothing but a faint echo, as if the darkness were swallowing him whole. Soon I'd be alone, facing my biggest fear: abandonment.

"Noah, I'm scared!" I stifled a cry as his voice became inaudible.

Beep… beep… beep…

Where is that sound coming from?

It sounded like a heart monitor. Nothing made sense. I called out to Noah, but even the sound of my voice had faded.

That's when it happened… Everything faded to black.

CHAPTER TWENTY-FOUR
ARIA

My body was sucked violently through a portal. I was no longer in our haven of paradise. I had fallen deep into an abyss of nothingness. I wanted to scream. I wanted to cry out at the top of my lungs, but nothing came out. A random flicker of memories flashed before my eyes as everything went in reverse: making love to Noah, walking backwards to the elevators, sitting by that fountain, watching the dollar flip out of the water, finding the note, dancing with Ryan, dancing with Evan, kissing Evan, arriving at Prom, Noah unclasping my necklace, writing in my diary, and…

I couldn't rewind any further. That's when I realized I'd lost a huge chunk of time. Having written some key events in my diary, I couldn't remember them taking place, as if it were a dream.

"Aria, can you hear me, angel?"

Noah's voice echoed in my mind, but I still couldn't see him.

I was falling in the darkness; the way Alice had fallen through the rabbit hole.

"Aria?"

Metal scraped against metal, tires screeched to a halt, and then the startling sound of shattering glass splintered into shards, scattering over the pavement. My body suddenly stiffened with a jolt, and I found myself strapped into my passenger seat… upside down. Car horns were blaring as the never-ending siren of an ambulance got louder. I wanted to cover my ears, but I couldn't move.

"Hold on!" a man shouted. "We're gonna get you out, hon! Stay conscious!"

I couldn't recognize that voice.

How… did I get here? Where's Noah?

My recollections abandoned me as soon as I felt blood oozing down my right temple. I wanted to turn my head toward Noah's seat, but the pain was agonizing; my seat belt was almost choking me. Covered in broken glass, the potent smell of gasoline irritated my lungs as I coughed uncontrollably.

Noah…

Twisting my neck in his direction, I groaned in pain and passed out.

Sirens, screaming, car horns… all of it stopped, except for that annoying beeping noise.

Beep… beep…

"Aria, listen to my voice, sweetheart. Squeeze my hand if you can hear me."

My eyelids felt so heavy.

"Please, baby… try."

I don't understand what's happened.

The reality I knew had evaporated. I wanted to run back to that hotel room and hide myself in Noah's arms, but there was nowhere to go. All I could see was black.

"Aria, I love you so much…"

Is he crying? Oh, my god…

I had never heard such devastating cries of agony in my life. I had to open my eyes. I had to comfort him.

Come on! Just wake up! I scolded myself, commanding my body to move.

"I can't live without you," he painfully expressed.

Something wet dripped onto my forearm before I realized it was Noah's tears. He was holding my hand and talking to me.

How come I can't move?

I couldn't lift a finger, which paralyzed me in fear.

"I can't pull the plug, Aria. Do you hear me? I can't do it! So you better fight! You better fight for your life, because you're fighting for mine as well!" He squeezed my hand harder and murmured in my ear, "I can't exist without you. I don't know how to after finding you. Please… please come back to me."

He needed to know that I could hear him—that I was conscious.

"Please." He sobbed. "Please don't punish me this way. I know you can hear me. Don't make me suffer like this. I'm already broken. I'm desperate, Aria. I've never been so desperate in my life. I've never felt this way about anyone. Please open your eyes. I won't ever let you go if you do." He cried like a man who had scarred his soul, pressing my hand to his cheek.

My heart had shattered. There was nothing I could do. I couldn't understand what was going on with me. I had no choice but to listen to the agonizing cries of the man I loved.

"Baby, *please*… I've been at your bedside for the past five weeks. I've been playing your music on your iPod, talking to you, praying you'll wake up." He kissed my hand, sniffling. "The doctors said the chances of you waking up are very slim and that I should prepare to say goodbye to you. But I can't, Aria. I can't say goodbye." He broke down. "You came into my life like a miracle eight months ago. And now, I don't know how to survive in this world without you. You're not supposed to die before me. I'm not supposed to bury you."

Noah's heaving sobs made me want to cry. I was screaming inside.

"Don't leave me… don't… leave."

What a cruel twist of fate this was. I would have much rather died than to have been consciously aware of my paralysis.

You're in a hospital bed, dummy! That possibility only scared me more as I listened to a heart monitor.

Composing himself, Noah blew his nose before he lowered his voice and spoke to me.

"I'm gonna tell you something, Aria. Take me seriously because I'm only gonna say this once, and one time only. If you love me like you say you do, if you're truly who I believe you are, then you'll wake up. Listen to my voice. Please try, baby." He sniffled, caressing my hair. "Aria Sophia Hunter," Noah murmured in my ear. "You are the love of my life. I fell in love with you from the moment I first saw you. To exist in this world without you is comparable to living without a heart in my chest. I would rather die, and I know exactly how I intend to destroy myself if you don't come back to me. If you really are my soulmate, then please open your eyes."

Everything in his voice revealed his true agony.

"I'm gonna play you a song." Noah released my hand.

A sad piano melody echoed around me, followed by an overture of cellos and violins.

"I know how you love music." He held my hand again. "These lyrics are special, and you know why."

My mind quickly filed through folders of memories, searching for a specific recollection connected to this song. And then I found it: I was standing at an outdoor benefit concert with Jade and Ally. One of our favorite rock bands was performing on stage: The Tea Party. Jeff Martin was singing "Heaven Coming Down" while everyone waved their lighters in the air.

Listening to his soul riveting voice again made my heart shiver. The song was about love, fear, strength, and faith. Jeff's lyricism was on another level of consciousness. There was so much depth in his music and soul frequency. His magical voice was like a spiritual awakening: a reflection of God's voice breaking through the darkness.

"Please"—Noah stroked my hand with his thumb—"open your eyes."

I suddenly felt as if an invisible tape was pulled off my eyes at last; they no longer felt heavy as I moved them side to side. A tingling sensation slowly returned to my fingertips while the numbness faded. I tried to squeeze Noah's hand.

"Aria?" His tightening grip seemed like resurrected hope. "Oh God, you can hear me… Baby, open your eyes. Squeeze my hand again, angel. Open your eyes!"

I had restored his dying faith, and it motivated me to find the exit out of the labyrinth I'd been trapped in. I felt like Aurora from *Sleeping Beauty*, desperately trying to wake up from what seemed like a hundred-year slumber. The only difference was that this was real life, not a fairy tale. I wouldn't wake up through "true love's kiss."

"Squeeze my hand again if you can hear me, baby. Come on!"

Struggling, I moved my fingers.

"Nurse!" Noah shouted. "Someone get a doctor in here!"

I could hear people rushing in and talking, and then something was pulled out of my throat.

"Keep talking to her," a man said.

"Aria." Noah kissed my hand. "Open your eyes and look at me."

The song had finally reached its bridge, as if it were a catalyst to my "great awakening." By the grace of God, my eyes finally opened, and the room flooded with blinding light. My surroundings were a blur. I blinked until Noah's handsome face came into focus. Those ocean eyes… I wanted to drown in them.

"Thank you," he cried. "Thank you, God."

In the short year that I'd known this man, I had never seen him cry in front of anybody. But here he was, breaking down at my side. My fallen angel had resurrected me from sleeping death. He pulled my weak body into his arms and begged for God's forgiveness. Deep down, we both knew it was wrong for us to love each other the way we did. But the truth was that neither of us could change it. Now that Noah had admitted his true feelings for me, he could never take them back. While I knew he desired redemption for his sins, a small voice inside of me yearned for the same.

Every angel in Heaven must have cried tears of agony. What they had witnessed was the most powerful force shared between two people: *love*; a love that was condemned between me and Noah from the moment I was born. We were wrong for each other. Our love was forbidden, but it was resilient enough to bring me back to him. The truth could no longer be buried. It was time to step into the light. We were soulmates.

CHAPTER TWENTY-FIVE
REALITY IN REVERSE

May, 1 2013
8:45AM

The sun had risen in New York City as Natalie rushed past pedestrians on 7th Avenue. She took the subway to work every morning before opening the women's clothing store she managed. Working in retail wasn't her passion, but it was a job she had settled for since giving up on her dream. As she opened the boutique and stepped inside, her cellphone rang.

Must be Mom checking in, Natalie thought.

Glancing at the caller ID, she immediately froze. Noah's name was at the top of the screen. The last time she had spoken to him was in January, and their conversation had been less than friendly. She wondered why he was calling as she finally picked up on the third ring.

"How nice of you to think of me on this fine morning, Noah—but I'm busy. Not all of us are multi-millionaires," she bitterly stated.

Switching on the lights, Natalie was prepared for a hostile conversation with her ex, but there was dead silence on the other end before her heart dropped when she heard sirens.

"Noah? Where are you? ... Hello?"

"I'm outside," he answered. "An ambulance just pulled up."

"*Ambulance?*" She panicked.

"Look, Nat, you're not driving, are you?"

"No. What's going on? Is Aria all right?"

Her daughter was the first person who came to mind. Noah's hesitation only made her worry more. "Tell me our daughter is okay!"

"Natalie, I'm sorry. We got hit by a car last night at an intersection. The driver was at fault. I'm still at the hospital. I'm fine, but—"

"What happened to Aria?" Her eyes welled up.

"She's in the intensive care unit… head trauma."

The news made Natalie break down in disbelief. She wanted to scream at Noah; she wanted to curse him and vent her anguish, but all she could think about was hopping on the next flight to LA.

"Nat, I—"

"I'll be there," she cut him off. "I'm going to the airport. Call you soon." Hanging up, she phoned her boss and explained the emergency before she contacted her best friend Candice and asked her to babysit while she would be away.

Money was tight and Natalie knew her husband would argue with her about taking money out of their savings to pay for airfare and hotel expenses, but she had to be there for her daughter. Her decision was not up for debate.

Locking up the store, she was back on the street, flagging down a cab as it pulled up to the curb.

"JFK airport, please."

CHAPTER TWENTY-SIX
NOAH

May 19, 2013

I've always been the type of man who never needed religion to elevate my life in a spiritual sense. I've never needed to get close to the *Heavenly Father* because it was simple: I didn't believe in Him. My religious upbringing had opened my eyes to the hypocrisy and contradictions of what we call "faith." There was a time when my mother used to force me and my siblings to go to church. But I can honestly say that I never felt the Lord's presence within the confines of such a "holy place." Our church minister had always tried to instill the fear of God in us. The bastard was a two-faced piece of shit who had been arrested for possessing child pornography. I remember how he'd be at church every Sunday, telling us we'll all burn in hellfire "if we refuse to follow the will of the Lord." Funny how he broke every rule he warned us not to break, and committed unspeakable sins behind that pious mask he wore. Someone should have wrapped those rosary beads around his neck and choked him to death. The scumbag had broken every holy covenant at the expense of the most defenseless. Most religious nut jobs project their inner demons. They use religion to assuage their fears because they're afraid of death and refuse to face their shadow side: the rejected, darker aspects of self. I'm paraphrasing Dr. Grey when I say, if you refuse to go within to heal your wounds and take accountability for yourself, then you will vibrate in fear, guilt, and shame *every day*, until you face the demons you hide in your closet. Only then, will you be liberated from the devil inside that keeps you in bondage. People use religion as a crutch to escape the pain and shame of doing the inner work: confronting the devil *within*—not as an outside entity, but an entity that lives within oneself.

I was young when I denounced my faith in Catholicism. Growing up, I made a promise to take no future generation of "Hunters" into a church. Ever. There was too much evil in the world. Why would God allow people to suffer so much? Was God so proud that he couldn't admit he'd made a mistake when he created Lucifer? Was Lucifer even to blame? If God is all knowing and wise, did he not know that by creating his inversion, he would rebel and plague the world in evil? Why not destroy him? If the Lord is truly omnipotent, how come he never showed that power? Oh right, he did… *eons ago* (supposedly). Clearly, I wasn't a monotheist; I had no interest in devoting my life to answering "theodicy's trilemma." Sometimes I wondered if suffering only existed to make the afterlife more attractive. Or maybe it existed just to increase our empathy. During times of crises, people and communities come together and try to find a solution… And somewhere along the way, they find compassion—that's the ideal vision, at least.

The human population is expected to eat up all kinds of religious mumbo jumbo. New Atheists like Richard Dawkins and Christopher Hitchens made more sense to me in explaining why religion exists and how it cultivates the seed that radicalizes people into committing evil deeds. If someone asked me what I thought of the Bible, I would have told them it sounded like fables. I had so many questions that always went unanswered, and any believers I conversed with regarding faith always said the same thing over again: "Walk by faith, not by sight. It's all part of the test. Trust in the Lord with an open heart, and He will bless you a thousand times over."

No, He won't. He just adds to your suffering with more burdens.

I refused to worship a god that allowed so much pain and suffering in this world. I had long waged a war with our "Creator" and vowed to curse his existence till my dying breath. In my eyes, he was nothing more than a mythological deity that long needed to fade.

But none of my past beliefs mattered when I stepped inside the small chapel on the fourth floor of Glenmore General Hospital. Three weeks had passed since that near fatal collision, and I was lucky to have survived with minor cuts and bruises. That pickup truck had T-boned my car at the intersection and slammed into Aria's passenger door. My Audi had been upside down when the firefighters came and used their hydraulic rescue tools to cut through the metal and get my daughter out. That accident could have easily been prevented. The person at fault had been driving drunk.

My injuries had not been serious, which was why I'd been discharged a few days later. But Aria had suffered extensive head trauma and internal bleeding. She had slipped into a coma, and I wasn't sure if I was ever going to get her back.

Uncertain whether to stay or leave, I walked up a narrow aisle and sat in an empty pew. There was no one around, but I preferred it this way. Hanging my head, I listened to nothing but silence. The minutes kept passing as I tried to find a part of myself that could somehow break through my ego and reach out to God… if He even existed.

I don't know how to do this," I began. "It's been such a long time since you and I had a heart to heart. What's messed up is that I don't really know if you're out there, but I guess I just have to believe, right?" I looked up at the big wooden cross and felt foolish for talking to it.

It's just an object. What am I doing?

"I didn't come in here today to pour my heart out and tell you about all the times I felt you failed me in life. I'm sure in your eyes, I'm the one who has failed *you*. All I know is that my daughter is in a hospital bed, and there's a real chance she will never wake up."

My throat swelled with pain as I sifted through my emotions.

"It's obvious I'm not a very godly person. I've sinned more times than I can count. I mean, where do I start? Pre-marital sex, ignoring my fatherly duties, drug addiction, promiscuity, sexual demons, bar fights, and finally, the worst of it…" I stared at my hands and watched my tears fall before I whispered, "I fell in love with my daughter."

There it was: the daunting truth. I noticed a Bible next to me as I stared at it.

"Why won't you speak to me, God? Why do you hide? What do you want from me? What are you trying to tell me?"

I felt foolish for asking these questions. Reaching for the Bible, I placed it on my lap and opened it at random. The first bit of scripture I read was a passage from *Leviticus-18:6*.

"None of you shall approach to any that is near of kin to him, to uncover their nakedness."

Is this a coincidence or a sign? I snickered under my breath, putting the book away.

"Thanks for the message. But I already knew that." Staring at the cross, I forced myself to consider the possibility that Christ had actually sacrificed himself on that thing for me—for humanity. Perhaps the crucifixion symbolized crucifying your toxic ego to resurrect your higher self: the true and authentic self. By forgiving your enemies, despite persecution, you achieve Christ consciousness—just a theory.

"Do you think I like to feel this way about her?" I ranted. "I don't! I hate it! But my feelings are real, and I don't know what to do!" Thrusting my hands in my hair, I tried to compose myself. "More than anything, I want her to carry out her life the way she is meant to. I want to see Aria graduate and establish herself… get married, become a mother… I don't want to bury my daughter. So please, please bring her back to me.

"I'm not here to strike a deal with the Devil. I'm here to make a divine contract with you out of blind faith and submit myself to eternal servitude. Please let Aria wake up, and I promise to love her the way a father should. I will repent and never touch her in a wrongful way. I'll do whatever it takes to live righteously by You. Just bring her back. Bring her back to me."

Closing my hands in prayer against my forehead, I parked my ego and broke down in quiet sobs. Perhaps this was my karma. Eight months… I had let this unlawful relationship carry on for eight months, and now I was reaping what I had sown. It had started out subtle. We had developed an emotional dependency and shared almost everything with one another, even personal things, as if we were best friends, not father and daughter. And it had only escalated from there: kissing her on that Ferris wheel, the secret make-out sessions… I hadn't been a good husband to Vanessa, nor had I been a good father to Aria. I had failed both women I loved in my life. This was truly an all-time low.

The chapel doors suddenly swung open and caught my attention as I whipped my head around.

"I never expected to find you in a place like this," Natalie said, approaching me.

"Desperate times call for desperate measures," I replied.

"I'm sorry. I just wanted to make sure you were all right." She moved down the pew and sat beside me.

After the accident, I contacted her as soon as I'd had the opportunity. She had a right to know about Aria's critical state.

"Any changes?" I asked, avoiding her gray eyes.

"No. I'm worried her kidney function will worsen."

"The doctors have her on dialysis. We can only hope for the best."

"Please tell me she'll wake up, Noah." Natalie cried. "Please tell me that our baby will survive this."

"She's a fighter, Nat. She's gonna wake up." I put our differences aside and wrapped my arm around her.

"Why did you have to take her away from me?" She cried on my shoulder. "If Aria was still in New York, this never would have happened."

Natalie sobbed, venting her anger as I stayed quiet and shouldered the blame because I truly held myself responsible for this tragedy.

"I'm so sorry." My remorseful apologies would never be enough. "It's all my fault"—I cried with her—"I'm sorry… I'm sorry…"

I couldn't confess my transgressions with Aria. I couldn't tell Natalie that I was in love with our daughter. My silent pact with God was between me and Him. No one else. I planned to honor our agreement if Aria ever woke up. That was the deal.

Strike me down if I ever look at her the wrong way again.

CHAPTER TWENTY-SEVEN
WHILE SHE LAY SLEEPING

May 27, 2013

It was a sunny Monday afternoon when high school seniors Ryan Taylor and Jessica Williams walked toward the front entrance of Glenmore General Hospital. They took a short elevator ride up to the head trauma unit and put on a brave face as they strolled down the hallway, heading toward Aria's room. The teenagers were on their lunch break and had an extra period spare, which gave them time to drop by the hospital and visit their friend.

Reaching the door, Jessica stepped inside and beamed at Natalie. "Hope we're not intruding," she said.

"Not at all. Please, come in," Natalie replied, sitting by her daughter's bed. She met Jessica's eyes and offered a weak smile as they hugged.

"I brought you a latté." Ryan handed her a warm cup.

"That's kind of you. Thank you, dear."

He sauntered toward the window and took out the daisies he had brought Aria last week; they had dried up and were dying. Ryan threw them into a wastebasket and went into the bathroom to fill the vase with water before he arranged the fresh daisies inside.

"Such charming flowers."

He met Natalie's exhausted gaze and said, "How are you holding up, Mrs. Mitchell?"

"Oh, the usual," she sighed, caressing Aria's cheek before she stood up and let Jessica have a turn to sit. "I'm trying to stay optimistic. But it's hard when the days keep passing and her condition hasn't changed." Natalie grabbed a tissue and wiped her tears. The poor woman looked like she hadn't slept in weeks.

"I understand," Ryan nodded.

"The doctor said it helps to talk to her, and that we shouldn't stop. There's a possibility she can hear us, even though she's comatose. This may be the only shot we have in getting her to wake up, but it's better than not trying."

Jessica smiled compassionately and said, "That's why we're here."

"I appreciate that." Natalie touched her shoulder. "It eases my mind knowing she has friends who love her."

"Your daughter's very lovable," Ryan admitted. "It's hard not to love her."

He and Jessica had been frequently visiting Aria, praying she would wake up.

"I'm gonna head back to my hotel and shower while you two spend some time with her." Natalie kissed her daughter's forehead and faced the pair. "Her uncle is gonna drop by around two. Would you mind staying with her until then?"

"We'll be here."

"Thank you." She hugged them tightly and left the hospital room.

When she reached the elevators, she finally let her tears fall freely. It was hard for her to stay strong throughout this ordeal, and her husband had not been as supportive as she would have liked. He was still upset about the way she had dropped everything and headed to California without confiding in him first. The last thing Rob had said to her was, "She's in a goddamn coma. There's nothing you can do for her! Come home!" His raspy voice echoed in Natalie's head as she took the elevator down in silence.

❦

Jessica docked her iPod and let her "Prom Tunes" play softly in the background. Even though Aria had missed their prom, she thought it was only fair to visit and describe all the exciting events that had happened. The room was bathed in sunshine when she opened the blinds. Pulling a chair toward Aria's bed, Jessica sat down and noticed the colorful prayer cards that were on display on a table and along the windowsill. Most of the students and teachers at their high school had signed a big glittery card that Jessica and Tammy had made for Aria; it was proudly displayed on the nightstand next to her bed.

Leaning against the wall, Ryan sat in a chair next to Aria and held her hand, praying she could sense his presence. He had never cared about someone the way he cared for her. He hated seeing his sleeping beauty so helpless with an endotracheal tube in her mouth. Aria's face was pale and sickly, but she remained beautiful to him.

"Hey there, gorgeous." Ryan smiled. "We're here... *again*... Mostly to annoy the hell out of you. Jessica just loves to talk your ears off."

She slit her eyes at him in annoyance and let out a little laugh. "Wherever Aria's traveled to in her mind, we need to give her a reason to find her way back to us." She took her hand and gently squeezed it, saying, "Hi, Aria... it's me, Jess."

"As if she wouldn't recognize *your* annoying voice." Ryan laughed.

"Oh, shut up! You're disrupting my connection with her!"

He rolled his eyes and stayed quiet about his skepticism.

"Aria," Jess began, "I'm gonna start off and tell you I love you and miss you. I wish you would wake up. But if you're not ready to, I understand. Ryan and I are here for you, and we'll keep bugging the hell out of you until you finally open your eyes. Won't we, Ry?"

"Yes." He gave Aria's hand a gentle squeeze. "We definitely will."

"We went to prom last Saturday." Jessica sighed. "It was amazing, babes. You would have loved the place our prom was booked at—a fancy five-star hotel. The banquet hall was enormous and perfect for the masquerade theme. I ended up going with Matt, and I swear, as soon as we stepped inside those double doors, there was this long grand staircase that led to the dance floor. And the way it was decorated... gosh... there were strobe lights, candelabras, chandeliers, fog machines... Oh, Aria, it was just so beautiful! It was like stepping into a time machine—full of vibrant colors and magic."

"*Magic?*" Ryan teased.

"Yes." She glared at him. "It was like time traveling to another realm. Everyone wore masks, though I couldn't really find any that were original enough to stand out." Jessica snickered. "You should have seen Steph's dress—actually, no… it's good that you didn't." She giggled at the memory. "It like was a ripoff of J-Lo's millennium gown at the Grammy's! Except it was black and way more revealing. Don't ask me how I know such details." She paused. "Okay, okay, I'm a diehard J-Lo fan—guilty as charged!"

Ryan looked amused.

"By the way… Ryan and Steph were voted as prom king and queen."

"Aw, come on, Jess!" He frowned. "Don't tell her that! Do you want her to wake up or stay asleep?"

"I'm just spilling the tea!"

"Well, stop! Spill it somewhere else! It wasn't like I wanted to be prom king. It's bad enough I had to dance with that crazy bitch."

"I'm trying to give her all the details here! I hoped that would have pissed her off enough to wake up." Jessica exhaled in frustration.

Ryan gazed at Aria's impassive face.

You're never gonna open your eyes again, are you? He pushed back tears.

"Talk to her," Jessica encouraged.

"I don't know what to say."

"Anything and everything—just talk."

Collecting his thoughts, he said, "Coach Carter wore this ridiculous looking tangerine tux."

Jessica's laughter filled the room. "Oh, my God! That was classic! The man's got a beer belly, but he totally pulled it off!"

Ryan couldn't hide his grin. He'd ended up going to the prom without a date because he hadn't planned to take anyone else but Aria. It was hard for him and Jessica to celebrate while their friend was in a hospital bed. Last week, Natalie had overheard them talking about canceling their prom plans. After lecturing the teens, she insisted they go because ditching their prom would have achieved nothing. It wouldn't have changed Aria's condition, and they would have missed out on a memorable moment in their lives. Her motherly love and encouragement had convinced them to go on her daughter's behalf and tell Aria all about it. They remained true to their promise and had returned to narrate that night.

"The hotel garden was so beautiful, Aria," Jess summarized. "We took a stroll with some friends, and there was this huge marble fountain… I made a wish and flipped a quarter inside. I won't tell you what I wished for, but I *will* say it was about you…"

"She wished you would wake up."

"Ryan!"

"What?" He crossed his arms in his chest. "You already gave her a big hint—might as well say what you wished for."

She shook her head at him and kept talking.

"Ms. Perez was chaperoning that night, and she had brought a date. Let's just say he was basically Mr. Universe—total hotty!"

Ryan rolled his eyes.

"He kind of reminded me of Evan." She giggled.

"The music was awesome." Ryan changed the subject.

"The DJ was phenomenal. He kinda looked like Pauly-D from *Jersey Shore!*"

"Calm down with your Pauly obsession."

"I *will* meet this man. It's happening."

"I wouldn't dare to interfere with your manifestation."

"Good." Jessica laughed and fixed her gaze on Aria. "I've put together a playlist of songs from prom." She docked her iPod.

"I can't believe you actually requested 'Gangnam Style.'" Ryan howled.

"Hey! Everyone danced to it!" Jessica's laughter died down as she looked at her friend with a weak smile. Squeezing her hand, she said, "I wore that royal blue dress we had eyed at the mall last month, remember? I felt like a princess, but you would have looked like a beauty pageant winner if you had come."

"I'm sure Steph would have died from jealousy," Ryan commented.

"Which reminds me… she got into a catfight with some girls that night. Ms. Perez had to break it up."

"She should have been crowned *drama queen of the class of 2013.*"

The two of them laughed and summarized whatever they could, praying that it would trigger their friend enough to regain consciousness. But sadly, that moment never came. Ryan left Aria's hospital room with a heavy heart and a mind filled with doubt instead of faith.

⁎⁎⁎

An hour had passed when Evan visited the hospital to see his niece. Her friends had left, and he was alone with her. Aria's iPod played in the background while he sat next to the woman of his dreams, admiring her in silence. Noah was not aware of Evan's secret visits. Even though he had warned him to stay away from her, Evan refused to listen. It killed him inside to think that she might not wake up, but he had promised to see her every day, no matter how long it would take; days, weeks, months, years… he would be there for her until she would wake up. Pulling the plug was not an option.

Gemma Hayes was singing "Wicked Game" while Evan held Aria's hand. Her energy put him at ease, even though she was unconscious. Turning his head toward the door, he noticed Jessica step inside.

"Sorry." She looked flustered. "I don't mean to disturb you, but I've been going crazy looking for my cellphone."

Greeting her with a smile, he pointed to a table in the corner.

"Thank God!" She sighed in relief. "Do you want me to get you anything—a coffee?"

"I'm good, sweetheart." Evan replied in his charming British accent. "Thank you."

"Anytime." She smiled shyly, turning to leave when she recognized the vocalist. "Oh, my God… what a crazy synchronicity! Aria loves this song—it was played at my prom."

"Is that right?"

"Yeah, I made her a prom-playlist." Jess paused and frowned. "I still can't believe she's in here like this."

"She'll wake up." Evan sounded confident. "You'll see."

"I pray she does."

The quirky teen lingered near the doorway before she said goodbye and left.

Evan had lost his train of thought, but he didn't want to talk anymore. Pulling his chair in closer, he brushed his fingers through Aria's hair and imagined her beautiful eyes staring back at him. Drawing his lips to her ear, he whispered, "I would be honored if you had this dance with me. Wherever you are… I'm with you, love. You're not alone."

Walking down memory lane, he reminisced about how he had ditched his prom and gone off to party with his friends at his family's lake house. Gazing at Aria's angelic face, he softly said, "I miss you so much. I have something to confess." He hesitated.

"Throughout my life, I've often felt so left out. I hated not being biologically related to my family. My adoption was more like a source of shame, knowing my biological parents rejected and abandoned me. I can't tell you how many times I sabotaged myself because of this. But right now, being here with you… it's made me realize how grateful I am to not share the same DNA. You and I… we have something.

"From the moment I saw you…" He let down his guard and told her how he truly felt about her, hoping she could hear him. But sadly, his confessions did not have the desired effect for which he was hoping.

CHAPTER TWENTY-EIGHT
PARALLELS: REALITIES COLLIDE

June 4, 2013

Hospitals had always been a place Noah wanted to avoid ever since his grandmother had died in one. He hated that sterile "hospital smell"—it only reminded him of sickness and death, as well as other unpleasant memories. He still felt horrible about the way he had walked out on Natalie when Aria was born. But for the past five weeks, Noah had been visiting her hospital room every day, to where all the nurses on the floor were familiar with him.

Carrying a dozen white roses, he walked into his daughter's room with a smile.

"I'm here to relieve you from your shift," he said to Natalie.

She put on a wistful smile as she looked up at him. "This place is gonna turn into a botanical garden by the time our baby wakes up."

"You should head back to the house and get some sleep. You look like hell."

"Not as bad as you look." Natalie stood up and stretched before she took Noah's roses and arranged them in a vase.

"I hate seeing her intubated like this."

"I know," she said. "Me too." Grabbing her handbag, Natalie caught Noah off guard when she gave him a hug. "Thank you for letting me stay with you and Vanessa."

"It's the least I could do."

He didn't want to be on a warpath, and neither did Natalie. Arguing was the last thing they wanted while their daughter was fighting for her life. Feeling lifeless and exhausted, their trauma had brought them closer together as they leaned on each other for support.

"I'll be back during visiting hours in the morning," Natalie stated.

"Take a day off to just catch up on sleep. I'll be here with her."

"All right. I might stop by in the evening, though." She started toward the door and turned around. "Noah?"

He looked at her.

"Are we ever gonna get our baby back?" she asked with tears in her eyes.

Burdened with guilt, he rushed to her side and pulled her into his arms.

"I abandoned you and our daughter eighteen years ago when you brought her into the world. I'm not gonna do that now. We'll get through this together, Nat. She's gonna come back to us."

"I'm sorry." Natalie sobbed. "I'm trying so hard to be strong… it's been five weeks."

"Don't lose hope. I haven't."

She calmly nodded and reminded her ex that she would return in the morning.

After Natalie left, Noah closed the door to drown out the noise from the hallway. Aria's hospital room had become his sanctuary and Hell. Removing his blazer, he folded it over the armchair next to the bed before he sat down and reached for his daughter's hand. He took a deep breath. Noah hated seeing her like this.

Loosening his silver tie, he unfastened his cufflinks and rolled up his sleeves to get more comfortable. The air was thick with the scent of fresh roses. He was thankful it didn't smell like death in her room, much like the sickly aroma of the hospital halls he remembered in the past.

Jessica's iPod was resting on Aria's side table. He slipped his daughter's hand in his and listened to the beautiful song that softly played in the background.

No ordinary love…

Staring at her impenetrable solitude, he felt compelled to speak, taking his time as he tapped into his heart space.

"I wish we were in Italy right now… standing on a hotel veranda… Don't you understand I need you here with me?" He squeezed her hand tighter. "When I look at you, I see my reflection, and it tears me up inside because I can't figure out how it's possible to be in love with a reflection of myself. It's narcissistic. It's wrong—but my heart begs to differ." He opened up, unaware of the way he was influencing the fantasy in her mind; a place where dreams and reality collided.

"You breathed life into my broken soul the first day I cast my haunted eyes on you." Noah paused, collecting his shattered hope. "You truly haunted me all my life, Aria. I always felt your presence and had long dreamed of reuniting with you. I just never thought it would be like this"—he hesitated—"this love I feel for you… it's so… forbidden. It sets my soul on fire."

He stayed quiet for a while and allowed himself to sink deeper into his mind before he said, "I'm never letting you go… Never."

০৩৮০

An overcast sky had darkened Aria's hospital room as Noah stared out the window with a coffee in hand. He had got very little sleep through the night. It seemed impossible to rest when his mind was a mess. Drinking his cup of dark roast, he thought about everything the doctor had told him. His faith was dying. Every day that passed, Noah died a little more inside the longer Aria remained unconscious.

"*… And our next track is by Amurai, 'Love & Light (Downtempo Mix)' taken from 'Armada Lounge, Volume six' album,*" a radio host announced from Jessica's iPod. "*You're listening to Anjunadeep, live on Digital Airway!*" a radio host announced from Jessica's iPod. He had let the music play through the night, hoping it would bring her back to him. She lay still, stuck in limbo.

Placing his cup on the table, Noah sat back down in the armchair next to Aria's bed, covering her hand in warmth before he kissed her wrist.

"I could stare at you for hours." He imagined her smiling while he continued to bare his soul. "That night when we fought in the car… I lied to you because I didn't want to admit the truth. I can never love another woman the way I love you, Aria. I hope you realize that. You've ruined me." He kissed her hand again and said, "What am I gonna do without you?"

Thunder rumbled in the distance as the sun took refuge behind the clouds. A storm was on its way. In minutes, a downpour of rain washed over Los Angeles, as if to clean the city of sin. Ignoring the crashing sounds in the sky, Noah focused on his daughter.

"You need to wake up... Please." He wasn't ready to let her go. "I'm right next to you. Wake up, sweetheart…"

The minutes kept passing, but no matter how much he cried and begged, she would not open her eyes.

"I'm gonna tell you something, Aria. Take me seriously because I'm only gonna say this once, and one time only."

He poured his heart out and finally admitted that he was in love with her.

"Please… open your eyes."

The storm had suddenly passed, and the sun was breaking out of the clouds, bathing the room in sunlight. Noah prayed in silence while Jeff Martin sang his evocative lyrics before a miracle happened.

His heart was racing, he looked down at his hand; Aria was gripping it tightly. Fighting through tears, he said, "Squeeze my hand again if you can hear me, baby. Come on!"

Noah shouted for a nurse and when they arrived, he explained what was happening before she left and returned with the resident doctor who was on call at the unit. He monitored Aria's motor and eye-opening response before he removed the endotracheal tube.

"Keep talking to her," the doctor instructed.

"Aria." Noah kissed her hand. "Open your eyes and look at me."

After five weeks of hell and hopelessness, she finally left her comatose world of slumber and returned to him from what seemed like a hundred-year sleep. Noah could no longer contain his emotions as he looked at his angel. Holding her palm, he broke down in tears. God had finally answered his prayers as he bowed his head and cried his heart out.

CHAPTER TWENTY-NINE
NOAH

Her voice… the sweet sound of her voice was all it took to pull me out of my sleep.

"Noah?"

"Hey," I replied, smiling at angel eyes. "You're awake."

"How long have you been waiting in that chair?" She sounded groggy, but at least she no longer had that horrific tube down her throat.

"That depends"—I pulled my chair closer—"Do you mean today?"

"Both?"

I held her hand and said, "I've been visiting this hospital room for the past five weeks. You were in a coma."

"*What?*"

Her heart monitor suddenly increased.

"Calm down, sweetie. I don't want you panicking. I'm gonna explain what happened, but I need you to relax first. Can you do that for me?"

Aria nodded.

"The worst part is over. You're awake. You're alive. And I'm here with you." When her heart rate relaxed, I asked, "Any memories of the accident?"

"Everything's still fuzzy."

"Do you remember when I picked you up from Evan's place?"

"You mean when you barged in, threw me over your shoulder, and kidnapped me?"

No memory loss. That's good.

"You're being dramatic about the kidnapping."

She smiled. At least she wasn't mad anymore. I felt relieved.

"Do you remember anything afterwards?"

Aria seemed to reflect while I caressed her hand. I had missed her so much. She was always beautiful to admire, even in her sleep. No one matched her energy. No one had her soul print. That's why it was so hard for me to cope with the silence of her comatose state. I missed everything about her—even our arguments.

"We were fighting in your car," she said.

"Right, and then I stopped at a traffic light, and once it turned green, your passenger door came in direct impact with a speeding pickup truck."

"No… that can't be right," she refuted in confusion. "We *passed* that intersection. I remember us driving through—it was literally a couple seconds later that the car behind us got hit by that vehicle."

"Aria, that's not what happened, baby."

"I looked back, and I saw the crash! You pulled over… we… we talked."

"Sweetheart, maybe you dreamed all of that while you were in a coma. We never made it past the intersection."

Her eyes darted side to side in confusion. Hopefully, reality was sinking in.

"Oh, my God!" Her face crumbled in tears as she clasped her hand over her mouth. "I told you I hated you!"

"It's okay, baby." I leaned in closer, moving her hand away.

"I didn't mean it!"

"I know that."

"I can't believe I said all those awful things!"

"Aria—"

"I'm sorry, Noah. I'm so sorry. I—"

"*Shhh*, don't cry."

She held on to me and wept in my arms. Our past arguments didn't matter to me.

"Stop apologizing," I said.

"I love you"—she sobbed—"I could never hate you."

"I know. You don't have to say it."

"But you could've died! I could've died! If I never woke up, you would have lived the rest of your life thinking I hated you!"

It was heart wrenching to hear her cry. I felt responsible for all her pain, and I couldn't take it away.

"I said some awful things too, Aria. So please, don't feel bad. No more tears. Do you forgive me?"

She nodded, drying her eyes.

"Good." I smiled. "I forgive you, too. I don't want to see you cry over an argument that happened ages ago. Let's just focus on your recovery." I kissed her head and relaxed in my chair.

"Can you tell me what happened?" she said. "Everything I thought was real has turned out to be nothing but a dream."

I was curious to know what those dreams were about, but I did as she asked and put together a chronological timeline for her.

"… After we left Evan's place, it was almost one in the morning— Tuesday, April 30th, to be exact. We argued in the car because… And then a white pickup truck started hydroplaning… the driver was speeding and driving drunk. We had the green light to go, and when I reached the middle of the intersection, it happened so fast. He slammed right into your passenger door and caused the car to flip and somersault sideways. I was knocked out at first, but regained consciousness when paramedics pulled me out of the car.

"The full crew was there at the crash site. Your injuries were more critical than mine. I remember not wanting to go on the stretcher, but they forced me."

"What happened to the driver?" asked Aria.

"He died during the crash."

"How old was he?"

"Twenty—a college kid."

"What was his name?"

"Jeezuz, Aria!" I scowled. "His name is insignificant. You're in this hospital bed because of that selfish idiot."

"But it was an accident."

"No, it wasn't. It could have been prevented. He didn't need to get behind the wheel while drunk." I tried to calm down. I didn't want to upset her with my loose-cannon temper.

"Did anyone else get hurt?"

"No."

"What happened when I was brought here?"

"You went straight to the intensive care unit," I replied. "Your injuries were internal: a collapsed lung, and your head was badly hit from the whiplash." It was hard to say these things out loud, but she had to know the truth. "Aria, you suffered a traumatic brain injury. You weren't conscious when they pulled you out of the car."

"I see my patient is awake!" said a voice from the doorway.

Dr. Patrick Peters had arrived. He'd been a long-time client at my firm, and was also a good friend of mine. Standing only a couple inches shorter than me, he had salt and pepper hair that was cut short, with brown eyes and a dimple in his chin. Rick was in great shape for a man in his late forties.

"You're a lucky young woman, Aria," he said. "Every time I've stepped in here, your dad's been sitting in that chair, praying for you. He loves you a lot. I'm Dr. Peters, by the way."

"Nice to meet you." She politely shook his hand.

"That's a nice firm grip you've got there." He chuckled. "I see you're gaining some of your strength back." Rick beamed at her before he looked at me. "How are you doing today, Noah?"

"Much better—relieved that she's finally opened her eyes."

"It's a miracle," he said.

"How come I'm still hooked up to all this machinery?" Aria asked.

Rick took off his stethoscope and hung it around his neck. "You suffered a brain injury, which caused you to slip into a coma once they rushed you into the ER. We've had to intubate you to help you breathe.

There was extensive injury to the cerebral cortex of your brain, as well as the reticular activating system in the brain stem. You scored a three on the Glasgow Coma Scale."

"What does that mean?"

"It means you were unresponsive, despite strong, painful, and verbal stimuli," Rick explained. "Your ribs are severely bruised, and there's internal damage to your kidney."

"My kidney?"

"Yes. You have acute kidney failure caused by the impact of the collision. Your right kidney was necrotic because of the trauma—completely gone. The other one has also suffered infarction."

"What's that?"

"Tissue death. A lack of proper blood supply and oxygen will cause it."

"What about my other kidney? Will it recover?"

"Well, if you're not aware already, you only need one kidney to survive. But since your other kidney is in a failing functioning state…"—he wavered a bit—"you're gonna need a kidney transplant."

I watched her expression to see if she would panic, but she stayed quiet and seemed to absorb everything the doctor had shared.

"We've been trying to introduce liquids back into your body," Rick said. "Diuretics were used to stabilize your blood pressure. But your case is so severe that dialysis was required to cleanse your body of toxins."

"Has that been helping at all?" she asked.

"Not enough to guarantee a full recovery," he replied. "A kidney transplant is the only solution."

And *that* was my cue to step in and reassure her that everything was going to be all right.

"Aria"—I held her hand—"Don't worry. Your mother and I will get tested to see if we can donate."

"Wait—Mom's in LA?"

"Yes."

"When did she fly here?"

"A day after the accident." I had a feeling this was too much for her to take in at once. "Look," I said. "It's almost four o'clock. Your mom will be here soon, and you can catch up with her." I was about to ask Rick something when I heard Evan's voice down the hall. He wasn't alone; Natalie was talking to him.

"I'll be right back," I said, stepping out of the room, only to regret it.

"What the hell are you two doing here?" I said, guarding the door while exchanging death glares at Evan and Rob. "Natalie, I thought I told you I don't want them here." I couldn't mask my anger.

"Noah, calm down. Doctor Peters mentioned it was best to get as many organ donors as possible in the family to volunteer and get tested, remember?"

"And that piece of shit would like to offer *his* kidney?" I was referring to that pathetic excuse for a husband she had. "Over my dead body!"

Rob leaned into Natalie's ear and muttered, "I told you this was a bad idea."

"Damn right it is!" I blasted.

"No." She shook her head. "It's not. Noah, please step aside. We came here to visit Aria, not argue with you."

"You're free to go inside, Natty. However, *idiot one* and *idiot two* can back off."

"Easy, bro." Evan glared.

Ignoring him, I cast my hostile gaze on Rob. "*My* daughter doesn't need your kidney. It's probably on the verge of failing from all that booze you've been chugging all your miserable life."

"You're one to talk!" Rob growled. "*Coke head!*"

"Get out of my face and leave this hospital before I put you in one of these beds myself!" I was ready to give him another black eye, but Evan stopped me.

"Noah, chill out!"

"Get your hands off me!"

I hadn't been sleeping or eating well for weeks, which explained my cranky mood. We took a breather when Aria called out to us. I guess our bickering was pissing her off.

Natalie looked at me with pleading eyes. "Please," she said, "for the sake of our daughter, keep the peace."

"Fine." I glowered at Rob one last time before entering the hospital room.

Evan embraced her first in cheerful spirits while I brooded in a corner. Natalie was next to shower her with affection. I had to resist my violent urges when Rob kissed my daughter on the head.

Rick caught our attention and told us he'd return in an hour after finishing his rounds with other patients.

"Doctor Peters," said Nat. "Before you go, I have to ask… when can we come in for testing?"

"We can schedule an appointment as early as tomorrow morning," he replied.

"Wonderful." She smiled.

I tried to bite my tongue but failed. "That excludes *Robby*."

Nat folded her arms in her chest and frowned at me. "No, it doesn't," she disputed. "He would like to donate a kidney to our daughter. And if he's able to, then you should be grateful."

I hated how quick she was to defend the jerk, despite everything that had happened.

"What's going on?" said Aria, sitting up.

"Nothing, sweetheart," Nat replied. "We're all getting tested tomorrow to see if we're a compatible match for your kidney transplant."

"Rob wants to donate?"

"Yes," he spoke up and cleared his throat before he sat in a chair beside her. "Aria, I wish I could take back all the horrible things I've said and done to hurt you."

You can't turn back the clock, asshole.

"I know I haven't been a great father to you. I've had my own demons to slay. Life's been so stressful. It's no excuse…"

Damn right it isn't.

"But I regret all the times I took my anger out on you and projected my inadequacy and shame."

She will never forgive you, and neither will I, I condemned him in silence.

Aria gave him the blankest stare, as if she couldn't believe what was coming out of his mouth. But that didn't stop Rob from apologizing.

"Maybe in the smallest way," he added, "I can make up for all the terrible things I've done by being an ideal candidate for you."

"*Wow!*"—I gave him a slow applause—"That *almost* passed for a half decent performance. You had me going there for a moment, Robby boy. I must admit." My blatant sarcasm couldn't have been more obvious.

"Who are you calling a *boy*?" he grumbled. "I'm older than you. Sit down, Noah."

"True." I titled my head. "You look pretty damn prehistoric."

"Noah!" Natalie shouted.

Rick seemed uncomfortable as he mentioned leaving to give us privacy.

"You're staying," I sternly stated, turning my focus back on fuckface. "When was the last time we saw each other, Robby?"

He stayed quiet.

"Well?"

"I'll answer you once you learn how to say my name properly."

"Oh, yeah!" I laughed. "Now I remember! I think it was at your apartment. Wait... weren't you in really rough shape? What the hell happened to you that night?" I chuckled, shaking my head. "*That's right...* I beat the shit out of you. Ah, good times! Would you like me to refresh your memory, Robby? Because I could—"

"All right," Evan cut in. "Enough."

"Will you stop doing that?" I glowered at him. "What are you, his bodyguard? Do you know what that SOB has done to my daughter?"

"Look, I know you have beef with each other, but you need to put your differences aside for Aria's sake."

My volatile temper stabilized when I met her gaze.

"You've been selfish," Evan said. "Forbidding me from visiting her. She's my niece, Noah. Her life is in danger, and I want to help."

I stared at my brother long and hard before I said, "Look at you, acting all grown up for once."

"You know I'm right, so stop being stubborn and let us help."

I was about to respond when Aria said, "You guys don't have to help. I don't want any of you to lose a kidney because of me. Put me on the transplant list, Dr. Peters. I'll wait."

"We only need one kidney to live, sweetheart," Natalie stated.

"I don't care. That's a major surgery. You're gonna be losing an organ—permanently."

"Aria," Nat sighed. "We're all getting tested. End of story."

Rick shared some medical knowledge.

"I should let you all know that transplant results are best when the donor and the patient are identical on the white blood cell antigen series. Because of inherited genes, this can only happen between brothers and sisters, where there is a one in four chance of a perfect match. Parents and children have a fifty percent match, because only half of the genes in a child come from each parent. One portion of the testing is called cross-matching.

"If both biological parents test positive by only a single antigen, that means the child would reject their kidney. But if they test negative, it means there's a minimal risk of organ rejection. With the antigens it's all tissue testing—keep in mind that those six antigens are out of 100 ones that are the most effective three out of the six that come from only one parent."

"I'm so confused." Aria frowned.

"I'll explain further," Rick said. "There are three major tests: blood type, the tissue one that is used especially, and the cross matching where the blood samples are literally mixed to see if one destroys the other."

"What about me and Rob?" asked Evan. "We're not her blood relatives. What are the chances of us being a match?"

"There is a one in a hundred thousand chances that you will both have all six antigens," Rick replied. "Transplants with living related donors are more likely to be successful than with unrelated because the body tissues are more likely to be closely matched. But to answer your question, even though the chances of being an ideal match are very slim, it is possible."

"See," I said to Aria. "Your mother and I will most likely be a perfect match."

I thanked Rick for his in-depth explanation and told Natalie that it was pointless to have Rob and Evan tested.

"I wouldn't rule out that option," Rick said. "There is a possibility that they could be a match—slim, but possible."

Natalie insisted this was all in our daughter's best interest.

"Fine." I relented. "We're all getting tested. I won't argue about it anymore." I was confident that I would be a match. She and I were connected in every way. I wanted to be the one to donate a healthy kidney to her. I had made a deal with God. This was the next part of our deal: giving her a part of me, selflessly, the way a father would. All I cared about was her wellbeing.

"Noah," said Nat. "May I have a word with you, please?"

I nodded, following her out of the hospital room. We stood in the hallway near the door to have a quiet conversation.

"You've been here since yesterday," she said. "Go home for the night and get some rest. I can stay with Aria until you come back"

"I want Rob and Evan to leave."

"She just survived a fatal accident. Let her be around people who love her."

"You expect me to believe that asshole really loves her?"

"He's willing to donate a kidney. Doesn't that prove he loves her and wants to help? I know he's not perfect, but he's changed for the better."

An attractive blonde nurse walked past us with a smile. Correction: she smiled at *me*.

"Fine," I sighed. "I need some sleep, anyway. If anything happens…"

"I will call you. Don't worry."

"Monitor Evan," I warned. "I don't trust him."

She rolled her eyes and said, "I don't think he's the one you should be worried about right now."

Ending our discussion, I walked back inside and told Aria I was heading home.

"You should rest, sweetheart."

"I'm tired of sleeping. I'm drowsy because of all these drugs they keep pumping in me."

"Your body needs to recover."

"When will you be back?"

"In the morning," I replied, standing up from my chair.

"Wait. Come closer," she said. "I have to tell you something."

Her lips brushed against my earlobe when I leaned in, sending chills down my body. She whispered her question before I met her beautiful eyes and smiled.

"Okay. I will."

"Promise?"

"I promise."

₧₧

Vanessa wasn't home when I arrived in the evening. She'd sent me a text earlier saying she was working late. Now that she was close to launching her swimwear store, her time was more occupied with business. I had encouraged her to stay focused, despite me taking time off from work after the accident. Lately, I had this rising suspicion she was having an affair, and that Aria had been right all along.

Before I went upstairs, I checked my voicemail on the landline. My mother had called and left a message. I knew my brother must have told her about Aria being in the hospital. She wanted to fly down and visit.

Now you want to be a grandmother? Not a chance in hell, I thought, deleting the message.

₧₧

I woke up an hour before my alarm and couldn't go back to sleep. My body was still worn-out but I couldn't get my mind to shut down. I was more worried about Aria than anything. I had promised her I'd stop by in the evening. I just couldn't say no when she asked me. Getting out of bed, I dressed myself, grabbed my car keys, and headed out the door.

It was almost 10p.m. and my wife still wasn't home. I tried calling her cell but went straight to voicemail. Minutes later, my cellphone vibrated with an incoming message from Nessa.

Sorry honey, I'm over at Hannah's place. She's in crisis mode. I'll explain later. Be home after midnight. Don't wait up. xox

Since when did she and Hannah become best friends? I found this odd but pushed it aside and drove back to the hospital.

CHAPTER THIRTY
NOAH

The hallway leading to Aria's room was quiet and dimly lit as I walked past a few nurses. Reaching the door, I opened it and stepped inside.

"What are you doing here?" Natalie looked surprised to see me as she talked in a hushed voice.

"I promised Aria I'd come back later in the evening. Rest for the night. I'll stay here with her."

"Are you sure?"

"Yes."

Natalie kissed our daughter's head before she got up and grabbed her handbag. I felt sorry for her. Our lives would have ended up so differently had I not broken her heart all those years ago. Her life with Rob only proved to have aged her faster. While my wife strutted around in heels, designer dresses, and fake tans, Natalie's everyday style was modest and conservative. Her dirty blonde hair was short and wavy and needed some touch-ups at the roots. There were dark circles under her eyes, and she seemed to have lost a bit of weight since I'd last seen her in New York.

That prick's probably putting financial stress on her—and this month of hell hasn't helped either. I made a mental note to have a private discussion with her later, to see if I could be of any help.

"Please call me if her condition changes," she said.

"I will. Don't worry."

Aria was sound asleep. Even though I knew she was no longer comatose, it was hard to see her with her eyes shut. I made my way over to the bed and sat down in an armchair, gazing at her. She had her mother's cute little nose and plump, pouty lips.

I was about to set my phone on silent when I noticed her stirring. Her beautiful eyes met mine, pulling me under a powerful wave of emotion.

"You're here." She smiled.

"Hey, gorgeous." I kissed her hand. "Don't fight sleep if you're tired."

"How long have you been sitting there?"

"I just arrived."

She ran her fingers through her long, dark hair and sighed. "I know, I look like crap."

"Don't be ridiculous. You always look beautiful, Aria."

She had no idea what she did to me. And I didn't think I could ever explain it.

"I'm so high on these pain meds they keep giving me, so I'm gonna enjoy the rush and pretend not to care about how crappy I look at the moment."

"You do *not* look crappy."

"I've looked better," she said, tucking a lock of hair behind her ear.

"Who are you trying to impress?" I teased. "Doctor Peters? He's happily married."

Her laughter made me smile.

"You don't need makeup and fancy clothes to impress me, Aria. Trust me on that. Everything about you is amazing."

The truth was, she could have walked around in a paper bag dress, and I still would have found her attractive.

"You're awake, living and breathing. It's a miracle."

"Everyone keeps saying that."

"Because it's true." I caressed her hand. Her genius mind was always a mystery to me.

"Ryan and Jess stopped by earlier," she said.

"I bet they were happy to see you."

"Yeah… everything still feels so surreal." She paused. "I won't be able to attend grad next week. It sucks that I've missed my finals."

"You don't have to worry about your SATs, since you already wrote it last fall. I've spoken to your principal and your teachers; they understand your situation, sweetheart. You can write your finals in late July."

"All right. I can handle that."

"I can always pay off your principal, though."

"Noah!"

"I'm kidding."

I was hoping this news would have made her happy, but she looked sad.

"Aria, I know it sucks that you missed your prom and can't attend your graduation ceremony, but we can host a party at our place once you're better."

"That won't be necessary. Thank you, though."

I was hesitant to open up the next subject, but eventually pushed myself since we were already discussing her academic future.

"There's something I've been meaning to discuss with you."

She met my gaze and said, "What's up?"

"How come you lied to me about accepting your offer of admission to Berkley?"

Expecting a detailed explanation, all I got from her was a shrug.

"When were you gonna tell me you were planning to go to Columbia?" I asked.

"How did you find out?"

"I received your registration package from the university two weeks ago. How come you changed your mind? I thought you were excited about going to Berkeley. They had offered you a great scholarship."

Patiently, I waited for a response, but all she said was, "Could you please pass me my mints? They're in that drawer."

"You're avoiding my question." I grabbed the mints and gave them to her.

"It seemed like the best choice," she explained.

"Then how come you didn't tell me? You know how much I value your education."

"Because I knew you'd try to change my mind and wouldn't be happy with my decision."

"I would have eventually found out. How did you expect me to react, then?"

"I didn't think you'd care."

She couldn't have been serious.

"Baby, come on now." I grimaced. "Tell it to me straight."

"You already know the reason, Noah. It's difficult to be around you, let alone be in the same state as you. I thought if I moved away, it would be easier on both of us."

Her reasoning was logical. It just hurt to think about being so far from her for the next four years.

"On a lighter note," I said, "they're offering you a thirty-thousand-dollar scholarship."

"Cool."

I'd been hoping for a more enthusiastic reaction, but she didn't look that excited. Perhaps she was too tired to talk.

"Why are you looking at me like that?" Aria said.

"I don't mean to make you uncomfortable. I'm just happy you're out of that coma. You don't know how hard it's been for your mother and me."

"I'm sorry."

"Don't be sorry." I took her hand. "I'm so grateful you're alive."

"Can we cuddle?"

"I don't know if I can fit next to you—it'll be a tight squeeze."

"I don't mind." She shifted over. "I can make room."

Carefully, I reclined next to her, stretching my legs. She felt warm as I wrapped an arm around her shoulder, pulling her to my chest.

"Are you comfortable?" I asked.

"Mm hm. Are you?"

"Yes." I kissed her head and cuddled her closely. "I'm right where I need to be."

"Can we listen to some music?"

"Sure, sweetheart."

Her blue iPod was resting on the nightstand next to me.

"So, I have a playlist of my own?" I noticed my name on the screen.

Aria smiled, hiding her face in my chest.

"You like doing that, don't you?"

"Doing what?" Her voice sounded muffled.

"Hiding yourself."

"Only when I feel embarrassed." She looked up at me. "If I could hide myself completely in you, I would."

"Oh, yeah?" I arched an eyebrow. "How come?"

"You know the answer to that question."

"No, I don't," I lied.

She fixated on the buttons of my shirt and fidgeted with them, saying, "Because you make me feel so protected. Hiding in your body would feel… familiar, as if it's the safest place ever. I can't explain it—like if I had to surrender to anyone, it would be you."

This moment was bittersweet. I felt good knowing I could protect her in a fatherly way. But I had failed to love her in the same sense.

Her lips were so tempting to kiss. I had to remind myself not to go there as I forced my gaze on her hypnotic eyes.

"Is this another 'I'm-hiding-my-face-in-your-chest-'cuz-I-feel-embarrassed' moment?" I teased.

"No." Aria giggled. "This is a: 'I'm-hiding-my-face-in-your-chest-'cuz-I-secretly-have-an-embarrassing-cologne-fetish' kind of moment." Her cheeks tugged upwards, revealing her beautiful smile. I couldn't help but chuckle.

"What did I miss out on these past five weeks?"

I couldn't tell her everything that was on my mind, so I settled for option two: a synopsis of what life was like for me last month.

"Well"—I stroked her hair—"ever since they moved you into the head trauma unit, I've been by your bedside, praying you would wake up."

"Praying?" She was shocked. "You don't believe in God."

I felt anxious as I tried to explain my newfound faith. "You made me a believer the second you opened your eyes," I admitted. "I knew there was no way I'd pull the plug if it ever came down to that. But I didn't want you to suffer in a vegetative state for years. I was going out of my mind, Aria. I didn't want to bury my only daughter. That's not the natural way of things. A parent should never have to bury their child."

"I'm not a child, though."

"You know what I mean."

She intertwined her fingers with mine and patiently listened while I spoke.

"I took time off from work so I could be here with you around the clock. I can't explain it, but I felt like you needed me."

That statement was not a hundred percent true; *I* was the one who needed her.

"Doctor Peters had encouraged us to talk to you as much as possible. He'd said that some patients have woken up from their coma while hearing their favorite music—that's why we had your iPod playing around the clock every day. Jessica had made a prom playlist for you as well."

"Yeah, I remember her telling me that." Aria paused. "What did you say to me?"

I'd told her a lot—too much, in fact. I had bared my soul and wasn't sure if God had brought her back out of pity for me, or because he wanted to test my faith.

"I whispered secrets in your ear," I said.

"I wish I remembered those secrets."

It was best she didn't.

"I remember bits and pieces of my dreams," she added. "It was as if I was living in an alternate reality… everything feels like a jumbled-up puzzle in my head right now."

"What can you remember?"

"I don't know… Life seemed normal."

"Maybe subconsciously you were suppressing the truth," I suggested.

"I think I altered the memory of the accident because I didn't want to believe we had crashed. In my dream, we passed the intersection, and the car *behind us* got hit instead. I remember freaking out... you pulled over once we were a safe distance away... You comforted me and tried to calm me down. I remember getting ready for prom in my bedroom... And that's pretty much it."

That was a relief. At least she hadn't been stuck in an endless purgatory of recurring nightmares. I often wondered if Hell was like that: a place where all your worst fears would come to life and torture you for eternity.

"I lost such a huge chunk of time," Aria sighed.

"Five weeks is better than five years."

"Clearly."

A quiet calmness crept between us before she muttered, "You showed up at my prom."

"Really?" I said in surprise.

"Yeah, I was planning on, um... doing something stupid—but you sabotaged my efforts."

"That sounds like something I'd do." I chuckled.

"You had read my diary. That's how you found out."

"Now *that* is something I would never do. That violates your privacy."

"I know. I was so mad at you."

"I believe it." My fingers took on a will of their own as I caressed her arm. Her skin was so soft. "Your friends often visited you," I said. "Did you read their cards?"

"Yes, I did." Her face lit up. "Jess and Ryan dropped by shortly after you left today. Apparently, prom really sucked. But here's the strange part... a lot of their descriptions of the events were like what I had dreamed about. Jess told me she and Ryan had visited me after prom and described everything. I think I still had some consciousness to a degree, because everything seemed to blend into my dreams. When I asked Doctor Peters about it, he said it was normal."

Now I really wondered if she remembered anything I had confessed to her.

"So," I said. "What happened when I showed up?"

Aria shrugged. "Nothing."

Nothing?

"Come on," I insisted. "Tell me."

"You dragged me home and lectured me. Typical you—per usual. And then I woke up, back to reality. No more warped coma-dimension."

Something told me there was more to it. Either she wasn't ready to share yet or had decided she would never disclose those details—ever.

"Noah?"

"Yes, baby?"

"Did you mean everything you said to me… before I woke up?"

Shit. She remembered. I couldn't lie to her, but I couldn't go against my promise to God, either. I refused to break her heart. I had done enough of that.

"Every word," I finally admitted. "I meant every word."

Releasing my hand, she wrapped her arm around my waist and hugged me tighter.

"Aria, this doesn't change our situation. You know we can't—"

"I know. But I have hope."

"How so?"

She flashed a sweet smile and said, "Maybe I'll tell you one day."

"Why not now?"

"Because I'd rather tell you when I'm not stuck in a hospital bed, poked with needles from left to right."

"Fair enough."

Humming a sigh, she snuggled up closer. "Thank you for being here with me tonight."

"I've been here with you every night." I kissed her head and shut my eyes as she placed her hand on my chest. It was hard to shut my brain off when all I could feel was that undeniable attraction between me and her.

"Noah?"

"Yeah?" I replied with my eyes closed.

"Can you tell me a story?"

"You know I suck at storytelling, Aria."

"But your voice is so soothing when you're not pissed off."

I had to laugh.

She looked at me like a sad little puppy and said, "Please?"

Back to being the caring father.

"Okay, okay," I yielded. "A story, hmm… did I ever tell you about how the sun fell in love with the moon?"

She shook her head.

"Four and a half billion years ago, while the moon was orbiting the Earth in the solar system, there was this incredible nebula in the galaxy… and within that nebula, the sun was born…"

The minutes passed as I rambled on about the science of astronomy, which seemed to have bored her to sleep. While life was changing around me, one fact remained the same: I was in love with Aria, and I knew it was wrong. When the last song ended, I turned off her iPod and rested my head against hers, till I eventually faded.

CHAPTER THIRTY-ONE
EVIL IS NOT BORN

It was Christmas Eve of 1988 in Hampden County. The city was covered in snow, which made the most rundown parts of the neighborhood look prettier. Lida Matein was a twenty-year-old single mother living in a studio apartment with her three-year-old son, Matthias. Despite her demanding work schedule, she was happy to have finally had the night off without worrying about drunken patrons grabbing her body while she would strip for them. A little piece of her soul died every time she exposed herself to a man she did not love.

Lida's dangerous love affair with meth had resulted from unaddressed childhood traumas. That year, all she wanted was to spend Christmas with her son and be an excellent mother to him, like she had always promised (whenever she tried to quit her drug addiction). Having stayed clean for six weeks, she was recovering from the withdrawal stage.

Bobby Helms was singing "Jingle Bell Rock" on the stereo—Lida's favorite Christmas tune. She played it every year on repeat during the holiday season. Dressed in a white robe and a Santa hat, she danced around with Matthias in her arms.

Snowflakes had frosted the windows of the apartment, revealing a white Christmas outside. The young mother had put up a small Christmas tree on the coffee table, decorating it with ornaments and mini candy canes. Red and green tinsel hung from the ceiling fan, with mistletoe hanging from the doorway in Lida's tiny kitchen.

Matthias's laughter filled the room as his mother kissed his cheek and playfully blew into his neck. A delicious aroma wafted from the oven, enticing the little boy's appetite. Lida had baked a homemade apple pie, her grandmother's famous recipe.

"Have you been a good boy this year, Matty?"

"Yes, Mamma." He smiled, wrapping his pudgy arms around his mother's neck. At three years old, he had developed a decent vocabulary.

"Santa's gonna bring you something special this year. Are you excited, Matthias?"

"*Yah!*" He let out the cutest laugh.

His cheerful giggling stopped when a loud noise made him jump in fear.

BOOM-BOOM-BOOM!

Lida froze and turned around, staring at the door. A foreboding presence crept into the apartment, shifting the frequency. She seemed to know who was waiting on the other side.

"Looks like we've got an uninvited guest." She placed her son in his crib.

Tightening her robe, she headed for the entrance door. Her excessive drug use had made her underweight, but she was on the road to recovery.

BOOM! BOOM!

"Hold on!" she shouted. "I'm coming!" Grabbing some cash from her purse, she unfastened a latch and opened the door.

A tall man with a bulky frame stood across from her, dressed in a black leather coat, dark trousers, and black boots. His neck was covered in tattoos, and he had short blond hair that was buzzed off. His dark, beady eyes pierced through hers as he glared at her. The crease in his forehead made him look like he had a permanent frown on his face. His left ear was pierced with a small golden hoop.

Lida was nervous. Readjusting her robe, she stared at the intimidating man towering over her.

"Where's my money?" he spoke with a thick Boston accent.

"It's here." She handed him the cash and tucked back a strand of her fallen hair.

He counted the bills and sneered at her. "You're kiddin' me, right?"

"I… I'll give you the rest next week—I promise."

"You're twelve-hundred short! Give me my money!"

"I don't have it! Please, it's Christmas Eve. I promise I'll get you the cash by next Friday."

"That's not how it works, bitch!" He clutched her throat and forced himself inside. "I'm gonna give you ten seconds to solve this problem. And if you can't, then I'll solve it myself. *Ten…*"

"I swear I'm telling the truth!" Lida panicked, backing away.

"Nine…"

"I don't have your money right now!" She bumped into a table.

"Eight…"

"If you just give me until tomorrow, I can borrow the money to pay you back!"

"*One.*"

Yelping in pain, she shrieked when he twisted her hair around his big, burly hand.

"*Mamma!*" Matthias stood up in his crib.

"I have a son. Please don't do this!" Lida begged, trembling with fear. A part of her already knew this would be the last time she would ever see her baby again.

The dealer looked around the apartment and let out a menacing laugh. "I don't see no bedroom."

"Take me to the bathroom. I won't put up a fight—just don't hurt me in front of him, please!"

"*Mammaaaa!*" Matthias started crying, sensing her fear.

"It's okay, sweetie! Mommy's gonna have a talk with her friend. He's just a little angry, but we'll work it out. Close your eyes and take a nap." She looked at her dealer and said, "Please don't harm my baby."

"I didn't say you could talk!" He was almost near the door when she grabbed a crystal vase on a side table and attacked him.

"You cunt!" The man dodged it in time as the vase shattered against the wall. He slapped her hard across the face, forcing her to the ground.

Turning his gaze on Matthias, he grinned and said, "I'm gonna teach you a lesson you're never gonna forget, kid."

Lida screamed in pain when he yanked her hair and dragged her to her son's crib.

"No!" she screamed, trying to free herself.

"Shut the hell up!" He punched her, causing Matthias to cry uncontrollably. "Never trust a woman," he muttered in anger, "because all they're good for is whoring themselves out! Know what that means?" He asked the terrified child. "I'll show you." The dealer laughed, unzipping his pants.

Lida fought to stay conscious. Before she could realize what was happening, her legs were forced apart and her panties were aggressively yanked down.

"GET OFF ME! STOP!" She struggled against him, but her efforts were pointless. He was stronger and heavier as he pinned her arms back and violated her.

"Take it, bitch!"

Wailing through the painful assault, Lida had no choice but to accept her fate while her only child witnessed the horror.

"Matthias, close your eyes, baby! Don't look!"

He cried, as diamond tears dripped down his chubby cheeks. The traumatized toddler squeezed his arms through the wooden bars of the crib, desperate to reach his mother. He couldn't be her hero and save her from the demon who was hurting her.

"Close your eyes, Matty!" she begged.

His heartbreaking cries turned into ear piercing screams.

"Listen to Mommy!" Lida pleaded.

"You won't shut up, will ya, whore?" The man pulled out a sharp blade from his back pocket, and just as she tried to reason with him, he slit Lida's throat like a sacrificial lamb before he continued raping her. Lida's blood curdling cries became garbled as her life slowly slipped away in seconds.

Looking up at her son, a dark, crimson pool spread beneath her as blood sprayed out on the carpet like a red fountain of sadistic suffering. Matthias's innocent face became blurry. His agonizing cries soon faded to faint echoes in the background. Lida exhaled her last breath before her heart stopped beating. Her nervous system had shut down, and her pupils were dilated. She was dead.

The minutes passed and Matthias was no longer crying. The poor child had gone into shock. He stared at his mother's lifeless body while the Christmas tune played on repeat.

"See no evil," said the assailant, "hear no evil. Speak no evil. I did you a favor, kid." He looked down at Lida's bloody body and spit on her. "She would've always chosen the drugs over you."

Walking back to the front door, he stopped and looked at the petrified child.

"Merry fuckin' Christmas." The door slammed shut before he left the crime scene.

... Jingle bell rock.

૪૦૭૪

Heart racing and drenched in sweat, Evan sat up in bed, shaking. It had been a second night in a row that his sleep was disturbed by nightmares about *her* again. He couldn't understand why it was happening; it had been years since he had them. Half disoriented, he made his way to the kitchen to get a glass of water.

A compilation of gruesome images flickered in his mind when he turned on the tap: the screaming, the thick pool of blood, garbled breaths... That lifeless look in his mother's eyes before her final breath escaped her lungs. Ignoring the dull ache in his arms, Evan gulped back his drink and noticed it was three o'clock in the morning when he glanced at the time on the stove.

Quenching his thirst, he returned to his bedroom and visited his secret shrine. The hanging light bulbs from the ceiling glowed when he turned on the switch and gazed at his "artistic mural." Standing before the collage of pictures, he lightly brushed his fingers against them and felt his heart sigh.

"I almost lost you," he whispered. "I won't let that happen again." He kissed his fingers and placed them on Aria's photographed cheek. "You belong to me, my beautiful dove." Evan smiled darkly, clasping the mini vial that hung around his neck. The crimson liquid inside was actual blood… Aria's blood. He had drawn it from her vein during one of his hospital visits. In his mind, it didn't seem wrong or sick to possess such an unusual accessory. He believed he loved her in his own way; he wanted to feel closer to her.

Sitting in the armchair, he opened the blood vial from his necklace and raised it to his lips, pouring a few drops on his tongue. Evan shut his eyes and savored the coppery taste. His cock stiffened below while he lost himself in a dark world of sexual fantasies: He wanted her to strip down in front of him and straddle his lap. He wanted Aria to cut any part of his body and lick his blood. His deranged desires aroused him.

Tomorrow morning, he would stop by the hospital, get his blood tested, and pray to be the best match for a kidney transplant. Knowing that Aria would live with one of his organs inside of her got him off.

I'll always be inside of you. Forever. You're mine.

CHAPTER THIRTY-TWO
ARIA

Almost a week had passed since I woke up from my coma—and maybe this sounds awful, but I wish I'd never opened my eyes. I would have died happy believing in a lie. How could I ever forget that night of eternal bliss with Noah? I wasn't sure if I would ever feel anything that could top that experience in real life. Since regaining consciousness, my mom visited me every day and lengthened her stays, especially since Noah was clocking in regular hours at work again. I didn't want him jeopardizing his job because of me. Sure, he was wealthy and could have retired, but he had a career he had worked hard to establish.

Last week, everyone went through a series of blood tests. Doctor Peters had said it would take another week for the blood results to arrive from the lab. These tests would determine if my cells would react well with the donor cells—cross-matching, that's what it was called. Lately, I had trouble sleeping because I kept dreaming about the night of the crash; a night I didn't want to remember anymore.

"*Uno!*" Mom shouted in victory. "I win!"

All my thoughts suddenly scrambled, as I looked up at her and accepted defeat.

"Mom, this game is so lame."

"Are you kidding? You love playing Uno."

"Yeah, when I was like—ten!"

"You always kick my butt whenever we play. It's nice to win for a change, so let me enjoy it!"

It seemed like forever since I last saw her smile. I never understood why she stayed with my stepdad; Rob was the biggest contributor to her unhappiness in life.

"You've been somewhere else all afternoon, Aria. What's up?"

"It's nothing."

"It's *something*. Come on, a mother knows when her daughter's in love. You're thinking about that cutie, Ryan, aren't you?"

"What?"

Oh God, she was so off—like *way* off.

"He used to visit you often while you were in a coma. I chatted with him here and there and thought he has feelings for you."

"We're just friends, Mom."

I *so* did not want to have this conversation right now.

"Hmm, I don't think he sees you as 'just a friend.' You can talk to me about boys, you know."

"I know."

"Good." She smiled. "We have a lot of catching up to do. Your father informed me about your plans to move back to New York. He said you've decided on Columbia for college. Why didn't you tell me sooner?"

I shrugged. "I guess I wanted to surprise you."

"Well, I told Noah that Columbia is a great university. You made the right choice, sweetheart. It'll be nice to have you closer again."

I was about to change the subject when I noticed the tears in her eyes.

"Mom, what's wrong? Why are you crying?"

She grabbed a tissue and said, "You're my first child, Aria. I almost lost you."

"Well, worst-case scenario, you'd still have another two kids to raise."

Frowning, she shook her head.

"Sorry. Bad joke."

"I love you and I want you to be happy"—Mom squeezed my hand— "I'm so proud of you for getting that scholarship. You worked so hard.

Don't let your finals discourage you. All your teachers have been very understanding about your situation. Noah said that he will take care of all your living expenses once you're in New York, so don't stress about money. Everything's gonna be fine. You're gonna pull through this."

There was so much optimism in her eyes, but I had a feeling she was masking her exhaustion.

"Mom, you look like you haven't slept in days. You really don't have to supervise me around the clock."

"I'm here because I want to be. I miss you, darling."

"I miss you too, but I feel bad. Who's watching over Terry and Tiff?"

"Your grandparents. They drove down from Boston weeks ago."

"I'm surprised Rob's here. He never closes up the garage."

"He's got Sammy running the place until he returns. He wants to be here for you as well."

"But Mom, you guys need the money—every dollar counts."

She raised her hand in protest to silence me. "I don't want you worrying about that kind of stuff. We've got it covered."

"What do you mean?"

"Your father's helping me out."

Oh, God… no. History repeating again. The dreadful thought plagued my memory and triggered a time when my stepdad's gambling had gotten so out of control.

"Mom, please don't give the money to Rob! You know what he'll do!"

"He's been getting help for his gambling addiction these past three months. It's a twelve-step program kind of thing, you know?"

He had tried AA last year and that clearly hadn't worked. How was this "program" going to make a difference now?

"Besides," she added, "he doesn't even know about the money. I'll tell him my parents helped us out if he asks. For now, I will deposit the check into my own separate account. Robert does not have access to it— those were Noah's conditions."

"How much money are we talking about here?"

"I had declined at first, because there was no way I'd be able to pay him back soon, not in weeks, not in months… *years?* Gosh, I don't know." She laughed nervously.

"Mom, just tell me." I grew impatient.

She took a deep breath, opened her handbag, and pulled out the check.

"*Wow…*" My jaw nearly dropped as I held it in my hand.

"I still can't believe it," she sighed. "He doesn't want the money back. He just wants to help me out."

"What are you gonna do with it?"

"I'm gonna deposit a portion into a trust fund for your brother and sister. Once they're eighteen, they can use the money for college, and the rest of it they'll receive once they graduate and get their degree. I was gonna do the same for you, but Noah told me not to worry about that. He's already contributed generously to you." She winked.

I guess this was gonna be another one of his surprises that I would have no choice but to accept.

"As for the rest of the money," Mom continued, "I'm gonna pay off all our credit card debt, cut up the plastic, and start paying for things in cash so I can get a better sense of how much I'm spending. I need financial stability at this point in my life. Noah's generosity is a godsend."

I felt this overwhelming sense of pride in him. He wasn't a big fan of my mother, but he knew I loved her a lot, and so he must have wanted to help in any way he could; that's what it meant to love someone unconditionally.

"Can I ask you a question, Mom?"

"Sure, sweetie."

"What was Noah like at sixteen?"

"I'm surprised he hasn't told you himself."

"Well, you know him. He's pretty reserved about his past. He hates talking about his family. Did you know about Evan?"

"Yes," she said.

"Why didn't you tell me?"

"I hardly ever talked about your father. Why on earth would I have discussed his adoptive brother out of the blue? I've tried my best to block out all the memories of his messed-up family."

"I don't think they're as dysfunctional as we are."

"You haven't met your Grandmother Olivia."

I could sense the animosity she felt toward this woman just by the change in her tone.

"Do you blame her for your breakup with Noah?"

"Blame?" she scoffed. "The self-centered shrew practically orchestrated the doom of our relationship. She was always so manipulative, and she had never been in favor of Noah dating me. According to her, my family was of a lower class and not fit to be in the same social circle as them. I remember her telling Noah he could do so much better, right in front of me! The nerve of that woman!"

Not wanting to open old wounds for her, I had to ask this last question:

"Mom, do you still have feelings for Noah?"

Her hesitancy made me uncomfortable.

"I… care about him," she admitted. "Lately, I've seen a new side to him. He's so caring and protective of the people he loves. I never expected Noah to be so kind to me. Funny how life changes a person." She sighed and said, "I'm gonna tell you a little secret, but please don't tell Rob or your father. Don't tell anyone."

"I won't tell a soul. I promise."

It seemed to take forever before she finally confessed.

"I think a part of me will always love Noah."

There it was: the confession I feared the most. I guess that explained why she never liked to talk about him; she never got over him.

"Mom, if you were still in love with Noah, why didn't you accept his proposal when he asked you to marry him all those years ago?"

"I didn't believe he was genuine. After everything his mother had said to me, I thought he only wanted to marry me because he had knocked me up. I didn't want to spend my life with a man who was uncertain of his feelings for me. Plus, I didn't particularly want to have a monster-in-law."

I supposed that made sense.

"Aria, when you get married you don't just marry your partner, you marry into the family," she emphasized. "Noah's father had always been a kind man, but Olivia was just cruel. I knew she would have never accepted me into the family if I had married her son. She would have made my life a living hell."

Maybe both women were just projecting their fears.

"I still remember that chat she had with me a day after you were born. She told me I could never make Noah happy, and that I was merely a passing fancy to him. She had laid out this horribly descriptive scenario about how he would meet the girl of his dreams at college and dump me; how he would inevitably cheat on me even if we got married."

"And you believed her?"

"I was sixteen, pregnant, and extremely insecure." Mom took a breath. "I'm glad you're far more responsible than I was at your age."

Reflecting on her words, I asked, "If you could turn back the clock, what would you do differently?"

"I wouldn't have got married so young."

"You don't regret keeping me?"

"Of course not, Aria! Never think that way. I am so proud of you! You're a bright young lady with your whole life ahead of you."

It was a relief to know that I wasn't on her long list of regrets.

"I wish I could get out of this hospital," I said. "I can't believe I've been bedbound this long."

"You're gonna have to take it easy for a while, especially after the transplant."

"I'm anxious about it."

"It's gonna be all right, sweetheart. Just keep a positive attitude."

Forcing a smile, I glanced at the clock that hung above the door; it was almost six in the evening.

"Mom, you must be starving. You should get out of here and get something to eat."

"Rob will arrive in half an hour with some sandwiches," she said, opening the blinds. "I love the sunshine."

"That's sunny California for you."

"How are things with you and your father? I'm sure you two have bonded." She walked back to my bed and sat in an armchair.

"Noah and I are close."

We've bonded in more ways than one.

"Your life is so different here, huh?" Mom said.

"Well, it's nothing like New York, that's for sure."

"Are you happy living with your dad?"

"Mom, can you stop calling him that? I'm not exactly comfortable calling Noah my father yet."

"Oh. Sure, sweetheart. I just thought… never mind."

"I'm not ready to call him 'Daddy,' you know? It's a little late for that. It makes me cringe."

"I completely understand."

Addressing Noah as my father felt so awkward because it never felt like he was.

"He honestly looks more handsome than when he was a teen." Mom giggled. "I feel so old in comparison."

"You're still a stunner, Mom. All you need is a makeover. Once I'm out of the hospital, we should go shopping and stop by at the salon."

"That sounds great, honey. I'd love a new makeover. But not until you're better."

"I'll get better—positive attitude, right?"

"That's right." She smiled.

I didn't like to see my mother sad. She and I had our differences, and she wasn't perfect, but I loved her; that would never change.

"Oh!" Mom exclaimed. "I almost forgot to mention I spoke to Vanessa yesterday."

"She swung by the hospital?"

"No, we had a friendly chat over lunch."

This can't be good, I thought in dismay.

"She told me about how she and Noah have been trying to get pregnant."

Definitely not good.

"… And after years of failed attempts, they finally have a baby on the way! Isn't that wonderful? You're gonna have a little brother or sister soon!"

I thought he had stopped screwing her… How could he?

I wanted to breathe into a paper bag before I'd hyperventilate.

"Aria, are you okay? You've gone terribly pale."

"I'm fine."

No. I wasn't. I hated feeling things so deeply, as if my heightened humanity were unbearable to feel whenever I was sad.

"How far along is she?"

"Eight weeks."

That means conception must have occurred around April. Noah and I had been fighting a lot that month, I thought to myself.

"I think I should get a nurse in here," she said. "You really don't look so good." Mom touched my forehead to check if I had a fever.

I tried to convince her I was fine as I smiled and opened the pack of vanilla pudding I had no intention of eating.

"See?"—I ate a few spoons—"Just hungry."

Despite how nasty it tasted, my mother looked satisfied.

"What else did Vanessa say?" I asked.

"Well, she mainly inquired about childbearing advice. I told her you were my most difficult birth. The first child always is—usually."

"Has she told Noah the big news?"

"I imagine he's absolutely thrilled about it by now."

I wanted to puke—literally vomit all my intestines and die. Okay, that would be painfully graphic, but I wished I had never woken up. I wished I could have stayed in a coma. At least I would have been stuck in my little paradise with the man of my dreams, even though everything was just a figment of my imagination. Hearing this news about the pregnancy felt like a betrayal. I had no right to be angry at Noah. I guess I just thought what he and I had was stronger and more meaningful than what he shared with Vanessa. Now she would have a part of him… forever.

"I'm gonna get a nurse in here," Mom said. "You've gone white as a ghost."

"I'm just tired."

"Are you in pain?" She looked worried. "Why are you crying?"

"I'm not." I wiped my tears and lied. "I'm just scared about the transplant surgery."

"You're gonna be just fine, sweetheart"—she held my hand—"you'll see."

I couldn't open up to my mom. What could I say to her?

I'm devastated because Noah's knocked up the woman I despise, and I wish it was me who was having his baby instead? She would have had me admitted to the psych ward before I could even explain my feelings.

"I'm sorry," I uttered, grabbing a tissue.

"It's okay to be scared. You're in the best hospital in the state with the best team of surgeons. Have faith. You'll be all right, darling."

I didn't want to be all right. I wanted to die. Noah would never leave Vanessa now. The wicked witch of Beverly Hills had won.

CHAPTER THIRTY-THREE
NOAH

I was sitting in the back of a Lincoln luxury car with Amir as our driver weaved through evening traffic. We had gone out for some celebratory drinks because we closed a case that almost went to trial, which could have damaged the reputation of our client's company if it became public knowledge. I rarely ever hit the bars after work, but that day I couldn't bring myself to walk into Aria's hospital room and plaster a smile on my face as if life were just "swell." Last night, I had found out that my wife was eight weeks pregnant, and I was going to be a father. I'd noticed that she had been gaining weight, but I never suspected pregnancy—especially since she showed no symptoms. You would think it would have made me happy to know I had another shot at fatherhood, but I felt so torn and disappointed in myself. My sex life with my wife wasn't great, and we hadn't been intimate for a while. The few times we were, was just to keep me distracted; to relieve the sexual frustration I felt toward Aria (unbeknownst to my wife, of course). It sounds disturbing, but it's the truth. I knew deep down I wasn't happy anymore. Maybe this was God's way of locking me into a loveless marriage as punishment for everything I had done wrong in my past. Sharing this life altering news was going to crush Aria… And if it just so happened that I could donate a kidney, I was sure she'd be hell bent on refusing my organ just to spite me.

I really got myself into a mess. There's no way Doctor Grey can help me here.

"Hey, buddy!" Amir snapped his fingers in my face. "Wake up!"

I apologized for zoning out.

"Where the hell is your head?"

"I'm just stressed out and worried about Aria. My mind's all over the place."

"You need to take it easy, bro. Maybe coming back to work this early was a bad idea."

"No, it wasn't. Craig is counting on me to help him close that Rochester case."

"I can handle Craig, *and* I can handle your other cases."

"You've got enough on your plate," I stated. "Trust me, I've got this."

"That's right, I forgot… you're *Noah fuckin' Hunter*." He rolled his eyes.

I flashed an arrogant smile and said, "Don't you forget it."

Amir chuckled and continued with his usual small talk.

"Tomorrow's my ten-year wedding anniversary," he said.

"Congrats! Do you have anything planned for Chelsea?"

"Yeah, I'm about to go and pick up her gift." He leaned over the seat and asked the driver if he could pull over after the next light.

"Well, this is me…"

We were parked across a high-end jewelry store.

"You can head back to the firm," he added. "I'm gonna take a cab home."

"Are you sure?"

"Yeah, it's gonna take me a while in there." Amir got out of the car and leaned toward my passenger window. "Women are like prostitutes. You spend money and buy them fancy shit, and they drop their panties! If you don't, they won't spread 'em!"

He had a crude sense of humor that most people did not enjoy.

"Don't tell your wife that," I said. "Get outta here, man."

"You're looking at Casanova reincarnated!" he exclaimed, backing away. "Don Juan, baby!"

"Watch where you're going!" I hollered out the window as he disappeared into a department store.

Facing the driver, I told him to take me back to the firm so I could head home in my car. When we stopped at a traffic light, I heard something vibrate near my shoe. Looking down, I realized Amir had left his cellphone behind.

It must have slipped out of his pocket, I thought, reaching down.

Suddenly, it vibrated again. A pop-up window appeared on the screen; someone by the name of "Hot Bitch" had sent him a text. Thinking nothing of it, I opened my briefcase and put the phone inside. I didn't want to violate my friend's privacy.

Ten seconds passed, and again, his phone vibrated. Then again, and again, and…

It's probably Chelsea, I concluded. But that buzzing sound wouldn't stop.

"Christ," I muttered under my breath, opening my briefcase and grabbing the phone.

I won't read it.

What I had decided instead was to scroll down his contact list and see if Chelsea's name was there. Feeling tense, my condition worsened when I discovered my assumption had been wrong.

I need to find out who this chick is.

But you already know, another voice answered in my mind.

I never thought of Amir as the type of guy who would have an adulterous affair. From my perspective, he was a loyal family man who was in love with his wife.

Have I been wrong all this time? I questioned.

Avoiding further assumptions, I locked the phone away again in my briefcase, but quickly opened it when I remembered to set it on silent. Right when I was about to adjust the setting, the phone vibrated in my hand. Aria's voice randomly echoed in my consciousness as I stared down at the cellphone in contemplation.

Why won't you believe me, Noah? She's cheating on you with your best friend!

"Fuck it," I cursed out loud, clicking on the name to read the following texts:

Hey sex machine, r we still on for 2nite?

My husband won't be home this evening. We should hook up. Let me know if u can. I'll wear that sexy lingerie u bought me ;)

Last chance before I make plans without u...

You know that voice in your head that gets louder, urging you to investigate, even though you don't want to learn the ugly truth? Yeah, that's called instinct—intuition, whatever the hell you want to call it. The phone number was unfamiliar to me, but I knew I had to text this woman back and find out who she was, even though a part of me already knew. I wrote:

Hey sorry. Was driving.

A few seconds later, I got another text.

I wish I was there stroking u while u drove.

We both know how I LOVE that ;)

This wasn't sexually stimulating to me, but I responded with:

Naughty girl. I should punish u.

She wrote back:

U can 2nite... if ur free ;)

Pausing, I tried to think this through before I started punching letters into the phone and asked her where "the husband" was tonight.

Her response came back instantly, and what I read... shocked me.

Noah's @ the hospital with little miss teen bitch. The brat is so spoiled.

Freezing up, I read her text over. An overwhelming sense of betrayal sagged over me. How could I have been so blind? Feeling furious, I knew I hadn't been faithful either. But I needed to know how long this affair had been going on, so I texted her back and tricked Vanessa into meeting me at a hotel of my choosing. She was in for a surprise... a surprise of her life.

CHAPTER THIRTY-FOUR
CHEATER, CHEATER

It was seven o'clock in the evening when Vanessa stepped out of an elevator at the Seascape Hotel. Strutting in red stilettos and painted lips, her expensive handbag bag swung from her arm as she walked down a narrow hallway. Reaching room 407, she took out her keycard and inserted it into the security lock. The door clicked once before she opened it.

"I'm here, lover!" Vanessa took off her trench coat. "You better be ready for me… because I'm *so* ready for you!"

What she didn't know was that Amir was not there.

"Where are you?" she called out. "And where's my surprise?" Stepping into the spacious suite, she wore nothing but heels.

A quick minute later, Vanessa gasped in fright when she was randomly blindfolded. Unaware that her husband was standing behind her, she laughed.

"Amir! You scared me!" Vanessa relaxed, feeling a pair of hands on her shoulders. "*Oooh*… I like a little bondage-play! Nice to switch it up for once. Usually, you prefer to be the submissive one." She giggled while her hands were tied behind her back.

Her vulgar language shocked Noah, but he controlled his anger and led her to the bedroom. Once inside, he sat her down on the mattress and gave her a gentle shove so that she lay flat on her back.

"*My, oh my,*" she breathed in anticipation. "Aren't we a little rough today?" Vanessa giggled with excitement. "I love being manhandled by you!" Parting her legs, she felt the slightest sensation on her thigh. "Are you planning on teasing me forever? Fuck me like the dirty whore I am!"

Her world came crumbling down when her blindfold was finally removed, revealing her husband's blazing eyes. Vanessa went white as a ghost.

"N-Noah... I... it's not what it—"

"Shut up, Vanessa," he said, walking towards the digital camera resting on the television.

"You were recording me?"

"Not anymore. I got what I needed," he calmly replied, switching off the camera. "So, here's what's gonna happen…"

She nodded compliantly, wishing she had never stepped foot into that hotel room.

⊱⊰

The tension between the two lovers seemed unbearable as Noah stood by a window, glaring at his soon to be ex-wife. She had dressed herself and was sitting on a sofa in the living room.

"Don't look at me with those judgmental eyes!" She cried out in anger. "You've been screwing Dianne behind my back throughout our entire marriage!"

Noah scoffed and folded his arms in his chest. "Is that your pathetic attempt at justifying your actions? I never realized how badly your insecurities have deluded you."

"Don't deny it!"

"*One*: Dianne works for me professionally; she's not my adulterous secretary. *Two*: she has zero interest in me because she's an open lesbian. *Three*: you are so screwed, and our marriage is officially over."

"Nothing is over!"

"How long has this affair been going on?"

Vanessa stayed quiet.

"How long?" Noah asked again.

"Nearly two years."

He cursed in his head, staying composed.

"Remember that infidelity clause in our prenuptial agreement?" he reminded her. "You broke it, and you know what that means…"

"I'm gonna fight you tooth and nail for all you're worth!" Vanessa shouted. "You neglected me for years! I cheated on you because you always gave me a reason to doubt your fidelity to me." She broke down in tears. "All I ever wanted was a baby! But you kept putting it off—made excuses! And now you're gonna divorce the mother of your child?"

"Paternity is yet to be determined," Noah calmly replied.

"This baby is yours!"

"*If* the child is mine, you will want or need for nothing. I'll make sure you're taken care of. But as far as our marriage is concerned, it's over. We're over. I can't live this lie with you anymore."

"When did you stop loving me?" Vanessa said in tears. "Did you ever really love me? Or was I just a convenient option at the time?"

"Stop it."

"I told you I've been sleeping with Amir for almost two years, and you haven't even shed a tear over my betrayal! You're not angry—you're not yelling or breaking things… you don't give a shit about me at all, admit it!"

"Enough!" Noah sternly raised his voice. "Compose yourself, Vanessa."

"No! Don't you *dare* tell me to compose myself!" She became more hysterical as she buried her face in her hands and sobbed. "I never meant for this affair to get dragged out for so long. It had started out as a one-night stand."

"When?"

"When you had gone on that work trip to Sweden two years ago… And then things got worse as we became more distant. I justified my actions because I thought you were cheating on me, too."

"If you were doubting my fidelity all this time, you could have talked to me about it; that's what married people do, Vanessa—they communicate!"

"You were always busy with clients and traveling. I was convinced you would have lied to me, even if I asked!"

"You know what?" Noah breathed out his anger. "Let's stop pointing the finger at each other. You're not happy. I'm not happy. Why stay together when we're both so miserable?"

"Our marriage isn't perfect, but I love you, Noah. Amir was just… He means nothing to me."

"Two years isn't 'nothing.'"

"I wasn't with him every day!"

"Just *every other day*, right?"

"No! Please let me explain. Ever since my plastic surgery—"

"*Surgeries.*"

"You don't find me attractive anymore."

"You're right, I don't," Noah said. "Because you butchered the face and body of the woman I married! I mean, come on! Open your damn eyes, Vanessa! I tried my best to love you, even though you never really loved yourself. Nothing can keep this relationship alive anymore. My trust in you is broken. This marriage is over. I'm filing for divorce."

"Noah, please—"

"You can have sole ownership of the company I helped you build, but I will no longer invest in it."

"Please don't do this!"

"You can keep your car, and I'll split the money with you once I sell the house."

"No!" cried Vanessa. "I won't let you do this!"

"Let's make this process as painless as possible."

Weeping inconsolably, she paced the living room. "Tell me there's no other woman."

"What?" Noah scowled.

"Tell me you're not rushing for a divorce because of another woman."

"It's not because of another woman," he sighed in frustration.

"I have one last request"—she wiped her tears—"tell me you're not in love with me anymore."

"Why are you making this harder on yourself?"

"I need to hear you say it."

Turning away, he stared out the window again and thought of Aria.

"Just say it, Goddamnit! Tell me the truth!"

After a long pause, Noah opened his eyes and faced his wife. "I'm not in love with you anymore."

A daunting silence fell upon them. Vanessa stepped closer to her husband and searched his lifeless gaze, desperately hoping his confession had been false. But he was telling the truth.

Collecting herself, she stopped sobbing and wiped away the black tears that had smudged her face. "Thank you for your honesty. I'll sign whatever you need after a paternity test is done."

"Fine," Noah replied. "We'll get you in vitro tested. Make an appointment with your obstetrician." He picked up his briefcase and headed for the door, but before he walked out, he looked back at Vanessa and said, "I'm still going through with this divorce. I've got you on camera, and I've got a witness. Don't forget that. If you try to fight me on this, you will lose."

"I don't want to spend my life with a man who doesn't love me anymore, so don't worry, I won't fight you on this."

"Good."

Check and mate.

CHAPTER THIRTY-FIVE
ARIA

Evan dropped by in the evening to visit, which was nice because I had missed him. However, I hadn't seen Noah all day, and I had the faintest feeling he was avoiding me. Maybe the fact that my stepmom was pregnant had changed everything between us. It sucked my optimism right out of me. My misery was all-consuming as I pretended to pay attention to what my mother was saying.

"… I'll be back in the morning," she said to Evan. "Are you sure you have no plans tonight?"

"I'm sure," he replied. "Get some rest, Natalie."

"You guys don't have to do this every day," I said. "I'm fine now."

"We're your family, Aria." Mom smiled. "And families stick together during a crisis—no matter how dysfunctional they may be. I'll be back in the morning."

After my mom left, Evan held my hand and asked, "How do you feel today?"

"Okay, I guess. I just want to get out of this hospital more than anything."

"Patience, love."

"That's not exactly my best virtue."

"I can relate." He chuckled.

"I'm tired of lying down and getting poked with needles every day—and I hate these horrible hospital gowns!"

"It'll all be over soon, Aria. Stay positive." He paused briefly and frowned. "You don't know what I went through while you were in a coma."

He was right; I didn't know. We never talked about it.

"I feel responsible," Evan said. "It's my fault. I never should have let either of you leave—not while Noah was so upset."

"Evan, please don't blame yourself. We got hit by a car. No one could have predicted the accident."

"I'm just glad you're conscious again. I hope you don't feel like this organ transplant will cripple you in any sort of way."

"I don't know," I sighed. "I feel like my life is ticking on the clock."

"You're gonna get a healthy kidney. I promise."

His effort to cheer me up was working. I spent the next ten minutes gobbling down some freshly baked Cannoli that Evan had brought me; they were bite size, and that delicious cream filling was to die for.

"I'm sure you're sick of all this hospital food."

"You have no idea," I said, chewing with my mouth full.

He took another piece from the pastry box and fed me as I slowly took a bite and savored the delicious taste of ricotta cheese, whipped cream, and semisweet chocolate chips.

"Does she approve?"

"She *definitely* does… *mmmm*… How did you know this is one of my favorite Sicilian desserts?"

"I didn't." Evan smiled and fed me another pastry. His dark eyes were seductive, but I guess that was the effect he had on people.

"Aren't you gonna have some?" I asked.

"I bought these for you. I don't have a sweet tooth, anyway. I'm strict about what I put in my body."

"Are you training for *Ironman* or something?" I laughed, feeling bashful.

"No, just keeping fit."

"I'm so jealous. At least you can move around and stay active. I'm not doing so well with this whole bed-rest thing." I loosened my scrunchy and shook out my hair. "It's just me, myself, and my mattress, day in and day out... *Wow!* That sounds like a horrible sitcom. How depressing is that?"

Evan chuckled.

"Sorry," I said. "Wallowing in self-pity at the moment."

"Finish your cannoli and stop drowning in misery. You're not allowed to—not on my watch, at least. I'm not here to throw you a pity party"— he leaned forward—"so suck it up, Aria. You're a Hunter, remember?"

"And what are we Hunters like, exactly?"

"Well... we can be incredibly stubborn, selfish, bossy, and a downright dick."

I laughed. "Okay, please tell me you weren't subliminally describing Noah."

"That obvious?"

"A little."

"He hasn't exactly been the best brother of the year."

"I'm sorry."

"Why should you be sorry?"

"I don't know. I've complicated your life more since you met me."

It wasn't just his life I had complicated, but the lives of many. I hated feeling as if I was a burden to anyone.

"You're the only person in our family who doesn't judge me," Evan said. "I know we've just got to know each other, but I care about you a great deal, Aria."

"You're sweet."

"No, just being honest."

We both smiled at one another as he reached into his pocket and said, "Before I forget, I have one more thing I need to give you." Evan pulled out a long red box.

"A present?" I said, looking surprised. "What's the occasion?"

"Consider it a grad gift."

"But I haven't graduated yet. I still have final exams to write before I get my diploma."

"You'll ace those exams with flying colors," Evan said, opening the box. "That's white gold," he added. "And that crystal is special; it has healing energies, which is why I thought I'd give it to you now while you're still in here."

"It's beautiful!"

The necklace was a pear-shaped crystal pendant, clasped to a silver chain. It was stunning—like nothing I had ever seen before.

"My mate's girlfriend runs her own custom-made jewelry shop. I swung by last week and had this made for you."

"I love it!" I pulled my hair up so he could fasten the pendant around my neck.

"It looks perfect on you."

Kissing his cheek, I gave him a big hug and breathed him in. But as soon as I pulled back, my heart dropped when I heard Noah's voice.

"Where's Natalie?"

We turned our heads in his direction.

"She left not too long ago," I answered.

Noah was dressed casually, which meant he must have gone home and changed after work. He stepped inside the room, keeping his hostile glare on his brother as he asked him what he was doing here.

"My niece is in the hospital," Evan replied. "Why wouldn't I be here?"

"Well," Noah said. "You can leave now."

Here we go again.

I had so much I wanted to say, but held my tongue. I had to hide all my heavy artillery and open fire once Evan was gone. Honestly, I was afraid of that moment. Having Evan around was best for damage control. Both brothers continued to argue as if I were invisible.

"Will you lighten up?"

"No!" Noah scowled. "I will not *lighten up*. She's *my* daughter, and you're clearly a bad influence."

"You afraid I might blaze up and pass her a joint while she's bound to this bloody hospital bed?"

"I wouldn't be surprised if you had drugs in your pockets right now."

Their constant bickering had no end.

"Says the former cokehead."

That was a low blow. Worried that Noah would snap, he seemed calm when I tried to read his reaction. It was scary.

"Get out," he demanded, never blinking.

"I think you should ask Aria what she wants." Evan defensively folded his arms in his chest.

"Guys," I weakly spoke. "Please stop arguing. I want you both to be here."

Noah gave me his usual stare down that made my insides twist like Twizzlers. But I was determined to win and refused to look away until he yielded to my will.

"Fine." He surrendered. "He stays." Dragging a chair next to me, Noah sat down and ignored Evan.

The energy in the room was still horribly tense. There I was, lying between two men I loved; brothers bonded through pain and broken by unspoken grudges. I looked at each handsome face and observed the way they glowered at one another. Caesar and Antony, oddly, came to mind.

"How are you feeling?" Noah asked.

"I'm all right."

"That's a pretty necklace." He reached out, holding the crystal pendant. "Did your mom give that to you?"

"No." I smiled. "Evan did."

"How sweet of him." He sounded more sarcastic than sincere. Clearly, Noah was struggling to play nice.

Evan took the chance to ask him about the pregnancy rumor.

"I heard you and the Missus are having a baby on the way. Congrats!"

"Who told you?"

"Natalie."

The reality of him having a baby with this woman was heart wrenching to hear. I felt like Vanessa had stolen him from me for good. I was about to say something to Evan when his cellphone chimed.

Checking his phone, he told me he had to go because "something came up."

"Another convenient booty call?" Noah said in a patronizing tone.

Evan dismissed the comment and kissed my cheek before saying he would visit me tomorrow.

After he left, Noah got up and shut the door.

"Good riddance." He sighed, returning to his seat. "I know you're upset."

Really? I thought in annoyance, staring out the window.

"Aria, look at me."

"No."

"Please."

"If I could get out of this stupid hospital bed, I would!"

"I know, but I'm glad I have the advantage at the moment. Look at me, please."

"You should get home to your pregnant wife." I avoided his eyes. He would not pull me into his ocean. I refused to let that happen.

"I doubt the baby is mine."

Whoa… pause.

"You were right all along."

I finally met his gaze.

"I'm so sorry for not believing you. I can't express how stupid I feel."

"Wait," I said in confusion. "What are you talking about?"

"You were right… about the affair. She's been sleeping with my best friend for two years. I feel like such a fool."

It seemed like a miracle that he finally accepted the truth.

"How did you find out?"

Noah recapped the whole scenario for me.

"I'm filing for divorce first thing in the morning—and that includes getting a paternity test done."

"They can do that while a woman's pregnant?"

"Yes. As long as she's over eight weeks into her pregnancy—and that's almost where she's at right now."

"What if you're the father?"

"Then you'll have a baby brother or sister, and I will love and provide for my child. But I'm still going through with the divorce. My marriage cannot be repaired at this point. So many things have complicated my relationship with Vanessa. Reconciliation is impossible."

I was afraid to ask my next question, but I did anyway. "Is it because of me?"

"She's been cheating on me for two years, Aria. I could spend a fortune on marriage counseling, but the truth of the matter is…" He paused, staring into my eyes. "I'm not in love with her anymore. Staying in a loveless marriage not only makes me unhappy, but I'm robbing her of happiness too because I'm not able to love her with all my heart. I can't even love her with half of it, at this point."

He doesn't look heartbroken, I thought. *But maybe he's just hiding his hurt.*

Noah was an expert at masking his pain.

"Can I hug you now?" he asked. "I've missed you all day."

"I've missed you, too."

Leaning in, I snaked my arms around his neck and pulled him into a warm embrace. I didn't want to let go, but all good things always come to an end. Sadly.

"I thought I wouldn't see you today," I said.

"You know I can't stay away from you."

He got up and closed the blinds before lying down beside me in bed. This was my favorite part of the day: cuddling with Noah. A soothing heat radiated from his body as I molded myself into him.

"What are you thinking about?" I asked.

"You don't want to know."

"But I do—otherwise I wouldn't have asked."

"True."

"You just don't want to share. You're always such a mystery."

"I think you're the only one who's ever come close to solving me."

Noah touched my hip, sending shivers down my spine. Our physical attraction would never go away. No matter how wrong it was, it was always there and noticeable. The sexual tension was killing me.

"What's on your mind?" he asked.

"Just thinking about you and I."

"What about us?"

"I miss you."

"I'm right here."

"I know. I mean, I miss…" I stared at his attractive mouth, hoping he'd kiss me.

"Aria." He touched my face. "We can't."

My heart sank.

"I promise we'll figure this out," he stated, gliding his fingers through my hair. "Do you trust me?"

"Yes."

Noah kissed my forehead and told me to focus on getting better. But that was impossible when he was lying so close to me. I wanted to caress him and kiss him. I wanted him to be mine.

CHAPTER THIRTY-SIX
THE DEPTH OF MY LOVE

"… A body has been found and identified in Terrance Park this morning…"

"Mom, wait! Don't change the channel!"

"… Eighteen-year-old Stephanie Cohen was brutally murdered last night in cold blood. A local jogger and his dog had been passing by the park on their routine run when the German Shepherd made the grisly discovery… Police detectives could not identify and incarcerate the assailant, and are still investigating the crime scene… A memorial will be held by Stephanie's family at the park tomorrow evening."

"Oh, my God!" Aria gasped. "Oh, my God…"

"Sweetheart, what's wrong?"

"I know her! I *know* her, Mom! She… I can't believe…"

"Oh, honey"—Natalie held her daughter's hand—"I'm so sorry."

"We weren't close. We just went to the same school."

Natalie was about to ask a question when Evan walked in.

"How are my two favorite ladies doing today?" He smiled, handing Natalie a cup of coffee.

"We've heard some very sad news," she said. "One of Aria's high school classmates was murdered last night."

Evan looked at his niece with concern. "Are you okay, love?"

"It was Stephanie."

"As in the same Steph who…"

"Was a complete bitch to me? Yes."

She didn't know how to feel.

"Steph was a mean girl, but she didn't deserve to be murdered," Aria expressed.

"Of course not, darling." Natalie frowned. "I hope they catch the person who did this. What a sicko."

Evan set his coffee on the table and hugged his niece. "I'm here if you need to talk about it, love."

"Thanks. I'm just in shock more than anything," she replied, noticing the gauze wrapped around his forearm. "Did you injure yourself at work?"

Sitting down, Evan glanced at his arm. "Baxter went kind of bonkers this morning. I was trying to get him out of his litter box because he had been crouching in it since last night. He scratched me badly when I picked him up. I figured he was sick, so I took him to the vet before coming here."

"What's wrong with him?" asked Natalie.

"He's got a clean bill of health, so the only conclusion she made was that he's anxious about something. It's probably because I had my friend's dog stay with me the other day. I was looking after him for the night."

"I pray Baxter will be okay," Aria said. "Did you at least disinfect the scratches?"

"It's nothing to worry about." He smiled reassuringly.

"I need to make a phone call." Natalie stood up and took her cellphone out of her purse. "I'll be back soon."

"Take your time. Your daughter's in excellent hands."

"I hate feeling so tired," said Aria.

"Go to sleep, sweetheart."

"But I don't want to sleep."

"You'll feel better when you wake up," he encouraged, stroking her hand until she finally closed her eyes.

∞

Almost fifteen minutes had passed when Natalie returned and asked Evan if he could stay with her daughter for an hour, which he was more than happy to do. She needed to have a private conversation with her husband.

The television was distracting, even though it was set on a low volume. Flipping through channels, Evan noticed that most of the news networks were covering the murder case of Stephanie Cohen. He switched it off and stared at his niece while she slept. His brown eyes cascaded from her face to her neck as he fixed his gaze on the necklace he gave her. He liked that she was wearing it. His blood was inside of that pendant, and Aria did not know.

Smiling darkly to himself, Evan leaned into her ear and whispered, "I will kill anyone who hurts you, because I love you, and I know you love me, too. You don't know it yet… but you will… soon."

Pulling back, he stared at her sensuous mouth. Temptation got the best of him as he edged closer and grazed his lips against hers, leaving the softest kiss. Being affectionate was foreign to him; normally, he'd kiss other women roughly. However, he enjoyed that moment of stolen intimacy and tried to control himself before he kissed her again.

Slipping his hand into Aria's, he softly whispered, "I am so in love with you. If you only knew to what depth…"

His sleeping goddess stirred as she mumbled, "*Mmm*… I love you… Noah."

CHAPTER THIRTY-SEVEN
ORIGINS

George and Olivia Hunter were a successful power couple. Living in New Castle, New Hampshire, they lived in a beautiful mansion on a large, gated property. From the beginning of their marriage, their life had been lavish and comfortable, but unlike Olivia, George had not been born into money. Being an only child, with no living relatives, he was the last living Hunter to extend the generation. George had gained his wealth through a dedicated work ethic, starting from the bottom and building his way to the top. By the time he was twenty-four, he had made many investments that had made him a vast amount of wealth. George Hunter was an ambitious, self-made multi-millionaire who had attained the American dream.

Olivia Blackwood had a privileged upbringing, being raised in an upper-class family. Her father was American and her mother was of British descent. Ever since she was six years old, Olivia dreamed of becoming a ballet dancer. She had trained vigorously through her adolescent years, hoping to join the Imperial School of Ballet in St. Petersburg. She wanted to travel the world and dance for a living, and that hadn't changed when she fell in love with George and married him at nineteen. There was a six-year age difference between the pair. Even though Olivia had married young, her parents had approved of the union, knowing she would be taken care of. George had promised to support Olivia's endeavors before she had agreed to marry him, but her ballerina dreams were only to be abandoned after she injured her ankle and was told she would never dance again.

Devastated by the news, Olivia focused her efforts on starting a family. She got pregnant with their first child before she miscarried and got pregnant again… miscarrying once more. The poor woman had four miscarriages before Isaac, Breanne, and Noah were born. George had wanted to fill his home with children, but Olivia was satisfied with three. What he hadn't expected was Olivia's postpartum depression. She was diagnosed after Noah was born.

As the children grew, Olivia occupied her time with interior design, organizing parties and charity events. Her mother had never nurtured her with love, so that same style of parenting continued with her own children. She felt emotionally distant from them. Despite her husband's efforts to help, Olivia could never bond with her children. She often felt guilty for not being emotionally involved during their primary stages of life. Isaac, Breanne, and Noah were raised by nannies, and Olivia's first two children were sent to boarding school by the time they were twelve. Her guilt had caused her to consider adoption and start her road to redemption. But more than anything, Olivia feared she would slip back into depression if she adopted an infant. She preferred to adopt a toddler: a child that had already passed the diaper changing, bottle feeding, and incessant crying stage. Gender was not of importance. All she wanted was to connect with a child and offer them a better life.

After weeks of deliberation over the subject, her husband had finally agreed and supported her decision. It was on May 22nd, 1991, when the married couple drove two hours away from their home to an orphanage in Massachusetts. That day, they met the orphaned children who seemed happy and healthy. Out of all the youngsters, Olivia had noticed one little boy who was extremely withdrawn and not as sociable as the other kids; he reminded her of herself when she was a child. She often felt socially awkward around others, like an outcast in society. Olivia spent some time with the boy in the playroom and instantly fell in love. He was smart for his age. The little boy's name was Matthias Andrews. The six-year-old had thick brown hair that resembled Noah's hair color. His big brown eyes were alluring but haunted by pain and trauma.

The Hunters had learned about his past and the tragedy that had happened to his mother on Christmas Eve two years prior. Child protective services had put him into a foster home, but it was later discovered that his foster parents were neglecting and physically abusing him. They had starved Matthias for days as punishment for misbehaving. His foster mother had often pressed a scorching hot spoon on the soles of his feet for his temper tantrums and bed-wetting. The doctor that treated Matthias's wounds at the hospital contacted the police. His foster parents had lied about the cause of his injury, which led the doctor to put two and two together. The man and woman were immediately incarcerated, and Matthias was treated for third-degree burns before his arrival at Sunny Hill Orphanage in Hampden County, Massachusetts.

George and Olivia felt bad for him. The orphanage director had informed them he did not like to be touched by anyone; it triggered fear and anxiety within the child and made him cry or become violent if physical contact was forced upon him. He missed his mother's touch, and she was gone.

Olivia understood his trauma. For the longest while, she did not desire any sort of physical affection, either. Despite this information, the strangest thing happened that day as the Hunters stood in the hall. Matthias walked up to Olivia, stared into her blue eyes, and hugged her like it was the last time he would ever hug another human being again. Olivia felt as if the little boy was embracing her with his soul as she got emotional.

Crouching to his level, she held him in her arms and felt an activation of maternal energy within her: a deep connection that she had never felt with her own biological children. She could not understand it but was convinced that God had put Matthias in her path for a reason.

After completing the paperwork in the oncoming weeks, they officially adopted Matthias into the Hunter family. Olivia had legally changed his name to Evan Michael Hunter—for his own protection. The man who had murdered his biological mother had still been at large.

Noah was excited to have a baby brother. He and Evan got along well for the first couple of months until Evan showed behavioral problems. On his sixth birthday, they gave him a pet cockatoo. A week hadn't even gone by, and he ended up killing the bird by squeezing its throat until it choked to death. Olivia had believed it was an accident, thinking her son didn't know his own strength... But Noah had witnessed his brother killing the bird. Evan had gone right up to the cage, took out the cockatoo, and killed it, right before he looked at his brother and said, "Look, Noah! I made him go to sleep!"

Their family pet Bosley was a big St. Bernard who had always been a friendly dog, but was old and sickly. When Evan turned nine, the dog went missing. Breanne had put up posters all over the neighborhood, offering a generous reward if someone returned the dog to the family. But no phone calls came. Six months later, George hired some contractors to landscape the yard, and they ended up finding Bosley. He was dead... buried in a black garbage bag.

The family could not understand how this had happened—and when Noah had accused Evan of doing it, they questioned their son, to which he denied all accusations. Olivia could not believe that a child could physically kill a dog that size and shovel a hole in the yard to bury the carcass.

Ever since that incident, George had felt it was in Evan's best interest to place him in long-term therapy. He was constantly concerned that his son's dark past had psychologically affected him. They didn't know that Evan had found the dog struggling to breathe as he lay dying beneath a tree. He wanted to end his suffering... so he shot him with his father's pistol in the woods. The child was intelligent enough to cover his tracks.

After this tragedy, the therapy sessions were successful, and Evan stopped his violent behavior toward animals, but that didn't stop him from being aggressive with other family members.

Noah's cousin, Felix, was the same age as Evan. He used to come over to play when they were children, but Evan never liked him because the boy would always bully him when no one was looking. Most of Noah's maternal cousins were mean to his brother and teased him for being adopted. One day, while Felix was playing in the playroom, Evan lit a match and set the curtains on fire before he rushed out and locked his cousin inside. He was twelve years old. Luckily, Noah had been home and kicked down the door to rescue their traumatized cousin. *This* was the part that Evan had left out when he had told Aria about his "fascination with fire."

When George and Olivia confronted their son about the upsetting incident, he had told them he was only playing with matches and the curtains had caught fire by accident. To reinforce his innocence, he said that he had left Felix to get help, unaware that his cousin had been locked inside. Unfortunately, many "accidents" had occurred within the Hunter mansion, and Evan was responsible for most of them. No matter what he did, Olivia loved him through it and always felt the need to defend her son. Evan settled down eventually, but by that time, Noah was getting ready to move out and start college. There was a six-year age gap between them.

The neighbors that lived next door to the family had been a married couple with no children. The husband was a lawyer who had remarried, and his wife resembled a platinum haired Playboy Bunny. She was also twenty years younger than her spouse. At sixteen, Evan lost his virginity to this woman, as they engaged in a scandalous, secret affair for two years. Lola Rutherford had given him his sex education. She had trained him to be the perfect lover by introducing him to the world of BDSM. She taught Evan how to be a dominant master, since he showed signs of aggression during sex. Lola's intention was to help Evan tame that monster within, so that he wouldn't be a danger to others, nor to himself. Through Lola's training, he could master discipline and control his aggression, which made sex more pleasurable. What Lola didn't know was that she was only feeding a demon that had grown stronger inside of Evan.

When her husband discovered the affair, he went straight to George Hunter's home, demanded to speak to his son, and punched Evan in the face. In the weeks to follow, the man put his house on the market and moved out of the neighborhood with his unfaithful wife. Evan never saw Lola again, but he was far from heartbroken. In fact, he was indifferent about his ex's sudden departure. Being young and good looking meant he had plenty of options to date attractive women.

By eighteen, Evan started college, but dropped out in his second year because he could not cope with his father's death. He blamed himself for the tragic accident.

After realizing that college was not for him, Olivia encouraged her son to travel, hoping that he would find peace. Evan left the country and backpacked all over Europe, documenting his travels. What Olivia didn't know was that her favorite son had taken a human life, despite returning in better spirits.

The first woman Evan had murdered was an illegal immigrant living in Italy. Her name was Oksana Volkova; she had met Evan at a bar on Christmas Eve. While they got to know each other, she told him about her modeling dreams, and he promised to help her because he thought she was stunning and didn't belong dancing in a strip club. He brought her to his studio that night and took some photos of her. One thing had led to another, and Oksana found herself in Evan's bedroom. During their torrid love making, Evan got aggressive. The young woman resembled his mother so much and had told him she was a recovering drug addict— heroin addiction. Something had snapped inside of him. He choked her with his bare hands until she was no longer breathing. After realizing what he had done, he panicked. He had not meant to kill her—it was a psychotic break. Calling the authorities was not an option. The only choice Evan felt he had was to dispose of the body. He cleaned up any traces of evidence and took a boat all the way out to the Tyrrhenian Sea in the middle of the night. Forcing Oksana's corpse into a large suitcase, he tied an anchor around it and dumped it in the dark waters below. The following morning, he booked a flight to Spain and fled the country.

Since Oksana's murder, Evan had killed five more women, choosing one victim each year. He performed his ritualistic killing in Europe every Christmas Eve, so that he was less likely to get caught. This pattern never broke until the night he murdered Stephanie Cohen. For weeks, he had been stalking her, planning and waiting for the perfect moment to murder the girl. The kill had been personal, though he hadn't killed her for pleasure; he'd done it for Aria. In his sick, twisted mind, Evan felt it was the greatest act of love: to eliminate all her enemies; people who refused to take accountability for the ways they had hurt his niece. When Aria had told him about what Steph had said to her at the Velvet Lounge, he had immediately placed the girl on his hit list without hesitation.

Stephanie had put up a fight when she had regained consciousness that night. Desperate to escape, she scratched his arm, but couldn't save herself. Evan cleansed her body properly before he buried her in the woods. The police did not know who to investigate, nor did they have any witnesses or evidence. Stephanie's tragic murder would become a cold case. Evan was sure of that. He had no regrets. His passionate love for Aria had driven him beyond obsession. He believed he was the only man who was worthy of her love because he would kill and die for her. If a man was not willing to make this sacrifice, then he didn't know what love was; this was Evan's distorted view on romantic relationships.

CHAPTER THIRTY-EIGHT
NOAH

Two days ago, I discovered I was not the father of Vanessa's baby. Relieved by the news, I was still upset, knowing my wife had been having an affair under my nose for so long. My confrontation with Amir had been far from violent. I told him to fuck himself and ended our friendship without losing my cool. To recap: after I had received the paternity test results, I had gone to work the next day and shook the bastard's hand to congratulate him on fatherhood. Taking the high road, I advised him to head home to rescue his belongings since his wife was most likely destroying everything as we spoke. I'd called her earlier and revealed her husband's transgressions with my wife. Now that I confirmed Amir was the father, I wasn't sure how his marriage would survive.

My goal was to get the bastard fired. There was no way we could work side by side in peaceful coexistence. But when it came down to a vote, the other senior partners had me outnumbered. Ending his employment at the firm meant we would lose a lot of our high paying clients. That SOB was good at his job, and we needed him. Amir was great at being a professional bullshitter. I could have taken notes from him in that department.

Vanessa ended up signing those separation papers, which meant this was going to be a quick and painless divorce. It shocked Natalie when she heard the news. I took her out to lunch one afternoon and had a conversation with her about our daughter and my marriage problems. She sympathized with me. On a positive note, we established a newfound friendship with one another.

To dampen things, a storm cloud had hovered over sunny California, and that "storm cloud" was my mother; she flew in yesterday. Apparently, she wanted to meet her granddaughter and be here during my time of "need." I was strongly against the visit in the first place and had communicated that to her, but Olivia Hunter does what Olivia Hunter likes. Being around my family was not good for me.

The routine hospital visits seemed never ending. All I wanted was to take Aria home. We were huddled inside her hospital room on a Wednesday afternoon, waiting for Patrick to arrive. I desperately prayed I'd be an ideal match. The two week wait felt like forever.

"Dr. Peters," Natalie said. "Finally, you're here!" She stood up from her chair, looking nervous like the rest of us.

"Please tell me you have good news," Rob said, holding her hand.

"I do, indeed. But first, I'd like to have a word with Noah, if you don't mind." Rick turned his line of sight on me and signaled to meet him outside the room.

"Hey," I said, shutting the door behind me. "What's going on? Are there any complications with—"

"No." He shook his head. "Aria's gonna be fine. We have a match."

"Then what's the problem?"

Rick seemed hesitant, which only made me crazier.

"Are you gonna tell me or not? Am I dying of cancer or something?"

"Noah, what I'm about to share with you puts my career in jeopardy. I'm revealing this information because I believe it's the ethical thing to do, despite its accidental results."

"Okay..."

He faltered a bit, and said, "I did a series of blood tests to assess the hematological system, clotting mechanism, and baseline kidney function. We screened for abnormal electrolyte balance and for glucose intolerance, which might occur post-transplant..."

"Look, Rick, you're losing me here. We're good friends, so can you just get to the point and skip the fancy medical lingo?"

Releasing a sigh, he glanced at Aria's hospital room and faced me. "Noah... Aria is not your biological daughter."

I stood there, motionless, while his words repeated in my head. Was I dreaming? Was I hallucinating? I wasn't doing drugs again, so I couldn't have been experiencing a psychotic hallucination.

"Noah, listen to me—there's more."

"Huh?" I snapped out of it. "Oh. Sure."

"I know this is a lot to take in, but I have to explain how this happened."

Staying focused, I pulled myself out of shock.

"The phlebotomist who had drawn your blood accidentally discovered Aria's paternity. To break it down in simple science, a child inherits genes from each parent that determine their blood type. This makes blood typing convenient in paternity testing. When our phlebotomist noticed inconsistencies between your blood and Aria's, they took it a step further and compared the blood types between you, Natalie, Aria, and Robert, and... we discovered that Robert is Aria's biological father. I'm not sure what you want to do with this knowledge, but you have a right to know."

What... how?

I stared at him with a blank expression.

"Will you please say something? I'm concerned."

"Excuse me for a moment."

"Where are you going?"

"To get some air. I'll be right back."

Rick caught up to me and said, "What should I tell the family?"

"The truth." I stepped into an elevator.

The doors closed shut, cutting off our communication.

⊂⊃

Standing on the roof of the hospital, I stood over the edge in the open air, staring death in the face. No, I was not suicidal. I had no reason to be.

Being an adrenaline junkie, I had long retired from my extreme forms of "fun" after marriage. It felt good to feel that rush again. I was overwhelmed, and I needed adrenaline to override my racing emotions. I had this burst of energy transforming inside of me, and I didn't know what to do with it. My hand trembled as I took one last puff of my cigarette before I stomped it out.

The sun was rising on the horizon; a new day to start over; a new beginning for me and Aria. Looking out at the city, I gazed up at the sky. Rick hadn't given me bad news. He had given me a miracle. On second thought, he was only the messenger. Maybe God was the one who had performed the miracle. She wasn't my biological daughter. I almost wanted to have another paternity test done, just to be sure of that fact— but surely that was my paranoia talking.

All this time, I had carried so much guilt inside, thinking I was never there for my child. Natalie had lied. Either she lied or she didn't know. I realized I hadn't been the only person she had slept with throughout our relationship.

Did she know Rob was the father? Did she stay quiet about it because of the money my mother had offered?

So many questions were in my head. I had trouble connecting the dots, but I didn't care. The past didn't matter anymore. Twisted as it was, I wanted to thank Natalie for cheating on me because this meant I could finally love Aria without a guilty conscience. Our attraction wasn't wrong anymore, and it seemed impossible to believe how this sudden turn of events would change our lives forever. I was happy.

If God had had a hand in this, then he had made me a devout believer. If not, then I guess it was destiny. Whatever powers that existed in the universe were finally on my side. All this suffering had not been for nothing, because it led me to her.

CHAPTER THIRTY-NINE
NOAH

I was speechless when I walked into Aria's hospital room. Evan was holding her hand, and Mom and Natalie were quietly sitting while Rob paced the floor. Rick wasn't there, and judging by their silence, no one knew the truth yet.

"What did Dr. Peters say to you?" asked Nat.

What could I tell her? I didn't know how to break the news. I was relieved when Rick appeared next to me.

"Sorry about the wait, everyone," he announced. "I was paged and had to check on a patient."

My mother regarded him with her resting bitch face stare.

"Frankly," she began, "I'm not impressed with your hospital or your staff." Her stony gaze found mine. "Please tell me you're not donating any money to this place, Noah."

"I assure you, Mrs. Hunter," Rick said, "this hospital is California's best."

"Mom, quit harassing Dr. Peters and let him speak." I glared at her.

Holding a clipboard, Rick cleared his throat. "First off, I'd like to inform you all about the good news... We have a match—two, in fact."

"Oh, my goodness!" Natalie's face lit up. "That's wonderful!"

"Based on the blood work and other evaluations, we could determine that Mr. Mitchell would not be an ideal candidate because his kidneys are not in the best condition." Rick looked at him and added, "I would advise you to follow up on this with your family doctor or a specialist."

"It's all right, honey." Nat touched Rob's shoulder. "We knew the chances were already slim with you."

That's what years' worth of alcoholism will do to kidney function: it destroys it.

"Fortunately, Mrs. Mitchell, through cross matching results, we found you are a qualified candidate for kidney donation."

"Oh, I'm so happy!" She stood up and hugged Aria with tears in her eyes. "See, sweetheart? You're gonna be just fine!"

"However," Rick continued. "We have an ideal match that showed better post transplantation success compared to Mrs. Mitchell's results."

Everyone stayed quiet and waited for the doctor to elaborate.

"If you recall, I had mentioned that donors who have no biological ties to a patient still are a match—it would be very slim, but possible."

"One in a hundred thousand," Evan said.

"Yes," Rick replied. "With that said, the blood results revealed Evan has all six antigens. His body tissue is closer matched to Aria's than her mother's."

"What?" I nearly shouted in disbelief, glancing at my brother. He was grinning, overjoyed by the news.i don't want to see

"The success rate following transplantation depends on the closeness of the tissue match between donor and recipient," Rick informed us. "For example, a kidney from a brother or a sister with a complete match has a 95 percent chance of working at the end of one year. A kidney from a parent, child, or half matched sibling has an 85 percent chance of functioning correctly. And last, a cadaver donor kidney has an 80 percent chance of proper kidney function within a year. But I must admit, these miraculous results have left my medical team baffled and amazed at the same time."

"What about my son, Noah?" Mom asked. "He's Aria's father. How come he was not an ideal match?"

"I was just about to get to that, Mrs. Hunter."

Things were going to get uncomfortable, *fast*. Rick met my gaze in confusion, uncertain whether to reveal the truth.

"Actually," I said. "The reason the good ol' doc here had wanted to speak with me is because…"

Here it was, the big reveal. Life as I knew it would change forever. Everybody's life was about to change.

"According to the blood tests…"

All eyes were on me now, making me more uncomfortable. I felt anxious and wasn't sure how to get straight to the point—other than, well… *getting straight to the point.*

"I'm not Aria's biological father."

I had finally said it. If the truth was supposed to set you free, then how come I felt like the walls were closing in on me? I needed someone to guide me through my emotional traffic.

"I knew it!" Mother snapped, standing up. "I knew you were never the biological father! You should have demanded a paternity test from this lying harlot ages ago! She was nothing but a penniless tramp then, and she still is!"

"Stop it!" I yelled. "Control yourself!"

There was no need for her to rage at Natalie in front of Aria. I was not her biological parent, but Natalie was.

"Mom, get out," I demanded.

"No, I will not leave! It's about time this sneaky little heretic hears what I have to say! She swindled our family and lied for money!"

"That is not true!" Natalie protested. "You offered me that check to stay away from Noah!"

"Shut your mouth, you filthy whore!"

"Hey! Calm down, Mother, or I'll have security remove you from this room right now," I angrily asserted.

She muttered to herself and sat down as Rick cut in to speak.

"These paternity results were stumbled upon by accident. I felt it was wrong to turn the other cheek after reviewing these findings. In addition, I would like to say that we discovered who Aria's biological father is."

"Rob," Nat uttered, sinking into her chair as she stared into space.

"Yes, Mrs. Mitchell," Rick said. "Robert is Aria's biological father."

"Are you kidding me right now?"

Rob seemed just as perplexed as I was. Finally, we had something in common.

"What more do you expect from a two-timing tramp?" Mom said hatefully. "You should be ashamed of yourself for making my son suffer all these years for nothing! His drug addiction was *your* fault! You almost ruined him!"

"All right, Mother, you've said enough." Grabbing her arm, I was about to force her out when Evan intervened.

"I got this," he reassured me and told her it was time to go.

"Justice has been served today!" Mom gloated.

There was nothing short of me losing my temper, but my brother finally got her out of the hospital room.

Natalie had stayed quiet throughout the humiliating confrontation. I guess she knew if she said anything, it would have fueled my mother's hatred even more.

I apologized to Rick and asked him to explain the DNA results now that the room was calm. My eyes wandered over to Aria; she looked as if she had zoned out of the conversation. If only I could open that secret vault in her mind: the place where she stored all her private thoughts about me. She wouldn't look at me, and I wasn't a mind reader.

When Rick finished his medical discussion, I thanked him and told him he did the right thing by revealing the paternity results. The awkwardness of my family drama was not something I wanted him to witness.

"I'll give you a moment to yourselves," he politely said. "Is your brother coming back?"

"I think so."

"Excellent. I'll return with the paperwork for the organ donation."

I still couldn't believe it; the chances were so slim. Maybe this was part of "God's plan." I couldn't gamble with Aria's life, but I trusted Rick's expertise. If he said that my brother was the best match, then I just had to deal with it.

After he left, I looked at my ex and said, "Could you do me a favor and backtrack eighteen years? I'd like to know how this 'mix up' happened."

CHAPTER FORTY
THE ONE NIGHT STAND

New Hampshire
1994

August heat in New England was unbearable, but for sixteen-year-old Natalie Miller, she had the luxury of having an air-conditioned home. Her friend Candice was visiting her that evening, painting her nails, when the telephone on her nightstand started ringing.

"Oh, my gosh!" Natalie got up. "That's probably him!" Turning down the radio, she dove for the phone over her bed and tried to control her excitement. "Hello?"

Candice rolled her eyes when she heard Noah's voice on the other end. Knowing that Natalie would talk his ear off, she busied herself by rummaging through her closet for outfits. They had been best friends since first grade.

"So," said Nat. "You're canceling our date tonight?"

The green-eyed, red head whipped her head around and shot Natalie an irritated glare. Candice had never been a fan of Noah, and this wasn't the first time he had canceled on her best friend.

"I just thought… No, I understand, but… Can't you tell your mother to back off? Why is she always filling your schedule with stupid errands every time you've got plans with me? This isn't fair, Noah!"

Candice noticed the crack in Natalie's voice and sat next to her when she noticed her crying. "Nat, break it off! He keeps doing this to you! It's ridiculous!"

"I… I'm not happy, Noah." Natalie wept. "I'm tired of you putting me on the back burner." She steeled herself and let him speak before she said, "It's a Saturday night, and I'm supposed to be out with my boyfriend, but he's canceled on me for the hundredth time… Yes, you heard me… Yeah? Well, maybe I don't wanna be your girlfriend anymore!"

Candice gently placed her hand on Natalie's shoulder and encouraged her to tell him off.

"What's the point in seeing each other, if we don't even *see* each other?" Natalie argued. "… Fine! It's over! We're over! Thank your precious mother for that!" She slammed the phone down and cried.

"You did the right thing," Candice said. "Noah's just a rich asshole on Mommy's leash."

"He called me selfish for not understanding his situation. I've been nothing but understanding throughout this relationship! His mother hates me! She insults me right to my face, and he hardly ever takes my side!"

"All the more reason to move on from the jerk."

"This is so not how I imagined spending my weekend."

"It's still not over. Come on, we need to get you all dolled up so we can go to that house party. You don't need a boyfriend to have fun. Let's celebrate your first night of freedom from Noah and that psycho mother of his. I don't want to see you lock yourself up in this room and cry over a guy who's totally not worth your tears."

But Natalie couldn't help it; she broke down. "I hate loving Noah— it hurts. I wish I never met him!"

"Stop crying, Natty. I doubt he's this upset over you. If he really loved you, he would have called right back. I don't hear your phone ringing."

The troubled blonde sniffled and dried her eyes. "You're right—screw him."

"That's the spirit!" Candice grinned and stood up. "Now, let's get dressed and go to Vicky's party. I'm sure we'll meet lots of hot guys who are way better than Noah. How does that sound?"

It took a while for Natalie to answer, but she finally said, "Let's do it."

ⅎ⅋

Vicky Hewitt's house was vibrating with music as Candice and Natalie stepped on the porch and rang the doorbell. They were greeted by their host and invited inside. Natalie figured there were at least a hundred people at the party.

"Are your parents out of town?" Candice asked.

"Obviously!" Vicky replied. "Make yourself at home, ladies. There's plenty of booze in the kitchen."

She was a beautiful brunette with brown eyes and part of the popular crowd at their high school.

After an hour of drinking and socializing, Natalie was introduced to a young man who had had his eye on her all evening. He was best friends with Vicky's brother and went to a different high school than Natalie; his name was Robert Mitchell. Natalie seemed to have forgotten about her troubles as she played pool with him and danced the night away.

By 1a.m., she was tipsy drunk and ended up in a bedroom with Robert—alone. Unaware of her vulnerability, she was desperate to forget about Noah, so she let Robert kiss her. Seconds turned to minutes, as Natalie lost herself in the heat of the moment and ended up sleeping with someone she had known for less than six hours.

When the party was finally over, Robert drove Natalie back to her place since she had work the next day. The drive to Natalie's residence wasn't long, and once he turned down her street, he parked in her driveway and asked if he could see her again.

"Sure." Natalie smiled.

"Can I get your number, then?"

"My parents don't like it when my friends call the house. They're strict."

"Oh. Well, how did you come to the party then? Won't you get in trouble?"

"They're out of town tonight."

"Ah."

"Give me your number," she said. "I'll call you, okay?"

He searched for a pen and scribbled down his digits on a piece of paper.

"Can I pick you up and take you out tomorrow when you're done with work?"

"I have to attend a family dinner, so I can't—sorry."

"Oh," Rob said, feeling rejected. "Well, all right. I had an amazing time with you. Call me when you're free."

"I will." She kissed his cheek before she left his car.

The reality of the situation was that she had no intention of contacting him at all. Natalie felt guilty for sleeping with Robert, even though she and Noah had broken up. She felt so regretful and thought she would have been able to move on from Noah much easier if she rebounded. But evidently, she was wrong.

;=

The next morning, a tapping sound ripped Natalie away from her restful sleep. Tired and hungover, she rose from bed and found the source of the noise: someone was throwing pebbles at her window. Drawing back her floral curtains, she let the sunshine bathe her room and got emotional when she noticed a handsome young man standing in her backyard, holding a big sign that read:

I LOVE U NATALIE
I CAN'T LIVE WITHOUT U

The lovesick boy gazed up at her and shouted, "Natalie Rose Miller, please be my girlfriend again!"

John Miller suddenly appeared out the backdoor in his robe and slippers. "Hunter!" he yelled. "What in tarnation are you doing on my property at seven o'clock in the morning?"

"Trying to marry your daughter, sir!"

"You better be joking!"

Natalie appeared behind her father and apologized as she slipped past him. Her long blonde hair had fallen around her shoulders in a charming mess. While she had no makeup on, she still looked beautiful. Running barefoot across the lawn, she ran straight into Noah's arms.

"I love you!" she confessed in tears. "I'm so sorry about yesterday. It was stupid of me to break things off."

"No, *I* was the stupid one." He gripped her tightly. "I don't want to lose you, Natty. I love you too much. Forgive me?"

"Of course, I do." She kissed him and ignored her guilt.

In her heart of hearts, Natalie knew she was the one in dire need of his forgiveness, but she was afraid to tell Noah the truth, because the truth would hurt. If he had found out about her one-night stand, he would have left her for good, or so she thought. Natalie loved him too much to lose him over a regrettable mistake; one she would never repeat, she told herself.

"I better go," Noah said. "I don't want to piss off your dad any more than I already have."

"Call me later."

"You can count on it." He caressed her cheek.

Stealing one last kiss, she hurried back inside, feeling elated.

Erase the past twenty-four hours. It never happened, Natalie told herself, hammering the final nail on her coffin of shame. She was unaware of how badly this karma would affect her life down the road.

CHAPTER FORTY-ONE
NOAH

I'd had enough of listening to all the sordid details about how Natalie had wound up in bed with Rob during the time we had dated. The truth was out now, but it didn't matter. We couldn't turn back the clock, nor did I want to.

"Please believe me, Noah," Nat pleaded. "I never considered that Robert could have been Aria's father. We had hooked up only once—and I was drunk when that had happened… You showed up at my house the next morning, and I just couldn't tell you. I was too ashamed. I didn't want to lose you."

Aria's silence bothered me. But that didn't last.

"How could you cheat on him?"

Natalie hung her head and wiped her tears. "Sweetheart, I am so sorry."

"How could you claim to have loved him when you hooked up with some other guy hours after a breakup?"

"Aria." I reached for her hand, hoping to calm her down.

"Don't touch my daughter!" Rob warned me.

"Oh, so *now* you want to act as if you actually care about her? Please," I scoffed. "You're just mad you were Natalie's second choice. She settled when she married you. She was never in love with you."

"Shut your mouth, you sly bastard!" Rob shouted. "This is a family affair now and *you* are *not* family, so leave!"

I was prepared to retaliate when Aria came to my defense.

"If you think I'm gonna start calling you 'Dad' and respecting you, you've got another thing coming. I hate you, Rob! Noah's been more of a father to me than you ever were! Being related to you sickens me! Thank God I won't be receiving your kidney; it's tainted and toxic, just like you! All you ever did was abuse me—and for what? Because I wasn't your biological child? *The irony.*" She laughed, wiping her tears.

"Maybe we should handle this elsewhere," I said to Nat. "She doesn't need to hear all this crap."

"I've got a better idea," Rob said. "How about you leave?"

"Listen, jerk. From the moment Aria was conceived, I believed I was her father because Natalie had never mentioned sleeping with you. For seventeen years, I carried a heavy burden with me and felt horrible about not being there for her. I don't have to explain myself to you, nor am I looking for pity. I attained custody of Aria in court fair and square. She's been living under *my* roof for nearly a year, and I've been there for her more than you've ever been. The sad part is you had the chance to raise her; you could have been an amazing father, and you wasted the opportunity."

He finally had nothing to say, so I continued.

"I feel sad for Aria. You watched her grow up. You could have been there for her, but you treated her as if she was worthless to you. Why? All because she wasn't your 'actual daughter?' Is that how you're supposed to treat a child? If they're not related to you, they don't deserve your love? Or is there another reason? What are you hiding, huh? What's your biggest shame?"

"You don't know what you're talking about."

"Why unleash all your rage on a child? You're a cowardly man, Rob. I hope you know that. You abused and neglected Aria. Now that you've found out she's biologically yours, that changes everything? It doesn't wash away the past."

He looked remorseful, but I wasn't finished.

"You don't deserve the privilege of being her father. She doesn't need you now because she has me. She will *always* have me."

"I know I've made mistakes," Rob said. "But I want to—"

"Seventeen years! You might as well have never been there from the start. The difference between you and me—among the long list of the obvious—is that I genuinely care about her, and you don't. You're nothing to her. Do you hear me? Nothing!"

"Stop it!" Nat cried out. "Stop fighting!"

Aria looked at us and said, "I want to legally change my last name. Mom, I don't want to take your maiden name, and I don't want to be a Mitchell, either."

"Sweetheart." Natalie frowned. "I know you're hurt about the paternity results, but I swear I never even considered the possibility that Rob could be your biological father."

"Stop calling him that! He's not my real father! I don't care that we share the same DNA!"

"Robert and I didn't date until after you were born. He had promised to take care of us."

"So that's all I was to you?" Rob said. "A one-night stand?"

"No, I didn't mean it that way."

I gloated, watching that asshole realize he was never her epic love. *I* was.

"I was in love with you!" Rob admitted. "I could have dated anybody! Instead, I married you and took care of you… started a family with you. I stepped up to the plate, even though that son of a gun had denied what he believed—what we *all* believed was his own flesh and blood!"

"I was sixteen, Robert!" Nat cried out. "Did you honestly believe I'd fall in love with you overnight? You took advantage of me while I was drunk!"

"I did not! Nobody forced all that booze down your throat! Take accountability for yourself!"

"I was a confused teenager who had broken up with her boyfriend and was trying to get over him!"

"You never called me back until you were about to pop out the kid! *Golden boy* over there didn't want you, so you used me!"

"That's not how it went down, and you know it!" she countered. "Robert, I've always been grateful you were there for me when my life was a mess. I never lied to you. I didn't know that Aria was yours. No one forced you to be with me! Why don't *you* own up to your shitty decisions for once?"

This was turning into a bad episode of *Family Court.*

"I'm so mad, Natalie! I can't even think!" Rob rubbed his temples, wandering toward the window.

"Why don't you stop being a selfish asshole for a couple minutes and be happy she's your biological daughter instead of dwelling on ancient history?"

"Why are you still here?" He erupted in anger. "You've said enough! Leave!"

"No!" shouted Aria. "*I* decide who stays or goes. I want *you* to leave!" she said to him.

"Robert, let's just take a time out," Nat suggested. "We'll get something to eat and talk this over like civilized adults."

Finally, she said something sensible.

"Or better yet…" Aria said. "Leave and never come back!"

Nat paused at the door and looked at me. I knew I had to speak to her one on one, eventually. But right now, I just wanted to have a moment alone with angel eyes.

CHAPTER FORTY-TWO
ARIA

I was in shock, feeling so many things at once, and the whole turn of events was mega strange, as if I had woken up from my coma, only to realize the reality I knew was nothing but a dream. And now I was on a completely different dimension of normal: *Twilight Zone* normal… if you could even call it that? I almost expected Morpheus to show up with his long black trench coat and killer shades, holding out his palms with this serious look on his face, saying, "The red pill, or the blue pill?"

Okay… I was obsessed with *The Matrix*. I didn't need to take a red pill to stay in wonderland. I wasn't Alice, and this wasn't a sci-fi flick I was sucked into. Regardless, I would have followed Noah through any "rabbit hole," no matter how deep or scary it was. It could have been a bottomless pit for all I cared. As long as I was falling with him, that's all that mattered.

"I hope those are happy tears," Noah said. His voice sounded so warm, contrasting the way he'd sounded earlier.

"They're *what-the-fuck*-tears." I laughed uneasily.

"Don't cry." He reached for my hand.

"I just can't believe that man is my biological father. I'm nothing like him!"

"I know you're not."

"I don't even look like him!"

"Thank God for that."

He made me smile and laugh, all amidst my pathetic moment of self-pity. The fact that I was genetically related to Rob made me want to vomit.

"I wish I was a test tube baby with a question mark sperm donor."

"I know how much you hate him," Noah said.

"Hate doesn't even come close to describing the ways I despise that man. I can't believe my mother hid this from you… from me."

I felt so angry knowing my mother had cheated on Noah. I didn't care if they had broken up for a day or not. Maybe I was a fool for believing that humans could be loyal to one another.

"I can't believe she had cheated on you with *him*."

"It doesn't matter anymore, beautiful." Noah squeezed my hand. "It's in the past."

"How do you feel about all this?"

"Relieved."

"Was I that bad of a daughter to you?"

"Oh, yes. You certainly were, young lady," Noah teased in a playful tone of voice. "I felt like the world's most perverted father for almost a year, questioning my morals everyday thanks to you. I'm surprised I didn't kill myself. Maybe I am just that selfish."

My tears flowed as I laughed and found comfort in his presence. He was right. The truth about my paternity was an immense relief—but it also made me sad. What if our bond would never be the same? What if he would leave me? There would be no way to stay connected to him anymore, now that our blood ties were severed. I just wanted to get inside his head and dissect it without actually having to ask him to reveal his detailed thoughts.

"You know that if I could kiss you right now, I would."

I hadn't said it. As usual, Noah was being his typical sexy self: charming to a fault.

"What's holding you back?" I asked.

"Several things."

"Like?"

"Like the fact that I haven't kissed you in what feels like forever. Do you really think I'd be able to pull back so easily? We both know what happens when we… you know. Someone might walk in, and then we're busted."

I knew exactly what would happen when our lips collided. The idea of kissing this man made my heart palpitate. The feeling was always so intense; he left me wanting more. I had contracted the "Noah Hunter Kiss Curse." Any woman who is lucky enough to kiss this man will never be the same. Locking lips with another contender would only result in extreme disenchantment. Kissing Noah was like breathing his soul. It was beyond euphoric and had changed me inside.

Everything seemed to be in perfect alignment for once (where he and I were concerned), but I wasn't happy at all about Rob being my biological father.

"This changes things for us, doesn't it, Noah?"

He nodded, smiling faintly.

"All of this seems so unreal," I expressed. "I can't explain it."

"I know the feeling." He kissed my hand, looking deeply into my eyes.

"Now I know why you don't talk about your mother."

"I'm sorry you had to hear all that earlier."

I was worried. What if our relationship got so serious and he popped the question? I didn't want to have a monster-in-law. I was jumping ahead of myself. It was possible that Noah would never propose to me because of the inevitable loss of interest.

"Do you still love me?" I murmured, hoping I hadn't sounded insecure. But the question itself revealed nothing but insecurity.

Noah studied me, leaning in as he guided my fingers to the side of his neck, underneath his jaw. I felt his pulse racing, pounding against my fingertips.

"Do you feel that?" he said.

"Yes."

"Do you know what that vein is?"

"Um… jugular?"

"The jugular veins bring deoxygenated blood from the head to the heart. That's how deeply you are embedded inside of me."

"I'm a vein in your neck?" I giggled.

"No, you're a *pain* in the neck. But…"—he pressed my hand against his heart—"You possess this part of me."

Melting and blushing, it was a terrible combination; the more I'd blush, the faster it added to the melting process.

"I want to possess all of you," I confessed.

"What makes you think you don't already?"

"Well, we haven't exactly, uh…"

Noah's lips curved up into a devilish smile as he said, "I'm not sure if you're ready for that yet."

"Are you kidding me? I've been ready for the past eight months."

"Answer me one question, Aria. Will you?"

"Of course."

"Why do you love me?"

"It's too long of a list."

"Don't start with: 'because you're hot.'" He chuckled.

"That's only number two on the list." I grinned.

"What's number one?"

"You're sexy."

"Smartass." He laughed.

I didn't want to analyze my love for him, so I changed the subject.

"I feel as though my identity's been stripped away. I'm no longer Aria Hunter. I'm a Mitchell. I'm *Aria frickin' Mitchell.*" I groaned.

"Well"—Evan leaned against the door frame—"you could always legally change your last name."

How much of our convo did he overhear? I wondered.

"I wasn't always a Hunter," he added, walking toward my bed.

"You're not here as an ambassador of our crazy mother, are you?" said Noah.

"I'm here because of the obvious," Evan winked at me as he sat in a chair. "You know Mum's gonna keep calling until you pick up, right?" he said to Noah.

"What do you think voicemail is for?"

"I don't think you can avoid her that easily."

"I want nothing to do with her. And if I were you, Evan, I'd keep that hateful woman out of my life for good."

"We're not that close as you think we are."

Noah shrugged, looking unconvinced.

"Where are Natalie and Robert?" asked Evan.

"Working out their drama somewhere," I answered.

"Well," Noah said. "It looks like you're not her uncle anymore."

"And technically, *you're* not her father anymore."

Here they were, acting childish again. I wasn't sure why there was so much rivalry between them; it frustrated me. In a perfect world, they would get along just fine and maybe even have a bromance? *In a perfect world,* I sighed in my head. But it wasn't a perfect world.

My hospital door suddenly opened, and in walked Mom and *the monster.* She looked like she had been crying.

"I'm sorry to intrude"—her voice cracked—"but could we have a moment alone with our daughter?"

Noah seemed reluctant to leave, but eventually let go of my hand and stood up.

"I'll be back," he said.

Evan kissed my head and followed his brother out.

"How are you feeling?" asked Mom.

"How do you think I feel?"

"Aria," Rob said. "Your mom and I had a long talk earlier. I want to make things right." He sat in an armchair and reached for my hand, but I pulled it away. "Please, just give me a chance. We want to take you home with us once you're well enough to leave the hospital."

"Absolutely not," I stressed. "Nobody's taking me anywhere. I'm staying with Noah."

"He's not your father, sweetheart," Mom said. "He's not even your stepdad."

"So? He's taken better care of me than Rob ever has. I'm not moving back with you guys—and you can't make me."

"Where will you live then?" Mom frowned.

"With Noah."

"You can't live with him," Rob argued. "He's not your family."

"He is to me!"

I had lived with him long enough to form an attachment.

"Darling," Mom started again. "Isn't there a way we can compromise? Please consider coming back to New York. You could start your school year at Columbia, and if you don't want to live with us, you can live in a dorm. We'd be happier knowing you're closer to home. We just want to be more involved in your life."

"I don't want you involved in my life! I can look after myself."

She seemed hurt by what I said, but I couldn't hold back my resentment any longer. It was years' worth of pain, overflowing out of me.

"You never protected me, Mom. You never defended me." I fixed my scornful gaze on Rob and said, "You should have left this jerk the first time he laid his hands on me! Do you really think I've forgotten? Remember the nights when you used to remove the light bulb in the bathroom and lock me inside while I screamed in terror because I was afraid of the dark? Or the time you beat me black and blue because I accidentally spilled milk on the floor? Do I really need to mention the rest, Rob? Should I expose that demon inside of you? Or are you gonna tell me to shut up and scare me into silence?"

"Aria, stop." Mom started crying.

"Why? Is it too painful to hear the truth? How do you think I felt enduring his abuse on a weekly basis?"

There were tears in Rob's eyes, but I didn't care.

"Funny," I snickered. "I seem to recall him being more than happy to dump me off at Noah's nine months ago."

I wanted them to leave. I wanted to be with Noah and escape everything.

A soft knock at the door caught everyone's attention; Doctor Peters had stepped inside.

"I apologize if I am intruding at a bad time."

"Not at all," Mom said, wiping her tears with a tissue.

"I've brought some forms that Aria needs to sign before I can schedule her for surgery."

"Wait," I said. "Has Evan spoken to a psychiatrist regarding the transplant operation?"

"Yes, he has," Dr. Peters replied. "All potential donors must undergo a psychiatric evaluation during the testing process."

"He's right," Mom said. "Your father and I had to speak to a professional, too."

Dr. Peters handed me some documents before he explained the medical procedures to my parents. If I survived this surgery, I didn't know if I wanted to pursue an academic career. I just prayed to God that the operation would go smoothly. Everything that had happened in the past three months had been hard to deal with, but this moment felt like a second chance for me and Noah. If that car crash didn't happen, then the paternity results would never have been discovered. Maybe the universe signaled that Noah and I were meant to be. Fate couldn't have been so cruel as to give me a glimpse of the possibility of happiness and then have me die on the operating table… or months later. I wanted to live. I wanted to experience life with the man of my dreams.

When Dr. Peters left, I was alone again with my parents. They gave one last attempt at convincing me to move back home with them, but the only person I needed was Noah.

∞

A few hours had passed before the man of my dreams entered my hospital room.

"Hey, beautiful." He smiled. "How are you feeling?" Sitting next to my bed, he placed his coffee cup on the nightstand.

I was on the verge of having a nervous breakdown. Everything was hitting me at once.

"Noah, I'm scared. I've never had surgery before. What if I don't survive this?"

"Don't think that way." He leaned forward, hugging me while I sobbed in his arms.

"I don't want to die."

"You won't." Noah rubbed my back. "We didn't go through everything we've gone through to lose each other now." Stroking my hair, he wiped my tears when I pulled back. "I know you're scared, but everything's gonna be just fine."

"You can't guarantee that."

"I can guarantee that I love you and would do anything for you. I want you to be strong, Aria. Be strong for me because I rely on your strength as much as you rely on mine."

"What if the transplant is unsuccessful?"

"Then you're getting another kidney. I'm not gonna let you die on me. Do you understand?" He cupped my face as I stared into his clear blue eyes. There it was: the tidal wave. It kept rising while I stood at the shore, surrendering to its power as it washed over me. This is what it felt like to love this man: knowing he could destroy me and break my heart. Every day, I had to trust that he wouldn't. Love was a risk, a leap of faith.

"I love you, Noah."

He pressed his lips near the corner of my mouth, avoiding a kiss. My body tingled, listening to his seductive voice.

"I love you more than anything in this world," he admitted. "As soon as this is over, I promise I'll take you on that trip to Italy once you're better. I want you to imagine walking on cobblestone streets and arched bridges by my side. Think about our trip to Venice, the floating city of romantic Italy. I'll take you on the gondolas… shopping sprees at designer shops. You'd like that, wouldn't you?"

"You don't have to spend extravagant amounts of money on me to make me happy," I said. "Just being with you is enough. Have you been there before with anyone?"

"Yes… Milan—it was work related, but my ex was with me."

Wonderful.

"Forget Italy."

"Aria, come on. I have Italian ancestry down the family tree—not to mention relatives who live there. I'll always want to go back, regardless."

Italian, Scottish, British, and American, I recalled a previous convo, adding those countries to our list of travels.

"I don't want you being reminded of romantic moments with your ex while you're with me."

"That won't happen."

"I'm no longer interested."

"You're so stubborn." He sighed. "We'll have breakfast on the patio and walk by the palazzos. Do you know what that is?"

I shook my head.

"It's an architectural style in the 19th and 20th centuries based upon the palaces built by the wealthiest families during the Italian Renaissance. I'll show you some pictures next time."

"Not interested."

"We'll walk the city streets together… breathing in delicious Italian food… I'll take you wine tasting at a countryside vineyard. Can you see it in your mind, Aria?"

Crystal clear, I nodded.

"We'll stroll through St. Mark's Square, Piazza San Marco."

God, his Italian sounded so sexy.

"… Listen to street musicians perform…"

"I'd love that."

"I'll take you to Rome—the Eternal City. It received its nickname because ancient Romans believed that no matter what happened to the world, no matter how many empires would fall, Rome would always live forever."

"You know so much about the country."

"I just know my history."

There was something about Italy that called out to me… Scotland, too. I couldn't explain it.

"There's so much to see," Noah said. "I want to show it all to you."

"When can we go?"

"During your spring or winter break."

"I wish we could leave tomorrow."

"I wish that too, but you're gonna need the rest of the summer to recover from surgery."

"I want to be with you. I don't want to live with Mom and Rob."

"You won't have to. I promise." Noah paused and changed the subject. "There's something I've been wanting to discuss with you."

"What's up?"

I hoped it wasn't bad news. Then again, nothing could be worse than being Robert Mitchell's daughter. To be fair, there were worse things compared to my situation, but I didn't want to think about poverty, war, and underground pedophile rings at that moment.

"I got a call back from a prominent law firm in New York earlier this afternoon," said Noah. "They've offered me a position. A friend of mine is the co-founder and senior managing partner of Keller & Trent. I accepted the position today."

"What? How come you never told me you were job hunting?"

"Because I wasn't sure I'd get hired at that firm. I guess my credentials helped."

"Oh, my God!" I gasped. "You didn't get fired, did you?"

"No, that's not what happened. I'm resigning because my senior partners refused to fire that asshole. I'm blind siding them and handing in my letter of resignation tomorrow. I'm not gonna offer my legal services and expertise to a team of people I don't believe in anymore. I'm their best asset. They need me, but I couldn't care less. My contract never had a non-compete clause."

"So… you'll be living in New York?"

"It'll be good for me—a fresh start." He seemed hesitant to continue, but said, "By the way, I've done a bit of research about Columbia, and I think it's a great university."

"But I don't want to be anywhere near Rob!"

"You won't have to see him. I want you to move in with me, eventually."

Say what?

"We'd have to stay off the radar for a while. I can get you an apartment and—"

"Oh, my gosh, no!" I cut him off and he looked confused. "I can't let you do that."

"Why not? I love you. I want to help."

"Don't take my independence away from me, Noah."

"How am I doing that?"

"By doing everything for me and being the hero all the time. I can work on my own."

"Are you too proud to accept my financial support now? Is this about Rob?"

"No." I lied.

"He projected his shame on you all your life. Release it, baby. You need to trust me to take care of your needs."

"I'm not even yours biologically. You don't owe me anything."

"I still feel protective of you, Aria. I still feel responsible. I want to take care of you because I can, and I love you. You can't expect me to just shut that off like a switch overnight. I'm older than you. I'm established, and I have the means to help."

This was so frustrating.

"I can go to school and work part time," I said. "Ally, Jade, and I can get our own place and split the rent and expenses."

"You want roommates?" He seemed to be against that idea.

"They're my best friends. It wouldn't be like they're strangers living with me."

"I guess I should be relieved you don't want any 'boyfriends' shacking up with you."

Ryan and Evan were the only guys that were my best friends, and Noah already had enough issues with them.

"When are you planning on moving?" I asked. "Will you sell the house?"

"I start on the job the first week of September. I've put the house on the market—it'll sell quickly."

Everything was changing fast. I could hardly keep up.

"Well," I sighed. "I guess I'm going to Columbia U."

"*Or…* you could stay here in California and go to Berkley."

"I don't want to be away from you, Noah. I'd rather endure being in the same area code as Rob, if it means I get to see you every day."

I just couldn't imagine my life without Noah. He made it worth living.

"Please don't abandon me," I said.

"Never." He kissed my hand and massaged my palm.

"This sucks. We find out we're not related, and we *still* have to keep our relationship on the low."

I was expecting Noah to laugh, but he seemed troubled by what I'd said.

"Hey." I frowned. "What's wrong?"

"I don't want you to commit to me so soon, not while you're young and have so much to experience. I want to love you selfishly, but I can't. It would be so unfair to you."

"How could you even say such a thing? I love you, Noah. You're the only man I want to be with."

"That may change once you start college. I don't want to restrict your freedom and prevent you from exploring your options. You should meet young men your own age, not sixteen years older."

Didn't he understand how crazy I was about him?

"First, our age difference doesn't matter to me. I hardly even notice it. Second, I don't want to date other guys. If I wanted to date someone my age, I would have dated Ryan."

"There's no point in changing your mind is there?"

"I'm insulted you would even try."

"I've never loved anyone like I love you, Aria. This is unfamiliar territory for me."

I wanted to kiss him, if only to make him believe I wanted him, every part of him.

"If we have to keep us a secret, I'm fine with that," I said. "I don't care if we must hide from the world. Just don't leave me."

"I can't, even if I wanted to," Noah assured.

"And please don't decide for me. I can do that now."

"I'll try not to be pushy. Sometimes you don't know what's best for you, but I do." He kissed my hand.

"So, we're going to New York?"

He matched my smile and said, "We're going to New York."

"I'm gonna survive this?"

"You're gonna walk into my brand-new penthouse; you're gonna let me wine and dine you; and by the end of the night, I'll throw you over my shoulder, take you to bed and…"

Oh. My. God.

"You're gonna survive this, beautiful."

CHAPTER FORTY-THREE
THE FINAL NAIL IN THE COFFIN

Natalie felt so depressed. The past ten years of her life flashed before her eyes as she sat across from her husband and drank a cup of coffee. They had gone to a local diner to talk but were struggling to communicate. Natalie did not know where to begin. She felt terrible about the way everything had turned out in her life. Ever since Aria was born, she believed Noah was the father. A tear rolled down her cheek as she fondly remembered her relationship with him. He was her first love. After eighteen years, Natalie realized she had never got over him. Spending time with her ex at the hospital had triggered her to self-reflect. The accident had brought the former lovers closer in ways she had never expected.

While Aria was growing up, she often saw traces of Noah in her, since she didn't have Robert's brown eyes.

The truth was always in front of me. I just didn't want to see it.

It was hard to console her husband and be happy about the paternity results when she wasn't deep down. Noah had been right to confront Robert with all his shortcomings, Natalie thought.

He's never been a good husband to me, much less a father to Aria.

She often wished she could turn back the clock and have married Noah. Natalie had refused his proposal because she believed Robert was the safer choice. By the time she got pregnant with the twins, she realized he did not make her happy. But it was too late to consider divorce when she had newborns to raise, and she did not want to do it alone. Every year that passed in her passionless marriage, Natalie felt as if she was losing pieces of herself. Living with Rob had changed who she was. She lived from paycheck to paycheck, taking care of a man who was abusive. Robert's poor qualities outweighed the good.

For years, Natalie felt trapped in her marriage. Her fear of being poor as a single mother had always been incentive enough to make her work through her marital issues. She was about to ask her husband a question when a server came by with Robert's meal. Natalie politely declined a refill and took her time finishing her coffee. She kept replaying the conversation she had had with Noah. His financial help was a godsend; she was grateful.

Staring out the window, Natalie remembered Noah's charismatic smile and hypnotic blue eyes. She could never forget the way he had held her hand, reassuring her that everything would be okay.

He's still the love of my life.

Her heart ached knowing she was no longer his.

"This steak is dry!" Robert complained.

"We're not exactly sitting in a five-star restaurant, are we?" Natalie said, ignoring his rant.

You never protected me, Mom. You never defended me. You should have left him the first time he laid his hands on me!

Aria's voice echoed in her head like a phantom. Natalie felt as if she was stuck in a never-ending maze—lost, with no direction. But now she had finally reached a door she had avoided for years: a door she should have walked through a long time ago if only she had had the courage.

Scarfing down his food, Robert released the loudest belch before he wiped the corner of his mouth with a napkin. Natalie stared down at her empty coffee cup in contemplation.

Time to walk through that door.

Looking lifeless and numb, she lifted her head and met her husband's eyes. "I want a divorce."

CHAPTER FORTY-FOUR
EVAN

Another sleepless night. I wasn't sure why these nightmares were haunting me again. I hated having to watch my mother die in front of me. I could never save her. My train of thought was suddenly disrupted when my cat hopped on my bed. Most men opt for a dog as a furry companion, but there were a lot of things to appreciate about felines. Ancient Egyptians used to worship them. Maybe that's why they can be such arrogant assholes—possibly an adaptive trait.

Baxter started meowing as he pawed at my stomach.

"All right, you little bastard. Let's get you some food."

Careful not to trip over boxes, I made my way to the kitchen, fed my cat, and poured myself a glass of water before hitting the shower. All I could think about was Aria. I woke up every morning with this girl on my mind, and I went to bed the same way. If I wasn't having nightmares about my mother getting raped and murdered, I was dreaming about Aria. I needed her in my life. I don't think she had the slightest clue how I truly felt about her. I worshipped her. Her photos on my walls were proof of that. There's nothing wrong with loving someone possessively and obsessively… it only reveals the depth of your love. You would kill and die for them. I would have done both for Aria in a heartbeat. I'd already killed for her, and I felt bloody amazing doing it, too. Strangling that bitch to death… the rush was indescribable. All my rage and resentment… my darkness poured out of me and seeped into her lifeless body. Burying her had been a relief, as if I had buried my darkest demon with her before he would rise out of the grave and re-spawn. The most insidious part of me was now rotting away with that corpse. I had purified my darkness within like a divine alchemy, all in the name of justice. That's what my rituals were, *a cleansing*… spiritual purge. A death and rebirth.

I didn't regret killing Steph. She deserved to die. Anyone who hurt Aria deserved an agonizing death. She possessed my soul, and I did not know how that happened, but I couldn't change it. No matter what it took, I had to be with her.

More than anything, I wanted to be inside her… making love to Aria would fill a void. It wouldn't be empty sex. Yes, I wanted to take her in all positions… everywhere, anytime I wanted, but my heart would be in it from beginning to end. Once we'd consummate our love, Aria would own me, just like I would own her—forever. Loyalty. This is what it meant to love: here is my darkest of dark. Love me. Accept me.

One of my darkest fantasies was to penetrate her in her sleep. I was confident I could please her. I'd spread those thighs, rub my cock on that sweet, tight pussy and ram it in. She might even try to fight me off, but deep down, I'd know she'd want me. Women love to get their back blown out and manhandled. They act like they don't want it, but they're just lying to themselves. It's the quiet ones who are usually the *biggest* freaks in the bedroom. The truth is, every woman loves a deep, hard, cock pounding. And the ones that say they don't are muffin-munchers or too much of a prude to admit it.

Fuck, if only she knew how badly I wanted her. I'd kill that cocksucker sperm donor of hers if it made her happy, though I'd torture him first. I had been contemplating that for the past few weeks, and I knew exactly how I would orchestrate his murder. I needed proper preparation to take out that abusive prick. Someone had to do it. I was more than honored to be the one to carry out this divine justice on my niece's behalf. That SOB had put her through enough. I planned to torture him first, until he would beg for death, only to resuscitate him and snuff out his existence.

Rinse. Repeat.

Oh… what a treat. One day soon, my dark goddess and I will kill people together… before I take her with passion.

I wouldn't cage her. She would have the freedom to flirt, lure guys in, and beguile them with her beauty to bring them back to our place afterwards. Then the *real* fun would begin. I'd teach her what to do, how to kill, how to be the perfect psycho sex slave—and she would learn fast—it's what I loved about her: her intellect. Studying her had become a passionate hobby of mine.

I planned on taking her to nightclubs with me, pick up a willing participant for an "m/m/f threesome," and bring him back to our place. I'd drug him up and instruct Aria to tie the poor bastard to a chair and make him believe he was getting a strip tease of his life. And once he'd be close to combusting, I'd hand Aria my favorite blade—the one with her name engraved on it… and I'd tell her to stab the bloke repeatedly. I'd stand behind her, kissing her neck, fondling her perky tits, whispering dirty talk in her ear before I'd bend her over, pound her out, all while the poor bastard is bleeding profusely. I'd be her glorious angel of death with white wings stained in blood—except I'd always protect her. Forever. She would never fear me or my darkness. She would embrace it and love it as if it's her own.

I never had a partner join me in my killing rituals. I wanted Aria to experience the extraordinary power of taking a life; it transforms you as you realize your own godhood. It wasn't a psychotic fetish, it was an evolution of mind (consciousness). Most people are so bloody stupid and programmed to remain that way. They can't think for themselves—easier if someone else does it for them. I mean, really, they're all morons… a mass flock of sheep determined to accept their own slavery.

FUCK. THAT.

I don't like to follow the rules and never will. Our government is not our friend—they never have been. Capitalism and consumerism control the "fine citizens" of Western society. Maybe if everyone smoked weed, they'd finally pull their heads out of their arses and realize that economic elites are the ones controlling the world, not presidents, prime ministers, or "God." It pisses me off how idiotic societies are. Freedom is a lie. We're all living in a camouflaged cage. However, *my* lifestyle is freedom in its purest form. I do whatever I want, and I get away with it because: (1) I have a superior intellect; (2) I'm rich. Simple as that.

Society is broken down as a pyramid of social classes, with a taxonomy for everything. If you're at the bottom, you're screwed and a waste of space. If you're higher up, you can live like a king or queen. And if you're in the top one percent... well, then you can live like a god. Who do you think supports the foundations of that pyramid? The slaves who work hard, not knowing that their everyday existence is to keep those elites ahead of everybody else. Any American who thinks that wealth is distributed fairly is a bloody moron. Free election of new world leaders does not abolish a civilian's status as a slave. What's the difference between slavery in ancient Egypt and the contemporary world? "Freedom" is the new slavery. If our government and media advocate our freedom, then surely we must be free, right?

Anyone who believes that is just another fool in our duped society. Fuck everyone and fuck the rules, including the false prophets and hypocritical "holy saints." Churches and cathedrals are full of rapists, robbers, pedophiles, and liars; it's the devil hiding behind religion, disguised as "God." We live in a godless country. People masquerade behind faith. I've concluded that this world is a cosmic egg for a reason— it's a prison planet that recycles souls. It's the "circle of life." In other words, once you die, you're just reincarnated back to this shithole.

I wanted to initiate Aria into my liberating lifestyle and empower her. I wanted her to feel that surging rush that was indescribable. I wanted to free her. I wasn't a monster. Monsters weren't capable of love. But I loved her... so deeply. I saw her inner demons, and I wanted to nurture them. When you love someone, you don't make them resist or change their true nature. You accept them as they are. You help them embrace their darkness, and you drown in it together. If the shadow was entirely corrupt, then at least we would drown in that corruption together... our love would be the light to guide our way in the darkness. Love would be the catalyst that would balance our light and dark; it was alchemy. I would be right there by her side. I knew she had been through a lot, but I could take her pain away. I could fuck the pain away. Aria belonged to *me*. Sex would be healing, and I was confident I could heal her wounds if she let me in.

I didn't like the idea of potential competition. That's why I often went through her phone while she was sleeping at the hospital, deleting Ryan's texts. I was tempted to kill him and get him out of the way. I even went as far as premeditating his murder, but there was no need to follow through. Aria wasn't staying in LA anymore. The kid couldn't love her like I did. No man could ever love her the way I do. I would allow no one to impede our future. She and I were connected. We had a bond—an understanding. I knew that if I showed her the darkest parts of myself, it would traumatize her... But she would grow to love me... because I believed she had the same darkness. It was there, only hidden. All I had to do was remove her mask and make her face her true self. I possessed Pandora's Box. I wanted to place it in front of her and encourage her to open it.

And when she does... she'll be mine, I thought, wrapping a towel around my waist.

I boxed almost all my things. Tomorrow would be moving day, and I would not sell my loft. I had purchased property in some other states and South America. I was going to leave LA and fly out to NYC. Three years ago, I had purchased an apartment downtown and was moving back in. As for Aria's shrine of photos... I had a beautiful mural waiting for me in a secret room I had created—identical to the one in my LA loft—my original masterpiece. When I moved to California, I knew I'd have to renovate, and it was worth it because it was her story. *Our* story. Maybe I'd even show it to her someday.

Most people worship the god of their Abrahamic religion; others worshipped science, sports, music, Instagram baddies... I worshipped Aria. She would worship me too once I'd give her back shots while tugging her luscious hair and awakening her shadow like a dark initiation. My goddess needed to be freed. I always got what I wanted, and I wanted her. She was marked. She was mine.

CHAPTER FORTY-FIVE
ARIA

NYC: the most crowded city in the United States. This place had a significant impact on commerce, finance, media, art, fashion, technology, and entertainment. I was back in the big apple, surrounded by skyscrapers and diverse little towns on every street corner. Some people might think this city is a cesspool of evil, but it was home to me. I grew up here. My best friends lived here, and I had amazing memories with Noah in New York.

Back tracking a couple months… my kidney transplant was a success. My body hadn't rejected the kidney Evan had donated to me. Doctor Peters had said I was in the clear and on the road to recovery. I was worried I'd have to take medication post-transplant, but because of medical advancements, Evan and I were vaccinated with a miracle serum that would eliminate lifelong dependency on medication for the kidney donor and recipient. We had two things in common now: one functioning kidney and matching scars. At least we wouldn't have to pop pills every day for the rest of our lives.

Leaving the hospital, I studied for my finals at home and recovered from the surgery. I had missed graduation, but eventually received my high school diploma. My friends were sad when they found out I was moving, but I promised I'd keep in touch. Jessica made me this beautiful scrapbook full of pictures of us and our friends. I hadn't been able to go to that Tiesto concert with Ryan; the event was in July, and I was still recovering in the hospital. I had given my ticket to Jessica and insisted she go with Ryan instead. I often felt like he and Jess would have made a beautiful couple. It was nice leaving LA knowing I had friends who genuinely cared about me, even though it was a few.

To celebrate my academic success, Noah had surprised me with three gifts: a pair of diamond-studded earrings, first class tickets to Rome, and a key to his new penthouse in New York. I didn't know what I had done to deserve these presents, but he just loved spoiling me. Our life was changing so fast… Just the thought of sleeping in Noah Hunter's bed made my heart explode. He was genuinely committed to me—to us. Yet somehow, I was always afraid he would change his mind and leave. My rejection and abandonment trauma still plagued me.

By mid-August, I parted ways with my exciting life in California and drove to New York with Noah. Mom had insisted I move back into our old apartment so she could take care of me, but I wanted to stay with Ally and Jade; they had already moved into a townhouse for the summer. Technically, the duplex belonged to Allyson's mother, Mrs. Jones. When Ally's grandparents passed away last year, Mrs. Jones inherited the family home. Jade and I were still going to pay her rent, but at least Mrs. Jones was kind enough to lower the cost. Living on a measly student income meant careful budgeting.

Our townhouse was on the West side of Manhattan—about a ten-minute walk away from Columbia University, in a wonderful neighborhood near the shopping district. The Apollo Theater and Marcus Garvey Park were just steps away, with some amazing restaurants and museums within walking distance. The three-story brownstone had a small staircase leading to a red entrance door. Mrs. Jones had placed some flowerpots on the front steps. The backyard garden was small but beautifully landscaped—perfect for summer barbeques and cocktail parties. Moving in with my friends was a big decision. I always knew these girls would be my besties for life.

My parents and Noah had sorted out all the legal stuff that needed to be changed (government documents, my birth certificate, etc.), which had been little of a hassle since Noah was a lawyer and had connections. It was hard to abandon his last name, but I ended up keeping my father's surname, even though I'd been against the idea a month ago. My name didn't define my identity; it was just a label. Aria Mitchell sounded foreign to my ears, but at least the name liberated me. I was free to love Noah the way I desired.

Returning to New York hadn't gone how I wanted… because Noah was not in New York with me. When he accepted his position at Keller & Trent, it was on the condition that he work at the firm's second location in London, England. He was to be there for three months to assist the legal team with a big case that was going to trial in January. They required his expertise, since he was the best at his job. He had told me he would be back in no time, but every day that passed seemed long and torturous.

Being thousands of miles apart made me sad, even though we communicated regularly through emails, texts, and phone calls. Just when I thought we could finally be together, our plans got sidetracked. I should have been happy he wouldn't be away for twelve months. It was only ninety days, but felt like ninety years to me.

On a positive note, by the time Noah would return, the renovation of his penthouse would be done. We constantly exchanged pictures and ideas on home decor. I loved browsing through interior design magazines. Though I enjoyed that more than he did. I appreciated how he put effort into things I cared about. Noah made me feel like I was still a part of his life; he wanted me involved in every aspect—including decorating his home… *our* home. I was in love with him, and those feelings only intensified every day. No one had clued in about us. We decided it was best to keep our relationship to ourselves, at least until he came back to the city. Then we would figure out how to tell our family and friends. I got extremely anxious every time I thought about telling my mom the truth. How would that conversation even go down?

Um, hey, Mom… I'm in love with your high school sweetheart. We've been in a secret relationship for months. I know you had him first, but he's mine now.

Yeah… no.

Allyson had started dating someone in June. I liked her boyfriend, but sometimes they'd stay up all night going at it, and I'd have to turn up my music to drown out their noises. It was frustrating because I was missing Noah. Did I have a guy brain or what? It wasn't normal to think about sex so much. Jess would have simplified it for me: "Aria, you need to get laid."

It sucked being in a different time zone than Noah. He was five hours ahead. Sometimes he stayed up late to work and we would talk on the phone, or I'd distract him on FaceTime and get a little naughty. I was still insecure about my body, especially since I was fashioning a surgical scar along the left side of my abdomen. Knowing I had taken something from Evan made me feel guilty. That horrible accident could have been avoided if I had just stayed home that night instead of driving to Evan's. I blamed myself.

I had fallen in love with the California sun, but I also missed the crisp fall air of New York City… Leaves changing color, fall fashion; it was the perfect season to wear boots, scarves, and warm pea-coats. Hot chocolate and homemade stews were also a favorite of mine during this time of year. It seemed like yesterday that I had fled from my big city life, but I could never take the city girl out of me.

CHAPTER FORTY-SIX
ARIA

I loved October rain, especially when I had to study. It was a Friday night and instead of going out, I was sitting in bed, listening to music and "partying" with piles of textbooks. My favorite track on Cary Brothers' *Who You Are* album was "Ride." I listened to it all evening because it made me reminisce about the three-day road trip I took with Noah from LA to NYC. Driving with the top down, feeling the wind in my hair, Noah's hand in mine… I was happy to be out on the open road after spending so many weeks in a dull hospital room. It was the first time I felt free to be with him minus the guilt. We stayed at a few hotels along the way, but we never made it past "first base" in the bedroom. I was still healing from a major surgery, so our sexual activities were limited to PG kissing and cuddling. Noah had more self-control than me, which was a good thing.

I had a paper to write on Friedrich Nietzsche and was about to begin my first body paragraph when I received a call. Noah's picture popped up on my screen and I instantly smiled. I was about to answer the call, but stopped when I realized I looked a bit disheveled. Brushing on some gloss, I got comfortable as I lay on my stomach and accepted his call on my laptop.

"Finally!" Noah beamed. "Took you long enough."

I blushed when I saw his handsome face.

"I was thinking you were trying to kick out a boy from your room." Noah chuckled.

"You're the one who looks like you have a serious case of sex hair going on. Dare I question *your* fidelity?" I teased.

"I always have sex hair going on, according to you."

That was true. His hair was just so thick and beautiful. The thought of running my fingers through it made me…

"You look gorgeous," he added.

"Are you kidding? Every time you see me, I resemble death more and more. Behold, your *Corpse Bride*."

He smiled, and I melted.

"I know you love Tim Burton films," Noah said, "but you're nothing close to the living dead. You just need to sleep on time, baby."

"Tell that to my professors who keep piling on the workload," I sighed, swinging my legs back and forth while I gazed at him.

"Why are you looking at me like that?"

"Like what? Am I not allowed to admire your hotness?"

"You're not admiring. You're studying me—suspiciously. Do I really need to show you there's no one under my desk?"

"Actually, I was just wondering if you've got a 'Curious Case of Benjamin Button' going on."

"Is that the movie where Brad Pitt ages backwards?"

"Well, Brad doesn't—but his character does." I giggled.

"Sorry to disappoint you, but I'm only getting older. And come to think of it"—he paused—"I'm not sure what would be worse: having you take care of a baby version of me, or having you care for me while I'm cranky and stuck in a wheelchair—in a diaper."

"Oh, my God!" I laughed.

Noah grinned, folding his hands behind his head. It was hard not to stare at his bulging biceps.

He really needs to take off that shirt.

"Well, at least I got you laughing," he said.

"You know I love you no matter what, Noah."

"You're determined to blind yourself to my flaws."

"I know you're not perfect, but your imperfections make you perfect for me."

"Careful now, if you keep this up, I'm gonna be a hundred times cockier than I already am. Most of these English folk have already labeled me as 'arrogant arse,'" he pronounced in an English accent. "I guess I have you to blame."

I smiled when he did.

"How's everything going on your end?" Noah sipped his drink.

"Pretty good. I'm just occupied with school, mostly."

"And how are you liking the new job?"

"I enjoy working at the bookstore."

"I really wish you'd devote your free time to your studies. I told you I'd take care of all your financial needs. You won't even share a bank account with me."

"I need to feel some independence, Noah. Please stop forgetting that."

"Yeah, yeah... I haven't forgotten," he sighed. "This isn't because of Trevor?"

"Please don't bring him up. He's my past. Anyway, it's good for me. I'm learning the value of the hard-earned dollar." I proudly smirked. "At least I'm not taking my clothes off for money—not judging, just grateful I don't have to do something I don't want to do. There's this girl in my human rights class who strips part-time, and she gets paid big bucks."

"Don't even think about it." Noah sounded serious.

"I would hate to piss off my temperamental boyfriend, even though he's outrageously sexy when he's mad at me." I spammed our chat window with green hearts and kisses—green for the heart chakra. Lovesick Aria, at her mushiest.

"You've seen me pissed off." Noah chuckled. "... actually, you've seen me *really* pissed, but what I'm trying to say is that I don't want you getting involved in the adult entertainment industry."

"You don't have to worry. I've already given up my modeling aspirations now that I have this ugly scar on my body."

"Aria, we've been through this before. That scar doesn't take away your beauty. You survived severe trauma. It should only be a reminder of what you've overcome."

I exhaled deeply and said, "I know."

Desiring intimacy, I dreaded taking my shirt off in front of him because of that unsightly scar that had been stamped on my skin forever.

"How are things with the family?" he asked, changing the subject.

"Everything's fine. I visit Terry and Tiffany when I can. I'm taking them to the movies tomorrow."

"That's nice of you."

"Mom and Rob are getting marriage counseling."

"Is that so?"

I nodded. "He still doesn't want a divorce."

"That doesn't surprise me. What woman in her right mind would want to marry that prick? Of course he'd want to keep her. He's nothing without Natalie—no offence."

"None taken."

"How do you feel about your mother's decision?"

"I don't blame her for wanting to leave. Rob's done a lot I can't forgive. Just because he's my biological dad doesn't mean he's been a real father to me."

"I know, baby." Noah frowned. His voice was so comforting. Every time we spoke, I felt better. "How badly do you miss me?"

I was about to answer him, but paused and said, "Do you remember that quote I used in that picture I told you about last year?"

"Of course."

"Well, it rains a lot where you are. You have plenty of rain drops you won't be catching tomorrow."

His smile touched his eyes.

"I'm supposed to be the charismatic one in this relationship," Noah said.

"There's no competition between us."

"I don't know… the last time we spoke, you brought up our zodiac signs—and according to some virtual 'oracle,' Leo and Aries are extremely competitive with each other."

"Only in the bedroom." I winked.

He laughed, gulping back his beer.

"By the way," I said. "Is it still there?"

"Is *what* still there?"

"You know…"

Noah arched his sexy eyebrow. "I'm convinced you always ask me this question to get me to strip."

I gasped dramatically. "Never! I wouldn't dare!"

"Right… she thinks she's so clever."

He snickered and slowly unbuttoned his shirt, flashing the phoenix tattoo. My name was still inked across his chest.

"I promise it's not going anywhere," Noah assured me.

"I hate this distance." I pouted.

"Remember what I told you at the airport before I left?"

I could never forget.

"You have me, Aria, no matter the distance. This is only temporary. I'll be back in New York next month."

"I know and I can't wait! I miss you so much it hurts."

"I miss you more, beautiful."

My cellphone suddenly rang.

"Aren't you gonna answer that?"

"Whoever it is, they can wait. I'm talking to you."

I was about to put it on silent when I received a text.

"You sure you don't want to check that?"

"It's from Evan," I said, reading his message. "He's showcasing some photos at a gallery next week and wants to know if I'd like to go."

"Ah. And?" Noah stared at me with a critical eye. I guess he expected me to decline the invitation. Regardless, I quickly texted Evan and told Noah I was going. He seemed to brood in silence.

"You're doing it again." I sighed.

"Doing what?"

"That annoying tapping thing you do with your fingers whenever you're irritated."

"I'm not."

"Yeah—because you stopped now." I rolled my eyes. "Look, Noah, your brother's finally following his dreams after abandoning them for so long. Be happy for him. Photography has always been his passion."

"I never said I'm not happy for him; I just find it strange he moved back to New York a week after we did."

"Does it matter? He's your brother. You guys used to be close."

"Keywords: *used to.*"

"Don't get grouchy on me now."

"I'm not, I'm just… frustrated." Chugging back his beer, he set it on the table. "Are you ever gonna take off that ridiculous necklace? It doesn't even match the outfits you wear."

"I don't care." My fingers clutched the pendant. "It's special. I still wear your wristband"—I flashed it—"If you haven't already noticed, it doesn't exactly compliment most of my outfits, either."

"There's no use in arguing with you over petty things."

"You should save your arguments for the courtroom. How's that case going on your end?"

"Our client is being difficult. He doesn't want to settle out of court, even though the offer is more than generous."

"Do you think you'll lose the case?"

"I never lose a case." Noah smiled confidently. "On a lighter note, did you know there's a Ferris wheel over here called the London Eye? It's also known as the Millennium Wheel."

"I've seen pictures."

"Every time I drive past it, I think of you."

I couldn't hide my smile. "We have a thing for Ferris wheels, don't we?"

He nodded with a smirk. "I had many sleepless nights over that kiss."

"It was intense."

The steamy memories flickered in my mind as I tried to play it in slow motion.

"You basically gave me an ultimatum and then jumped out of an airplane—without a parachute."

"You jumped out and came after me, though."

"You left me no other choice. Honestly, Aria, you have no idea how messed up I felt afterwards."

"I never forced you to kiss me."

"I know that. I felt guilty because I didn't want to stop," Noah confessed. "I don't regret it now. Maybe all of this was fate."

"Since when do you believe in fate?"

"I found God when you opened your eyes in that hospital bed. And I started believing in destiny when I found out you weren't biologically mine. Faith and fate go hand in hand."

I didn't really understand that.

"So, you're saying there's no way to fight fate? That a person's potential for great evil is preordained?"

"We all make different choices in life, and each choice leads us to a different destiny."

"Insightful."

"I could explain my philosophical views to you, but I have some work to finish up, and you need to study."

It was only 8p.m. for me, which meant it was 1a.m. over there.

"Before I forget," Noah said. "Did you get that delivery today?"

"Yes, I did." I turned my laptop toward my nightstand so that he could see the vase full of roses. "You really don't have to send me flowers every day, Noah."

"I know, but I meant it when I said you'd receive a single rose from me for all the days I'm not with you."

He was so romantic.

"Why red, though? You know white roses are my favorite."

"Because the red rose represents love at first sight."

"Says who?"

"Says me… What are you doing?"

"Googling something," I replied, clicking on a webpage that explained the meaning of rose colors. "According to this site, 'a white rose represents purity and innocence. When a man presents a lady with a white rose, he is showing her he is worthy of her love.' What do you think?"

"I think… I'm not worthy of you."

I grimaced. "I wish you wouldn't feel that way."

"There are many things about my past I haven't shared. I'm sixteen years older than you, Aria, and I've lived long enough to experience a lifetime of mistakes I deeply regret."

His eyes seemed so remorseful. I knew he had difficulty digging through his past, and I never wanted to force him to tell me, but I was curious to know everything about Noah.

"You can always talk to me about it," I said. "I would never judge you."

"I know, beauty." He smiled. "Give me time. I would prefer to open up about my past in person, not behind a computer screen."

"I understand. I love you, Noah."

"I love you, too. I always will. Don't forget that."

"Never." I kissed my fingers and placed them over the webcam.

"One more," he requested.

"*Mmmmuah*!" My lips almost touched the screen.

Noah grinned. "That hit the spot—gave me chills. Please tell me you're not walking around college boys with your shirt buttons undone. I'd been hoping that was just a high school phase."

"Maybe I'm trying to seduce my professor… am a divine confessor of love… an innocent dove."

He stifled a laugh and said, "Innocent my ass! That's way too much cleavage."

"Vanessa would leave the house with her tits out!"

"Don't compare yourself to her. You're outrageously beautiful, and I just don't want you attracting the wrong kind of attention."

"Are you gonna stalk me and show up while I'm walking down a dark alleyway?"

"I think you're watching too many psych thrillers. Don't go gallivanting alone at night—or else."

"*Gallivanting*?" I giggled.

"You're not the only one who's a walking thesaurus."

"For the record"—I cleared my throat—"I'd rather *gallivant* around you—in panties."

"Stop teasing. Promise me you won't go walking the streets at night on your own."

Now he was back to the "protective dad approach."

"Aria…"

"I promise," I sighed.

"Good—and sleep on time tonight."

"I'll try. Although, I wish I could make a cameo appearance in your steamy sex dreams."

"You already do. I promise." He simpered. "Good night, beautiful."

"Good night, Noah."

Reluctantly, I ended the call and signed out of Skype. Lying on my back, I closed my eyes and drowned in love drunk feelings. How was this man mine? I couldn't wait for that day when we could finally hold hands in public, introduce each other to our friends, and share a kiss on a bench in Central Park… in the rain, just like that couple I'd seen years ago. I'd gone through a series of tower moments in life, but I was happier than ever. Even though Noah was out of the country, at least we were no longer related.

There wasn't much to complain about. I was living with my best friends, my mother was finally leaving the sperm donor, and Evan was in the same area code as me. I felt lucky, but also worried that something terrible would happen, as if I was never meant to stay happy for too long. Perhaps I had done something horrible in my past life (if I had one), and I had to brace myself for karmic retribution. Or maybe I was still traumatized by my childhood.

My first year at Columbia was off to a great start. I chose psychology as my major. Studying human behavior and thought process was interesting to me, which included learning about different fields of psychology. My relationship with Noah was a head trip within itself. Our love story would have made such a controversial film on the silver screen.

I'd probably get attacked by religious fanatics, even though the Bible is littered with incest.

Transitioning from high school to university had not been as hard as I'd expected. I enjoyed having more freedom and meeting new people. There was this guy I met in my sociology class who was cute and funny; his name was Josh, and he had asked me out last week, but I told him I had a boyfriend who was "studying abroad." I hadn't told Noah about him because he would have worried for no reason. Noah was always paranoid about our age difference, especially since he believed it made things challenging for us. It was important for him to know that he was never holding me back. I knew I was much younger, but I was serious about my commitment to him. There was no way I'd mess up what we had by cheating on Noah. I often wondered if Vanessa's infidelity had hurt him, but he didn't seem depressed. He was a self-aware, self-actualized individual, all of which I aspired to be. I wanted to achieve self-mastery.

I need to quit daydreaming; I have a paper to write.

"Mrrrrowwww…"

Baxter suddenly hopped on my bed, demanding attention as I sat up and cuddled him. Evan had given him to me when I'd offered to take care of his kitty. His loft was not a great environment for a cat since he constantly had clients and models at his place doing photo-shoots. Baxter was skittish around strangers.

My stomach kept grumbling as I made my way to the kitchen; it had a retro feel to it: sky blue backsplash, white cupboards, and laminate countertops. Our refrigerator was lime green, with a round retro table set (also lime green). The girls and I normally ate breakfast there and had dinner in front of the TV.

I was about to fix myself a meal when the doorbell rang.

Weird. I'm not expecting company.

Heading downstairs, I glanced at the security cam and smiled.

"Evan!" I beamed, opening the door.

"Hey, love."

"Oh my God, you pierced your eyebrow!"

"And my cartilage." He grinned, flashing his piercing.

"Wow! I love it!"

"Thanks."

He looks… hot.

"Sorry about dropping in unannounced. I was in the neighborhood, and I thought I'd just swing by and give you these…" He held up some shopping bags.

"You really didn't have to go through all that trouble," I said, inviting him in.

"Aria, you're a student, and you're taking care of my cat. The least I can do is help with some expenses."

"I appreciate that, Evan. Thank you. Let me help you with those."

"Don't worry about it," he said, taking off his shoes. "Lead the way."

He followed me upstairs to the kitchen and helped me unpack.

"Are you hungry at all?" I asked, biting into an apple.

"Now that you mention it, a little."

"What do you feel like eating? I can make you some—"

My apple suddenly vanished from my hand.

"Sorry, love." He smirked, chomping on it. "I just wanted a bite. You made it look… delicious."

"You're lucky I don't have the flu."

"I'm not afraid of your 'germs,'" he teased, placing the fruit on the counter. "Now, where's my hug?"

Squeezing me in his arms, Evan lifted me up before I was on my feet again. Being affectionate was natural to him; I loved that. He was like this perfect cuddle bear; a super sexy cuddle bear with muscles—minus the fur.

"You feel lighter," he said, glaring at me with his penetrating brown eyes. "Are you not eating?"

"I've been skipping meals because of my school schedule."

"Okay, here's the deal: you're coming over to my place this weekend, and I'm gonna make you some fantastic Italian cuisine. I'm sure you'll be impressed with my amazing culinary skills."

"I love Italian food. It's one of my favorite cuisines."

"You should take better care of yourself, sweetheart."

"I am. Don't worry."

Something caught my attention as I fixated on Evan's neck.

"Is that a new tattoo?" I pointed at the black symbol. I hadn't noticed it earlier because his jacket collar was covering it.

"Yeah, I got it done last week." He rolled up his left sleeve and showed me the tribal tattoos that covered his arm.

"Wow! It looks amazing! What does the ink on your neck mean?"

"It's in Mandarin—it means *Humble*."

"What was the occasion?"

"I went to the tattoo parlor and read the meaning of this symbol… it just spoke to me. Sometimes a tattoo chooses you, not the other way around."

"What about all those people who get inked and then regret it later? How would you explain that?"

"Stupidity."

We both laughed.

"Well, I should probably get going."

"Stay. I'll make you a cup of coffee or hot chocolate."

"I don't wish to impose."

"I'm all alone in this house. I could use the company."

Removing his navy jacket, he hung it over a chair and stared at me. Evan was very fashionable. He never wore expensive Armani suits like Noah, but his style was just as attractive. Every time I saw him, he was wearing something new: designer brands in men's jeans, shirts, coats, shoes, accessories… you name it. I guess being rich and best friends with fashion designers had its perks.

"Tea, coffee, or hot coco?"

"Coffee, please—black, no sugar." He hovered close by while I got a pot of dark roast brewing.

"I'm excited about this exhibit next week! Is there a specific theme?"

"Yes." Evan hovered close to me. "*Innocence Interrupted*."

I smiled, meeting his dark, shiny eyes. "I'm sure it's gonna be amazing!"

"I'm happy you're coming. It means a lot to me, Aria."

Evan's eye contact was always so intense with me, as if he were trying to tell me something without actually saying it out loud: soul language. I had yet to become fluent. Jade's cheerful voice broke the spell as she entered the kitchen.

"Evan's here? Hi!"

"Hey, Jade!"

She greeted him with a lingering hug, blushing when he complimented her outfit. For a while, I sensed Jade had a crush on him, though the idea of them dating did not bother me. She and Evan would have made an attractive couple. Jade was stunning, but her beautiful heart made her prettier.

"Love the piercing and new ink!" she noticed, checking him out. "Boy, you are fine as hell! How are you single?"

He chuckled, leaning his weight against the counter. "I'm just waiting for the right woman to tie me down."

"Are you looking?" She flirted.

"Are you applying for the position?"

"Hmm…"—Jade bit her lip—"I don't know. The line up to date me is *long*. I'm not sure if you could handle the competition."

"I'd make you go exclusive with me. Don't worry."

"*Oooh*, he's cocky!"

"Not at all. Cocky is more like: if I took you out on a date, you'd delete all those numbers and edit my name on your phone as 'future hubby.' Why waste your time on a boy, when you can date a *real* man who knows how to treat a woman?" He stepped closer to Jade. "You've got the real deal standing in front of you."

"He's not messing around, is he?" Jade giggled. "You're intense, but I like that… and confidence is sexy."

Their chemistry was obvious, I noticed, fixing a cup of tea.

"You should come to my show tomorrow night! I'm performing some songs at Lavva Lounge—it'll be an intimate setting. Ally and Aria will be there. I'd love it if you came."

"You sing?" Evan seemed surprised.

"And dance." Jade smiled.

"Prove it."

She shuffled through some songs on her phone and played "Drunk in Love." Beyoncé was incredibly talented. I just never had the chance to have the concert experience and watch her perform. But this song was *definitely* something I would dance to.

Cranking up the volume, Jade started a full-on solo dance routine.

"It's hot, right?" She nodded to the beat.

Evan grinned as she wrapped an arm over his shoulder and said, "You got any moves?"

"Why don't you show me what you got first, love?" He held her hips, smiling as she danced on him.

It was like watching a scene straight out of *Step Up* or *Take The Lead* right there in my kitchen. Jade sang along with Beyoncé, finishing the last verse in *a cappella*.

"Wow!" Evan clapped. "I'm impressed!"

"Does this mean you'll come tomorrow night?"

"You can count on it."

She hugged him in excitement and looked at me with hearts in her eyes. "We should go club hopping tonight!"

"I can't. I have a paper to finish."

I reigned high as the queen of procrastination.

"You're totally taking 'academics' way too seriously, Aria," said Jade. "College life also includes partying and getting drunk on Friday nights!"

I would have gladly gone if Noah was here, but he wasn't.

"What about you, Evan? Wanna come?"

"I've got a photo shoot early in the morning."

"*Ugh!*" Jade groaned. "You guys suck."

"Why don't you ask Ally to join you?" I suggested.

"She's on a date with her man."

The coffee machine switched off before I poured a fresh cup for Evan.

"Thanks, love." He smiled.

"You're welcome."

Our eyes lingered on each other for far too long; I almost felt self-conscious.

"Well," Jade sighed. "I guess I'll draw a bath and do some reading tonight."

"Sounds relaxing," Evan replied.

"Feel free to ask me out on that date any time." She winked, walking out of the kitchen when he said, "Are you free Wednesday evening?"

Jade paused and smiled at him. "For you, I am." She smiled.

"I'll pick you up at six."

"Don't be late."

I was certain she would pump me for information about his likes and dislikes once he'd leave, but I was glad she and Ally adored him.

Hopefully, Noah will come around.

"I was right: you guys have a thing."

"I haven't taken a girl out in forever," said Evan, sipping his coffee.

"Just make sure you treat her right."

"I wouldn't treat her any other way. I'm always a gentleman."

We sat at the kitchen table and chatted about my studies and his photography for a while before the subject changed to my love life. Evan asked if I was seeing anyone. I wanted to tell him the truth, but I couldn't. I had promised Noah I'd keep our relationship under wraps. It sucked not having anyone to talk to about my secret boyfriend.

"Thanks again for the coffee"—Evan got up—"It's getting late and I'm keeping you up when you should be studying."

"I'll walk you out." I took our mugs and placed them in the sink before I followed him downstairs.

"Thank you for dropping by. I'm surprised Baxter hasn't come out to greet you. He's probably napping somewhere."

"Yeah, the furry bastard's living the life now—constant female attention."

I laughed.

"I'll text you tomorrow, love." He kissed my cheek. "It was good seeing you." He took my hand and kissed it.

"You're so affectionate." I tried not to blush.

"Does it bother you?"

"Not at all. Take care and drive safe."

"I will, sweetheart. Cheers!"

He gave me a big hug before he left.

When I was back upstairs, I got startled by Jade's sudden presence.

"Geez!" I flinched. "Don't sneak up on me like that!"

She was dressed in a bathrobe with a gold face mask on and a towel wrapped around her head.

"Sorry, just beautifying myself! I'm so stoked about this date! He finally asked me out!" Unable to contain her excitement, she grabbed my hand and dragged me into her zebra print bedroom for some girl talk.

⊰⊱

An hour into sharing everything I could about Evan, Jade brought up the subject of Noah and my parents while painting her toenails.

"I still can't believe how everything went down. I mean, you lived your whole life thinking your dad had abandoned you when he was living under the same roof as you. He treated you like crap just because he thought you weren't his kid. That's so sad."

It stung to hear her version of my truth, but I knew she hadn't said it maliciously. Jade was just outspoken sometimes.

"I'm still a bit in shock," I revealed.

"Yeah, I don't blame you."

"Noah promised to be a part of my life no matter what, so that's all that matters."

"What was it like living with him?"

This felt awkward. I didn't want to place him back in the "daddy" category. He was my man now, and throughout our relationship in LA, we struggled to resist our attraction. There was no way I could tell my friend that.

"Noah was a better father to me in the eight months I lived with him than all the years I'd lived with Rob."

The painful truth.

"Too bad Ally and I weren't able to visit in the summer. If you had told us about your accident, we would've been on the next flight out."

"I know. But I didn't want you girls to come all the way out there just to stare at me in a hospital bed. I wanted to get the surgery over with so I could recover and come home."

"You're lucky we've forgiven you for that." Jade peered up at me, offering a sympathetic smile. "Seriously, Aria, we're your best friends. No matter what situation or crisis you're in, we deserve to know. I'm just so happy you survived and are here with us."

"Me, too."

"But… back to the subject of 'Mister Hot-and-Available'… Tell me what I need to know. What are his pet peeves?"

"He hates traffic."

"Who doesn't?" Jade snickered.

"He loves a woman who takes care of her appearance, but is also not afraid to walk around in sweatpants with no makeup on."

"Okay, that's definitely me. Go on…"

"He's been in one serious relationship. He never went into detail, but the 'fatal ex' broke his heart."

"Poor baby." Jade frowned. "Who would want to hurt that man? He's gorgeous, talented, financially stable, has *mad* sex appeal… need I say more?" She giggled. "I just love his mysterious brown eyes. His ink and piercings—*mega* turn on. He's got the entire package!"

Jade was right. Evan was great boyfriend material—except he wasn't a boy. He was a man.

Man-friend? I wonder if we would've dated had I never met Noah.

"I'm so nervous about this date! What if we don't hit it off?"

"Well, from my own observations, you both have chemistry. I'm sure the date will go just fine. You'll come home with a huge smile on your face, and you'll tell me all about it while you glow and reminisce."

"Do you think he was waiting for me to turn eighteen before he asked me out? I mean, my birthday was two weeks ago."

"I'm not sure."

I honestly didn't know. The age of consent in New York was seventeen. So even if Evan had asked her out sooner, he wouldn't have been breaking any laws.

"I just need to relax and not psych myself out. He's a regular guy… who just looks like a hot model." Jade groaned and slumped down next to me. "I really hope he'll like me. Not like a friend, but *like* me, you know?"

"He already does. Just be yourself. You should never cut up your puzzle piece to fit with someone else's; that's like mutilating your identity and becoming someone you're not. You're outgoing, smart, funny, and beautiful. Jade, you have so many outstanding qualities. Any guy should feel lucky to date you or even have you as arm candy."

"You're seriously the best!" She hugged me. "I'm so glad you're back in New York again, Aria."

"Me too."

"Please don't move away."

"I don't plan on it."

CHAPTER FORTY-SEVEN
ANYTHING FOR HER

Evan was dressed sharply that night as he walked through Diamond Collar Gentleman's Lounge with two middle-aged men who were notable fashion magazine editors. After meeting up for a formal business dinner, they were more than impressed with Evan's portfolio. He had entertained the gentleman, hoping to get hired as their photographer for their next big cover. Fortunately for Evan, the club owner was a close friend of his and had promised to offer his guests full VIP treatment.

The establishment was dark and hazy, which only added to the seductive atmosphere. A T-shaped platform served as the main stage, with patrons seated around, throwing cash at the strippers as they worked the poles.

The club owner, Antonio Ramirez, emerged from a door and walked toward Evan to escort his entourage upstairs. Inside his office, he offered them drinks before he passed an iPad around and asked them to pick out their favorite dancer for a private show. Afterwards, Antonio made a phone call and asked one of his bouncers to bring the women to his office.

Once the strippers arrived, all eyes were on them, as if they were a piece of prime rib at a buffet. They lined up next to their boss and waited for detailed instructions.

"All right, ladies," Ramirez said. "You're gonna show these fellas a good time tonight… Anything goes."

“”

Evan had been smoking a cigar while he sat in a private room and waited for his private dancer to return. A sexy playlist of explicit music played in the background, setting the mood for scandalous activities. The mirrored room was dark with neon orange lighting. A wide triangle platform was set up in the center, with a pole in the middle. Sitting on a half-moon sofa, Evan exhaled hoops of smoke in the air.

After a ten-minute wait, a dark-haired stripper returned with a fancy chest full of condoms and sex toys. Her sapphire eyes seemed to glow as she stood in front of her client and opened the chest, wearing nothing but sparkly nipple pasties and a G-string.

"Don't be shy, sweetheart." She winked.

"I've got my own," he said, retrieving a Magnum from his wallet.

"I'm gonna take *real* good care of you tonight, big boy."

Towering over Evan in eight-inch heels, her flawless body was free of tattoos and piercings, and her B cup breasts were not surgically enhanced. Antonio was aware of Evan's type, which explained why he had advised his employee to cover up her ink for her VIP client.

"What's your name, love?" Evan puffed a cloud of smoke.

"Roxy."

He smiled and said, "Your *real* name."

"Roxy."

"I see how it is." He looked amused. "Did you bring what I asked for?"

She nodded, pulling out a cosmetic item.

"May I?"

Handing it over, she eyed him in curiosity, watching as Evan smeared the sangria colored lip liner along the left side of her abdomen to create what was supposed to look like a six-inch scar.

"I've done a lot of kinky things for clients, but this has got to be the weirdest by far." She laughed, stepping on the platform. "You're pretty hot, though, so I can't complain. Most of my clientele are old guys who wanna spank me or get spanked."

Roxy turned on some music and swung her weight around the pole while Evan admired her perky breasts to her toned stomach, fixating on the imitation "scar" he had drawn, right where her kidney was located.

Aria.

She was all he could think about.

"Would you like to make a lot of money tonight, love?"

"*Oh, yes*"—the stripper slid down the pole into the splits—"I won't disappoint."

"Good." He blew out another ring of smoke and said, "Hair down, heels off, and saddle up on me."

Seduction dripped from Roxy's desirable body as she stepped off the platform and obeyed Evan's commands.

"I'm gonna take care of you, baby"—she straddled his lap—"I always go the extra mile for a buff daddy." She rubbed his chest with her manicured hands, planting a kiss on his neck, unaware that he was fantasizing about Aria the entire time.

CHAPTER FORTY-EIGHT
DARKEST DAYS

Cambridge MA, Oct 1999

Throughout Harvard's campus, Noah Hunter's loft was popularly known as the best place to party. The young man had established a notorious reputation that had got him into hot water—but there was nothing that money couldn't fix, according to him. Among his peers, Noah was the typical "rich boy" who appeared to have it all, but looks are deceiving. He was battling the darkest demons. Drugs, sex, and alcohol had become his way of life, and if he continued this reckless routine, he would end up on academic probation. It seemed a miracle he had made it to his junior year.

It was a Friday night, and Noah's place was packed with college students who were drinking underage and using drugs. The music was so loud that a neighbor was bound to make a complaint. Noah knew that by the end of the night, his loft would look like a dump once everyone would leave. But he never had to worry about cleaning up since he could afford maid services.

While everyone was partying on the main floor, Noah was upstairs with two women. His spacious bedroom was encased in frosted glass and uniquely designed with pot lights and blue LEDs around his bed frame. Taking off his shirt, Noah sat on the edge of his bed while his "friends" disrobed.

He made two neat lines of cocaine on his mirrored nightstand before he rolled up a twenty-dollar bill and snorted the powder. Sniffling a few times, he repeated the same method until all the "sugar dust" had disappeared, reaching the back of his throat. He didn't mind, though; it numbed his nasal passage, causing more of it to get absorbed at a faster rate. Using a credit card, he cleaned up the left-over coke and made one last line.

"Do you wanna play with us?" said the blonde, tossing her bra at his head.

"I'm game." Noah grinned. Lying back on his bed, both women slithered over his body like sly serpents.

"Who's Aria?" one of them asked, noticing his tattoo.

"No one you need to know." He tangled his fingers through her wavy hair, pulling her down so she could show off her oral skills while her other friend joined in.

"You're such a dirty slut, aren't you?" he said, shoving two fingers down her throat. "That's it… suck it for me."

Fully aroused and high, Noah was no stranger to recreational drug use and cheap hookups. His hedonistic lifestyle had only pushed him further away from opening his heart to love and faith. The compassionate young man he used to be had been destroyed by his addictions.

In that moment, amidst the moaning, groaning, and slapping sounds of flesh against flesh, he submitted to his carnal desires, not caring about how it scarred his soul. Noah was on a dark road to self-destruction, and he was fully aware of it. The long-term consequences were not on his mind. The importance of preserving sacred sexual energy wasn't even within his awareness. He knew nothing about it; all he knew was that he was suffering every day, and his vices made the pain disappear, but it never lasted; it was a temporary fix. There wasn't a day he abstained from sex— and that included his "precious" cocaine. He was a tortured soul, enslaved by lust and substance abuse.

After ten minutes of foreplay, Noah's confidence had skyrocketed from the fast effect of the drug; it induced an amplified feeling of superiority for the user. Both women prostrated themselves on his bed while they shamelessly teased Noah.

"Spank me! I've been a *bad* girl…"

"Give it to me first!" the blonde demanded, wiggling her bare bottom.

In this bedroom, nothing was forbidden. Releasing his shame, Noah gripped his manhood and satisfied their insatiable lust, working his way to a mind-blowing climax. Their sexual intimacy was far from passionate; it was raunchy, aggressive, and devoid of emotion; no heart to heart connections. The hours passed as they exhausted each other until they finally passed out.

⊂ℬ⊃

The next day, Noah was awakened by a pleasurable sensation down below. Sunlight poured in as he rubbed the sleep out of his eyes. Struggling to focus, he watched the brunette he had bedded bobbing her head up and down, engulfing his manhood in her mouth. Now that he had come down from a cocaine high, all he wanted was to be alone. The downside of regaining clarity was realizing how horrible he felt: guilt… shame… self-loathing: a cocktail of pain. It was too much for his soul to bear. He did not want to face himself and be reminded of his inner demons.

"What the fuck are you doing?" Noah said, sounding deliberately cruel.

"Don't you like the way I suck you off, baby?" she teased, swirling her tongue around his swollen tip.

"I want you to leave."

"That's not what you said to me last night…"

"Drop my cock and get the hell out!" he blasted.

His stiff demeanor offended her as she sat up and scowled at him. "Why are you being such an asshole?"

Ignoring her, he threw his legs over the bed and pulled on his jeans.

"Do you even remember my name?"

"No, and I don't care." Noah lit a cigarette. "Wake your friend up and take her with you." He sounded so harsh and distant: a stark contrast to how charming and flirtatious he'd been the night before.

"I liked you better when you were high." She dressed herself in haste. "At least you weren't such a jerk!"

Heading downstairs, he overlooked the pigsty in his living room and puffed on a cigarette. Noah made a quick phone call for house cleaning before the angry brunette brushed past him, kicking plastic cups aside to get to the door. Her blonde friend followed behind, but paused for a moment to speak to Noah.

"I had fun last night. We should do this again!"

"Not likely." He smiled condescendingly.

"Come on, Jen!" her friend called out. "Let's go! We never should have slept with that prick!"

"What do you expect when you're dressed like hookers, throwing yourselves at men?"

"You're not a man."

She cursed at Noah some more before they finally left.

"Happy whoring!" Noah shouted, slamming the door shut.

Standing in deafening silence, his loft smelled of booze and marijuana. He took one last drag of his cigarette and crushed it into an ashtray on the coffee table. Noah knew he was a hypocrite. He had insulted those young women in such a degrading way; and the worst part was that he was fully aware he was projecting his own shame and self-loathing. His first love and heartbreak had caused his downward spiral. Noah's painful history with Natalie had damaged him. He resented his mother for getting involved to prevent their union. But what troubled him most was how he had relinquished his parental rights and was not involved in his daughter's life. He had been too young to have understood what it meant to be a father.

Before moving away to college, he was confident in a reconciliation when he had proposed to Natalie. She threw him off when she had rejected him (because of her own fears and projections), and before he knew it… she had taken their daughter and disappeared from his life. He felt tremendous guilt for not being there for Natalie and Aria. Noah had got involved with the wrong crowd and developed addictions he never thought he would have struggled with.

I hate myself. He hung his head down, sitting on the sofa.

⊱✦⊰

By 9p.m., Noah's place had been cleaned and organized. He sat in his living room, typing away at his laptop and occasionally sipping a mug of coffee. He had a major term paper to finish and was hoping to make the deadline by tomorrow. Half an hour had passed when he finally got into the zone of writing, only to be distracted by a soft knock at the door. Clad in a pair of ripped jeans, he dragged his feet to the entrance, peered through the peephole, and let out an exasperated sigh before he opened the locks.

"What are you doing here, Cammie?"

"Well, hello to you too, *Mister Ruggedly Handsome.*"

A brown-eyed beauty with long caramel hair stood before him, wearing a white pea jacket, a black scarf, and blue jeans. Her boots were flat heeled since she was tall enough to be a runway model. The beauty mark on her left cheek only accentuated her full luscious lips. Her olive skin was flawless, with a healthy glow.

Noah stared into her rich mahogany eyes and leaned his weight on the doorframe.

"You missed Thursday's lecture," Cammie said. "I brought you the notes."

Eyeing her carefully, he resisted the urge to dismiss her by being deliberately cruel.

"Can I come in?"

He hesitated to respond, but eventually stepped aside.

Camellia Castellano was attractive, intelligent, and ambitious. Every guy at Harvard found her desirable—professors included. Even though she had many dating options, she only wanted one man: an emotionally unavailable young man by the name of Noah Hunter.

Cammie was half Cuban-American, raised by a wealthy family in Florida. She had moved to Cambridge when she got accepted at Harvard. Her major was in political science and she planned to go to law school once she received her bachelor's degree. Unlike Noah, she lived in a sorority house on Harvard's campus. The two of them had been friends with benefits on and off throughout their first year. From the get-go, Noah had clarified that he wasn't looking for a serious relationship, but Cammie was convinced she could change his mind. She desperately believed she could save him from himself. She was wrong.

Their relationship was extremely unhealthy. Cammie loved and hated a man who couldn't reciprocate her love for reasons unknown to her. They would break up and make up constantly. She would promise to keep things casual and then go back on her word every time because she wanted more; she always wanted more. Despite Noah's hot and cold nature, Cammie loved him in silence and refused to lose hope. She wholeheartedly believed that he would wake up and realize he was in love with her, too. She had yet to surrender to the fact that you can't save someone who doesn't want to be saved.

They often partied together and experimented with party drugs. When Cammie wasn't spending the night in her bedroom, she was sleeping next to Noah, naked beneath his sheets, where they frequently unleashed their sexual fantasies. There were many occasions where she had found out about his flings with other women, which caused her to sink into mild bouts of depression and distance herself for a while... But she always came back. She loved Noah too much to move on from him. Cammie believed they were destined to be together. Unfortunately, Noah was incapable of committing to her. His traumas had emotionally crippled him, and he refused to confide in Cammie or get professional help.

"I brought you some take out... Chinese—your favorite." She placed the food on his coffee table and removed her coat.

"I already ate," Noah answered wryly, walking into the kitchen to refill his coffee.

"Oh." Cammie frowned. "Just save it for later." She took the bag and put the food away in the refrigerator.

Noah watched her vigilantly. She was easy on the eyes, but he was far from happy to see her. Feeling agitated and moody, he didn't want any company and was tired of Cammie showing up at random. All he wanted was to be left alone so he could finish his paper.

"A smile would be nice now and then," she sarcastically muttered, returning to the living room.

"Look, Cam, I'm really busy."

"Working on an essay?"

"Yeah."

"I could help you," she offered with a smile.

"I don't need help."

"What's got you so tense?"

"Nothing. I just want to be alone. You didn't even call."

"I didn't think I needed to." She closed the space between them and wrapped her arms around his chiseled shoulders. He was tense, Cammie thought. She lovingly kissed Noah's cheek and hugged him for as long as she could. She had missed him so much and only wanted to be close to him. But Noah could not be moved inside. He did not return her affection; he rarely ever did.

"Why won't you hug me back?" She withdrew, staring into his icy eyes.

"We both know what will happen if I do."

"It's just a hug."

"And then a kiss, and then a caress, and the next thing you know, I've got you under me with your clothes off."

"So?" Cammie flashed a pearly white smile. "Why resist something we both want?"

He rolled his eyes and stepped back. "Do I really need to go through this again with you?"

"Noah, I care about you. Why do you get mad at me for expressing it?"

"Because I don't need or want you to care about me. We had agreed to be friends with benefits, remember? But clearly that's failed because you keep getting your feelings involved. I'm not on the same page as you, and I'm tired of looking like the asshole every time I can't give you what you want. You have these impossible expectations from me—expectations I can never fulfill. Do you understand?"

"Can't you just try?" She sulked. "Are you even aware of the things you say when we make love? You're so sweet to me, and—"

"We don't make love. We hook up. And I'm *high as fuck* the entire time! I say a lot of bullshit when I'm doped up. You already know that."

Cammie tried to reason with him, dismissing her shattered feelings. "I know you have demons inside," she said. "We all do. But I can't just forget about everything you and I have shared. We're like magnets, Noah—and magnets attract." She held his icy hands, hoping that the warmth in her voice would melt his frozen heart. But it didn't.

"Everything with you is always so intense," Cammie confessed. "We're both the same, you and me. The only difference is that I'm an emotionally developed version of you, while you remain an empty shell."

"You say it like it's a choice."

"It is, Noah."

Feeling triggered, he glared at her and said, "Get out, Cammie."

"Truth hurts, but you need to hear it."

"I said, *get out*."

"Stop pushing me away. I know there's a good man inside of you. I don't know what happened in your past to make you this way. I wish you would tell me and let me in."

He hung his head down and said nothing.

Hoping to get through, she touched his face and tenderly kissed his neck, then his jaw, the corner of his mouth until he finally kissed her back.

"You know you want this," Cammie murmured. "You know you want me."

Noah kissed her hard, and within seconds they ended up in his bedroom, snorting cocaine and engaging in mind blowing sex. He took her in his favorite positions till he was out of condoms.

After a couple of hours, the drugged-up lovers lay in bed together, sleeping off the rest of their high. Cammie enveloped herself around him, feeling elated to have her fix. He was her worst addiction. He was her undoing.

⚬

Around three in the morning, Cammie opened her eyes. She was happy to find Noah beside her, which meant that last night had not been a dream. Kissing his chest, she hugged his warm body and was careful not to wake him as she traced his phoenix tattoo and wondered about its significance. The first time Cammie had asked him about it, Noah had said the name belonged to someone he loves a lot; someone who was no longer part of his life. Even though it hurt to think he was hung up on someone else, his tattoo proved he could love. What she didn't know was that the name on Noah's chest belonged to his daughter, and that he had tried several times to get shared custody of her but failed because he struggled to get clean.

Despite his destructive habits, Cammie was only a social drug user. She wasn't addicted and stayed away from syringes. But whenever she and Noah were in the same room together, she was up for anything—and sadly, enabled his drug habit, too. He was addicted to cocaine, and Cammie was addicted to him.

"Noah, baby… wake up." She caressed his face. "You still have that paper you need to finish."

He was too exhausted to move. After several attempts to wake him, Cammie got up to shower.

When she returned to his bedroom, Noah was still fast asleep.

He's out like a light, she thought, dressing herself in one of his shirts.

She softly kissed his head before heading downstairs. His laptop was still on the coffee table and had been left on. Cammie sat on the sofa and started typing away. If anything, she was saving him from failing.

⚬

Around eight in the morning, Noah scrambled out of bed. Feeling panicked, he rushed down the stairs, wearing only a pair of faded blue jeans: the buttons were still undone, and his hair was a mess.

"Why didn't you wake me up?" He raged, startling Cammie.

"I did," she said. "You wouldn't wake up." Sipping on coffee, she calmly walked over to him.

"That paper is due today!" Noah thrust his fingers into his hair. Cursing out loud, he paced the floor.

"I think you should turn on your laptop." Cammie hid a smile.

Noah froze when he opened his saved word document. There were pages filled with words he had not written.

"I saved your ass," she boasted. "You can thank me with some amazing morning sex. Your class doesn't start until ten, so I think we've got plenty of time to kill."

"Why the hell did you finish my paper for me?" Noah sounded ungrateful.

"Um, because you refused to wake up—duh!"

"The professor will notice this isn't my style." He skimmed through the sections she had written. "My writing is a lot more advanced."

Hurt and humiliated, Cammie set her mug down on the table and folded her arms in her chest. "Are you saying I'm too stupid to write an academic paper?"

"No. I'm saying this is not my style. I was supposed to add five secondary sources, which you didn't include."

"Noah, I spent all night working on that paper just to make sure you would pass."

"I risk getting kicked out of my program if he gets suspicious!"

"Calm down, he won't! It's not like I copied and pasted from online sources. *I* wrote the paper. McPherson can search all he wants to see if it was plagiarized, but he won't find anything. Why don't you thank me instead of acting like a dick?"

Noah clenched his jaw and stood up. His mind was a mess.

"I need a shower."

"Can I join?" Cammie smirked.

"Look, thank you for last night and for writing my paper—even though I never asked you to, but I really need you to do me a favor and leave." He paused. "Like right now."

"You can't be serious," she said in disbelief.

His lack of response only hurt her more. Staring at him long and hard, she desperately tried to keep herself from crying. "You know what?" she said. "This is my fault. I'm the idiot who keeps showing up at your door like a desperate fool. I need to stop getting mad at you and be mad at myself for being so stupid!" She turned around and stomped up the stairs to get changed.

Noah's guilt crept up on him as he called out her name and followed her.

"Wait," he said, reaching his bedroom. "Will you just stop for a moment?"

Cammie ignored him, cursing in Spanish while she dressed herself.

"Please?"

"No." She brushed past him and went downstairs.

He followed her and tried to make her understand why he needed space, but she already had her coat on and was about to leave.

"I'm sorry, okay?"

"Sorry isn't good enough," Cammie said with tears in her eyes.

Before Noah could respond, she was gone in a flash.

ೞ

An hour had passed since Cammie had left Noah's place. Lying on the sofa, he smoked a joint while listening to Matthew Good Band's "Beautiful Midnight" album. "Suburbia" faded in as he turned up the volume and folded his hands behind his head. The guitar rift was sad with haunting lyrics, but Noah was already depressed.

Might as well wallow in self-pity, he thought, wishing to numb himself.

CHAPTER FORTY-NINE
CARRIE

June 2000, San Francisco CA

Carrie Castellano was Cammie's younger sister and a sophomore at Yale University. Throughout her life, she was labeled as the "introverted nerd." At only nineteen, Carrie had never had a boyfriend, had never been kissed, and was still a virgin. Her parents had got divorced when she was two years old, and her mother remarried three years later. Both sisters were raised by their mother and stepfather in Arizona. Throughout Carrie's adolescent years, she struggled to get along with her mother, so she moved in with her father in Miami, while Cammie stayed behind.

Both sisters were close, but they had opposite personalities. Cammie was confident and outgoing; while Carrie was shy, reserved, and struggled with social anxiety. For much of her life, she always felt her older sister was prettier and more accomplished than her. Throughout middle school, her classmates bullied her and made her feel like an ugly duckling. The teasing eventually stopped once she started high school, but she could never erase the image of "Plain Jane" from her mind. Carrie's hazel eyes were typically hidden behind dark-framed glasses, and her skinny figure was nowhere near as voluptuous as Cammie's. She was a petite young woman, with short brown hair that she usually dyed in different colors. Despite their differences, they had a healthy relationship and loved each other a lot. Carrie had always been the brightest and most ambitious. She aspired to be a lifesaving neurosurgeon.

Moving away for college had helped Carrie to come out of her shell and become more independent. She finally had a sense of autonomy—something she had rarely felt while living at home with her mother and stepfather.

It was in the summer of her freshman year when the most amazing event happened to Carrie: she fell in love. Her sister had invited her on a road trip, and although Carrie had been reluctant to go, she was glad to have suspended her fear, because as soon as she cast her eyes on Noah Hunter, it was love at first sight. He was attractive in every sense, but he was never mean to her like other boys had been in the past. Carrie thought he was charming to a fault and heartbreakingly good looking. Her sister had warned her earlier on not to get close to him because Noah was the bad boy type. But it was impossible for Carrie to believe that. Throughout their trip, she saw nothing but Noah's sweet side.

They traveled for three weeks, site sightseeing and partying along the Atlantic coast. By the time they reached Georgia, Cammie suspected her sister was crushing on Noah. When she finally had an opportunity to be alone with her, she cautioned Carrie not to let her feelings go beyond friendship. What she had failed to mention was that she was madly in love with Noah.

One evening while they were staying at a hotel, Cammie eavesdropped on a conversation Noah was having with her sister:

"You remind me of someone," he said. "Someone I used to love." Even though they weren't dating, Cammie couldn't help but feel a twinge of jealousy every time she saw her sister bonding with him. It boggled her mind how he found Carrie to be more interesting than her.

When they left Georgia, they drove to San Francisco and stayed at a summer home that belonged to the grandparents of their friend Miguel. After three amazing days of surfing, barbeques, and patio parties, the four of them went to a rave on their last day in the city. Carrie had mentioned that she had never been to a rave before, which was why Noah wanted her to experience it.

At 10p.m., Carrie and her friends parked near an abandoned warehouse that was transformed into a party capital for ravers. They got inside with no ID, since Miguel's cousin was a bouncer.

Carrie was in awe as she absorbed the flashy environment. Masses of people were covered in neon body paint, dancing under laser lights. The atmosphere was like live wire, full of amplified energy.

"This is so amazing!" Carried shouted over the music.

"Come on!" Cammie grabbed her sister's arm and led her through a crowd. It was going to be a night they would never forget.

₧∓

A DJ was spinning a live set for the past three hours, and the rave had got more crowded than before. Masses of glowing bodies danced in a large crowd, waving glow sticks in the air as the music cross faded to "Behind" by ATB ft. Flanders.

At some point, Noah and Carrie lost Cammie and Miguel as they danced close together. Noah had consumed no alcohol that night, but he was high on Ecstasy. Dripping in sweat, he took off his shirt and noticed the way Carrie's eyes widened when she saw his ripped physique; it made him smile as he lost himself in the melodies of heaven, heightening his euphoric state.

Carrie was clad in a plaid miniskirt and combat boots. She had knotted a white vest top at her stomach, showing off her midriff. It was the first time she wore heavy makeup; it was also a first for Noah to see her without glasses on. Carrie had never had this much fun before in her life. The rave was like an initiation, a rite of passage. Her parents always sheltered her from everything they believed to be harmful to her growth. But at that moment, under the strobe lights, she felt free, happy, and in love.

Noah yelled over the music. "This track is a vibe!"

"Never heard it before!" Carrie shouted back. "But I love it too!" She hung her arms over his shoulders as he reached for her waist.

"I wanna kiss you!"

"*What?*" Carrie wasn't sure if she had heard him correctly.

"I wanna kiss you!"

"I can't hear you!"

"I said, I—" Noah stopped mid-sentence and kissed her deeply.

His kiss was a powerful catalyst, awakening Carrie's inner dark goddess as her body came to life. Finally, she experienced her first kiss, and it was more than what she hoped it would be. Her young soul was too inexperienced to realize that her connection with Noah was just puppy love. She wanted to express her feelings to him before the trip ended.

Pulling back, Noah smiled and caressed Carrie's beautiful face before he led her away from the crowd. She followed him like a trusting angel and found herself pushed against a wall in a secluded hallway where Noah's demon trapped her with an insatiable kiss.

"I want you," he breathlessly whispered in her ear.

Carrie's heart pounded in her chest. The pleasurable pull in her stomach felt painful. Things were escalating quickly. She was certain she wanted Noah to be her first. She didn't care that they were both under the influence of alcohol and hallucinogens. Everything at that moment felt right to her. But that was the illusion of MDMA, Carrie thought; it gave a false sense of euphoria, and happiness. It was the devil's drug, or so she was told.

"Tell me you want me, Carrie."

She moaned when Noah pressed himself into her.

"I want you."

"Touch me," he demanded. "Pull it out."

Carrie blushed.

"Are you getting shy now?" Noah chuckled. He kissed her deeply, guiding her hand down his pants. "Look what you do to me."

Hiding her excitement, she curiously stroked his generous length, moaning softly as he grazed his lips along her jaw and let his hand travel to the source of her heat.

"Take me," she murmured.

Noah wasted no time, pulling out a silver foil from his pocket; he ripped it open with his teeth, rolled it onto himself, and thrust into her without warning.

◌◌

For the past twenty minutes, Cammie had been trying to find her sister through the crowd. She was worried, hoping that Noah was with her instead of some creep. But as soon as she walked through the exit doors, she froze in shock. Her heart shattered to pieces as she watched Carrie and Noah going at it like rabbits against the wall. They were too distracted to realize they had been caught. Feeling betrayed, Cammie's jealousy nearly consumed her. She was in love with Noah for years; she never thought he would do something like this. Overwhelmed with emotion, she turned away and rushed through the masses until she was finally outside.

◌◌

Labored breaths echoed in Carrie's ears as Noah's hard body tensed up against her. Achieving a mutual release, he groaned in pleasure and kissed her before he set her on her feet. She was already addicted. She only wanted more.

"That was incredible!" Carrie said. "You were my first…"

Noah's smile instantly faded and transformed into a look of panic and horror.

"What?"

"I've never had sex with anyone else."

He laughed. "You're joking."

Carrie shook her head, feeling self-conscious.

Noah's face went pale when he looked down and noticed a trickling line of blood dripping down Carrie's thigh. He cursed himself in his head and tried to stay calm.

"What's wrong?" She frowned.

"You're… bleeding." He cleaned the blood on her leg with his shirt.

"Oh, my God! I'm so embarrassed!"

"Don't be," he said with compassion. "Stay here."

"W-wait! Where… where are you going?"

"I'll be right back. I just need to clean up. Wait for me here."

He left her shortly to go to the restroom. But when he returned, Carrie was nowhere to be found. Noah was worried, thinking she had wandered off and got lost. Pulling out his phone, he tried to call her.

Maybe she had to use the restroom, he thought, hanging up.

Tracking his friends, he maneuvered through a group of ravers until he got to the center of the dance floor. Someone grabbed his arm and got his attention. Noah was relieved to see a familiar face when he turned around.

"She's having a seizure!" Miguel shouted in a frenzy. "I called an ambulance!"

"What?"

"Someone must have slipped her something!"

"Wait, who are you talking about?"

"Carrie! Come on!"

Noah couldn't move; he was stunned.

"We need to leave, man!" Miguel tried to shake some sense into him.

The two of them bolted out of the warehouse, where they soon found the girls. Carrie was on a stretcher, being led into an ambulance.

"We need to follow them." Noah rushed to the parking lot.

But his corvette was gone. Cursing out loud, he told Miguel that Cammie had his keys.

"She probably left to go to the hospital. I'll call us a cab."

Feeling guilty, Noah prayed Carrie would be all right. He felt responsible for what happened to her. He blamed himself entirely.

∽

At the hospital, they were promptly informed that Carrie was in the ICU and was getting her stomach pumped. She had MDMA in her system and had had an allergic reaction. Noah and Miguel sat in the waiting room for almost an hour before a doctor appeared and told them that Carrie was stable. Cammie eventually arrived, running down the hall in tears. It was three in the morning; everyone was exhausted.

"How did this happen?" she asked Miguel.

"Carrie was drinking a bottle of water when she found me. The next thing I knew, her eyes rolled back and she dropped to the floor, seizing."

"I never bought her any alcohol," Noah said.

"Someone must have sold her a roofied bottle or slipped her something when she wasn't looking," Miguel concluded.

"She was with me almost all night. I was looking out for her."

Cammie turned her furious gaze to Noah and let him have it. "I can't believe you hooked up with my sister! How could you?"

Noah froze up again, unaware that she had walked in on them.

"What kind of man are you? She was saving herself for marriage! Maybe *you* were the one who drugged her!"

"How can you say that? I'd never do that!"

"You slept with my baby sister!" Cammie exploded, shoving Noah's chest while she cussed him out. "How could you do that to me?" Her mahogany eyes misted with tears. "How?" She pushed him harder like a woman scorned, crying uncontrollably.

"*Cálmate*, Camellia!" Miguel said in Spanish, restraining her arms. "This isn't the place!"

"I hate you!" She screamed at Noah.

"I... I didn't know." Regret poured from his eyes. "I wasn't thinking."

"You asshole!"

"I'm so sorry."

"You're always sorry, aren't you?" Cammie wept. "We both know that's a load of bull—because you never give a shit! You don't care about anyone but yourself!"

"I didn't mean for this to happen."

"Just go!" Cammie hurled Noah's car keys at him with revulsion and said, "You mess everything up! Pack your shit and leave! I never want to see you or hear from you again!" She turned and took refuge in Miguel's arms.

Noah was so guilt stricken. There wasn't much he could say or do. He felt useless and powerless. Cammie's agonizing cries echoed in his ears as he shamefully walked down the hall to the elevators.

I can't get any lower than this, he thought, heading down to the parking garage.

He left an envelope full of cash on the coffee table to help cover his friends' travel expenses. Noah had already taken care of Carrie's hospital fees, but it still didn't make him feel any better. His summer vacation had turned out to be a nightmare, and he held himself accountable. He wasn't sure how he could ever make it right with his friends, especially the sisters.

CHAPTER FIFTY
GUESS WHO?

Cambridge, MA, 2001

Life as Noah knew it had gone back to normal, except a few things had
changed: he was six months clean from his addictions. Last summer's
haunting events had been the wake up call he needed to check himself
into rehab when he returned to Cambridge in August. It was during his
stay at the wellness center where he first met Dr. Alexander Grey. His
sessions with him hadn't been successful at first, but eventually, Dr. Grey
helped Noah overcome his cocaine and sex addiction to get him on the
road to recovery.

*Love, acceptance, self-respect: it must all start from within, Noah. How can you
love and respect another person, if you can't even show the same toward yourself?*

Noah remembered Dr. Grey's advice as he cooked in his kitchen on
a chilly Thursday evening in February. He only had two months left of
school before he would graduate.

*Learn to love and forgive yourself, Noah, so that you can forgive and love others
with a compassionate heart. You can't live the rest of your life punishing yourself and
pushing people away out of shame. That will only lead you down a dark and lonely
road.*

Grey's advice was useful, but Noah felt daunted when he thought
about the long road to redemption. His relationship with Cammie was
often discussed with Dr. Grey. Noah had sent her many emails

apologizing for what had happened on their road trip. He had mentioned his sobriety, but Cammie never replied. She avoided him for months and ignored him whenever she saw him on campus. Dr. Grey had suggested he email Carrie and apologize, but he didn't have her contact information. Noah had never meant to hurt Cammie or ruin her relationship with her sister. He didn't like the way things had ended last summer, but Dr. Grey had told him not to dwell on the past. Giving Cammie some space was for the best. He knew he needed to forgive himself for what happened in order to move forward with his life. And that's exactly what Noah was determined to do.

೮ು೧೮

By early March, Noah found himself in the middle of another custody battle for his daughter. While stressing over his finals, he worried about his case in family court. Tomorrow morning, he was flying out to New York with his attorney. Being seven months sober, his anxiety was through the roof, but Noah was determined to stay optimistic. He needed his daughter in his life. Seven years had passed since she was born, and he was finally ready to be there for her. Aria was the only person he loved unconditionally. He was confident if he was more involved in her life, he could be a better father and a better man.

It had been raining all day on that late Tuesday evening as Noah occupied his time with his studies. From the start of his senior year, he had stopped hosting parties and had become a social recluse. He was progressing well, determined to put his poor reputation behind him.

Setting his laptop aside, he got up to make some coffee when someone knocked on the door. Surprised by the unexpected visit, he sauntered to the entrance and looked through the peephole to see who it was.

Shit.

Anxiously, he unlocked the door and prepared himself for an argument.

"Cammie."

There was a five-second pause before she smiled and invited herself in.

"You're forgiven," she casually said, looking around his place. "I needed time to get to that stage. Missed me?" Cammie smiled. "I'm surprised you didn't go to any of Connor's parties last year."

"I've been in rehab. I mentioned that in my emails to you."

If you bothered to read them, he thought, put off by her indifference.

Cammie had ignored him for months, and now she was waltzing back into his life as if nothing had ever gone wrong between them.

"Are you okay?" he asked.

"I'm great."

Her brown eyes cascaded from his face to his muscled body: he was clean shaven, had put on some weight, and looked well rested, healthier than ever, Cammie thought.

"I'm sorry," Noah said. "I wasn't expecting to see you."

"Well, you can't blame a girl for hating your guts after what you did."

"Cammie, you know how horrible I feel about—" He sighed, rubbing the back of his neck.

"I know. I'm not here to guilt trip you." She stared at him for what seemed to be forever, untying her trench coat as it dropped to the floor, revealing the red lingerie that was covering her intimate places.

Noah's eyes widened in reaction.

"If you think we're officially over, you've got another thing coming, Noah Mason Hunter." Cammie stepped toward him. "I didn't go through Hell and back with you all these years for nothing." Closing the space, she left the softest kiss on his lips, as if to erase his intimate encounter with her sister.

Noah tried to resist her advances, but Cammie wouldn't stop. Reaching below, she rubbed her palm against his evident arousal.

"Come on," she whispered. "I know you want me. Take what you've conquered..." Her lustful stare enticed him as she unfastened her bra and dropped it behind her. "Take what's yours."

His cocaine addiction wasn't the only thing he was recovering from, but sex addiction as well... And here was Cammie, flaunting herself, tempting him to take "one last drink," knowing it would never be his last. She was the devil in disguise. Noah was an addict, and he was about to relapse.

"I want you"—Cammie licked his lips—"… inside me."

Heated lust flashed in his gaze as he lifted her up and dropped her on the couch. He quickly divested himself of his clothes and parted her thighs.

"*Oh, God*," Cammie moaned. "I needed this." She tangled her fingers through his hair and kissed him. "I so needed this."

Finally, she had got her fix. Her favorite drug had always been Noah. That would never change, she believed. She was determined to marry this man and convince him they were meant to be.

೦೩೮೦

At some point, they ended up in Noah's bedroom. Their sex was fierce but short-lived. Cammie looked more than satisfied as she lay beneath him. He supported his weight above her and stared into her eyes.

"We can't keep doing this," said Noah. "We're toxic to each other. I'm not good for you." He had more clarity when his mind wasn't impaired from excessive drug use.

"Take me again," Cammie demanded. "Hard and rough like you've always done."

"I don't want to be rough with you."

"We both know you do. That demon is still alive in you. I can feel it… sense it." She bit her lip. "Choke me while you…"

"So, you came here to give me a *sexorcism*?" Noah joked.

"Something like that."

He rolled off her body and lay beside her, regretting his impulsive decision to sleep with her. Rationalizing seemed too hard when his every instinct had been screaming to surrender and satisfy his sex drive.

Cammie mounted him and slowly sucked on his index finger to arouse him again. "Punish me for being such a bitch to you."

"Stop. You haven't." He pulled his hand away.

"Bend me over and…" she murmured dirty things in his ear, giggling as something pulsed beneath her. "Or maybe you'd like to—"

Using his strength, Noah flipped her on her back before he got up.

"This was a mistake." He dressed himself.

"Are you serious?" Cammie couldn't understand his rejection. She took it personally. "You always like it rough, though."

"Not anymore." He zipped his fly.

Getting out of bed, she put on her panties and followed him downstairs to the living room. Noah had been the only man to fully satisfy her sexual desires, and she would not leave his loft until she got *exactly* what she wanted from him.

"I've brought something for you." She reached into her handbag and dangled a small bag full of white powder.

His blue eyes darted to his lethal lover, inducing excitement and anxiety. Something within him was desperate to escape its cage. His cocaine addiction had robbed him of happiness and had caused him more pain than good.

"Come on, babe," Cammie pleaded. "Sex always feels so amazing when we get high together."

This was her last-ditch effort in making him revert to old patterns. In her twisted mind, being with "asshole Noah" was better than no Noah at all. If she had to sabotage his efforts to stay sober, she would live with that on her conscience; Cammie was selfish that way.

"Why would you bring that shit to my place when you *know* I've been trying to stay clean?" He looked at her accusingly, controlling his rage.

"It's just cocaine, Noah—not heroin." She sat on the couch, turned on his stereo, and fixed a few lines on the coffee table.

"I don't touch that stuff anymore." He watched her snort up. "I can't keep doing this with you." Noah hated having to be a jerk again, but if it was necessary to break her heart to end their toxic relationship, then he would play that role for the greater good. "Whatever we had… it led us nowhere."

"What do you mean?"

He rubbed his forehead in frustration and shouted, "I don't love you, okay? I'm not in love with you! I never was and never will be! You're just an easy lay! That's all you ever were to me!"

Cammie was stunned. "You don't mean that. I know what you're trying to do, and it won't work this time, Noah."

"You really are daft, aren't you?" He scoffed. "I'm bored with you! You'll never get me to commit, so just stop wasting your time and leave me the fuck alone!"

They argued back and forth until Cammie finally broke down in tears. "Why are you always so heartless to me? After everything…"

This was more than Noah could handle. It gave him no pleasure to hurt her, but he had to remind himself that a permanent separation was for the best. His sanity and sobriety were on the line.

The minutes passed, and her crying only worsened. Sitting down, he tried to reason with her through a more civil approach.

"Cammie, listen to me. I'm seriously messed up—that's why I'm seeing a shrink. You deserve to have someone who will love you and treat you right. I've got too much baggage."

"All of which I've accepted time and time again!" she wailed with tears in her eyes. "I'm the only woman who gives a damn about you! Not your ex, not the whores you casually hook up with, and not even your family! I deserve a chance, Noah—after everything we've been through!"

Consumed with guilt and self-loathing, he pulled her in his arms and let her cry in his chest.

I'm nothing. I'm nobody. I'll always be a fuckup. It's better to stay out of Aria's life. Look at all the people I've constantly hurt: it's a never-ending pattern. I should be selfless for once and stay away from her. I know where this road will end. I'll destroy her just like I destroyed Nat, Carrie, and everyone else who knows me. I'm a selfish, heartless bastard, and a narcissistic junkie. I can't kick my addictions. I need to stop deluding myself. I'm too far gone. This is as good as it's gonna get for me.

Drowning in despair, he watched himself sinking into a void until he could no longer see the light. He felt empty, lifeless, and alone.

When Cammie finally quieted down, Noah stared into her mahogany eyes and caressed her face. She was beautiful, seductive, and unquestionably desirable, but he just couldn't get his heart to connect with her in the way she wanted.

If the Devil is real, then he's sitting beside me right now… as a woman, Noah thought.

"I just want to be with you." Cammie wiped her tears.

"I know, baby." He kissed her and embraced his demons. "Fix me some lines."

The high was instant, a bittersweet reunion. Reclining against the sofa, he exhaled deeply, feeling invincible, like he could conquer the world again. He had welcomed chaos into his psyche and somewhere in his muddled awareness; he knew he would regret it.

☙❧

Noah never made it to the courthouse the next morning. His attorney had left many messages on his answering machine, but he avoided returning his calls. He spent the next the next two days spiraling on a drug binge with Cammie. They only got up to rehydrate, use the restroom, shower… and then it was back to sleep, sex, and snorting coke repetitiously.

On the third night, Cammie woke up around two in the morning to find that Noah was still asleep. Caressing his chest, she was startled when he clutched her wrist.

"Go back to bed," he muttered with his eyes closed.

"I just love touching you."

"I'm trying to sleep."

"Are you ever gonna tell me who Aria is?"

Turning away, he mumbled, "The only girl I love more than anyone."

Cammie's envy stung her like a hundred scorpions. Unable to sleep, she angrily threw the covers back and strode into the bathroom to shower and leave.

This was their tragic tale of unrequited love. Their toxic relationship continued until they finally parted ways for law school.

CHAPTER FIFTY-ONE
ARIA

I was so excited to go to the photo exhibit tonight and see Evan's creations. I had been looking forward to it since the day he told me about the special event. Jade and Ally couldn't attend because they both had an evening class they couldn't miss. Around 6pm, I stepped out of my apartment wearing a white double breasted straight cut jacket with a wide collar. It took ages to put my outfit together, but I decided on black skinny jeans, a coral-colored tunic, and black suede ankle boots I wanted to wear on a special occasion. Straightening my hair, I wore it over my shoulders and wrapped Noah's scarf around my neck: the same one he had given me last year when we walked down Central Park. My makeup was minimal, but I had brushed on some peach colored lip gloss.

Headed for the subway station, my cellphone suddenly rang. I beamed when I looked at the caller ID.

"Hey, you!"

"Aria, I've got a bit of an emergency."

"Is everything all right?"

"I need you to do me a favor."

"What's up, Daddy?"

"I'm 'Daddy' now?" He laughed.

"Yes! Now I can say it, since we have no blood ties."

"And what does 'Daddy' mean in this context?"

"Rich, older man who is sexy A.F. and possesses all the qualities of an ideal father and lover."

"I'm reminded of my old age, if you call me that."

"It'll grow on you, Daddy Noah."

"Good lord…" He chuckled. "I'm not sure how I feel about you calling me that in public."

"Only in the bedroom."

"Definitely *not*."

I cracked up.

"Do you still have the key to my penthouse?"

"Yes."

"I need you to go there and go inside my office. I—"

"Wait—*right now?*"

"Yes, it's urgent."

Crap, I'm gonna be late for Evan's exhibit!

"Look," Noah said. "I know you haven't seen my place yet because of the renovation, but if you just get there now, you'll know which room is my office because it's the only room I told the contractors not to touch. Once you're there, text me and I'll call you back to tell you what I need. It's just a case file—but an important one. Can you please do that for me?"

I couldn't say no. He needed my help, and I would not let him down.

"On my way."

"Thank you so much. You're literally saving my job here."

"I'm glad to help."

"I'm sorry I called at a bad time. I haven't forgotten about my brother's big event tonight. I just really need you to get that file, scan it and email it to me."

"Don't worry, Noah. I'll find it." I signaled a cab and got inside. "I'll text you once I'm there."

"Thank you—oh, and Aria?"

"Yes?"

"I love you, baby. You're mine. Don't you forget it."

I would never tire of hearing that. Ever.

ঙ৪৹

The cab ride to Noah's penthouse condo took about twenty-five minutes. I was deep in the heart of the city now, in an upscale neighborhood in Manhattan called SoHo. Paying my fare, I stepped out on the street and couldn't help but gape at the high-rise building across from me. It looked like a luxury plaza hotel I'd seen in a magazine. The exquisite cast-iron architecture seemed revitalized, which explained why it appealed to commercial clients. Noah wasn't too far from the townhouse I lived in. A half-hour drive was better than being thousands of miles apart.

Using the key through the lobby door, I let myself inside the main entrance and looked around. The concierge was an elderly gentleman sitting behind a desk. We exchanged smiles as I headed toward the elevator. At the top floor, I walked down a wide hallway with windows leading to a tall brown door. Three gold plated numbers were mounted in the center, just above the peephole:336. Inserting the key, I opened it and stepped into the darkness.

The city lights glittered from the floor to ceiling windows across from me, and the penthouse had a fresh paint smell, though it wasn't too overpowering. I was pleasantly surprised when I turned on the lights and found a fully furnished living room, exactly the way I had envisioned. It was identical to the way we had planned to decorate it together. All those DMs we had exchanged back and forth bouncing décor ideas had been so much fun. He must have hired a professional interior designer. I remembered him saying the penthouse was five thousand something square feet, which meant the market price was somewhere in the high millions.

The spacious living room had dark hardwood flooring with an impressive cityscape view. The walls were painted in the same color I had told Noah I wanted: moon mist. I adored the white sofa set. They built a contemporary fireplace across from it. Designed in a simple monochromatic color scheme, it accented the suite with dark shades of brown and green. A giant television was mounted on the wall, and it made me think of all the movie nights we would have together, kissing and cuddling… possibly more. I smiled at the thought.

The ceiling was outrageously high, but it suited the open concept design. I loved the spiral staircase that led to the second level, where the bedrooms were located. I had been expecting to walk into an unfinished renovation, but everything looked perfect: a breathtaking palace in the sky. Standing in awe, I had to remind myself that I had an urgent task to attend to.

I sent Noah a text, and he quickly called me back.

"How come you never told me the renovation was finished?" I asked. "The penthouse looks amazing!"

"The upstairs level isn't done yet. Where are you right now?"

"In your giant living room."

"*Our* giant living room. Are you facing the windows?"

"Yes," I answered.

"Okay, do you see a hallway to your right?"

"Uh huh."

"Walk to the end. There's a door to your left."

I did as he instructed and opened the door to his office.

"Okay, I'm here."

"There's an oil painting mounted on the wall behind my desk. Do you see it?"

I switched on the light. "Yep!"

"Behind it you'll find a safe. The passcode is: 18-6-39-75. Punch in the digits and open it. There's a silver key in a black box."

"Okay… I've got the key. Now what?"

"Go to my desk and unlock the first drawer on the right—you'll find a bunch of files. Look for the one that has the label: *Jung vs. Matthews*. I need you to fax it over to me. Do you know how to work a fax machine?"

"Uh…"

I did not want to screw this up.

"Look," Noah said. "Don't panic. I'll walk you through it." He seemed much calmer than I was.

When I opened the drawer, I froze. There were no files inside… nothing. The only thing I found was a long stem rose—a red one.

"Did you find the file?" he asked.

"Um… no."

"What do you mean 'no'?"

"I found a rose in the drawer, not a file." I grabbed it and closed my eyes, smelling its intoxicating scent.

"Hmm, that's odd," Noah said.

Music suddenly echoed all around me; it had a progressive house beat. *What the…*

He must have installed a Bluetooth sound system somewhere.

"Noah, what's going on?"

I paused a moment and recognized the song: "Dream of Love" by Nox Vahn and Mimi Page.

"Consider this your anthem… and what's going on is that…"—he paused and appeared by the door with his phone to his ear—"I'm standing right in front of you." Tears filled my eyes as I dropped the call and rushed toward him. He was dressed in semi-formal attire: white shirt, gray formal trousers, and dark loafers—handsome, as usual.

"I can't believe you're here right now… you sneaky bastard!" Rushing with excitement, I flung my arms around him. "I thought you wouldn't be here for another month!"

"I wanted t—"

My lips collided with his before he could finish his sentence. Kissing Noah was like experiencing the most euphoric state of ecstasy; it was Heaven coming down. No scientist could ever create a hallucinogenic drug to duplicate what I felt, as if trillions of fireworks were going off in the atmosphere at the same time: a supernova blast of sun and moon energy. It was a cosmic crescendo every time we kissed. He breathed life into my soul. I only prayed he felt the same when he kissed me.

"Why'd you stop?" I said, as he pulled back.

"For breath." He kissed me again with reckless abandon, tracing my curves.

This was the best surprise ever. I wouldn't wake up in a hospital bed again, only to be torn away from a beautiful life. This was the real deal. This was Noah Hunter in the flesh. All mine.

"I missed you so much," he murmured, kissing my neck.

"I missed you more. You have no idea. I've cried myself to sleep most nights hugging your shirt."

"My beautiful baby. It feels so good to just hold you. I'm half a soul when I'm far from you, Aria."

He held me in his arms while I stared at his handsome face, caressing him.

"Was this whole 'emergency' a setup?"

"I'd like to think of it as a sentimental gesture."

"I still can't believe you're really here." I kissed him softly, hugging the life out of him.

"*Need... air... Aria...*"

"Sorry!"

Easing my grip, I held his face and let our lips melt, relaxing in his protective energy.

"Are you gonna... let me explain?" Noah laughed between kisses.

"You have my undivided attention."

"Long story short... I closed the case earlier than expected."

"So, bringing me here for that case file was—"

"A white lie. I could tell you were panicking as soon as I mentioned the fax machine." Noah chuckled.

"You are so devious!"

"My intentions were good. I'm just happy to hold you again."

His brilliant sea eyes bore right into me, reflecting love, passion, and desire at the same time. He always took my breath away.

"Please tell me you won't be leaving the country soon." I pouted.

"Trust me, I don't plan on it. The only time I'll be flying out of here is in December with *you...* to Italy."

"You've made me the happiest woman in the world right now."

"I know a hundred different ways I can make you happier tonight." His crooked grin was so sexy as he picked me up and threw me over his shoulder.

"Put me down! I need to be at Evan's photo exhibit tonight!"

"Call and cancel," he said, marching into the living room.

"I can't. I promised him I'd be there. Please don't make me go back on my word. I never break my promises."

Noah seemed reluctant to listen, but eventually stopped. Releasing a heavy sigh, he placed me back on my feet.

"Do I really have to share you tonight?"

"I'm afraid so."

He smothered my neck in kisses and squeezed me in his arms.

"Noah…" I giggled. "I'm serious. I'm already running late."

"I heard you"—he glided his lips to my shoulders—"we'll go together."

"You really want to come?"

"I'm sharing you tonight, remember? I deserve at least half of your attention—seems only fair."

"I wish we could go out in public as a couple."

This dampened the mood a bit.

"That day will come, baby," he said. "I promise." Caressing my cheek, he kissed me softly before he pulled back and held my hands. "In the meantime, let's establish a code—a secret lingo."

"Okay… like what?"

"For instance, every time you hear me criticizing Evan's work, it just means I'm secretly expressing my love for you."

Oh boy.

"If I say, 'Wow, Evan… did you take that photo with the lens cap on?' I'm really saying: 'You're a goddess, Aria.' And if I also comment with: 'A gorilla would be more competent with a camera…' I'll really be saying—"

"Definitely *not*. You're not gonna use me as an excuse to hurl crude insults at your brother. This is his first exhibit. Be nice, be supportive, and if you refuse to be, then just quietly brood in a corner somewhere—you're good at that and you're still sexy. I won't mind." I grinned.

"Are you forgetting who wears the pants in this relationship?" Noah raised his eyebrows.

I looked down at my legs and met his eyes with a smile.

"Point proven." He exhaled.

"I'm gonna find a vase for my rose, and then we need to leave your place."

"Again, it's *our* place. I gave you a key, Aria. This is your home, too."

Noah was my home. As long as I was with him, I was happy.

CHAPTER FIFTY-TWO
KINGDOM AT WAR

Cambridge, MA, April 2002

Noah's cellphone was ringing nonstop in the morning. In a drugged-up haze, he reached for his device and accidentally knocked an ashtray off the nightstand. Without bothering to glance at the caller ID, he switched off his mobile, pulled a pillow over his head, and went back to sleep. Two young women were tangled in each other's arms next to him; a bisexual couple he had picked up at a bar last night. His pattern of nocturnal activity had not stopped since he graduated last year. Constantly relapsing, he took a year off before enrolling in law school, though he hadn't been too productive with his time. His constant partying and drug use was taking a toll on his health.

Once again, Noah was woken up by stimulating pleasure. His eyes snapped open as he looked down and saw a woman with pink hair devotedly giving him a morning blow job—something he was used to. She expertly swirled her pierced tongue around his base, amplifying his arousal.

"You have the most beautiful... I've ever sucked." She giggled, pleasuring him.

"Wanna go for a ride?" He raised himself on his elbows and met her sea-green eyes.

"*Mmmmm...* yes." She simpered, mounting him.

Noah reached into his drawer and tossed her a condom. "Wrap me up." He folded his hands behind his head.

Abandoning his self-indulgent lifestyle was more challenging than he thought. He could not reform himself. Enslaved by sexual demons, almost nothing was forbidden inside his bedroom. Flesh was slapped and whipped, bodies were penetrated; and hair was pulled. Labored breaths and lustful moans always echoed from that room every night.

Having satisfied his sex drive, he finally collapsed on his back and felt like the dirtiest scumbag alive. Every time he had sex with random women, all he felt afterwards was intense self-loathing. The "wind down effect" after sex was especially unpleasant for him. He felt as if pieces of his soul were decaying day by day.

His flawless body glistened with sweat as he lay motionless. But his internal world was a mess. No amount of showering could cleanse his contaminated soul from the dark energies that had attached to him because of his promiscuous lifestyle. He needed spiritual purification. Feeling lost, Noah knew he had wasted the past four years on casual encounters and drugs. It was getting harder to maintain his double life. He desperately wanted to get back on track, but his cocaine addiction was derailing his progress. The path he was on was a destructive one. He was fated to crash and burn if he didn't get help, and this scared him because he had a daughter to fight for and live for.

𝄢𝄢

Around six in the evening, someone knocked while Noah was sitting in the living room. Not bothering to check who it was, he opened the locks.

"Well, well…" He sneered. "The gods must really hate me since they keep bringing *you* to my door."

"The *gods* have blessed you, which is why I keep *showing up* at your door." Cammie matched his sardonic smile.

"Right… a 'blessing.'" Noah rolled his eyes and let her in. His sarcasm never seemed to bother her.

"It wouldn't kill you to pretend to be happy to see me, you know." Her heels clicked against the hardwood floor as she paced his living room.

"When did you get back from New York?" he asked.

"Yesterday." She faced him. "I see you have your usual 'just got laid look' going on."

Noah was dressed in a white undershirt and faded blue jeans that were a little loose around his waist. She secretly enjoyed his unkempt appearance.

"Take a shower. Let's go out."

"I don't believe we have a date scheduled for today." He folded his arms against his chest.

"Be spontaneous!" Cammie pulled out two tickets from her purse and waved them in the air. "Let's go to the Madison Art Gallery. There's this new artist in town—brilliant paintings, from what I've heard. Get ready and go with me."

"I'll pass."

"Oh, come on, Noah! Try something new and fun for once! All we ever do is stay at your place, get high and smash."

"I never force you."

"Well, obviously. You're incredible in bed... that's why I always end up with my panties on the floor whenever I come over." She giggled. "But seriously, *please* come to this gallery with me tonight." Cammie wrapped her arms around his neck. "I just feel like we're closer now, especially after everything you told me last week. It meant a lot that you shared your past with me and told me about your daughter. You kept me in the dark for years, but now we're so—"

"I don't want to have this conversation right now."

"Why are you getting upset?"

"I've told you time and time again that I can't do the whole boyfriend thing."

"Who said I was asking you out as my boyfriend? Friends go out. They have dinner; they talk; they enjoy their time together. Why can't you just be a normal person like everyone else?"

"Because I'm *not* like everyone else."

She paused and glared at him. "Most guys would kill to take me out."

"I'm not most guys."

"Thank you for pointing out the obvious."

Noah looked more irritated than she was. He was about to say something when a woman walked past him down the stairs; they had slept together the night before.

Cammie whipped her head around and was stunned to see a raven-haired woman standing completely nude.

"Do you have any more coke on you?" she asked.

Cammie scowled at Noah. "*Really*? You're still banging basic bitches?" Pain and betrayal poured from her eyes while he gave her a stony stare.

"Look, I told you not to show up unannounced like this."

"Keep your whores." She tore the tickets in his face. "Keep your drugs. I'm done."

Noah couldn't feel anything. He was numb. He had no capacity to care anymore. After Cammie left, his booty calls approached him.

"What the hell was her problem?"

"Fuck if I knew"—he rubbed his neck—"I'm all outta snow."

"Shit, really?"

"Sorry."

Noah watched her disappear upstairs before she returned with her girlfriend. Both women were fully dressed.

"It's been real, but we gotta go."

He didn't stop or ask for their numbers. In Noah's mind, they were just junkies looking to have a good time at his expense. His bedroom had turned into a cheap motel, and the vacancy sign was always on. Standing at the threshold, he observed the chaos: messy sheets, ripped condom wrappers, empty liquor bottles, clothing all over the floor… He had created his own version of Hell, and he couldn't blame anyone but himself.

Stepping over a pile of laundry, Noah hovered by the window and lit a cigarette while staring out at the city. For the past five years, his drug addiction had robbed him of happiness and ruined any chance of being there for Aria.

I should just end it, he thought in despair.

A bottle of vodka was resting on his windowsill; he hurled it at the wall in anger, watching shards of glass shatter in the air, like the pieces of his shattered life.

CHAPTER FIFTY-THREE
ARIA

Pulling up to a curb, Noah paid our cab driver and joined me on the sidewalk. We couldn't hold hands or kiss, and I hated it. I would have preferred his arm around my shoulder as we walked together, but that would have looked too intimate. Instead, I shoved my hands in my jacket pockets to avoid touching him.

"Did I tell you how beautiful you look this evening?" Noah said.

"Yes, you have. A few times, actually. But feel free to repeat yourself. I don't mind," I flirted with a smile as we entered the exhibit.

The gallery director escorted us down a hallway that led to Evan's showroom. Progressive house music got louder when we approached a giant hall full of mingling art lovers. My expectations were subverted when I looked at the photographs on the walls.

"Son of a gun," Noah snickered. "Did you know you were his muse all this time?"

"Are you kidding me? I'm just as surprised as you are!"

There were blown up photos of me... *everywhere.*

Why didn't he ask me first? I thought, feeling uncomfortable.

All my pictures were in black and white—mostly shots of me staring off at something or doing everyday tasks. There was one specific photo of me staring into the camera: it was black and white as well, except for my eye color. I remembered when Evan had taken that photo. He had called out to me, and as soon as I had turned around… *flash!*

"Aria!" Evan waved at me, abandoning the person he was talking to.

He looked so handsome. It was the first time I'd seen him dressed in semi-formal attire. He wore a black dress shirt that was tucked into his black tailored trousers and a white tie. A dark leather belt was fastened around his trim waist, and his black smart shoes complimented his outfit. I especially liked how his piercings and his tattoo gave him a nonconforming edge. He gave me butterflies when he approached. According to my psych professor, it was a normal reaction that almost everyone felt around attractive individuals.

"I'm so glad you made it!" Evan said. "I was thinking you wouldn't show up." He embraced me in a lingering hug.

Noah never missed a chance to be the "protective dad" and grilled him.

"What the hell is this?" He glared. "Did you even ask her for permission before you plastered her photos everywhere?"

"Relax, bro. I'm not selling her photos—they're just part of my show for a limited time of viewing pleasure."

That was a relief. I didn't exactly like the idea of someone hanging a giant photo of me in their bathroom or something.

"You still should have asked her first."

"Noah, it's fine," I said. "It's definitely a surprise, but I'm extremely honored."

"I think London life only made you crabbier than usual," Evan said.

"Hmm, yes—must be because of the constant rain," Noah sarcastically replied.

I felt myself blushing when I noticed random people observing my photos with drinks in hand.

Are they admiring or critiquing? I wondered.

A few gallery goers were staring right at me. I guess they had connected the dots and realized I was the mysterious girl in the photos. When I located the bar in the corner, I was tempted to order a martini to calm my nerves.

Too bad I'm underage.

"Do you like them?" Evan asked. "I took pictures of you at every opportunity when you weren't looking."

"I guess that explains the random flashes from time to time." I laughed uneasily.

"You're beautiful in how you have this innocent allure. I wanted to capture that."

Me? Innocent? Oh, if he only knew.

I looked over at Noah; he was still grumpy.

God forbid that a man compliments me in front of him!

It wasn't like Evan had my naked body on display for the world to see. There was nothing racy or sexual about my pictures—not even a hint.

"You inspired me, Aria, and I just wanted to share your beauty with people who would truly appreciate it."

What a sweetheart, I thought, beaming at him.

"I don't care how 'innocent' this all looks," Noah said. "She could sue you for this."

"Are you giving her legal advice now?" Evan laughed as he slid his hands into his pockets.

"Noah, don't be so dramatic," I said. "I think it's sweet that he displayed my photos for his opening night."

"He's got your pictures pinned up everywhere. What if some psycho strolls in, sees what he likes and stalks you? I'm not letting you out of my sight."

Now he was just exaggerating.

"Why did it have to be her?" he said to Evan. "You know plenty of models you could have worked with."

"I did. If you'd look around, you'd notice their pictures. At least I care about Aria's modeling dream. There could be a modeling scout among us right now as we speak." Evan winked at me.

I didn't want that dream anymore. How could I model after having nothing to show but an unsightly scar on my body? I hoped he hadn't gone out of his way to get an agent interested in me.

"I won't waste my breath justifying all the ways I care about her to you," Noah said in a hostile tone.

"Fine—don't. Just stop threatening me for no reason."

"I'm not threatening. I'm stating facts. You simply have no legal right to display her photos without her permission."

"Are you hard of hearing?" Evan scowled. "I already said I'm not showcasing Aria's photos for profit. I'm tired of repeating myself to you all the time."

Noah looked like he was about to punch him. They exchanged death glares while I became a barrier between the feuding brothers.

"Please, don't make a scene here."

"You should have got her consent. That's all I'm saying."

"You want to leave the protective father act outside? She's not upset. Why are you trying to argue with me?"

"Guys, please just try to get along. Do I really need to quote Mahatma Gandhi? *An eye for an eye—*"

"Stay out of this, Aria," Noah warned.

"Why are you even here?" Evan glared. "Aria's old enough to ride the subway. She doesn't need you chaperoning her. Get over your daddy instincts because you're not her father, and she's not a child."

"That's it," Noah snapped. "We're leaving." He grabbed my hand, but I pulled it back.

"I'm not going anywhere!"

"Forgive me for trying to look out for you."

"You're overreacting as usual, brother. I know you think I'm a colossal failure, but I would never hurt Aria."

"How virtuous of you."

It was a good thing their argument was drowned out by music and chattering background noise. These people were here to admire and purchase artwork, not to spectate an episode of *The Maury Show*. I tried to calm them down when Evan pulled out his cellphone.

"I need to take this. Be right back."

Noah was somber.

"Why are you like this?" I said, looking cross with him.

"Like what? Look around you. Don't you find this all a little… creepy?"

"He's a professional photographer. Taking pictures of people is part of the job. Yes, it's a bit of a surprise to walk in and see photos of me everywhere, but these pictures are harmless."

"He lacks professionalism." Noah scanned the gallery.

"Can we please just enjoy this evening without you provoking him?"

"That's not what I'm doing." He met my eyes again and grimaced. "I just find it strange how he's switched occupations so suddenly."

"There's nothing wrong with following your passion."

"That statement is not always true."

"Are you gonna argue with me now? We're not at a deposition. You promised you would get along with Evan this evening. I don't want to ruin his night."

He seemed so frustrated. I just couldn't understand why he couldn't leave the past behind him and reconcile with his brother. Evan was not his enemy.

"Noah, can you please keep a level head?"

"I'm sorry for losing my temper. I'll back off."

୭୫୭

My evening was going smoothly, despite how it had started when Noah and Evan were arguing an hour ago. They weren't exactly friendly with each other, but they weren't fighting either—which was good. The three of us hovered near a photo of me that was mounted on a wall. My hair was up in a messy bun as I gazed out the window of my townhouse apartment.

"You look sad here," Noah said.

"I was."

"What were you thinking about?"

"My parents."

Since returning to New York, Rob had tried to repair our broken relationship, but I wanted nothing to do with him. I felt like he wanted to use me to keep his marriage together with Mom. She should have divorced him years ago.

"Well"—Evan cleared his throat—"Hopefully all these people will pull out their checkbooks tonight."

I was relieved he changed the subject. Maybe he knew I was uncomfortable talking about my "mommy and daddy issues."

"I'm trying to raise funds for my friend's charity," Evan added.

"I didn't peg you as the charitable type," Noah said, never missing a chance to insult him.

"What would I do with the money? It's not like I need it."

"Of course you wouldn't. Dad left you a generous trust fund—your biggest achievement in life. Too bad you didn't earn it."

"You're such an arrogant bastard."

"*I'm* the bastard?" Noah sneered.

"Just because I dropped out of college doesn't mean I'm stupid. You always think you're better than everyone else because you have this 'fancy law degree.' Dad gave you almost everything he owned. You're the wealthiest member of our family, and here you are judging me, saying I've never earned my living."

"Are you calling me a hypocrite?"

"Guys!" I cut in. "*Please.*"

There was a moment of silence before Evan said, "Nice to have you back in town, big bro." He grinned at Noah.

My temperamental lover reciprocated the gesture with a patronizing smile.

A caterer came by, holding a tray full of fizzy champagne glasses. Alcohol: that's exactly what we needed. Evan grabbed a glass and handed it to Noah before he grabbed another two for me and him.

"She's underage." Noah pointed out the obvious.

"Seriously?" I raised a brow. There was no way I was going to allow him to be the "over-protective father" tonight. I took the champagne glass out of Evan's hand and thanked him with a smile.

"Lighten up, Noah," he said. "It's just a glass of champagne. I propose a toast since it's a special night for me. None of us are biologically related, but I consider you both my family, and that will never change."

"To family then!" I gave Noah *the look,* since he seemed reluctant to join in.

Raising his glass in the most unenthusiastic tone ever, he said, "Cheers."

The sparkling wine tasted sweet. I could feel Evan's eyes on me. I knew if I stared too long, I'd get sucked into a black hole. God only knew what waited on the other side.

"Come," he said. "There's plenty more artwork to admire."

We were about to follow Evan when someone called out, *"Noah Mason Hunter?"*

Turning around, I instantly regretted it. A tall, leggy brunette started toward us, dressed in a tight, long sleeve dress. She had long caramel hair that was highlighted. Her dress had a short hemline which showed off her killer legs. Her curvy hips swayed as her heels clicked against the marble floor. She had a beautiful tan and her makeup looked flawless.

"What are the chances of running into you here, of all places?" She flashed a stunning smile, hugging Noah. "I never thought I'd see you again!"

I could feel my snakes slithering out from my hair as they hissed, waiting for my command before they'd bite this strange woman. That would have been an interesting *Springer* episode: "In Love with My Best Friend & Medusa Wants to Kill Me!"—I would play Medusa, of course.

"You haven't aged a bit!" She cupped Noah's face. "What's your secret?"

Noah seemed uncomfortable, as if he hadn't been expecting her to be so affectionate. Or maybe he just felt awkward because I was there while this woman (an ex?) was all over him. Now that I had seen her up close, she was a real head turner. I wasn't sure if she was the same age as Noah, but she was gorgeous. I was envious of her seductive presence. Funny how we question ourselves, our own beauty, skills, and talents when confronted with a mirror of who we aspire to be (or so we think).

"What are you doing in New York?" Noah said.

"Long story. Why don't you introduce me to your friends?" She smiled, glancing at me and Evan.

"Cammie, Evan—Evan, Cammie."

"So… *you're* the infamous brother! I can't believe I had to wait around a decade to finally meet you!"

Evan shook her hand and hovered close to me like a protective uncle while Noah introduced me to his old acquaintance. I couldn't help but wonder just how much of a "friend" she really was.

"Aria, this is Cammie. She and I had gone to Harvard together back in the day."

"Oh, my God! You finally got in touch with your daughter?"

"Uh, sort of." Noah nervously rubbed the back of his neck.

Ugh, this was getting awkward. I did not want to have *that* conversation with someone I hardly knew. Not wanting to leave Noah's side, I didn't want to be the "clingy girlfriend" either. Cammie continued to talk up a storm while I stood there feeling left out. They seemed to have so much history together and I couldn't stay present in their conversation. I wasn't a part of Noah's past—maybe just a small piece. Ten years ago, I was only eight years old, and he was probably dating this vivacious woman.

Maybe now is a good time to separate for a while, I thought, turning to Evan. "Hey, why don't you show me the rest of your artwork?"

"I'd love to."

"It was nice meeting you, Cammie."

"You too, Aria!"

"Wait," Noah called out.

"Catch up with your friend. I'll be close by. Don't worry." My reassuring smile wasn't convincing, but at least I tried.

CHAPTER FIFTY-FOUR
NOAH

We had been alone for only a minute, and Cammie was already flirting with me.

"You look great, Noah! Then again, that shouldn't surprise me, right? I've always known you were blessed with amazing genes."

"What are you doing in New York? Weren't you working at a law firm in Chicago?"

"Yes, I still am. But I'm here because Carrie's getting married. Her wedding is this Saturday."

"Ah. That's great! Good for her."

"Not really. I think she's settling down way too fast. But since we're on marriage, I'm hurt you didn't send me an invitation to your wedding!"

That's right, I hadn't. Our relationship had always revolved around one thing: sex. Knowing Cammie, she would have given me a blow job right before walking down the aisle. It was common sense not to invite her.

"How'd you find out?"

"You know me." She smirked. "I have my sources."

"Well, if it makes you feel any better, my marriage didn't last. I'm getting a divorce."

"Oh. I'm so sorry."

She wasn't. I bet she was gloating inside and happy that I got a mean dose of karma for hurting her so much.

"I'm a divorce attorney now," Cammie said, "and I know it's never a simple process to go through. I hope you two are working it out amicably."

"As amicably as possible," I sighed. "How long has Carrie been dating her fiancée?"

"About three years."

"That's not so bad. I always thought of her as the traditional type of girl."

"Yeah, until *you* corrupted her and practically robbed her of—"

"Do we really need to go there? I apologized, and she forgave me. Let's keep the past where it belongs."

"I'm sorry," Cammie said. "I didn't mean to drag up the past."

"Yeah, well, I paid my karma in full—trust me."

I didn't want to be here anymore. I wanted to leave and take Aria with me. This gallery was enormous, but I felt like the walls were closing in on me. My angel was no longer in my line of sight. I kept scanning through crowds to find her. I wasn't sure why I felt anxious whenever she was on her own.

Where is she? I wondered, hiding my distress.

"Walk with me a bit," Cammie said. "Let's catch up." She grabbed my arm, but I withdrew.

"What's wrong?" She frowned. "Does it scare you to see the 'ghost' of your hottest girlfriend?"

I didn't know what to say. Cammie was still beautiful, but Aria's beauty was unmatched. No one could take her place in my eyes.

"I guess I still have that effect on you, Mister Speechless—especially when we touch. Not your fault, though." Cammie giggled.

"I'm seeing someone," I said.

"Moving on from the ex really fast, wouldn't you say? Tell me, who's this unlucky woman? She must be a rebound."

She was aggravating me. I didn't want to be reminded of my past. Nothing about her had changed—except that she was no longer on her father's payroll. Then again, maybe she still was.

"My love life has nothing to do with you," I replied.

"Don't get so defensive. I'm not trying to pry. I'm just curious. You know, I've often thought about getting in touch with you again. But I guess my ego always got in the way."

Her pride had never stopped her from showing up at my door in the past.

"I just didn't like the way we ended things," she added.

You mean the way I ended things.

"You moved on, Cammie. I moved on. It's what people do: they move on." I looked behind me to see if I could find Aria. Something seemed off with her, and I was worried.

"Looking for someone?"

"Aria."

"What a protective father. You're not gonna lose her in this place, Noah. When did you two reconnect?"

This was going to be hard to explain.

"Last year," I answered.

"Did you go to court to get custody?"

"Yes."

"How old is she now?"

"Eighteen."

I hated feeling older than her.

"Wow, so it's recent."

I bet she thought I waited too long to get custody.

"Well, I'm happy you have your daughter back in your life. She's so pretty."

"Listen, Cam…" I rambled for a minute before I finally said, "to make a long story short … she's not my biological daughter."

Her brown eyes widened in disbelief. "*No-freaking-way.* Natalie had lied to you?"

"She didn't know. It's too complicated to explain."

"Does Aria know?"

"Yes."

"Okay. Wow… all this time… after all that pain you went through…" She placed a sympathetic hand on my shoulder. "You know you can always sue your ex for emotional damages and stress. I could even represent you."

"No one had forced me to be a drug addict. I self-medicated my pain away all on my own—that was never Natalie's fault."

Cammie stayed quiet, as if to verify my admission of guilt.

"We had some amazing years, you and I," she said.

"Most of which I regret—because of my addiction."

Walking at a leisurely pace, we stopped in front of a blown-up photo of Aria.

"Her eyes are so blue," Cammie noticed. "She's very beautiful."

"Her eye color could be brown, green, violet—doesn't matter. It's Aria's heart that makes her so amazing."

"I believe you." She turned her head in my direction. "Are you her stepdad now?"

"Well, she spent a year with me before we found out about the paternity. It's kind of hard to break that bond, especially since I thought I was her father ever since she was conceived."

"I can't even imagine what that feels like."

A caterer came by with some more champagne, which gave Cammie the opportunity to grab a glass for herself.

Where the hell did Evan take her?

I had become a possessive partner and an over-protective father—no denying that; at least I was aware.

"Are you working in New York?" Cammie asked.

"Yeah—just got back today, actually. I was working a case with our partnering firm in London for two months."

"Sounds exciting." She sipped her champagne. "Have you ever lost a case?"

"No, and I don't intend to."

"You're still cocky as ever."

"Interpret my confidence however you wish."

We strolled past a small crowd of people, admiring Evan's artwork.

"How long have you been dating this mystery woman?"

I paused and gave Cammie a look, as if to say it was none of her business.

"Fine… I'll lay off on the personal questions. By the way, I'm recently single—just in case you were wondering."

I wasn't interested.

"Maybe we were meant to run into each other like this. I mean, what were the odds?"

It seemed like a coincidence to me.

We stopped to look at another photo. An attractive model was holding a white butterfly in her hands as she stared into the camera lens. I couldn't read her expression, though I guess that was deliberate.

"I almost got married last year," Cammie said.

Too lost in the photo, I stayed quiet and let her share.

"I ran out on the groom on my wedding day."

"You what?"

"I was in my dress and everything… Ready to walk down the aisle and become *Mrs. Abbot*. I can't believe I waited until the last minute to realize I was making a mistake."

"How come you didn't marry him?"

"I wasn't in love with Kaleb," she answered with a shrug. "We dated for a year and were engaged for three months. It was all so fast, really. I think I just wanted to settle down. I thought he was everything I wanted, but he wasn't. I guess I just knew if I married him, we would have ended up divorced. Anyway, I did the right thing in the end." She finished her drink.

"I see I'm not the only one who has a reputation for breaking hearts."

"I blame *you*. You damaged me."

There it was: the piling guilt.

"Cammie, I'm sorry. I really am—for everything."

We locked eyes for a moment. Her smile seemed forgiving as she leaned in and gently kissed my cheek.

"I forgave you a long time ago, Noah. It's impossible to stay angry at you and even more impossible to hate you. I guess you'll always be my weakness."

I took her hand and squeezed it gently. "I just want you to be happy, Camelia. I know I put you through some shitty chapters in your life, but I want you to close them and move on."

"My life is better than what it was ten years ago. Let's just be grateful that we made it out of law school alive."

I *was* grateful. Had I continued my addiction, I would have wound up dead.

We spent the next half hour strolling through the exhibit, talking, and admiring Evan's pictures. Most of the photos were of Aria, so I had a lot to appreciate.

"It's kind of ironic that I spotted you at an art gallery." Cammie giggled.

I still remembered that night when she had surprised me with tickets to an exhibit. She had given me the silent treatment for weeks after discovering that I had women over. But Cammie came back. She always came back, and I always let her. That's just the dance we did around each other. But things were different now. *I* was different. I had moved forward, and I wasn't ever going back. I had no intention of breaking Aria's heart. Ever. She had been through enough, and I couldn't live with myself if I resurrected that demon within; a demon who wanted to drag me into a life of sex, drugs, and chaos. At what cost? Losing my soul? Losing Aria? I refused to be my own worst enemy. Cammie was no longer my temptation; this is what she had to accept, regardless of the ego wound. My kryptonite was Aria, and my biggest struggle was convincing the woman I love of this truth: she had the power to make or break me.

CHAPTER FIFTY-FIVE
EVAN

I've always been immune to pain. The only agony I can recall is when my biological mother was murdered. Ever since that night, something shut down inside of me. I remember having countless accidents as a child: scraping my knees, cuts, bruises, broken bones… But I never cried—not a single tear was shed. I fell out of a tree once and broke my arm. Most eight-year-olds would have screamed their lungs off, but I'd marched straight into the house, looked my parents in the eye and told them I did something funny to my arm. The bone had been probing out of my skin. It hadn't ripped through the flesh, but the bump was visible. Mum had fainted when I pushed it back in. Why was I retrieving these memories now? Because I realized how vulnerable I was with Aria; she had the power to hurt me.

Which is why I need to kill her.

No. Worst-case scenario, you keep her captive, and make well use of her. Think with logic. Not emotions.

The voices were back again. Why was this happening now? Shutting my eyes, I tried to find my quiet place. I don't think I ever knew what it felt like to be in love until I met Aria. She gave purpose to my existence. I just wanted to be accepted by her. I wanted her to embrace all parts of me, especially my darkness. The truest path to liberation is when you reveal your shadow self to the one you love. By unveiling all parts of you, you open yourself up to receiving authentic, unconditional love; it's the greatest reward you receive by risking vulnerability. If you hide your dark side, you rob yourself of reconciling your shadow, and coming into alignment with your true love. You may even live a double life because of cognitive dissonance. I didn't want to hide my shadow from Aria. I was just taking my time, revealing my monster in doses. The last thing I wanted was for her to run from me.

If I took off that mask right now, she would head for the hills. I had to wait. The opportunity would come—I would make sure of that, even if I had to manipulate my way into getting what I want.

For years, my life had been so empty. The only time I felt a rush was when I'd kill; the adrenaline was indescribable.

She's just a whore like every other woman, a voice said in my head. *Slit her throat and kill her! Kill her, you twat!*

"Evan, these pictures are amazing!"

Aria pulled me out of my past, disarming me with her seductive eyes.

"The models are so beautiful."

"Not as beautiful as you." I smiled.

"You're flattering me. We're all beautiful in our own way."

"I don't give empty compliments."

"I'm sorry for what happened with Noah earlier."

"You don't have to apologize for him."

"He's just really protective of me."

"I noticed"—I sipped my champagne—"I hope you're not upset that I displayed your pictures tonight."

"Not at all. I really appreciate the effort you put into all of this."

"I have plenty more events lined up in the upcoming months. I expect you to be there."

"I wouldn't miss it." She smiled warmly.

"How's school going, by the way?"

"Great."

"Are you dating anyone?"

"No… but there is this one guy in my sociology class. He's asked me out a few times. I feel bad for making excuses."

"What's keeping you from saying yes?"

I already knew. I knew everything about Trevor and had dug into his past, pulled up as much dirt I could find, and had targeted the bastard as my next kill. What Aria didn't know was that he had been cheating on her throughout their relationship with multiple women… including a drunken one-night stand with her best friend Ally. She was also on my hit list. Anyone who had maliciously lied to Aria deserved death in my eyes. The most disturbing part about my personality was how quickly I could shut off my emotions in the name of justice. If I couldn't get an admission of guilt out of my targets, then I would eliminate them from the face of the earth. It was divine justice served. Someone had to be God's executioner. I was happy to take on the role as her angel of death in the name of love; it was violence channeled properly.

I knew what it was like to be cheated on and lied to. I still fantasized about murdering the fatal ex who broke my heart. If she wasn't in an unhappy marriage with three kids, I would have finished the job. She was suffering and had let herself go; it gave me peace.

"I guess I just want to focus on school instead of a relationship."

Aria's soothing voice pulled me out of a red mist of murderous thoughts. Someone seemed to have caught her attention as she peered over my shoulder. Turning around, I saw Noah and Cammie laughing together. She seemed to be cozying up to him.

"Did Noah and Cammie date back in college?" Aria asked.

"Sort of. They have history together."

Based on the gossip my sister Breanne had shared, those two had an "intense friendship."

"Did Noah love her?"

"Let's just say that whenever they were alone together, they ended up with their clothes off."

Her face went pale.

"Hey, you all right?"

She fixated on the reminiscing couple and looked at me. "I'm fine."

I think I just figured out why she's been keeping me at arm's length.

"Did you want to catch up with Noah?"

"I'd rather stay with you."

"Nothing would make me happier, love." I smiled. "Come on, I want to show you something."

Slipping her hand in mine, I moved through the crowd of socialites, absorbing her beautiful energy through my palm.

"Where are you taking me?"

"Somewhere."

We approached a door and before I opened it, I asked her to close her eyes as I pulled out my phone and turned on my Bluetooth. Opening my music playlist, I played a special song that reminded me of Aria.

"Don't peek."

"I won't." She giggled. "Wow… who is that artist? The music sounds amazing!"

"I discovered this new artist by accident last week while surfing YouTube: 'OFTEN' by Maji."

"Beautiful."

She had the voice of an angel.

Unlocking the door, I stepped into a dark room and guided Aria inside.

"Keep those eyes closed until I say…"

"Don't worry."

I headed to the back and pulled on a lever.

"What was that sound?"

"You'll find out soon."

"What are you doing?"

"Just trust me."

"Can I open them now?"

"Not yet."

There was some equipment I had set up on a table earlier. All I had to do was turn on some switches and I was good to go.

"I'm getting anxious! I really wanna see!"

"Patience is a virtue, sweetheart."

I attached a missing cord to my laptop and opened some software. Music echoed around me as the walls lit up. I had used 160 LCD screens to create a 5D-360-degree video room. Sixty-inch monitors were mounted on the walls, ceiling, and floor. The image transmission system controlled all the screens to offer a 5D visual experience of video footage. This was her big surprise: she was about to view a time lapse of a starry sky from sundown to sunrise.

"Open your eyes, Aria."

Her reaction was priceless as she looked around in amazement.

"*Oh, my God,* Evan! This is incredible!" Stepping toward the monitors, she watched as the clouds rushed by at turbo speed. "It's like I can actually *feel* the earth's rotation."

"Are you awestruck?" I chuckled standing behind her, touching her shoulders.

"I have no words!"

Standing behind her, I touched her shoulders.

Don't worry, Little Red, this wolf won't bite… yet.

"This is so surreal."

Now that I had gained her trust, all I had to do was lure her to my bedroom.

You'll be addicted to me. I'll make sure of it, love. I promise you.

CHAPTER FIFTY-SIX
THE LAST STRAW

Robert and Natalie were having a shouting match all evening. They had argued through their therapy session; they had argued in the car; and they had argued during the elevator ride to their apartment. Natalie was resolute about leaving him, and there was nothing stopping Robert from getting violent.

"I want you to pack your things and move out!" she shouted.

"This is my goddamn home! I pay the rent! You're not kicking me out!"

"I'm not happy with you, Rob! I'm tired of trying to make this marriage work when it's clearly over! Why can't you just throw in the towel and make this a painless separation for our children?"

"Because I love you!"

"No, you don't! You don't know what love is! I feel like I'm in a cage living with you! I'm so unhappy that my heart physically hurts! Don't you want to be with somebody who can make you happy?"

"*You* make me happy, Natalie! Remember our vows? Does that mean nothing to you?"

"We're always fighting! We never get along anymore!"

"Because you don't want to get along with me! Can't you see I'm trying my best?" he yelled in frustration.

Natalie stole a moment to calm herself. "If you won't move out, then I will—and I'm taking the kids with me, too."

"Like hell you will!"

"I've tried doing this your way, Robert. Our last counseling session is next week, and I won't change my mind about the divorce."

"You mean you won't change your *heart*." He stared at her accusingly, violating her personal space. "Who have you been screwing behind my back?"

"How dare you insult me!"

"You cheated on your high school lover boy, and you know what they say… Once a cheater, always a cheater!"

The next thing he felt was a hard slap in the face.

"Bitch!"

Natalie strode past him in haste and headed for their bedroom.

"Don't you walk away from me!" Robert's footsteps pounded behind her.

"I'm taking the kids and leaving!"

"Over my dead body!"

The twins were terrified as they hid in a closet. Terry tried to comfort his sister as she cried in his arms.

"*Shhh*, don't be scared."

"I want Aria." Tiffany whimpered.

"Remember what she used to tell us?"

"We stay in the closet until it's safe to come out."

They flinched when they heard glass breaking.

"Put the suitcase away!" Robert yelled, entering their bedroom.

"I tried doing this the peaceful way with you"—she raided the closet—"But you're just impossible to live with!" Grabbing some essentials from the bathroom, she returned and finished packing. "Step aside please, Robert." Her voice sounded shaky; she was afraid. "Please, move."

"Or what? You'll bulldoze your way through me?" He chortled.

"Let me leave!"

"Don't make me raise my hand to you, Natalie!"

"Nothing you say or do will make me stay. So please, just let me go."

"You're not taking the kids! They're my children too! Do you understand?"—he shook her shoulders—"Do you understand me or not?"

Natalie started crying, which only angered her husband more as he slapped her in the face.

"How do you like that? Doesn't feel good, huh? I'll smash that pretty face in!" He punched her across the jaw with a heavy right hook, causing Natalie to fall to the floor from the impact. "You wanted this, you stupid cow! You're nothing but a lying whore!" He continued his merciless abuse, shouting profanities like a shameless demon.

What Robert didn't know was that Evan had set up surveillance equipment inside his apartment. He was watching him.

"You two-faced bitch!"—he punched her—"… That's why you want to leave me… because you're a cheating slut!"

Natalie was bleeding from her nose, and her lip was cut. Curling into the fetal position, she tried to protect her face from further damage. No matter how much she begged, he wouldn't stop.

"Happy now?" Robert kicked her in the stomach and yanked her ankle to trip her when she tried to get up.

He enjoyed seeing her helpless, crying and crawling like an injured animal. He often projected his own inferiority onto her.

"I tried so damn hard, Nat. I really did. But I think you like this, don't you?" He laughed insidiously. "You love pissing me off!"

"Let me go!" she cried in terror as he flipped her onto her back.

Robert was about to thrash her with his belt when she kicked him in the testicles, paralyzing him in pain.

"I will kill you!" He groaned.

Natalie got up while he was still incapacitated. With trembling hands, she abandoned her suitcase and ran into her children's bedroom.

"Terry! Tiffany!" she cried out in panic.

The little boy opened the closet, gasping in fear when he saw his mother's injured face.

"Mom, you're bleeding!" His brown eyes filled with tears.

"I'm scared!" Tiffany bawled.

"Why does Daddy keep hurting you?"

"Because he's sick and needs help."

Crouching in front of her children, she hugged them both.

"Don't be afraid, my babies." Natalie wiped her bloodied nostrils with her sleeve and put on a brave face. "We're going on a vacation, kiddos, all right?"

"Where?" Terry asked.

"Just follow Mommy, come on!"

She got them out of the apartment before her husband could interfere.

When they reached the parking garage, Natalie strapped her children in their seatbelts and got behind the wheel of their old station wagon.

This is it, she said to herself. *I'm leaving him for good this time and never going back.*

The engine fired up, and soon they were gone.

CHAPTER FIFTY-SEVEN
ARIA

I don't think I had ever felt so intimidated standing next to another woman. Cammie was stunning—she could have easily won the title of "Miss Universe."

"It was nice meeting you, Aria." She smiled. "Good luck with your studies."

"Thank you."

"We should have lunch while I'm still in the city," Cammie said to Noah. "You have my number now."

"Yeah, I do."

"Don't be a stranger then!" She kissed his cheek and hugged him before she left.

I was irritated. This was the worst time for my "jealous diva" to come out from hiding. The only difference between her and I was that she was in a constant state of PMS and passive aggressive to the core. I wasn't proud of this version of myself, nor did I enjoy envying Cammie, but seeing the way she had interacted with Noah made me feel insecure about us. They had obvious chemistry.

Noah needed a real woman in his life, not some insecure teenager that made metaphorical comparisons to Disney characters. Perhaps my inner child desired vengeance: *Aria never had a childhood, so Aria doesn't get to step into adulthood, because Aria could not grow up.* God, what the hell was wrong with me? At least I didn't express those thoughts out loud.

"Aria?" Evan's voice was faint.

"Sorry, I zoned out"—I looked at him—"What were you saying?"

"I was just thanking you for coming here tonight."

"Oh, it was my pleasure." I tried to smile convincingly, but I felt like I was taking more of an awkward *selfie*—minus the camera.

"I'll see you later this week." He hugged me.

"Don't cancel on Jade again."

"I don't intend to."

"I'm gonna take her home now." Noah cut in. "Good work on the exhibit." He wrapped his arm over my shoulder. I wanted to shrug it off but changed my mind.

We said goodbye to Evan and parted ways.

℘

A yellow cab pulled up to the curb as Noah opened the door for me. I moved into the passenger seat and stared out the window, determined to keep conversation to a minimum.

"You're so quiet." Noah broke the silence.

"Nothing on my mind."

Tension lingered between us, and I knew I was responsible for it. Amidst my rampant jealousy, I still had some functioning logic. It wasn't Noah's fault that Cammie had thrown herself at him. Yes, that was an exaggeration—but I was sure she wanted all that sexy Hunter hotness all over her.

"Is it just me or is it colder than Alaska in here at the moment?" Noah said.

"I'm just tired. I can't wait to get home and sleep."

"I'm not taking you back to your place. We're going to the penthouse."

"Are you sure you don't want to take Cammie up there instead?"

So much for hiding my jealousy.

"Is that why you're giving me the cold shoulder?" He smiled amusingly, which only annoyed me more. This wasn't a laughing matter. Cammie was a threat; a lethal *watch-her-like-a-hawk-or-she'll-steal-your-guy* kind of threat.

"Come here." Noah stretched out his arm.

"I'm good. Thanks." I stayed apathetic.

"Cammie's just a friend, Aria. You don't have to be jealous—waste of energy."

"I'm not jealous! I just don't feel like cuddling!"

"Okay… sorry."

I had failed at doing the whole "nothing's wrong, I'm good, I'm fine" kinda deal. My insecurity was obvious, and my natural reaction was to act indifferent and pretend like I wasn't bothered at all. It was a tough front I put on to protect myself: a defense mechanism.

"Are you feeling hungry at all?" Noah asked.

"No."

"Thirsty?"

"No."

He reached for my hand, but I pulled away.

"You know, Aria, sometimes I forget how old you really are."

Ouch.

I had three choices now: sob in silence, unleash my fury, or give him the ever-torturous silent treatment. I was tired of option one… didn't particularly enjoy option two, and option three wasn't all that great either, because I knew he absolutely hated it.

Noah's done nothing wrong. I'm overreacting.

Our relationship was not a game of chess, yet I was deliberately placing myself on the opposite end: a black queen vs. an army of white. I'd lost all my pawns, knights, rooks, and bishops. The king that I was supposed to protect symbolized my pride, and I knew it would be an easy victory for Noah since he had me as a checkmate. I didn't want to be his opponent. I wanted to be on the same side protecting him, not my puffed-up pride.

"I'm sorry," he sighed in frustration. "I just need you to communicate with me. How can I know what I did wrong if you don't tell me?"

"You did nothing. It's me—it's just that time of the month."

It definitely wasn't.

"You're a terrible liar."

"That's right, I am. You're the biggest liar, so of course you'd be able to tell. After all, isn't it your job to twist the truth?"

"Are you calling me a crooked lawyer?"

I went too far.

"Judging by your lack of a response, I'm gonna assume you didn't mean what you said."

My wounded ego had made things worse. I hated going "cave-mode," and I wished he could realize how it was hard for me to step out of my cave when I was afraid. Not of him... of having to reveal what hurt me. I felt stupid and was mad at myself.

"We're heading home and we're gonna talk about this, Aria—whether you like it or not."

CHAPTER FIFTY-EIGHT
NOT OVER YOU

Natalie was staying at a hotel that night with her children. Leaving Rob and calling the police was the best decision she had ever made. An officer had informed her they arrested her husband for felony assault and battery; he was spending the night in jail. Natalie knew that someone would eventually bail him out, but at least now she could prove that he was not fit to have shared custody of their children.

The twins were sleeping peacefully in bed when their mother stepped out of the bathroom. Having taken a shower, her body was still sore from the assault. Natalie was in shock. The bruising around her face made her feel ashamed. She had promised herself that if Rob would get violent again, she would leave him for good. Following through on her word, she was proud of herself for finally having the courage to leave. But her mind was exhausted and still racing. She needed someone to confide in. Phoning her mother was not an option since she was against divorce. Natalie got her iPad from her bag and connected it to her wireless keyboard before she sat at the desk. Opening her email, she noticed a message from her friend Candice; it had been sent two days ago. They had always kept in touch, even after Natalie had uprooted her life to New York. Scrolling down the page, she read Candice's letter.

From: Candice Hartwell (candi.h@flymail.net)
Sent: October 23, 2013
To: Natalie Mitchell (mitchell-nat08@inbox.com)

Hey Natty,

You never emailed me back or returned my calls last week. I'm worried. Please get in touch when you can. I'm in St. Petersburg at the moment—Russia's amazing! I'm visiting Dimitri's family tomorrow and I'm kind of nervous. I don't regret marrying him. I never thought I would leave Joey, but people change, right? I know things are rough between you and Rob. I just want you to know you have my support, no matter what you decide. I want your happiness. I'm your best friend. Please don't shut me out. Once I get back, come to Florida with the kids and stay at our place. You could use a vacation. Please let me know how you're doing.

Love you lots,

-Candi

A sad smile appeared on Natalie's lips as she clicked the reply button and started typing away. She made a mental note to create a new email address. She no longer wished to be associated to Rob.

From: Natalie Mitchell (mitchell-nat08@inbox.com)
To: Candice Hartwell (candi.h@flymail.net)

Hi Candi,

I'm sorry for not getting in touch with you sooner. I've had a hectic couple of weeks—I'm all right though, so please stop worrying. Rob and I have been to marriage counseling and things aren't going so well. He tried to change his ways, but the problem is that I don't love him anymore. I'm not in love with him. He's hurt me more times than I can count, and the only reason I stayed is because we have children together. It's sad how resentment can kill a partnership.

Natalie wondered if she should reveal how Robert had put his hands on her, but decided not to. She did not want to upset her friend while she was on vacation. Releasing a deep breath, she continued writing.

I'm tired of being in this loveless marriage. I want to be happy; I think I deserve that much. I know you're probably going to shake your head when you read what I'm about to tell you, but I have to tell someone. Seeing Noah again has stirred up feelings I thought were gone. I'm still in love with him. Now, before you send me an email listing all the reasons Noah is bad news, let me tell you this: he helped me pay off my debts and gave me a generous amount of money to put away for my children's college fund when he didn't have to. Let's just say that it's more than enough to help me start a new life. I hadn't accepted it at first because there was no way I could pay him back in this lifetime, but he had insisted that he didn't want the money. He sincerely wanted to help me. And here I thought he hated me all this time… But I was wrong. He's given me hope. Noah was never the bad guy, Candi; his mother was.

I need a fresh start. My kids deserve to live in a safe and loving environment that is free of abuse, and I can't pretend to be happy when I'm not. I'm seeing a divorce lawyer this week and looking for an apartment. It's about time I moved to some place new. By the way, I got promoted to top sales manager at work yesterday! My boss is opening another boutique, and she wants me to manage the store. I'm taking this all as a good sign. It feels right. Hopefully by January, I'll be in better circumstances.

This is the best decision for me right now. I know Aria will emotionally support me through this, since she knows how hard it's been to live with Rob. She's shown no interest in wanting a relationship with her father ever since we got back from California. Honestly, I don't blame her. I know she still talks to Noah. She feels closer to him, despite the paternity results. But with Robert, she wants nothing to do with him. She looks up to Noah. He's been out of the country because of work. I can't wait till he's back in New York. I really think there's a chance he and I could rekindle what we once had. There's still something between us—I feel it.

*Now that he's single, and I'm single—well, **soon** to be—we can have a second chance. Aria adores him. I doubt she would have a problem with us dating again; I think she would jump for joy. It saddens me knowing that Robert was rarely a good father to her. I constantly turned a blind eye to the abuse. But not anymore. This time, I'm putting my foot down.*

If I'm lucky enough to have my happily ever after, maybe I can finally give Noah that baby he's always wanted. I'm probably getting ahead of myself, but it's what I truly want. I've had to sacrifice so much for Rob. Sometimes I don't even recognize who I am anymore when I look in the mirror. I used to be so beautiful, vibrant, and happy.

Now I feel like I'm just a ghost of my former self. Robert has damaged me in more ways than one. I don't mean to trouble you with my problems, Candi… I just need someone to talk to while I go through this divorce. You've already been down that road, so your support would mean the world to me.

I think I need a complete life makeover: a new car, a new place, new look… new me. I just want to look and feel young again. Most of all, I want Noah back. I believe he and I are meant to be together. He wouldn't have given me all that money if he didn't still care about me, right? We have history. Maybe the universe is pulling us together. I'm filing for divorce soon. He's moved back to New York… I don't know, Candi. I just have a good feeling about us getting back together again. This can't be a coincidence. My New Year's resolution is to pursue my personal happiness, and that's exactly what I'm going to do.

Please visit once I'm situated and settled. Have fun on your trip, sweetie, and stay safe. I'll call you once you're back on American soil.

Sending you lots of love and hugs,

-Natalie xox

She sent the email and felt lighter inside. Her evening had been terribly dramatic. Robert had never gotten this violent. Natalie was still in shock that it had happened, but the bruises on her face didn't lie. He could have killed her. Tears rolled down her cheeks as she got ready for bed.

I don't know how I ever lived with this man; she thought in dismay.

Tomorrow was a fresh start. She considered writing Noah an email. She wanted to connect a bridge between them and pull him closer, worried that he'd be taken off the market if she didn't move fast. Noah had all the qualities she desired in a man. She was committed to reigniting their romance, unaware that her daughter had already captured the heart of her first love. Noah and Aria's secret relationship would have crushed her… *if* she ever found out.

END OF BOOK 2

ACKNOWLEDGEMENTS

Thank you to my friends, family, and readers who were there from the beginning of Noah and Aria's love story… it's been a long road getting here, and my heart is full of gratitude.

To my dear friend Chuck, thank you for always believing in me, even when I struggled believing in myself. I love you forever, my guardian angel.

A huge heartfelt thank you to Patti, Brian, Sammi, Bella, Charzi, Theo, Kimmie, Amber, and everyone else who offered me encouragement, support, and constructive criticism. I am so grateful. Thank you to my angels who worked behind the scenes to help me with marketing. Sending you all love and light.

Thank you to my readers who were there from the start of my writing journey and to my new readers who have discovered my work. Your support means the world to me.

I'd like to thank my publisher Reagan Rothe for taking a chance on this controversial love story. Thank you for believing in me and my potential. I'm so grateful to the Black Rose Writing team. I appreciate all the help with this publishing process. It's truly an honor to be part of this family.

NOVEL SOUNDTRACK

- Koven – More Than You
- ATB feat. Sean Ryan – Killing Me Inside (Acoustic Version)
- Andy Moor feat Betsie Larkin - Love Again (LTN Remix)
- Above & Beyond presents Ocean Lab – Sirens of the Sea
- Korn - Freak On A Leash (Josh A's Beast On A Leach Mix)
- Papa Roach – Between Angels and Insects
- Papa Roach – Getting Away With Murder
- Sky Ferreira – Everything Is Embarrassing (Krystal Klear Remix)
- Armin van Buuren feat. Fiora – Waiting For The Night
- Gemma Hayes – Wicked Game
- Christina Perri – A Thousand Years
- Aiiso – Your Love Is An Echo
- Art of Noise – Moments in Love
- Amurai – Love & Light (Downtempo Mix)
- Sade – No Ordinary Love
- Cary Brothers – Ride
- The Prodigy – Firestarter
- Matthew Good Band – Suburbia
- The Chemical Brothers – Hey Boy Hey Girl
- Motorcycle – As the Rush Comes (Gabriel & Dresden Chill Mix)
- Tiësto feat. Cary Brothers – Here on Earth
- Maji – OFTEN
- Marsh – sleep (feat Jodie knight)
- Jeremy Olander- Crossed
- Dee Montero – Polaris
- Way Out West – Tuesday Maybe (Modd Remix)
- Alex Metric & Ten Ven - Otic
- Fluida - Awaken
- Red Axes - Sun My Sweet Sun (Konstantin Sibold Afro Tech Mix)
- Above and Beyond – On My Way to Heaven
- Nox Vahn – Tribute
- Hraach - Aurores [Saisons]

- Super8 & Tab feat. Jan Burton – Who Needs Pain
- Aiobahn- Tonite
- Oliver Smith – Curiosity
- John Castel & Xan Castel - Face to Face (Nayio Bitz Remix)
- Grum – Pattern Recognition
- Ilan Bluestone ft Giuseppe De Luca – Frozen Ground (Cosmic Gate Remix)
- Above & Beyond feat. Richard Beford – Northern Soul (Spencer Brown Remix)
- Andrew Bayer feat. Asbjorn – Super Human
- Grum & Josep – The Love you feel
- Oliver Smith – Make Me Feel
- Azari & III – Hungry For The Power (Franky Wah Edit)
- Above & Beyond and Mat Zo 'Always Do' (Anjuna Beats)
- Röyksopp – Breathe (ft. Astrid S) (Röyksopp Remix)
- Star Slinger – Ladies in the Back (feat. Teki Latex)
- Just Her —We Dance
- Qrion – 11-11
- Eli & Fur – Where Do We Go From Here
- Eli & Fur – Skyway (Rewind Edit)
- Fancy Inc – Nightmare
- Corren Cavini - Steps Away From The Sun (Extended Mix) [DAYS like NIGHTS]
- Just Her – Depend On Your Love
- &ME, Black Coffee - The Rapture Pt.III
- Nox Vahn ft. Mimi Page – Dream of Love
- Röyksopp, Pixx - How The Flowers Grow (Jan Blomqvist Remix)
- Avoure - This Feelin
- James iD - Kaleidoscope (White) [Anjunadeep Edition]
- James iD – Can't No More [Anjunadeep Edition]
- James iD – ID [Anjunadeep Edition]
- Tagavaka – Tear My Heart Apart (White) [Anjunadeep Edition]
- Christoph x ADZ ft. Artche – Strangers Much
- Jay Aliyev – Everything You Need (Slowed)

- Sian Evans - Hide U (Tinlicker Remix)
- Tinlicker – ID
- James iD – Need You
- Curt Reynolds – Rolling Heart (White) [Anjunadeep Edition]
- New Order - Blue Monday (My Friend Bootleg)
- Sultan + Shepard – Indigo
- Ashibah & Bakka - So High
- Sultan + Shepard – Avalanche
- Scorz feat. XIRA – Fascination
- MOGI – Give Me A Sign (Mattsu Deep Remix)

ABOUT THE AUTHOR

Mina Alexia was born in Tehran, Iran. She moved to Canada with her family at the age of three and was raised in a small town in Ontario. She graduated from Wilfrid Laurier University with a bachelor's degree of Arts, Honors English.

Having faced many adversities in life, she decided to use her artistic gifts to heal through the medium of creative writing. Mina uses her social media presence to spread awareness on trauma recovery and mental health. Her novels include trauma-informed themes that are rich with emotion. She believes "we need to feel to heal."

I SHOULDN'T
FEEL
THIS WAY
MINA ALEXIA

NOTE FROM MINA ALEXIA

Word-of-mouth is crucial for any author to succeed. If you enjoyed *I Shouldn't Love This Way*, please leave a review online—anywhere you are able. Even if it's just a sentence or two. It would make all the difference and would be very much appreciated.

Thanks!
Mina Alexia

We hope you enjoyed reading this title from:

BLACK ROSE
writing™

www.blackrosewriting.com

Subscribe to our mailing list – *The Rosevine* – and receive **FREE** books, daily deals, and stay current with news about upcoming releases and our hottest authors.
Scan the QR code below to sign up.

Already a subscriber? Please accept a sincere thank you for being a fan of Black Rose Writing authors.

View other Black Rose Writing titles at
www.blackrosewriting.com/books and use promo code
PRINT to receive a **20% discount** when purchasing.